THE
Murrumbidgee
Kid

Peter Yeldham's extensive writing career began with short stories, radio scripts and a column for a weekly magazine. He spent twenty years in England, becoming a leading screenwriter for films and television, and also wrote plays for the theatre, including the highly successful comedies *Birds on the Wing* and *Fringe Benefits*. Since returning to Australia he has won numerous awards for his mini-series, among them *1915*, *Captain James Cook*, *The Alien Years*, *All the Rivers Run*, *The Timeless Land* and *The Heroes*. He is the author of seven previous novels, which include *A Bitter Harvest*, *The Currency Lads*, *Against the Tide* and *Land of Dreams*.

PETER YELDHAM

THE
Murrumbidgee
Kid

VIKING
an imprint of
PENGUIN BOOKS

VIKING
Published by the Penguin Group
Penguin Group (Australia)
250 Camberwell Road, Camberwell, Victoria 3124, Australia
(a division of Pearson Australia Group Pty Ltd)
Penguin Group (USA) Inc.
375 Hudson Street, New York, New York 10014, USA
Penguin Group (Canada)
90 Eglinton Avenue East, Suite 700, Toronto ON M4P 2Y3, Canada
(a division of Pearson Penguin Canada Inc.)
Penguin Books Ltd
80 Strand, London WC2R 0RL, England
Penguin Ireland
25 St Stephen's Green, Dublin 2, Ireland
(a division of Penguin Books Ltd)
Penguin Books India Pvt Ltd
11 Community Centre, Panchsheel Park, New Delhi – 110 017, India
Penguin Group (NZ)
Cnr Airborne and Rosedale Roads, Albany, Auckland, New Zealand
(a division of Pearson New Zealand Ltd)
Penguin Books (South Africa) (Pty) Ltd
24 Sturdee Avenue, Rosebank, Johannesburg 2196, South Africa

Penguin Books Ltd, Registered Offices: 80 Strand, London WC2R 0RL, England

First published by Penguin Group (Australia), 2006

1 3 5 7 9 10 8 6 4 2

Design by Marina Messiha © Penguin Group (Australia)
Cover photography by Sasha & China Tourism Press/Getty Images and Tim Hixson/photolibrary.com
Permission to reproduce the poems by Kenneth Slessor, originally published as 'Darlinghurst Nights',
from Tom Thompson & ETT Imprint, Sydney
Typeset in 10.5/16.5pt Sabon by Post Pre-Press Group, Brisbane, Queensland
Printed and bound in Australia by McPherson's Printing Group, Maryborough, Victoria

National Library of Australia
Cataloguing-in-Publication data:

Yeldham, Peter.
The Murrumbidgee kid.

ISBN 0 670 02977 7.

I. Title.

A823.3

www.penguin.com.au

To Marjorie,
who is always there, from the first page

Author's Note

My deep thanks are due to the Australian actor Bill Kerr. While this is a work of fiction and all the characters imaginary, Bill's reminiscences of his boyhood were the sparks that first kindled my interest and led to the character who became Teddy Carson.

PART *One*

Chapter one

Belle Carson was a good-looker, the best looker for miles around; even those who didn't like her (which included most of the women in town and quite a few of the men) had to admit that. But they also agreed she was as nutty as a fruitcake, and in the manner of small communities the bush telegraph – which spread any gossip the least bit unusual or outrageous – frequently carried news of her.

Five-feet-seven, slim as a reed with soft dark hair and blue eyes to drown in, Belle couldn't help it; she was always unusual, and often outrageous. It was a recurrent nightmare for her eight-year-old son, Teddy. Whenever he and his dad were with her, he'd notice the sly looks and the way people raised their eyebrows and muttered to each other. Gabbing, George called it, a bunch of old boilers cackling, which meant his dad felt it too – the talk about them, the constant chitchat.

But it was worse at school. Teddy was on his own there. Piggy Morgan said Belle was a dingbat. Tom Parkes said she was as mad as a blue gum full of galahs. The rest of the class sniggered agreement and pronounced her a loony. Got tickets on herself, they said, even if she *had* been on the stage in the city, and was supposed to be famous. This was in frequent dispute, for none of them had ever heard of her and neither had their parents, so she couldn't have been all that famous. Bill Burwood, the son of the bank manager, reckoned the biggest part she'd ever played was probably the arse-end of a horse in a pantomime. So Teddy, though two years younger and three inches shorter, fought him.

Big or small, each time a boy made an insulting comment or a dirty joke about his mum, Teddy felt compelled to fight them. He'd lost count of the number of fights he'd had in Belle's defence, and was painfully aware he had managed to win none of them. He had suffered cut lips, bruised ribs and greater humiliations: his head held down the black pit of the school dunny by the big boys until the stench made him sick; treacle spread on his seat in class; and once an agonising Chinese burn on his wrist while the teacher, Mrs Lassitter, wrote on the blackboard with her back turned. Daily he went to school in dread, enduring more torment than he dared mention at home.

Meanwhile he kept wondering if one of the taunts levelled at him could possibly be true – that George was not really his dad at all and therefore he was a bastard. It was hard to know how to ask Belle about this, but ask he must. He thought about it when trying to sleep at night, rehearsing what he could say, and several times braced himself to try, but his mouth felt dry and his tongue too thick to pose the question. Then one day it just happened.

Belle was making a stew, peeling carrots and potatoes in their tiny kitchen, which seemed even smaller since the delivery of the new Hallstrom refrigerator earlier that week. It was an invention that ran on kerosene – Teddy couldn't understand how, but it kept food and drinks colder than their old icebox – and they no longer had to have the iceman call each day. George had been able to buy the machine at a special price on easy terms because he was in the sales department of Gable's of Gundagai, the big local emporium, and Belle had been in a good mood ever since it arrived, so this was the moment.

'Am I a bastard?' he blurted out, then was terrified when her face changed from shock to anger. For a moment he thought she might hit him. She never had raised a hand against him, but there was always a first time, so he was on the back foot and ready to run, in case. But her anger was not directed at him.

'Who said such a thing?' She knelt and put her arms around him, and he could feel her shaking.

'Just some kids,' Teddy mumbled, wishing he had said nothing.

'Who? Little brutes. Give me their names, darling.'

'I can't, Mum. I forget who it was.'

'No, you don't, my pet.'

'I do, honest.'

'Don't say honest like that when you're not telling the truth. We both know you're not.' She hugged him so tightly he could feel her whole body trembling, and he had a strange feeling she was going to cry. 'I won't make you tell, but you must promise me one thing.'

'What, Mum?'

'Not to believe them, or their nasty, stupid lies.'

He gladly promised, because it was the answer he had wanted. What a relief. It meant George really *was* his dad, so he couldn't be a bastard. After another hug Belle released him and stood up. There were tears in her eyes, but she quickly looked away so he knew he was not meant to see them.

'I'll get you a cold lemonade.' She went to the new machine. 'I hate this shitty little town,' she said, but it was more of a whisper, and he knew he was not meant to hear this either.

The gate always squeaked. George kept oiling it, but after a few days the squeak returned. It was a sound they lived with, like the rows every Friday night next door when Harry Lucas came home from the pub and started belting his wife Essie. Like the dog across the road that yapped when anyone walked past, or Mr Miranda cutting his grass at the same time each Sunday morning, the clatter of his mower waking people trying to sleep in. When he finished they knew it was an hour before church time, because Mr Miranda was a verger at St Thomas's who carried the collection plate, and he'd be showered and in his best suit – his only suit – before the bells rang.

George said Mr Miranda's lawnmower drove him batty, as did Harry Lucas yelling abuse at his wife, while the dog catcher ought to sort out the bloody yapper opposite, whereas the squeaking gate at least had its uses. After all, nobody could arrive out of the blue and catch them having a bit of a feel, or even doing it in the cot. Belle told him not to be so coarse in front of you-know-who.

Her name was really Arabella; Teddy had once heard old Aunty Ethel call her that, but Belle said she'd changed it when she was twelve, after her parents died. Even at that age she'd known Arabella was not the right kind of name for a theatrical poster. And now that Aunty Ethel herself had gone to heaven, no one called her anything but Belle.

On the porch behind their house was an almost-inside lavatory that had replaced the old thunderbox in the backyard, because Teddy's mum, who feared no man or woman, was terrified of spiders. One day while Belle sat there, absorbed in the local paper, a lethal red-back crawled across the page and onto the editorial she was reading. She emerged from the tin shed with a scream, spent the day in constipated discomfort, and that night said it was time George arranged for something a bit more civilised.

So George put on his best suit (the one the army had given him on his discharge, which he only wore to weddings or funerals) and went to see Clarry Burwood at the Bank of New South Wales. After a lot of talk and having to sign second mortgage papers, he managed to borrow enough money so they could install the new chemical system called a Hygeia Dissolvenator, which meant the dunny men did not have to call each week to empty the pan. Theirs was the only house in the neighbourhood with such a contraption, the only place the cart drove past on its weekly collections, and it made them different.

Teddy didn't like being different. It meant people talked about you, which was the worst thing that could happen in the town. Although, he had to admit, Belle truly *was* different from anyone else in Gundagai. Nobody else who lived there could say they'd been on the stage – a star. He'd seen the photos in her scrapbook and heard her friends talk when they came to visit. So whatever else he had to put up with – even the taunts and fights at school – Belle really had been famous; her name was on theatre posters and programs that hung in neat frames all over the house, and no other kid in town could claim that. At nights even after the worst days, trying to sleep and forget the teasing or the punches, he could at least rely on the fact his mum was celebrated.

It was a word she used, and he'd asked her what it meant.

'Well known,' she told him. 'A sort of fame, if I can venture to say that. What I mean is, if I walked into the Theatre Royal even now, Jimmy the stage doorman would know me. He'd remember. Jimmy used to say he never forgot a pretty face. My darling, it was a wonderful time in those days, so stimulating and exciting. Good audiences, packed houses, and after the shows at night there'd be chaps outside, waiting.'

'Waiting for what, Mum?'

'For my autograph, dearest heart.' She said it with a wistful sigh, as if there was more to it, but it was not something she could explain, not until he was older.

Behind their house a strip of land straggled down an unruly incline, a wilderness of paspalum, lantana and wild blackberry bushes. Almost obscured where the land ended was a muddy stream. Sometimes, on the far side of town this trickle of water managed to reach the Murrumbidgee, but only when aided by a downpour of torrential rain. Not that this mattered to Belle. She said it was a tributary of a majestic river on which paddle-steamers had once sailed. She never ventured close enough to see the stagnant seepage and the tadpoles that bred in it.

'Our house by the river' she was given to calling it, and some nights, after a few extra glasses of wine, she would refer to their tiny two-bedroom fibro cottage with its peeling paint and rusty iron roof as *Notre maison près de la rivière*. This was invariably said with the trace of a laugh and it always sounded a bit peculiar, as if she was talking with a clothes peg on her nose – a fact Teddy was once unwise enough to express aloud, only to be promptly told off by Belle in her most scathing style.

'Darling, try not to be a Philistine,' she scolded, 'even if we do dwell among Goths and Vandals.'

'Who, Mum?'

'Never mind. It happens to be the way the French speak, using the correct Gallic accent, *mon petit*, and I won't allow you to be an ignoramus like others in this desolate district who deprecate France, which is a cultured, civilised place . . .'

Teddy wondered what deprecate meant, and whether he should ask, but Belle was in full flow and there was no chance.

'. . . an aesthetic country, full of fine intellectuals and artists – quite unlike here – after all, it was the birthplace of Racine, Debussy, Voltaire and Molière. Not forgetting Zola, Chopin or Claude Monet.'

He had never heard of any of them. But from that time on, *Notre maison près de la rivière* it was, which became awkward. Such things travelled swiftly through the town. It meant another three fights at school, all of which he lost.

Chapter two

On the day of the annual Riverina Talent Quest, the local park was bedecked with flags and bunting. The Gundagai brass band, hot in unsuitable serge uniforms and looking like members of the Salvation Army, played melodies from favourite musical comedies, rendering these with an enthusiasm that could be heard all over town. Rows of folding seats were set up adjacent to the war memorial, where a dais had been erected to serve as a stage. It would also provide a platform for the mayor, together with the master of ceremonies and the adjudicator. It was barely ten o'clock, and the quest was not due to begin until noon.

Belle had risen early and washed her hair, but had not yet decided what to wear. It was a choice between the organdie skirt she had worn in a revival of *Rose Marie* or the blue dirndl from *The Maid of the Mountains*. She thought perhaps the blue, with a big straw hat she had worn in *No, No, Nanette*. Priding herself on never leaving a show without at least one item from the production wardrobe, she had acquired a collection of diverse and extraordinary outfits, rarely failing to give the locals a chance to comment on her appearance. Aware of this, she chose with an eye to attracting attention – and invariably received it because of her striking looks, plus a certain hauteur with which she regarded her fellow citizens.

The blue dress and straw hat, she eventually decided, would make a dazzling display amid the dreary Sunday-best floral frocks that the ladies of Gundagai wore to occasions like this. A drab lot they were, and today she wanted to be notable. Today was special. That decision taken, she dressed in slacks and a shirt, left the blue dirndl out to iron, and persuaded George to come for a walk to the park.

'But it's far too early,' he said.

Of course it's early, she agreed; after all, she was still in her old clothes and hadn't really made up her mind what outfit she would choose, but didn't he wish to escort her? Just a leisurely stroll together, down to the park to see the venue. When George asked why, she told him it was simply being professional to check the stage and the seating. He looked puzzled, but that was George, to whom all things theatrical were a puzzle. A good-natured man, his tanned face was more amiable than handsome. He was of barely medium height, just an inch taller than her, and six years her senior. At thirty-seven his sandy hair was receding slightly. They had met by chance in Sydney, at Greenwich, where Belle had gone to stay with her Aunt Ethel after a traumatic love affair. Two weeks later, to the surprise of those who knew her, and the delight of her elderly aunt (who thought she need a stabilising influence), they were married. Despite their obvious disparity and the conjecture of her friends, the marriage had lasted.

Belle took his arm as they walked along the footpath and crossed the dusty road, passing identical small fibro houses where washing sagged on clothes lines. Bored men hosed parched lawns; others weeding vegetable gardens nodded to George while slyly running their eyes over Belle. Their wives, from front porches or behind the lace curtains of their windows, scrutinised her with as much dislike as she felt for them. It was always a relief to leave the shabby neighbourhood and reach the centre of town, where there were paved roads and an occasional fine stone building with traces of Victorian opulence.

In the park where the brass band was now butchering a Jerome Kern song, Belle opened her handbag and produced three squares of cardboard. On each she had printed the word RESERVED. She attached them to the most prominent seats in the centre of the front row.

'You can't do that,' said George, looking around uneasily in case the mayor or anyone in authority was observing her.

'Of course I can,' she said, and took his arm again, ready to leave. George was rigid with apprehension.

'There's Percy Bates,' he said anxiously, spotting a familiar face beneath a peaked cap.

'He's supposed to be a friend of yours. For goodness' sake, relax and give him a wave like you usually do.'

George waved. The bulky policeman promptly headed towards them.

'Oh gawd,' George muttered, 'now what?'

'G'day, George.' Percy Bates was a florid-faced man, already sweating in the rising heat. He touched his cap in Belle's direction; it might have been a gesture of respect. 'Mrs Carson.'

'Mr Bates.' She smiled in automatic response.

'Warm day. Be real hot later,' the policeman forecast. 'There'll be a mob in soon. Good idea, bookin' yourselves a decent seat before they overrun the place like a plague of rabbits.'

'We thought so. I'm so glad you agree,' Belle said.

'Your young bloke takin' part in this, is he?'

'Yes, it'll be his first public performance.'

'Nervous?'

'Not him. He's very excited and looking forward to it,' Belle replied, conscious of George's slight frown, while thinking this was by far the longest conversation she and the local policeman had ever had.

'What's he do? Sing?'

'He can sing beautifully. But not today. He's entering the speech section, doing a special recitation.'

'Oh,' Bates said vaguely, 'is he? Well, good luck to him.'

'He has so much talent he doesn't need luck. But we appreciate the sentiment.'

The policeman looked bemused, unsure if he was being thanked or insulted. 'Good-o,' he finally said. 'So long, George.' He nodded rather carefully to Belle, and resumed his leisurely patrol.

'There,' Belle said, 'we're not going to be arrested for reserving seats.' She noticed George frown again, and smiled at him. '*Now* what are you bothered about, worry-guts? Come on, let's go home and find Teddy.'

'It's wrong, what you told Perce.'

'What did I tell your friend Perce that's wrong?'

'Ted's not looking forward to it at all. He's scared.'

'Nerves, George.'

'He couldn't sleep. Didn't eat his breakfast.'

'That's nothing. I knew people who'd throw up before they went on stage. Part of the pressure.'

'Jesus Christ,' George said.

'Nerves are natural, almost essential for a good performance. He'll be wonderful. You'll see, you'll be proud of him.'

But when they reached the house Teddy was not there. Nor was he down by the stream. With Belle growing increasingly anxious, they searched the neighbourhood for almost an hour, but could not find him.

It was amazing. Like a miracle. For so long Teddy had been on his own, an outsider with hardly any friends, apart from Herbie Bates. He and the policeman's son had begun school on the same day and, after enduring some bullying initiation ceremonies, had become good mates. But when Herbie was not around, Teddy rarely found himself invited to join in with the others. Often forced to play games by himself, he tried to pretend it was fun. Only an hour before he had been slouching along the river bank, feeling sick with fright at the thought of the ordeal ahead, when Ginger and Norm came past. He was hardly aware of them at first, immersed in wondering what it would be like up there on the stage, all those people looking at him, ready to laugh if he made a mistake. And it was such a complicated verse, and he had to say it real fast, had to keep to the tempo Belle had taught him night after night . . .

'You a snob?' Ginger asked.

Teddy turned in surprise, ready for combat, even though they were both older and bigger than him.

'What do you mean, am I a snob?'

'It means stuck-up,' Norm said.

'High and mighty,' Ginger added for good measure.

'I know that.' Teddy was anxious not to appear ignorant. 'I meant, who said I'm one?'

'Plenty of kids. They reckon yer up yerself, think yer too good for us.'

'They're wrong,' Teddy replied, stunned. 'Why do they say that?'

''Cos yer won't join anyone's gang. Too much of a know-all.'

'But I'm not. I'm not in a gang 'cos nobody's ever asked me to join.'

'I told yer,' Norm said to Ginger, and they both looked at Teddy as if they were trying to make up their minds about something.

'What if *we* asked yer?' Ginger said eventually. 'Would yer like to join us?'

'You haven't got a gang.'

'We're startin' one.'

'I thought you were in Piggy Morgan's mob?'

'We're sick of Pig. He bosses people around.'

'So, what do you reckon?' Norm asked. 'Want to be in it?'

'Bloody oath,' Teddy replied, because it sounded grown-up to swear, and he knew he'd said the right thing when both boys grinned.

'Good stuff,' Ginger said. 'You're our first recruit.'

Recruit was a popular word, because most of their fathers had been in the war, some of them fighting in France or Egypt, and a few special ones had been at Gallipoli, which was supposed to be the best war of all. But some of the men who had been there didn't talk much about it, except when they put on their medals and marched on Anzac Day, and afterwards went into the hotels to remember mates who hadn't come back. They often sang as they trailed home when the pubs shut; sometimes by then the songs were sad ones. Teddy had even heard a man say he'd been mad to put up his age and go 'over there', but that had been after the celebrations, and he told it to everyone who went past him as he sat in the street surrounded by empty beer bottles.

'Didyer hear me?' Teddy realised Ginger was still talking. 'We're gonna be the top mob round here. What we'll do is pinch kids from the other gangs, one at a time, till we're the biggest and best. By the time they latch on, we'll be ready to bash 'em up. Right, Norm?'

'Right, Ginge.'

'I'm the captain,' Ginger said, ''cos it was my idea. Norm's the first lieutenant. You can be a corporal.'

Teddy felt disappointment. It didn't sound very exciting, being a corporal. 'Can't I be an officer?'

'Ted, yer gotta work yer way up. Yer can't expect to start at the top,' Ginger replied.

'Besides,' Norm added, 'we gotta have troops. Lots of troops. The next recruits will be privates, so you'll be in charge of them.'

'Promise?'

'Solemn oath. They'll be known as Teddy's privates.'

Both boys choked back laughter. He wondered what the joke was, but decided it would be good tactics to grin, as if he understood.

'My privates,' he said, and was rewarded when they roared with laughter.

Ginger slapped him on the back. 'Yer a good sport, Ted. One of us – we made the right choice.'

'I could recruit Herbie for the gang,' Teddy offered.

'Good thinking, Corporal.' Ginger approvingly gave him another slap on the back. 'Now let's go and we'll show you our hide-out.'

'Is it far?' Teddy knew he would soon be expected back at the house to get dressed in his costume for the talent quest, but he could hardly tell that to his new comrades. It would sound sissy, and might ruin everything.

'Not far,' Norm assured him. 'Along the other side, till we get to the main river near the bridge. You wait till you see our lair. I bet no other gang's got a headquarters like this.'

The main river near the bridge, Teddy thought with dismay. That was a fair walk through the bush, and might take half an hour. Then another half-hour back again . . .

'What's up, Ted?' He realised they were both watching him. 'Don'tcha want to see it? Got somethin' better to do?'

'No,' he said. 'Sounds beaut to me. Let's go.'

They waded across the tiny stream, sinking almost to their knees in the mud, their shrill voices excited and in pursuit of adventure as they began to imagine the ooze beneath their feet to be dangerous quicksand. Teddy gave only one swift glance behind him, and to his relief saw no one. They were out of sight amid undergrowth on the far bank before a worried George came looking for him.

It was a massive kurrajong tree, hidden by tangled vines of morning glory and surrounded by a profusion of red gums on the slope above the river. So thickly foliaged, its branches almost obliterated the sun as they stood below it. It had taken longer than expected to find their way there, and they were dishevelled and scratched by blackberries. Teddy was remotely conscious of time passing, but he was now part of a gang, one of the founding members, and that made the day important and time somehow irrelevant.

They gazed up at the kurrajong.

'This is HQ,' Ginger said. 'Up there's our command post.'

Ginger was fond of military terms. His dad had been one of the first volunteers to join up, and had been at the famous battle of Long Neck fighting against the Turks, and then later against the Germans in a place called Pozières. Ginger said he hoped that in about ten years, when he was old enough, there'd be another war so he could fight in it, then he could join the RSL, the Returned Services League. His dad belonged to it, and so did his grandpa, who had been in the Boer War, and he'd be able to march with them both on Anzac and Armistice Day.

'Was your old man in it?' Ginger asked Teddy.

'Of course,' Teddy said, but he had learnt not to enlarge on this. He knew – George himself had explained – he'd been a clerk at

Victoria Barracks in Sydney, which most people felt wasn't being a proper soldier at all, it was just pen-pushing. Not that it was necessary to say he'd been a pen-pusher, George had advised, but it would be sensible not to skite about him, or make him out to be a hero or anything silly like that. Teddy had been told this a year ago when he was still only seven, and he was proud that he'd kept the secret ever since.

'Whereabouts did he fight? France or Gallipoli?' Ginger was eager to know more.

'Both, I think,' Teddy said. 'He doesn't like to talk about it.'

'Mine talks about it all the time.'

'Some do, others don't.' Teddy was pleased with his quick-witted response. 'Now where's the hide-out – our command post? All I can see is a big tree.'

'Stand clear and watch this.' Norm pulled on what seemed like a tendril hanging from a branch in the kurrajong. A rope ladder secured in the foliage above slid down beside them.

'One at a time,' Ginger said. 'The leader leads.'

He climbed the ladder and vanished into the green overhead. After a few minutes they heard him call, and Norm began the ascent. Left alone, awaiting a signal, Teddy had a fleeting moment of concern. He wished he owned a watch so that he knew the time. But he reassured himself the talent quest wouldn't start for ages. First there'd be the brass band and boring speeches, and all sorts of things.

'Righto, Ted.'

He carefully climbed the swaying rope. High in the tree was a wooden platform where Ginger and Norm waited. Some branches had been trimmed back to afford a view across the river towards the town. They could see for miles.

'What do yer reckon?'

'It's great,' Teddy said, 'did you make it?'

'Yep – me and Norm. Pinched planks from the scrap yard. Took weeks, but from up here we can see every single thing that's going on. No other gang could possibly attack us – we'd spot 'em coming.'

'Pin 'em down with catapult fire,' Norm added. 'Ain't it a beaut view? You can see all over the town – our school, even the park and all them people at that stupid talent quest, or whatever it's called.'

That was when the distant band struck up a fanfare. Teddy could see the crowd and hear the trumpets. He felt sudden dismay, a moment of such panic that he thought his stomach would empty and he might disgrace himself.

Chapter three

'He's nowhere in the town. Not at the hospital; I've even been to the police station, in case he had an accident. No one's seen him. I've asked everywhere I can think of.'

George was out of breath as he reached the gate, explaining all this. Belle was waiting there, wearing a vivid crimson dress and a large picture hat, having changed her mind and her clothes three times as her growing disbelief became a troubled concern, finally turning to anger.

She shook her head helplessly and went back into the house, leaving George to follow. On the dining table lay a brand new pair of short pants, a white shirt and Teddy's tiny clip-on bow tie. She could hardly bear it. She had saved so carefully from the housekeeping to buy them – had put them on lay-by for weeks, which was hard enough in these times, but she'd kept up the payments. And because today was to be Teddy's first public appearance, and because Belle had been so certain of it being a triumph, she'd saved up to buy fresh prawns and a flagon of wine so they could celebrate tonight, as well as a cream cake with icing on it for Teddy.

'How could he do this to me?'

'We don't know what he's done, Belle.'

'We know he's not here,' she said despairingly. 'That's what he's done. We know he's forgotten, he's just wandered off somewhere, daydreaming. All the tuition, the weeks of rehearsals . . . so much work for nothing.' She felt as though she was about to be physically sick with disappointment. 'Where in the name of Christ can he be?'

'I'll keep looking,' George said, but knew it was unlikely he could locate the boy in time. 'You go down to the park.'

'What's the use of that?'

'Ask the judges if he can be put later in the program.'

'They'll never agree.'

'Yes, they will. Use your charm. You'll persuade them,' George assured her. 'You look really beautiful in that red dress.'

'No, I don't. It's too tight and the colour's awful,' Belle replied unhappily. 'In this heat I'll sweat and my mascara will run. I'll look like a melting strawberry tart.'

The river was much wider than Teddy had thought. It had looked so easy at first. After he heard the fanfare he knew he must make the decision; there was no choice except to be positive, so he told Ginger and Norm he had to get back to town, had to meet his mum and dad or he'd be in big trouble, and he was going to take the shortest way back and swim across. Both boys had been startled, then tried to prevent him, saying it was too wide and he might drown. But Teddy had put a stop to that, telling them he'd been taught to swim by his dad who used to be a Bondi lifesaver, and who was secretly training him for the school sports.

'You watch,' he had said with a bravado that impelled him to swing his way down the rope ladder, run to the river's edge and dive in without even stopping to remove his shorts and shirt. When he surfaced he had turned to look back at them, their scared faces visible high in the tree, and while treading water he had cheerfully waved to them before starting to swim.

Now – it felt ages later – the opposite bank seemed as far away as ever. Teddy wondered if he should try to slip out of his shirt; it was filling with water and becoming heavy, making him feel it was weighing down his body. But it would be even harder to swim while holding his shirt, and he would get into trouble if he lost it. He kept thinking about dangers that might be in the river: floating logs that could stun him or, far worse, slimy eels or water snakes below that might attack . . .

He began to thresh wildly, feeling the onset of panic. If he drowned they'd drag the river. Percy Bates or one of the other local cops would row out, while a crowd from town would watch from the boat ramp as a diver searched for his body in the mud and reeds. There'd be an ambulance waiting and they'd take him to the hospital with the siren blaring, but it would be too late for a doctor to save him. He'd be dead, and everyone would be sorry, especially those kids who had teased him or bashed him up at school. Belle would sob and put on her black dress. George would be sad, and Gable's Emporium would have to give him the day off work to attend the funeral. Ginger and Norm might even be questioned by the police.

'Why did you let him swim alone like that?' they would ask.

'We were frightened,' they'd have to admit, 'and he was a far better swimmer than us. But the current was against him. Even the best swimmers couldn't have made it.'

As he struggled, feeling weaker with each futile stroke, he wondered why he had told the lie about his dad being a Bondi lifesaver.

George Carson had never been a swimmer. As a child growing up in the city, summer outings to the beach had been a treat for the rest of the family and a source of dread to him. His brother and sister swam effortlessly; his father had once been a finalist in the State titles, and the prospect of a son who could not swim was anathema to him. His solution was to throw him into the deep end of the local pool, again and again, until he stopped sinking and learnt to survive. In time, George graduated to a rather desperate dog paddle, but became deeply afraid of the water.

As an adult, able to make his own choice, he had never swum since, and thus had not progressed beyond the despised dog paddle to a more fashionable overarm, let alone the stroke admired as the Australian crawl. Neither the town baths nor the river had ever tempted him. It was one of the advantages of living in a country town far from the coast – he had no contact with the beach culture that was so alien to him. So it was with a feeling of terror that he stood on the river bank and watched eight-year-old Teddy's failing attempt to swim across the Murrumbidgee.

George was there by accident. Having exhausted all possibilities and unable to face Belle's disappointment, he had walked past the park where the talent quest was well under way, and heard the master of ceremonies – a prominent Sydney comedian – announce that the next performer had not yet appeared. It was to be hoped that local lad Ted Carson would arrive in due course, but meanwhile they would continue with the next artiste, the delightful Catherine Carr, aged ten, from Wagga Wagga, who had chosen to sing 'Danny Boy'.

George had heard the band begin, the young and rather thin voice nervously trying to follow the musical tempo, as he crossed the road. Willed by some instinct that he would never understand, he walked beneath a canopy of flame trees, past a grocer's shop and a garage – both of them shut – down to the river. There seemed to be no one in sight until he saw the flailing figure in mid-stream. George knew at once who it was and stood frozen in fear and a heart-stopping panic, unable to move.

It was only for seconds, but seemed longer. Then, in some astonishing way, his shoes were discarded, jacket and trousers flung on the ground, his shirt and tie wrenched off, and he was in the water. There was scarcely time to be terrified.

He tried to call. The boy, struggling for his life, gave no sign of hearing. 'Teddy!' he shouted. Disregarding his fear, George focused on the thought that Teddy would sink and he'd be unable to find him in the murky depths. An image of the mud and slimy black depths spurred him, if only to avoid the prospect of it.

'Teddy!'

It felt unreal, but George was out there in mid-stream, grabbing the boy and shouting into his face, glimpsing Teddy's startled recognition, manhandling him and desperately dog-paddling them both back to the safety of the river bank.

'You're not to tell her,' George said, 'or else I'll chuck you back in. Did you hear me? She's had enough upset already. Got it?'

'But what'll I say?' Teddy had showered, and was now in his new shirt and short pants as George stooped to fit the bow tie.

'Don't say anything. Just get up on stage and do it. Right?'

'Right,' Teddy said. 'But Dad . . .'

'What?'

'I think I was drowning. And you saved me.'

'Rubbish. Get your shoes and socks on, let's hurry.'

'But Dad —'

'Hurry! I hope, after all that, you can still remember the words.'

A plump twelve-year-old boy ended his mechanical tap dance with a flourish, poised with arms flung wide, awaiting applause. It was polite but perfunctory and he left the dais disappointed. The comedian acting as master of ceremonies came to the microphone and dutifully thanked the dancer. He was a tall, skinny man with a toothy smile, and shiny hair plastered down with brilliantine. The committee thought they were lucky to have such a popular name, and after much debate had agreed to pay his exorbitant demand of a ten-pound fee plus first-class train fares.

'And now, our youngest contestant in this year's quest has arrived, and may I say just in time. Please put your hands together and welcome your very own local lad – eight-year-old Teddy Carson!'

Belle heard the applause and had a moment of pride, convinced it was louder for him than for any others. She watched as the tall comic made a performance of leaning down to shake hands with the small figure of her son, and heard the wave of amusement as he milked an easy laugh by lowering the microphone to Teddy's height, then kneeling alongside him to complete his announcement.

'Young Mr Carson tells me he will be doing a recitation of a poem. I leave you in his good hands.'

'You great dopey clown,' Belle muttered angrily. 'Piss off and stop hogging the limelight.'

Only George could hear this indignant sibilance. 'Shh,' he said. He took her hand and held it, trying to calm her. There had been no chance for explanations when he and Teddy slid into the seats beside her a few minutes earlier, no time to reply to her puzzled look as she saw George's change of clothes; his soaked and muddy best suit was at home, and he was now wearing an old sports jacket and flannel trousers. At last the visiting MC retired to the background, and Teddy was a very tiny figure alone in front of the microphone, facing the crowd in the park.

'Bow,' Belle whispered, and almost as if he might have heard her – but this was surely impossible – they saw Teddy turn and bow to the adjudicator, who sat waiting to judge his performance.

'Kindly proceed with your recital,' the adjudicator said. He was a rather prim man in his late forties, a teacher of English grammar at St Bartholomew's College in the town of Cootamundra. Belle wondered what his qualifications were for evaluating the merits of singers, dancers and the acting ability of her son.

From the improvised stage, Teddy looked down at his mum. She gave him an imperceptible nod of encouragement. He took a deep breath, smiled engagingly at the audience as if they were his friends, then just as they were expecting a sweet childish verse, he dropped his voice a full octave and launched himself into the recitation:

> A bunch of the boys were whooping it
> up in the Malamute saloon;
> The kid that handles the music box was
> hitting a jag-time tune;
> Back at the bar, in a solo game, sat
> Dangerous Dan McGrew,
> And watching his luck was his light-o'-
> love, the lady that's known as Lou.

The adjudicator looked surprised. He started to frown, and lightly tapped the bell on the table in front of him. It was a signal to

stop the performance, but Teddy paid no heed. He hardly heard the
sound. He was capturing the beat, the feel of the rhythm, the way
he had rehearsed it so often with Belle, increasing his tempo as he
warmed up to the exciting bits:

> When out of the night, which was fifty
>   below, and into the din and glare,
> There stumbled a miner fresh from the
>   creeks, dog-dirty, and loaded for bear.
> He looked like a man with a foot in the
>   grave, and scarcely the strength of a louse,
> Yet he tilted a poke of dust on the bar,
>   and he called for drinks for the house.
> There was none could place the
>   stranger's face, though we searched
>   ourselves for a clue;
> But we drank his health, and the
>   last to drink was Dangerous Dan
>   McGrew . . .

The adjudicator was hitting the bell firmly now, and he kept on
banging it repeatedly. 'Stop it!' he shouted. 'Stop this at once!'

Teddy turned to look at him, bewildered. 'But sir, I'm just starting.
There's ten verses. It's a famous poem called "The Shooting of Dan
McGrew".'

'I'm perfectly aware of its title. You will do as you're told and
stop now!' He rose from his chair. 'This choice of material for a
young boy is totally unsuitable. It's nothing but crude doggerel. He
should have been given something more appropriate for a child of
his tender years.'

There was a sudden outbreak of excitement. Amid it came a voice that dominated the hubbub, demanding with a piercing clarity to be heard. Belle was on her feet, outraged.

'Who says it's unsuitable?'

'I do.' The adjudicator looked down at her. He was brick-red with indignation. '*I* say so. "The Shooting of Dan McGrew" is coarse and vulgar verse, inappropriate and totally improper for a recitation by an eight-year-old, or by any child on a public occasion like this. He's disqualified.'

'He's *what?*' Belle stared at him, disbelieving.

'Disqualified, Madam.'

'Belle, love —' George, by now alarmed and embarrassed, tried to take her arm, begging her for all their sakes to please sit down, but he was too late. She was climbing the rostrum steps to confront the adjudicator. Teddy realised this with sudden dismay.

The audience, who had dutifully tolerated the heat and the long program, now sensed the advent of a happening. They all knew Belle, but none had ever seen her in such a rage as the moment when she faced the teacher from St Bartholomew's.

'How *dare* you criticise the material!' Her voice carried to all corners of the park, picked up by the microphone because she was now standing alongside it. '*How dare you! I* chose that poem.'

'Then you should be ashamed of yourself,' he snapped at her.

'This is supposed to be a talent quest,' she shouted in his face, 'not a church picnic!'

The mayor rose to his feet, conscious of impending disaster. Despite the warmth of the day he was wearing his ceremonial robes of office. Some of the crowd were laughing, calling encouragement to Belle, others felt clearly scandalised by her intrusion and were starting to complain. The afternoon had been a tedious one, relatives and friends dragooned into obligatory attendance, compelled to sit through mediocre performances by far too many children, and His Worship's political antennae warned him they were only moments away from chaos. His authority was required to defuse the situation.

'Mrs Carson,' he sternly ordered, 'kindly leave the platform at once and stop disrupting the proceedings. Step down and resume your seat.'

'Shut up, Pinocchio,' Belle replied, which brought a great roar of laughter, for the mayor was distinguishable by an elongated nose, and had threatened to sue opposition aldermen who used this nickname when accusing him of telling lies in council. He was even more infuriated by the public hilarity, and lost all sense of civic dignity.

'Sit down, you bloody bitch, or I'll have you chucked off this stage.' He couched his threat in what was meant to be a ferocious whisper, but unluckily for him the microphone picked it up and broadcast it to the crowd. Despite their diverse opinions of Belle, a large number of women in the audience gave voice to a unified echo of disapproval that promised to cost him votes at the next election.

Belle enjoyed the mayor's look of dismay, then took no further notice of him. She turned back to the adjudicator. 'Before this buffoon interrupted, I was about to say you're an impostor. You have no qualifications, no talent, and no right to be here trying to evaluate artists. You're just a jumped-up ponce.'

'And you're a madwoman,' the adjudicator hissed at her.

'What's more to the point,' Belle said, as if he had not spoken, 'you're an imbecile, an amateur! Disqualify him, would you? I'm here to tell you this boy is going to be a great actor. He's going to be a star. And you and Pinocchio the mayor and anyone else who disagrees can shove your opinions up your arse!'

George sat wishing he had drowned in the river. On stage Teddy heard startled laughter – but it was only from a section of the crowd. Most had faces like stone. He knew his mum was defending him, although he was unsure from what. He put out his hand and found hers. She clung to it like a lifeline.

Fingers locked, they left the platform amid uproar.

Teddy watched as Belle carefully poured herself another glass of wine. It was the last one, draining the flagon which had been full when she began, and George made an ineffectual motion of protest, but said nothing. She seemed not to notice, and sipped her drink.

The house was quiet and dark, like her mood; just two lamps alight, one on the piano, which occupied pride of place in the cluttered living room where they sat, the other on a chest that lit the main wall where all Belle's photos and playbills were displayed. Among them were pictures of her as a young soubrette, or in costumes for dramatic roles; these, together with the many theatrical programs and her neatly kept scrapbooks of press clippings, were what one of her friends, Teddy remembered, had called 'the memorabilia of her life'.

Whatever that was supposed to mean, they sat there among it, Belle drinking steadily but not drunk, and George looking tired and perplexed, which was how he often looked, especially when she was upset. Teddy had heard another friend say that George had a perplexed look on his face most of the time, ever since he had first met Belle. Although he was only eight, Teddy was good at overhearing things he wasn't meant to, and expert at storing them in his memory.

'Unsuitable.' She almost spat the word, gazing into her glass.

Neither of them said anything, as if they were her captive audience. 'Un-bloody-suitable! How would *he* know? How in the name of Christ would that weedy, wretched man know? Is he anyone?'

'He's a school teacher, love —'

'I know that. A second-rate teacher in a third-rate college.'

'Yes, well, but —'

'I mean, is he anyone of substance? I hardly think the instruction of elementary English at a school in Cootamundra gives him the right to publicly humiliate us – and disqualify my son.'

'*Our* son,' George murmured softly, but Teddy realised she was brooding and appeared not to have heard him.

Huddled in a chair in the corner, feeling invisible because his parents seemed oblivious of him, he watched them both. The room felt strange and unreal. The events of the day had drained him, yet he was determined to fight off sleep. So much had happened, and he did not want to miss anything else that might occur.

'I blame myself,' Belle said. 'The fault is mine.'

'Is it?' George sounded surprised to hear her say this. 'You mean the choice of the wrong poem?'

'*Of course* I don't mean that. It was a considered choice, to demonstrate his versatility and his range, despite his age. I blame myself because he has talent but no chance of showing it while we moulder in this backwater.'

'Fair go, darl,' George said, 'it's not such a bad place, really.'

'It's a dump.'

'You didn't think so when we first came here. You were keen enough just to get the hell out of Sydney, away from everyone, and forget about the past.'

'All right,' Belle said, and she slid a glance at Teddy, almost hidden in his chair. Unable to see him clearly in the shadowed room, she seemed to assume he had fallen asleep. 'Just watch what you say. Leave things that happened back then out of this.'

'Be glad to,' George replied, showing sudden spirit, 'provided you quit blaming all your troubles on this town. We have to live somewhere.'

'Do you call it living?' She drained her glass and put it on the table.

'I know you're cranky about today, and it's understandable. I'm upset too. But nothing will ever please you here, will it? You've never given this place a chance.'

'A chance? For God's sake, it's been eight years! Isn't that long enough to be suffocated?'

'At least I've got a decent job here. A hell of a lot better than I'd get in any damn city, where half the people are out of work.'

'Ah yes, the job,' she said. 'The steady and reliable job with Gable's of Gundagai.' Teddy could hear her voice beginning to rise and knew the signs: she was angry again. 'Is that our shining future? Will we sit and decay in this house, count off the years and grow into antiques while you carry the flag for the Henry Gable Emporium? Perhaps you'd like that to be Teddy's future, to follow in your footsteps as the assistant manager, kitchenware.'

'I didn't say that. But there are worse things to be.' Teddy could tell that George was equally upset, which was rare. 'Plenty of no-hopers in your game. Most of 'em on the bones of their arse, pretending things are dandy. An awful lot of pretence goes on in your weird world, Belle.'

'We all know your opinion of show business,' she said, 'but I personally don't give a bugger what you think. I happen to believe Teddy has real talent, and it's a sin to waste it.' She went to refill her glass, and seemed surprised the flagon was empty. 'Talent is like gold, it's precious and it's rare. If I do one thing with my life, I'm going to see he uses it, that he becomes someone. And I don't mean a star of Glorious Gable's in bloody Gundagai.'

'We can't leave here,' George pointed out. 'There's my job and the cheap mortgage. We'd never get another loan as good.'

There was silence while Belle considered this remark. Then she shrugged. 'We'll give it a while longer,' she promised.

At least Teddy *thought* it was a promise. But later that night, tucked in bed and unable to sleep for thinking about the eventful day, he wondered about Belle's words. In a way, they had sounded more like a threat.

Chapter four

'Smile,' the photographer said, perspiring as he slid in a new plate. His tiny studio, up a flight of stairs above Wilson's Drapery and Soft Furnishings – 'your sofas covered and curtains made to measure' – was like an oven.

Teddy obediently relaxed his face into a polite smile, but Belle shook her head vehemently. She moved in front of the lens to prevent the shot being taken. The photographer sighed. He was accustomed to simple portraits, or comfortable events like weddings and baptisms. He was also used to being the one who issued instructions.

'Don't smile,' she said, and she turned to the photographer. 'If I wanted a little photo for the family album, I'd have borrowed a box brownie and not wasted my money. I want some depth and feeling. Some intensity, not a bland, meaningless, grinning snapshot. I want him to look ethereal . . .'

'Ethereal, Mrs Carson?'

'Have you ever heard of the word?'

'Has *he*?' the photographer retorted, now fed up by the demanding session and feeling thoroughly bad-tempered.

While they argued about which posture he should adopt (Belle kept insisting that by ethereal she meant a solemn and spiritual study, but certainly not a silly, angelic look), Teddy sat hoping that none of his mates had seen them coming in here. Especially Norm and Ginger, for they were now his best friends, ever since the big day when they had at last recruited their tenth member – ten being considered the right size for a gang – and they had issued a proclamation and an open challenge to Pig Morgan and his mob. Apart from a slight skirmish and an exchange of insults, no real battle had yet taken place. The closest they had come to wartime action was arming themselves with lots of stones and setting up snipers with catapults, but then Percy Bates had cycled past in his police uniform and they all had to hold their fire and pretend to be friends. Since then plans were constantly being discussed about how to engage the enemy.

It would be terrible if Norm or Ginger or any of his own gang found out, but far worse if Piggy's riffraff knew he was here, dressed up in a velvet costume Belle had made for him, looking like Little Lord Fauntleroy. He'd be a joke at school. It would spread around the whole district. They'd never let him forget it. He'd have to run away, there would be no alternative . . .

'Teddy, darling,' his mother said, 'are you listening?'

'To what, Mum?'

'I thought not. I want you to look pensive, serious. Now, can you do that?'

He nodded. It was easy. The best way to do that was to empty his mind, just gaze at the lens with a trace of confusion.

'Lovely,' Belle said. 'Just perfection. Don't you think so, Mr Lucarotti?'

'Perfection,' the photographer said, visualising the prospect of an early release from the claustrophobic heat of his studio. It would be followed by a visit to the saloon bar of the Imperial Hotel, where the vision of a schooner of cold draught beer was like a treasured mirage that would efface this tyranny.

'Last one,' Belle said. 'This time he's crying.'

They both turned and gazed at her. Mr Lucarotti managed to suppress a sigh.

'Crying?' Teddy asked. 'Why do I have to cry?'

'Because it's different.'

Different, Teddy repeated to himself. Why must we always be *different*?

'For a very simple reason,' Belle said, as if she had read his mind, which he had come to believe she could, 'because no one else will have a portfolio with a young boy shedding tears. And casting directors notice such things. You must realise, my pet, they see dozens of hopefuls. Probably hundreds. They're bored with smiling faces and rows of white teeth that look like well-kept tombstones. Posed, artificial pictures. What we have to do is create an instant impact. Make them be aware of us. That way, they'll remember you. So you take a moment or two, darling, and then cry.'

'But . . . how?'

'You're an actor. Actors can cry when they want to.'

'But what'll I cry about, Mum?' Teddy was bewildered.

'Think of something sad,' Belle said.

'I don't know anything sad.'

'Of course you do. Like . . . your little puppy, remember?'

'Winnie the Pooh . . .'

'What happened to him?'

'You know.'

'Yes, but you tell me.'

'He was run over.'

'And . . .?' Belle persisted.

'He died.'

'Think of how you felt, Teddy,' she murmured to him, 'think of that poor little dog, your wonderful friend Pooh, slowly dying.'

Mr Lucarotti was mesmerised, gazing from mother to son. Teddy's face startled to crumple. Tears filled his eyes and began to roll down his cheeks. Belle nodded to the photographer, who was so shocked by this display of parental ruthlessness that he almost forgot to click the shutter of the camera. By now, Teddy was openly sobbing, hardly aware of the flashlight.

'One more,' Belle said, and Mr Lucarotti took a last shot, then watched in wonder as his client ran forward to kneel and wrap her arms around her son. She hugged him, murmuring soft contrite phrases, pleading that she was sorry and to please forgive her. However, the photographer felt certain that if his prints should fail to satisfy, she would be quite capable of making the child do it all again.

The car looked almost new – streamlined and heavy with chrome that shone like silver, despite the street dust that enveloped it. They saw it as they walked home from school, engrossed in plans for the advancement of their gang, with Norm and Ginger debating the best time to launch an attack that would completely skittle Pig Morgan and his mob of losers.

'It's got to be a real shock,' Ginger said. 'We want to make Pig look like an absolute dingbat. If we do it properly and leave him stranded like a shag on a rock, then most of his gang will desert the sinking ship and come over to our side.'

Teddy was not sure if he should say so, but he had a notion how to achieve this, his own secret idea of how to make Pig look a real dill. The trouble was, he wondered how the other two would feel about him making the suggestion, since they were now firmly established as the natural leaders – the captain and his first lieutenant – and frequently it had been made clear to him that he should remember he was only a corporal. It had been said so often he was getting sick of hearing it. Now that they had the numbers, Norm and Ginger had become what George would call a bit stuck-up. So although it was a good idea, a perfect way to make Pig Morgan look stupid, he debated whether to broach it, which was when they drew near his house and saw the car.

'It's a sports tourer.' Norm knew all about cars, for his father served on the petrol pump at the main garage in town. 'A Fiat 19S. Made in Italy.'

They both nodded as if already knowing this, but Norm was determined to assert his authority in such matters.

'I s'pose youse know where Italy is?' he asked, and after receiving a blank look from them, grinned triumphantly. 'It's in Europe, yer drongos, and full of Eyeties. That's what they call Italian people. They eat garlic, my dad says, and make pricey cars. Whoever owns this must be worth a few quid.' He turned to Teddy. 'It's somebody you know, 'cos it's parked in front of your house.'

But it wasn't anyone that Teddy knew. When he went inside he found a stranger, a tall man in a tan summer suit, with Belle's lipstick on his mouth and his blond hair in disarray.

'Darling,' she said, for he had come in quietly by the back door, 'you do sneak up on people. This is a friend of mine from when I was in vaudeville. His name is Dan.'

'Dan, Dan the comedy man,' the visitor said. Teddy caught a glance between them. He thought his mother was frowning – as she sometimes did when she was sending him a warning – and he saw the man take a sideways look at himself in the mirror that hung over the mantelpiece, then pat down his hair and wipe his mouth with the back of his hand. The smears of lipstick were transferred there. Teddy saw them when Dan stretched out to shake hands.

'Dan Hardacre. You wouldn't remember me, young shaver. The last time I saw you, you were knee-high to a grasshopper.'

Teddy nodded politely, although he didn't like being called a young shaver, and wondered what the man was doing there, apart from kissing his mother when no one else was home.

'She was good, your mum. Great dancer, terrific legs, the best in Harry Larsen's revues. Belle was the youngest and prettiest girl in the chorus.'

'Dan!' This time Belle was definitely frowning. Teddy himself was puzzled. He felt sure the chorus was not very important, but that couldn't be right because his mother was quite famous.

'Not that I like to boast,' she said hastily, 'but the chorus was just a start. We did other shows together. Not only Harry's shows. Proper theatrical plays.'

'We sure did,' Dan now quickly agreed. 'Your mum and I go way back.'

'Not too far back,' Belle said. 'Speak for yourself.'

'You were only sixteen when we met. Sweet sixteen, so by my reckoning you can't be a day over thirty-two.'

'Thirty-one,' Belle promptly corrected him, which was when they heard the gate squeak, and the sound of the key in the front door.

Teddy had hardly ever seen George in a bad mood, but that night after Mr Hardacre had gone (which was what George had called him, making no attempt to shake hands, Teddy had noticed), Belle was in a sulk and George was cranky. They had their tea in complete silence, which was much worse than shouting at each other, and the two hardly spoke a word until Teddy had gone to bed and they thought he was asleep.

'You might've at least tried. Put on a show of making him feel welcome.'

'Why?' he heard George ask belligerently. 'Why the hell should I make that prick welcome?'

'Watch your language,' Belle said, which was strange because people in town were always saying her language was awful, a real disgrace, and Mrs Audrey Stevenson, the Methodist minister's wife, told church friends that Belle should wash her mouth out with soap. To this Belle replied she was a frustrated old chook who minded everyone's business but her own, or else she'd know about her husband and the new choir soprano in the organ loft.

But Dan Hardacre in his expensive sports car . . . that was something else. He and Belle had exchanged secret looks before he left, peculiar looks, and Teddy had seen George watching them. Belle waved as he drove away in a cloud of dust, and when she came back inside she said Dan was doing all right for himself these days. Never much of an actor, but with films now all the rage Dan had been smart and hopped on the bandwagon. Not acting – he'd hardly be driving a car like that if he was still an actor; he'd seen the light and got a job as the manager in Australia for the American film company United Pictures.

George had shrugged as if he wasn't in the least interested, and had gone outside to water the garden. Belle followed him, as though determined to explain the visit.

'You must have heard of United Pictures. They plan to make films here in Australia and Dan is in charge of production. It's his job to find the directors and actors. Listen to me, George, will you?'

'I'm listening.'

'I didn't tell you before, but I sent copies of those photos Mr Lucarotti took to Dan's office in Sydney. He really likes them. Thinks Teddy's big brown eyes and his freckled face would look great on the screen. Dan's on his way to Melbourne to a conference, but he was so impressed by the photos he did a detour to see for himself. He thinks someday there might be a part in one of his movies. How about that?'

George just grunted and went on hosing the cabbages, as if he did not believe a word of it.

Teddy didn't quite believe it either. And now he lay in the dark, listening to them quarrel.

'Don't you care that he might get work? A role in a film?'

'How could he? It'd mean missing school.'

'So what, if it's a chance to prove he's really good. I've always said he could be as big a star as that kid in America, Jackie Coogan. A few weeks off school won't matter.'

'Why don't we just drop the subject, Belle. How do you think I feel, coming home and seeing that bastard here?'

'Will you please listen for a minute?'

'I'm sleepy.'

'Well, sleep on this. You're a fool, thinking there's anything between Dan and me.'

'There was once. I'm bloody certain he's the one —'

'Shut up about that,' Belle said hastily, 'and just believe me, you're wrong about it. He's not.'

'You swear that's true?'

'I swear. Before God. On the Bible. I promise, George.'

'Next you'll try to tell me you were just good friends.'

'No, I won't lie about that. But it was long before I met you. You silly bugger, there were a lot better prospects than Dan Hardacre hanging around me back then. But I married *you*, didn't I?'

Teddy struggled against sleep, waiting for George's answer. Instead there was a long silence, then Belle's voice again.

'There,' she said, sounding different, so much softer he could barely hear her, 'that's more like it. Better shut the door.'

The house was dark and quiet, and while he tried to fathom what it all meant, Teddy fell asleep.

Chapter five

The station guard blew his whistle; the train began to shuffle out. Belle stood on the platform waving, then gradually became a small distant figure until Teddy could no longer see her, and he felt his first trace of homesickness.

'Cheer up, old chap,' Sam Swallow said, 'it's an adventure.'

His wife Mabel fossicked in her voluminous bag to produce a packet of sandwiches wrapped in greaseproof paper. She and Sam each took one, and she broke another in half and gave Teddy a portion.

'Remember, dearie,' she said, 'if the conductor comes along, you hide under the seat, there's a good boy.'

The train clattered past the signal box on the outskirts of town and picked up speed. This really is an adventure, Teddy thought. The pair sat opposite him, facing the engine. Second class, 'cos there ain't no third on this line, Sam said, and he announced they liked to travel with their public, 'cos that way you got to know 'em and he and Mabel had always been close to their fans. Around them the luggage racks were filled with their baskets of theatrical costumes.

It had all happened in the space of a few days.

Belle had been pleased and excited, showing George a postcard when he came home from work. 'From Sam and Mabel,' she said. 'Sam and Mabel Swallow. You remember – The Swallows.'

'Struth,' George had said with a frown, 'they're not coming to stay with us again?'

'Just for a night. Teddy can sleep on the sofa. Go on, don't be a grouch.' She hugged him. 'It'll make a change to hear all their news. Couple of troupers doing it tough on the vaudeville circuit. We can give them a bed.'

'Sure it's only one night? Last time they stayed a week.'

'They were broke then. Look what it says on the card, "just overnight to see you and George, and dear little Teddy who probably won't remember us. Then we're off early the next day to Wagga and Albury on a two-week tour". It can't be any plainer than that.'

'Off the next day.' George had smiled and tucked his arm in hers. 'In that case, it'll be nice to see them again.'

Sam and Mabel arrived from the station by taxi, because of the amount of luggage they brought. They were much older than Belle, even older than George, Teddy thought, and he guessed they must be at least forty. Sam had a ruddy face, tufts of ginger hair that didn't quite cover all of his head, and an English north-country accent. Mabel was small and plump and referred to herself as 'just a girl'. 'Us girls', she said, meaning her and Belle. Teddy thought that a bit peculiar, but he decided not to say so.

He knew Belle was really happy about their visit. She'd cleaned the house, picked flowers, cooked a big spaghetti and bought two flagons of wine for the occasion. Even George had enjoyed the evening, and laughed at Sam and Mabel's jokes; they seemed to have lots of them, Teddy thought, and they pushed back the furniture in the lounge room so it was like a small stage where they performed what they called their new 'routines'. Then Belle played the piano and Teddy sang for them.

'What'll it be, lad?' Sam had asked.

Teddy and Belle knew. She smiled and struck a chord. It was one of his favourites. He felt an easy confidence.

> In these hard times
> You gotta put up with anything,
> In these hard times
> You mustn't pick or choose,
> And if she's nice and you squeeze her tight,
> She'll ask you round tomorrow night
> If you don't mind sitting without a light
> In these hard times.

He tap-danced between the verses, as Sam and Mabel enjoyed more wine and enthusiastically applauded him.

'Bravo,' Sam shouted. 'Bravo!'

'He's a regular darling.' Mabel enveloped Teddy in a hug. 'I think we could use him.'

'What do you mean . . . use?' George asked.

'In the show, George dear. Does he have other numbers?'

'Dozens,' Belle said.

She refilled their glasses, and turned the lights low. Then she played as Teddy sang 'The Ballad of Kelly's Gang', after which he recited 'The Shooting of Dan McGrew', making them chortle, and finally Belle ran her fingers along the piano keys, and changed to a soft sentimental tempo. Teddy loved this song.

> There's a town beside a river,
> Running north from Rainbow Pond,

And the paddle steamers ply there
On their way to parts beyond.

When the people on the steamer
Ask what place it is, by chance,
The answer is, most likely,
It's a joint of some romance.

But sometimes they'll declare that
It's a spot of great renown,
Where a dog sits on a tuckerbox,
Just five miles out of town.

George had not been easy to convince, and not pleased when he found Sam and Mabel's plans had changed, and they would be staying three days after all. There were frequent arguments between Belle and George, some of which Teddy overheard.

'He can't go off with a pair of strangers, Belle.'

'They're hardly strangers. I've known Mabel and Sam since I was a kid. It's only two weeks, for heaven's sake.'

'He'll miss school.'

'He'll be on stage, in front of a proper audience. That's worth a couple of weeks of dull old school.'

Whacko! Teddy thought. Fights in the playground could be forgotten while he found out what it felt like to be on a proper stage. A real live theatre, not the stupid talent quest. He felt sure he wouldn't be even a tiny bit scared performing to crowds of people.

The arguments between Belle and George grew until they included Sam and Mabel.

'All expenses paid, George.'

'What, no salary?'

'George, old thing, we're offering him experience,' Mabel trilled.

'You can't buy experience, George, old chap.'

'And we are known,' Mabel pointed out. 'He needn't ever be ashamed of appearing on stage with "The Swallows". We have a very loyal following.'

'And we'll bring him safely home,' Sam insisted.

Teddy could see his dad was losing. While he really wanted to go by that time, he didn't want George to be upset.

'I'll send you a postcard, Dad,' he promised, and George sighed and said to make sure he did. Belle smiled and said she'd wash and iron his stage outfit and pack his suitcase. Mabel hugged them all, and said she'd treat him like her own.

The School of Arts hall in Wagga Wagga was not Teddy's idea of a theatre. It wasn't a proper theatre like the ones in Belle's scrapbooks. It had a noticeboard outside, and on this was pasted one of the leaflets he had helped Sam and Mabel distribute to the shops in town. After two places had refused them, saying they had a policy against the display of free advertising, Sam suggested Teddy might like to try the next shop alone.

It was an ironmonger's store, and the man behind the counter took the leaflet and carefully read it. He was very tall, and looked down from a great height at the nervous small figure.

'The Swallows, eh?'

'Yes, sir.'

'Never heard of 'em.'

'They're quite famous.'

47

'Must be. Says here, vaudeville at its very finest. Sam and Mabel return to entertain by popular request. And you, young man, are you a Swallow?'

'No, sir. I'm Teddy Carson.'

'And what do you do? Apart from handing out these?'

'I'm in the show, sir.' Teddy thought he should keep calling the man sir, because he was so tall. 'I sing and dance.'

'Do you?' the ironmonger said. 'Well, I might come along and see that. Want me to display this, eh?'

'If you wouldn't mind, sir.'

When he met them further down the street by previous arrangement, Sam said it was well done, very well done indeed, and perhaps Teddy should keep on with the shops while he and Mabel visited the hotels and the bowling club. That way they could meet and mingle with the prospective audience, and thus make sure every night was a full house.

If the School of Arts did not resemble a real theatre, the audience was even less like a full house. Small groups of people were scattered so thinly that it was uncomfortable. The rare moments of laughter the sketches produced were no more than titters that lapsed into embarrassed silence. Sam and Mabel Swallow performed with a grim tenacity, as if engaged in combat with their audience, a battle to win a trace of warmth and interest – one which was undoubtedly being lost – while they tried to ignore the vacant seats, the coughs and yawns, the restless shuffling of people eager to escape, and the awful echo of their own voices in the dead auditorium.

Out of sight behind the draped curtain on the prompt side of the stage, after being told to remain there and be quiet until he was called,

Teddy felt anxious and afraid. He wished he was safe at home; all his life he had been fed wonderful success stories of huge audiences that laughed and sometimes even cheered. But not here; he could tell this was a failure. This wasn't how it was meant to be, it was nothing like it had been in Belle's scrapbooks or in her stories.

As another of their sketches ended without a laugh or a vestige of applause, the Swallows walked off stage to the prompt corner. Sam was furious and dripping sweat; Mabel seemed close to tears. In desperation they looked at Teddy.

'Quick.' Sam nudged him. 'Get out there. Give 'em something, a song or a dance. Keep 'em there, or the buggers'll want their money back.'

'But . . . there ain't a piano. How can I sing?'

'Stuff the piano, get on the bleeding stage. Give us a break.'

'Quick,' Mabel hissed at him.

'What'll I sing?'

'Any-bloody-thing,' Sam said.

Teddy felt a sudden and unexpected push from Mabel. Taken by surprise, he went backwards, waving his arms in the air in an attempt to keep his balance, then slipped and fell flat on his back in the centre of the tiny stage. He sat up and looked in abject terror at the audience. He had no idea what to do, until someone tittered.

Teddy stood up, a tiny figure in his shorts and shirt, and began to rub his bottom as if it hurt. He thought two or three people laughed at this. Then he pretended to adjust his bow tie, a trick that Belle had shown him, making the audience believe he was looking in a mirror. He twisted it one way, then the other. He looked puzzled and swivelled his head as if the mirror was crooked.

Because the show until then had been so bad, and here was this diminutive figure miming, people started to chuckle. Out in the semi-dark a man clapped. Teddy made out his features, it was the friendly owner of the ironmongery shop. All at once terror evaporated; in the cold and hostile School of Arts the audience had a recognisable face. He snapped to attention and saluted him. It brought a sudden wave of laughter and even some scattered applause.

He heard it with relief. At the same time came the realisation he had only been on stage a few seconds, and he had no idea what to do next. Should he stand on his head? Try some more mime? Do a tap dance? His feet twitched, and he tapped for a few moments, uncertain if this was what they wanted. It was then that the idea came to him.

'A bunch of the boys were whooping it up in the Malamute saloon . . .'

There was an instant response as he launched into the first verse of 'Dan McGrew'. He gave it the fast rhythmic beat that Belle had instilled into him during rehearsals, and he felt the audience responding – without even looking he knew they were leaning forward, listening and smiling. There was no adjudicator to ring a bell and stop him, and he began to tease them with long pauses, bringing laughter, making them think he'd forgotten the words, then galloping into the next verse.

At the end when they stood and applauded, he let it run, milked it, then took a penny from his pocket, screwed it into his eye like a monocle and waited for their silence as they resumed their seats. When it was quiet he adopted the mock-English accent Belle had taught him.

> I'm Burlington Bertie, I rise at ten-thirty
> and saunter along like a toff,
> I walk down the Strand with my gloves
> on my hand,
> Then I walk down again with them off.

I'm Bert, Bert, I haven't a shirt,
But my people are well-off, you know.
And everyone knows me, even Lord
   Rosebery,
I'm Burlington Bertie from Bow!
I am –

'Really!' he called out to the rapt and captive audience, 'Ai'm Burlington Bertie from Bow.'

He tap-danced between the verses. There was no piano, but he didn't need one. Teddy took the penny from his eye, flicked it in the air and caught it. Then he put it back as a monocle in his other eye. He felt their warm and friendly laughter, felt their affection reach up to him.

It was like magic; like the best of the bedtime tales that Belle had been telling him for years. The glow, the feeling of wonder at taking an audience by the hand, discovering that they liked him. Teddy knew, with absolute certainty, there could never be another moment in his life as good as this.

Afterwards Sam and Mabel walked home in a glum silence, punctuated by remarks from her that sounded like a quarrel. He tried to keep up with their brisk strides, wondering what he had done wrong. After all, the audience had cheered him at the curtain call when Sam finally heeded their shouts and beckoned him forward. But, for some reason, ever since then, Mabel seemed to be angry about it.

'Upstaged,' he heard her say, 'by an anklebiter. Sod that for a lark.'

'Later. Talk about it later,' Sam murmured, as though he was trying to calm her down.

Their boarding house was on the far side of town, close to the railway station. When they had first arrived, Mabel told him that although they normally stayed at the Grand Hotel, this was the week of the

Riverina Cup race meeting and the town was full, so accommodation there was out of the question. But they had been fortunate to find digs, even if it wasn't quite up to their usual standard, and the landlord had kindly agreed they could all share the same room.

'Nice big double bed,' Mabel had said, 'so there's plenty of space for all three of us.' Teddy could snuggle up on one side, Sam on the other, and she'd sleep in the middle. There was a bathroom down the hall, and Teddy went there to brush his teeth and go to the toilet while Mabel changed into her nightie. On his way back, he was about to open the door when he heard them talking.

'Stupid bloody idea, being landed with him,' she was in the middle of saying angrily. 'If you hadn't been half-pissed, you'd never have suggested it.'

'You always did have a bloody short memory, Mabel. You was the one half-pissed – *you* suggested it.'

'Well, you agreed. So what do we do?'

'Use him. After all, he made 'em laugh. We couldn't get a giggle out of 'em, and he made 'em laugh.'

'These yokels will laugh at anything.'

'Well, they didn't fucking laugh at us.'

'Because we're too sophisticated for them. Out of their league. Let's get one thing clear, Sam. I ain't playing second fiddle to no bloody kid.'

Teddy tiptoed away, then coughed loudly before he pushed open the door of the room. They were both in bed. He said goodnight, and climbed into the tiny space allotted to him.

He wished he had some money of his own so he could run away from them, back home to Belle and George.

George was always the last to leave the kitchenware department. When he reached home he pushed open the gate and reminded himself it was time to oil it again. Across the street Miss Limmington's dog yapped as the spring squeaked shut. He parked his bike in the lean-to and went inside the house. Belle was at the stove.

'Still no postcard from him?'

'Not a postcard,' she said, turning for the obligatory kiss.

'He's forgotten.'

'He hasn't,' Belle said, and George's disappointment changed to a smile as she gave him an envelope, addressed in Teddy's rather unsteady and laboured handwriting. Inside was a leaflet of the show: below the names SAM AND MABEL SWALLOW he had carefully printed 'WITH TEDDY CARSON'.

'Just this? No news?'

'There's a drawing on the back.'

George studied it, frowning. 'It's a woman who seems to be riding on a broomstick.'

'Wearing a witch's hat. Made me laugh. That's what I'd call a pretty good likeness of Mabel Swallow. I'll bet he has some tales to tell when he gets home.'

The audiences grew smaller each night. The district manager was unhappy, and made no secret of it. He told Sam and Mabel he had been totally misled by their sharp city-slicker agent. In his own opinion, they were about ten years past their peak. And the peak couldn't have been all that high. If it wasn't for the talented small boy, he doubted if anyone would've turned up at all.

'Ridiculous,' Mabel said in reply. 'We expected a theatre, and you booked us into a morgue.'

'It's a perfectly adequate performance hall, which *you've* managed to turn into a morgue, Mrs Swallow. I'm giving you notice.'

'You can't,' she snapped heatedly, 'you booked us in for two weeks!'

'And now I'm booking you out – tomorrow. And you can forget Albury and the rest of the tour. It's cancelled.'

'We'll sue,' Sam promised.

'See you in court,' the manager said, unperturbed.

Teddy felt sure he must be dreaming. He thought he was at sea; it was like being on a raft that seemed to be bobbing up and down, only it was the double bed they all shared in the boarding house, and he could hear strange sounds. Sam seemed to be gasping for breath, making peculiar grunting noises, while Mabel was panting and whispering excitedly. The bed rocked, it felt like someone was wrestling, then Teddy was bumped and jolted onto the floor. Half-asleep and confused, he looked up dazed. The room was pitch-black.

'What's happening?'

'Bugger it,' he heard Mabel's voice, 'you've woken him.'

In the dark above him Sam seemed to regain his breath as he said, 'Up you get and back into bed. Go to sleep, old chap.'

'But what are you doing?'

'Exercise,' Sam said, between gasps. 'Keeping fit.'

'Be a good lad,' Mabel told him. 'Here's a pillow. Why not curl up over in the armchair, there's a pet. Till we finish our exercise.'

'No use,' Sam muttered to her, 'I've gone off it.'

'You can't go off it. Not now.'

'Well, I have.'

'You're bloody useless,' Mabel told him, sounding angry.

'Tough tittie,' Teddy heard Sam reply. 'It was your stupid fault, trying to save on rent. I definitely couldn't raise it, not now.'

Teddy stood in the chill, wondering what they were talking about.

'Can I get back in?' he asked.

'Might as well,' Mabel snapped.

He crawled into his allotted space on the edge of the bed. Mabel hastily shied away as his knee touched her bare flesh, and that was when Teddy realised she did not have her nightgown on. He fell asleep trying to work out what had made her so furious. By now he had come to understand what 'upstage' meant, and he wondered if he had somehow upstaged her again.

Belle lay awake in their small bedroom, long after they had made love and George had fallen asleep. Teddy's drawing had made her laugh at first, and quite impressed her. It was a distinct improvement on his rather untidy handwriting. But George had voiced a concern, speculating on whether they were treating him properly; if they were, then why did he regard Mabel as a witch?

Belle had tried to laugh, and said Mabel could be a bit bossy at times, and this was just their son having a bit of fun. Nice to know he had a good sense of humour. She was sure he'd come back with some funny stories about 'The Swallows'. But at the back of her mind the same thought had been troubling her all day. He was only eight years old. And Mabel could be a real cow; they were both pretty tough, she reflected, they'd had to be. Not much chance of surviving these days in the Depression and what was left of vaudeville otherwise.

They shook Teddy awake. He was confused; they never got up this early. It was still pitch-dark, but the curtain was pulled back and the window open. He realised Sam and Mabel were both fully dressed, and something peculiar was happening. Outside the window there was a street lamp. By its thin light Teddy could see their suitcase as well as the baskets with the costumes and his own small case, all being carefully lowered out of the window.

'Get dressed,' Mabel whispered.

'What's wrong? Why are we leaving?'

'It's a game, young Ted,' Sam told him as they handed him his clothes. 'Get dressed, lad, quick as you can. Nice and quiet. Put on your socks, but no shoes till we're outside.'

'I need to go to the toilet.'

'Shh,' Mabel gestured. 'Later.'

'It's urgent.'

'So is this,' she hissed, shaking him, and he realised it was not a game.

Teddy fumbled as he tried to hurriedly put on his clothes while the pair waited with ill-concealed impatience. Sam helped him climb out the window, then he and Mabel followed. They picked up their cases. Teddy was shivering as they stood silently in the glow of the street lamp and listened. Far away there was the sound of a train whistle, somewhere out on the tenebrous edge of the countryside.

'That's the milk train,' Sam said, 'right on time. Grab your things and run like buggery.'

A light went on in a room at the far end of the building. A blind shot up like the sound of a pistol firing. With the experience of many such escapes Sam and Mabel were already on the run, despite being heavily laden with their belongings. Behind them the pyjama-clad landlord appeared, framed in the lighted window.

'Come back, you dirty rotten bastards,' he shouted, then climbed out and began to give chase. Teddy, burdened by his own suitcase and a bundle of props, lost sight of the others. He knew they were supposed to head for the station where the sound of steam hissed as the train arrived. Behind him he could feel the footsteps of the landlord rapidly closing on him. He felt terrified. The train had stopped; mailbags were being tossed out and milk churns loaded.

He did his best to run faster, but the semi-dark was his undoing. Fearful of the pursuit, he turned to glance back over his shoulder, and in so doing tripped on a paving stone and went sprawling. He heard the grunt of satisfaction behind him, then felt the weight of the landlord as he was pinioned.

'Gotcha!' The man was breathless but triumphant. He hauled the scared boy to his feet. 'Them bastards can't skip now. They'll be back for you.'

'No.' Teddy was winded and bruised by the fall. Despite his fear he managed to add, 'I don't think they will.'

They both heard the guard's shrill whistle and the engine blasting steam as the train started to move out. The landlord, with an iron grip on his captive, turned to watch it leave.

Chapter six

The bike was waiting for him outside the front door. Belle and George heard his shout of delight, and watched from the window as he mounted it and rode a short distance across the yard before losing his balance and falling off. They rushed out to help him to his feet.

'I'm not hurt,' Teddy said. 'Gosh, this is the beautest present I've ever had, and it's not even my birthday yet.'

Belle was about to say that beautest was not a proper word, but felt George touch her hand; instead she smiled and said it was a birthday present in advance, only he mustn't ride on the road until he'd had more practice.

'Definitely not on the road till we say so.' George was quick to support her.

'Right, I'll practise all weekend. Watch me this time,' he called, and rode twice around the yard without falling.

Belle realised George was still holding her hand. 'It was a lovely idea, George.'

'Bit of luck, getting it cheap from work. It was a trade-in on a Malvern Star, so I thought it too good to miss. The boss said I can pay it off, four bob a month. Pretty good that, a shilling a week.'

'With interest?'

'Of course. But we'll manage.'

Belle felt a sudden affection for him. This was the closest they'd been since the hideous day, weeks ago now, when she had been forced to take the train to Wagga to bring Teddy home. It had been Percy Bates who'd brought the news, arriving at their door and removing his cap, wiping the sweat from his face to say there'd been a phone call from the police down there. A landlord had made a serious complaint that his lodgers had done a flit, and left a child behind. He had caught the boy and wanted him held as security until his rent was paid, but he'd been warned such action was against the law.

The law, it seemed, had taken control of the situation. Her son was in protective custody, but according to the station sergeant who had telephoned, he was badly disturbed by the experience, and it was not lawful to simply put him on the train and send him home. Illegal, the policeman said, who seemed to relish stressing this. He must be properly collected by a parent or a guardian, or else it'd be a matter for the local magistrate and the children's court.

After that – as if that was not enough – there was the humiliation of finding money for the train fare, and having to go to Gable's Emporium to tell George. She still remembered his incredulity, his look of angry disbelief as he asked how her so-called friends could have done a thing like this. Belle, close to tears, pleaded with him not to quarrel about it in front of everyone, but to please ask Mr Gable for an advance against his salary, so she could catch the midday train to collect Teddy and be back before nightfall.

In the end it had been Belle herself who had convincingly lied to Gable, aware he had often eyed her with a look she knew well, especially when his plump wife wasn't watching. Belle glibly told him that some friends had taken their son on a trip, but this was an emergency because he wasn't well and she was anxious to bring him home in case it was serious.

'Better hospitals down there, if he's ill,' was all Mr Gable had said, eyeing her with the same sly look, while arranging for the advance.

After the anxious journey by train, she had to endure the ordeal with the disapproving Wagga police sergeant. He was blunt, asking her what kind of mother she was, and what sort of treacherous friends would do a moonlight and leave a young kid behind? He made it clear he thought she was mad, allowing an eight-year-old to go off with a couple of untrustworthy theatricals. Perhaps she was, she'd meekly agreed, but please could she see her son?

First he'd made her sign a form and told her that if anything like it ever occurred again, he'd personally see the matter was handed over to the welfare department. He had watched, unsmiling, while mother and son had a tearful reunion, and Belle had calmed Teddy and left the office with relief. She could still vividly recall the burly police sergeant's face at the window, his stare becoming a gaze of open contempt as he watched her walk away.

Only one thing had been salvaged from that awful day. On the railway platform, awaiting the return train to Gundagai, a porter had wheeled a trolley past the bench where Teddy was sitting on her knee, clinging to her as if determined not to be left behind. The porter had stopped and looked at them.

'I know who he is. Saw him in that crook show they put on at the School of Arts. Are you his mum?'

'Yes,' Belle said, wondering what sort of savage blow would next assault her.

'He was good,' the man said. 'Real good. Them other two, the oldies, they were plain awful, but he was great. Tell you somethin', lady, I seen a few shows in me time. He was easy the best kid I ever seen on a stage.'

All the long way home Belle had felt comforted by that. But in the time since, she had repeatedly asked herself, what did it really mean? The man was not a critic, he was a railway employee, a porter. Not a producer, not a director or a talent scout. Just a person pushing a luggage trolley up and down a country platform. Yes, he did seem genuine in his admiration: it had been spontaneous and sincere, and Teddy had basked in it, the first good thing to happen since the Swallows – proper scum of the earth they were, she decided, so-called friends who had no ethical standards – had done a moonlight and abandoned him. The porter's remarks had made the journey home more agreeable, but the truth still had to be faced. What was the point of having real talent when there was no chance it could ever be put to use? It was almost worse knowing that someone thought him so good.

'Let him have a proper childhood,' George had pleaded with her the night after their return. 'For God's sake, Belle, what's so wrong with him having an ordinary sort of life?'

Almost everything, she thought bleakly, but what was the use of saying so? An ordinary life was all her son would ever have, the 'proper childhood' George felt was so essential. Attending that awful school, where he seemed to be constantly fighting but refused to explain why; after that the high school, she supposed, until he was old enough to leave and find work; then growing up to become part of the town with its banal conventions and limited horizon. A mundane and ordinary existence was the only kind on offer in this district.

In her heart she tried not to blame George. It wasn't his fault that jobs were so scarce, the Depression biting deep, and thousands out of work. She knew he could not leave Gable's Emporium. All over the country men were tramping the roads, living on the indignity of the government's relief cards that offered a subsistence of food, enough to survive on for a week, as long as the recipients moved on to the next town. Awake late at nights, she secretly admitted to herself that George was right; they had a house and a basic wage coming in. Barely three pounds a week, but it was food on the table, even if there was not much money left over. Just enough for a loving father to afford an extra shilling a week payment on a bike, at an exorbitant rate of interest.

Yet Belle often dreamt of what might be. Remembering her own early life, she wanted it to be different for Teddy. Her parents, tragically drowned in a storm off Long Reef when she was still a schoolgirl, had been dismissive of her youthful ambitions. Sent to live with her remaining relative, Aunt Ethel at Greenwich, she had been told to apply herself to cooking, sewing and domestic science in readiness for life as someone's wife. At sixteen, breaking away from this family restraint, she went out on her own, taking jobs to pay for dancing and singing lessons. Then the real stage at last, real shows – at first the chorus, after that bit parts if a producer or director favoured her, although she had her own rules. There were strict limits: no old pervs; they had to be likable or attractive; and it needed to be mutual – not for her the hurried knee-tremblers after rehearsal at the back of the upper circle. She had standards. Well, most of the time anyway, she admitted in moments of singular honesty.

But how she missed it all. Even the tough times between jobs, with three or four girls sharing a single room, eating cheap, walking to the city from Darlinghurst to save the tram fare, queuing for auditions . . . fond recollections softened by the years, perhaps, but there was always laughter, she vividly remembered that. There was the fun of being seventeen; blokes at the stage door with small bouquets and big hopes. The array of live theatres, tiny amateur playhouses to the big-seaters: the Princess, where she'd appeared in a walk-on with Roy Rene and Nat Phillips; the Criterion, where she had two lines in a mystery thriller before becoming the corpse and having to lie on stage as still as death until the interval curtain. Not forgetting the Showcase Theatre, where she and Dan had been in the chorus backing 'The Great Delilah' – the world's most famous feminine magician, with her fifty amazing miracles, twice daily! And what a terrible bitch she was – what a dictatorial old tart, that famous Great Delilah.

Sometimes, remembering, it was like a jumble of exciting images, a moving kaleidoscope in her mind. The sheer vibrancy of the city with its crowds, the constant traffic, the splendid new picture palaces with orchestras on stage, or an electric organ rising like an illusion from the pit. And in the daily newspapers, page after page advertising films and their stars. Whereas in Gundagai there was just one lone cinema that, because of the Depression, few people could afford, and once in a while there was the advent of the travelling Picture Show Man.

Belle felt certain, were they able to live in one of the cities, it could be so different. There, with frequent auditions, Teddy would at least have the chance to prove his talent. The railway porter, after all, was part of an audience, and it was the audience's reaction that in the end created stars. But such dreams were out of reach. They were virtual prisoners in this country town, too far from anywhere; nothing could change that.

Until four months later, when the letter came.

Chapter seven

She waited by the gate, trying to hide her excitement as she saw Teddy wave from his bike at the street corner. Any moment George would appear from work. It was five-thirty, and he unfailingly reached the house at that time each afternoon. The store closed at five; he took fifteen minutes to tidy his department and another fifteen to walk home. Sure enough, his figure turned the corner with Teddy cycling beside him, expert enough now to be able to ride at walking pace while relating the events of his day.

But not of hers, she thought with an inner excitement, and took out the letter that no one else yet knew about, and read it again. Then she went inside to make sure there was a bottle of cold beer in the refrigerator, and that the stew was gently cooking so the meat would be tender.

'Guess what?' Teddy said, cycling alongside George and eager to tell him the momentous news. 'Pig Morgan's gang has been taken over by us. We trapped them, Dad; it was all my idea, and I've been promoted to sergeant. I'm number three after Ginger and Norm in the joint gangs. How about that?'

'Wait a minute,' George said, with a grin. 'Why not start at the beginning? How were they trapped, and what was your idea that worked this famous victory?'

That was what Teddy liked about George. You could tell him all sorts of things like this, whereas Belle thought kids' gangs were childish and dangerous. When he came home from school he'd thought about telling her, but she had only been interested in some letter she'd been sent. It was different with his father. He dismounted from his bike so they could walk together.

'I said we should ask Pig to a meeting under our secret tree. It meant we had to risk telling him our headquarters' location, and we made him promise to come alone, so we could have a peace talk. I told Norm and Ginger he was sure to agree, then he'd doublecross us. He'd bring his mob and surround us. They'd try to trap us up the tree.'

'And did they?'

'You bet. There were about twenty of them, all armed with stones and catapults, telling us to come down and surrender. Then . . . listen to this, Dad —'

'I'm listening,' George said, and as if to prove it he repeated, 'they told you to come down and surrender . . .'

'That's right. And we had to pretend we were scared they'd pull on the ropes to climb up and get us. They fell for it! They pulled the ropes, thinking they were ladders, and down it came.'

'Down what came?'

'Bags of cow shit – I mean manure – that we'd collected. It covered them and made them stink. You should've heard the row! They all blamed Pig Morgan, and pushed him in the river. Then the rest had to dive in to get rid of the pong, and we slid down the tree on our ladders, and let fly with catapults. After that they surrendered and we made a treaty.'

'Cow manure?'

'Heaps of it. Stank like the dunny cart.'

'Pretty fierce tactics, Teddy.'

'All's fair in love and war, Dad.'

'I s'pose it is, son.'

Belle waited until George was sipping his nightly beer before she produced the letter. She smiled and handed it to him to read.

'It came today,' she said. 'I was dying to go into town to tell you, but I thought it best to wait. Read it. They want him.'

'Who wants him?'

'George dear, read it. Remember the photos I sent to Dan Hardacre? How he promised there might be a part some day? Go on, read the letter. Aloud, so Teddy can hear.'

Teddy could see George frown, then he began to read. 'Dear Belle, we are in the process of mounting a local picture here at the White City Film Studios at Rushcutters Bay. American stars seem to be the policy these days, but there is a part for a young Australian boy. I suggest you bring Teddy to Sydney to meet the American director, who was very impressed by that photo of him expertly shedding tears. I've told the Yanks he's exactly what they are looking for . . .'
He stopped reading and shrugged.

'You see?' Belle said.

'What I see is that nothing's guaranteed. Meet the director, that's all. What I don't see is any offer of train fares or expenses.'

'Dan wouldn't waste time writing, unless it was a real chance.'

'You just said it – a chance. And we can't afford it.'

'We have to.'

'Belle, we haven't got the money. You know that as well as I do.'

'Ask the bank —'

'They won't lend us a penny.'

'They might.'

'Not a hope. If we had enough to pay fares and accommodation, I s'pose you'd talk me into it. But we haven't. So please just forget it.'

He handed back the letter. Belle looked stricken. Teddy felt she might cry, and kept hoping she wouldn't. Besides, he was not sure if he wanted to go away just now, not after his gang's victory.

'Write to your friend Hardacre if you want,' George said, 'and tell him to send expenses and train tickets. Then we might know if it's real.'

'Don't be stupid,' she replied bitterly, 'that's not how it's done. You don't make demands like that till they offer the job. They'll have half the kids of Sydney lining up for a role like this, so why would they feel obliged to send our fares?'

'I think,' he said, draining his beer and placing the glass firmly on the sink, 'you've hit the nail square on the head. It's only a very faint chance, and we don't have any money for faint chances. So that's the end of it.'

The Bank of New South Wales was, by consent, the grandest building in town. Dating from the 1870s and erected after a disastrous flood had forced the first settlement of Gundagai to be rebuilt on higher ground, the Georgian architecture with its fine sandstone enhanced the main street. The interior contained high ceilings with intricate plaster cornices and sculpted friezes. An air of reverent hush prevailed, and business was invariably transacted with the utmost decorum.

In his managerial office, portly Clarence Burwood was doing his best to preserve this propriety, but finding it a struggle. Some clients were more difficult than others.

'My dear Mrs Carson,' he said, determined to be affable, 'I'm trying to explain, in the simplest terms, that you cannot borrow money without security.'

'No need to treat me like a simpleton,' Belle told him.

'That wasn't what I meant,' he replied hastily.

'Well, that's how it sounded.'

'Look, I'm sorry, but I do have other appointments.' He pushed back his chair, waiting for her to take the hint. It was a tactic that usually worked, but to his annoyance Belle showed no sign of leaving.

'You haven't finished this appointment yet. I'm prepared to sit here till we work something out. For instance, I'll mortgage the house.'

'You can't mortgage the house, Mrs Carson,' he said, becoming terse, his hands fidgeting irritably.

'Why not?'

'Because the house is already mortgaged.'

'So forget about mortgages. Let's discuss details.'

'Let's not,' he snapped.

She felt anxious. There was no other way she could obtain the money. This was her only hope.

'Ten lousy pounds, Clarry. It's nothing to you. But it's life or death to me. Ten rotten quid. Are you going to stand in the way of a talented child's future for a measly tenner?'

'I'm not a benevolent society. Just a bank manager.'

'And a good one, everyone says so. But try to understand – it's just ten pounds. I might only use five, but I need the rest in case of emergencies.'

'You may as well ask for fifty.'

'But I don't *need* fifty. I only need ten. We'll travel third, and stay in cheap digs. I promise you'll be repaid,' she pleaded. 'Teddy's first money . . . it comes straight back to you.'

'Assuming he gets this role —'

'He will,' Belle asserted.

'I'm sorry,' Burwood said with finality, 'but that's nowhere near good enough. We require security.'

'I promise, on my word of honour, you'll be paid.'

'Banks just don't operate like that, Mrs Carson.' He began to rise again, determined she would take the hint this time.

'Right,' Belle told him, 'then I'll make you another promise.'

'Promises, my dear lady, are of no consequence.'

'This one is. I promise if I don't get this loan, your wife and the staff will be told how you put your hand up my dress at the amateur theatricals.'

The bank manager's face went bright red. He sat down with a force that made his chair clatter.

'Cut it out, Belle,' he retorted heatedly, 'that's bloody blackmail.'

'Of course it is.' Belle was calmness personified. 'But I tried it your way, Clarry. Now we'll do it mine.'

In the night the train whistle blew as it sped across the Riverina plain. Opposite her the small figure of Teddy stirred, opened his eyes as if to ensure she was still there, then fell asleep again. Belle smiled while she thought of Banker Burwood's alarm as his secretary came in to remind him two other clients were being kept waiting for their appointments.

'Er, thank you, Miss Barnett,' he'd said, taking out a handkerchief to mop his brow, the sweat on it obvious to both women, 'I won't be long.'

'In fact, I think we've probably finished,' Belle had said. 'Haven't we, Mr Burwood?'

'Yes, virtually.'

'Just the formalities to complete,' she reminded him.

'Quite. Er . . . Miss Barnett, please bring me a loan form for Mrs Carson to sign. And, er, ten pounds in cash.'

Bloody blackmail indeed, Belle thought, but the randy little bastard caved in, which was all that mattered. Miss Barnett had left with raised eyebrows and returned with ten crisp pound notes and the loan form. Belle felt certain that rumours and speculation would by now have enlivened the bank. She enjoyed the thought as she closed her eyes, lulled by the rhythm of the train. Three days, she thought. Time enough. George had been astonished, not exactly thrilled, but had no argument left when she produced the borrowed money without revealing her methods of persuasion. Just three days, she had promised him.

She slept for a while and woke early, with the dawn light revealing the drab sight of crowded suburbs, tiny backyards, a horsedrawn milk cart in the street, the train clattering through the rail stations towards Central. Teddy was now awake, looking with wonder at the congestion of houses, terraces bound by communal walls, their small strips of land bordering the railway embankment. At road junctions there were trams and lines of early traffic, with uniformed policemen preparing for the impending peak-hour chaos.

It was two hours before they managed to find a room in Paddington. A sour-faced landlady assessed them, silently priced their cheap luggage, and grudgingly agreed she had a vacancy.

'Top floor, two shillings nightly, plus sixpence for the child,' she said. 'Three nights minimum stay, and payment in advance.'

WHITE CITY STUDIOS was the name spelled out in huge letters across the building. It looked more like a warehouse than a film studio, most people agreed, and it stood like a landmark on the hill above the White City tennis courts and Rushcutters Bay boxing stadium. A high brick wall screened inside activity from public view, and there was a colourfully dressed guard at the gate to keep out the uninvited.

'Mr Hardacre, you say? That would be Mr Daniel Hardacre? Is he expecting you?'

'Yes,' Belle replied at her grandest, determined on some respect after the humiliation of the awful residential where the room was squalid and the shared bathroom was not only filthy, but required sixpence in the meter for barely enough hot water to bathe in, 'will you kindly tell him that Mrs George Carson from the country is here, with her son Edward.'

'Wait here,' the guard said, unimpressed, and after a delay to demonstrate his authority he sent a messenger boy to convey the message to the front office.

'Am I called Edward in Sydney?' Teddy asked in confusion, because it had been a perplexing day, trudging between residentials that were either full up or too expensive – as well as one that didn't take children, and another that Belle said was just a knocking shop, whatever that meant. When they did eventually find one and were told they had to pay the rent in advance she didn't like the room, and Teddy had to share a bath with her because it cost sixpence. When they'd tried to walk all the way to the studio to save the fare, she was limping. He'd noticed and pretended he was tired so they caught the tram after all. And now she talked to the uniformed man in a funny la-di-da voice, and called him Edward.

'It's all right, darling,' she said, 'just a bit of show in front of that silly dressed-up concierge. Looks like a leftover extra from *The Chocolate Soldier*. Acts as if he's guarding Buckingham Palace.' She saw her son's confusion, and put a consoling arm around him. 'Never mind me, love. It's been a long day, and we're both tired, but I'm sure that everything will be worth it when we see Dan Hardacre.'

After ten minutes the telephone rang, and the guard told Belle to go to the main reception hall. Mr Hardacre would see them.

They met in the echoing hall. It was busy with people working, women at desks were typing and young messengers were hurrying with cans of what Belle told him was celluloid film. To Teddy it felt like a strange place to talk, but Mr Hardacre took them to a sofa and sat them down. He seemed perplexed and upset.

'Jesus Christ, Belle,' he said, 'I had no idea.'

'No idea of what, Dan?'

'That you'd lob in here like this. No letter, no phone call.'

'But you wrote to me,' Belle said, 'so here I am. Here we are.' She smiled brightly, determined to believe that nothing was wrong. It seemed to agitate Dan Hardacre.

'I wrote in good faith, Belle. Please understand that,' he said, taking her hands and gazing at her, 'but I only found out in the past two days what my status is in this company.'

'You're their Australian manager, in charge of production.'

'So I was led to believe.' He shook his head. 'But what I really am is an office boy. I'm in charge of bugger-all.'

'What?' Belle's voice was more of a startled whisper.

Teddy felt confused. Mr Hardacre looked as if he was finding it difficult to explain. He released Belle's hands and avoided her gaze as he continued.

'I open the mail and write the letters so that if anyone claims that America has monopolised this industry, the Yanks can point to me and say one of our major companies makes films here, and it's managed by an Australian. The trouble with that is, it's bullshit. I'm just a cover to mask their invasion of our culture. I'm allowed to make cheap movies with small budgets, half of which don't get shown at all. This successfully shuts up the few politicians who actually give a damn. When they ask what's wrong with our industry, the answer is the films weren't good enough to be exhibited.

'But this one was to be different. I was told I was executive producer. I suggested a cast to be auditioned, including Teddy. The director and producer, both from Hollywood, said it was a big role but they agreed to test him. So I wrote to you. Then, last night, they told me they'd decided to cast the film their way, with all imported actors. His part will be played by a kid from one of their previous films.'

Teddy watched Belle. She was staring at Mr Hardacre, for once without a single word to say.

'Utterly wrong for the role, of course. Wrong age, wrong accent – but well known in the United States. That's when I realised I was no more than their local figurehead. I would have telephoned you, Belle, but I didn't know the number.'

'We don't have a telephone,' Belle said after a long pause. She felt sick with disappointment, but tried not to show it.

'I wrote to warn you this morning. It's probably being typed in the office right now. I can show you the letter, if it helps,' he offered.

'How could it?' she asked. 'Luck of the draw. It's what they call show business, isn't it?'

'Jesus Christ,' Dan said, 'get angry, will you?'

'No point, Dan. How will that change anything?'

'It'd make me feel better,' he answered.

'Perhaps it would.' She shrugged and contrived a wry smile. 'Well, I'm sorry. I can't do that.'

'Of course you can't. It was a stupid thing to say. So what happens now?'

'What I always intended, if he didn't get it. Spend a few days here. See some friends. Maybe even find him an agent – for the next time.' She managed to summon another smile for him. 'Don't feel bad about it. We'll manage. We'll be fine.'

Late that night Teddy knew Belle was awake, and heard a sniffle. Moonlight showed through the flimsy curtains. He could see her reaching for a handkerchief.

'Mum, are you crying?'

'Crying? Of course not.' She looked away to prevent him seeing the tears on her cheeks. 'Good heavens,' she continued, 'why on earth should I cry? We're going to have a lovely three days, and enjoy ourselves.'

'But what happens when our money's gone?' Teddy asked.

'When it has,' Belle replied, 'then we'll go home.'

Chapter eight

Belle took him on a tram ride to Bondi, and Teddy was enthralled by his first sight of a beach, the surf rolling in and swimmers riding the waves. They had an ice-cream and walked along the Esplanade, where a Salvation Army band was playing. When the tambourine girl started moving around the small crowd with her collection box, they managed to leave before she reached them. On the sand excited children were busy making castles, and although he gazed longingly at a stall selling buckets and spades, Belle pretended not to notice.

They shared a bag of fish and chips, and in the afternoon went to see a friend of Belle's, an agent in the city. If there was anything brewing, any auditions or shows planned, dear old Maurie would know about it, she told him. Leaving the tram at Queen's Square to save the cost of an extra section, they walked across the city. There were long queues at the St James, where a Greta Garbo film was playing. Those waiting for seats in the unreserved stalls extended in a line around the block. The more prosperous-looking people stood in a far shorter queue for the dress circle. Belle noticed most of the women were dressed in bright spring outfits, realising that in this part of town there were many who could afford the latest fashion. She felt like a country cousin in what were her best clothes, and envied their silk dresses with elegant longer hemlines. Their new chic hats and ankle-strap high heels were an added spur to her discomfort.

Teddy was amazed by the bustle of people in the streets. Belle took his hand so they would not be jostled and separated by the crowds. In Castlereagh Street she showed him the imposing facade of the Theatre Royal.

'Cecil Kellaway,' she said, indicating the name spelt out above the title. 'I was in a show with him once.'

'Let's go and see him, Mum,' Teddy suggested.

'Darling, he has a matinee. Besides, he's a big star now. I doubt if he'd remember me.'

'I bet the stage doorman would.'

'Perhaps,' she said, and squeezed his hand affectionately, 'but with the matinee he'll be busy too.'

David Jones displayed a galaxy of cajoling signs. One read: AMAZING SALE – LESS THAN HALF PRICE. OUR SACRIFICE IS YOUR OPPORTUNITY. Belle stopped to admire a smart coat, 'Given away at an absurd one guinea'. She gazed longingly at fashionable shoes: seven and sixpence. Despite these bargain prices, the store seemed almost empty.

The tough times are not just in the country towns, she thought, the only busy places here are the cinemas showing overseas films. As if to endorse this, they passed the Regent, where Ramon Navarro's name was illuminated in neon lights across the giant facade, and people stood waiting for the next session.

King George Chambers had once been a prestige address, but the building was now marked for demolition. To Teddy, Maurie Silver seemed immensely old. His office up two flights of stairs was small and cluttered with packing cases. A young male assistant was helping him to fill them with files and photographs.

'Belle Baker,' he announced with delight, 'as I live and breathe.'

'Belle Carson now,' she said, and hugged him. While he had never been a tall man, in the ten years since she'd known him he seemed to have shrunk. But his friendly face was unchanged. Around his eyes were the same good-humoured creases, and he still had the same warm smile.

'What a nice surprise. Not a day older.'

'I've got an eight-year-old son to prove I am,' she smiled.

'The looks, Belle,' he said, 'the looks, they don't get no older.'

Teddy could see how much this pleased her. Maurie Silver found seats for them amid the mess, and sent his assistant downstairs to bring a pot of tea, and a glass of milk for Teddy.

'Time to turn it in,' he told Belle, after she expressed dismay at learning he was not just shifting office, but closing down his agency. 'I've been at this game since they cranked the camera on *The Kelly Gang*, and all the other films we made here in this country. Top of the world we were then, truly the top of the film world. Sixty silent features in one year, can you imagine that?'

'Before I got married, I was an extra in a few,' Belle said.

'Exciting times, darling, but now the country's lost it.' He sighed, his wrinkled face reflective and nostalgic. 'We go backwards, Belle. A bit of government help, and we could've had a truly great industry. Equal to this Hollywood place.'

'No need to tell me.' Belle recounted their frustration of the previous day. Maurie sympathised. It was an all-too-familiar story.

'I wish I knew of something to help.'

'No auditions? Nothing around?'

'Nothing. Vaudeville's crook. Half the managements are importing their shows. The game seems over, Belle, that's why I'm giving it away. And let's face it, the stairs are getting beyond me. What'll you do?'

'Go back to Gundagai,' she said, not trying to conceal her despair. There had never been a need for pretence with Maurie. 'But first I promised Teddy we'd take a ferry. He wants to see this famous Harbour Bridge they've been building, so he can tell his friends. We may as well have something to talk about when we get back home.'

Teddy thought it was a marvel, unreal. Two huge spans of metal high above them built from opposite sides of the harbour had met with perfect precision in mid-air and locked together like a giant meccano set, the guide on the tourist ferry told them. Belle privately thought the ferry company were a bunch of robbers, charging a shilling for such a short trip, but it was a once-in-a-lifetime chance to see anything like this, so they had to afford it.

They sailed from the quay, out of Sydney Cove, beneath the almost-completed bridge, and across the harbour towards Blue's Point. The guide said the land was named for Billy Blue, the famous Jamaican-born ferryman and water bailiff, who had rowed the gentry in these waters over a hundred years ago, when Sydney was still a convict settlement and the harbour a trading centre filled with the sails and rigging of foreign vessels from all parts of the globe. His voice boomed out on a speaker as the group aboard the ferry looked up at the huge structure above them.

'The bridge is costing nine million pounds.' People on board gasped; it was a fortune, and no one could begin to imagine such an amount. The guide, who was a schoolteacher earning extra money in his spare time, always enjoyed the disclosure of this revelation.

'It was begun eight years ago, and will be finished within months. But the idea for a link between the town and the northern shore has existed for a long time. Believe it or not, that was suggested way back in 1815 by the convict architect Francis Greenway, who designed many of our finest buildings. You heard me correctly,' he said, as the group reacted with bemusement to this, 'back in 1815. After that the politicians debated it, and it took them a mere hundred years to make up their minds. Decisive people, our parliamentarians,' he said and was greeted by laughter, 'but at long last, there it is, ladies and gentlemen, boys and girls. The largest single-arch bridge in the world. The total length including approaches is two and a half miles. That arch, 390 feet above us, weighs many thousands of tons and rests on four steel pins.'

Everyone looked up.

'Don't worry,' he said amid the nervous giggles, 'they're very strong steel pins. They'll need to be; the bridge will carry trains, trams and cars. Motorists will no longer have to wait in queues for the car ferry to cross this stretch of water, not after the State Premier cuts the ribbon and declares it open. So there it is, folks, you can tell your grandchildren you were here when it was being built. One of the great new wonders of the world.'

Teddy could see distant figures above, men clambering on girders, or being hoisted up the metal arch in cradles. He went and tugged at the guide's sleeve.

'Did anyone fall or die?' he asked.

Just like the classroom, there's always one little bugger, the guide thought, and realised the question had been heard because the boy had a clear and resounding voice. He had to make the best of it.

'Our young friend asked if anyone fell or died.' He extended a hand to Teddy, and lifted him onto the bulkhead beside him. 'What's your name, son?'

'Teddy Carson.'

'And where are you from, Teddy?'

'From Gundagai.'

'Gundagai, eh? Where the dog sat on the tuckerbox?'

'Nearly right,' Teddy said, hoping Belle wouldn't think the man was teasing him and start a row, 'he sat on it five miles away.' He thought it'd be awful if she began to argue with the man while they were in the middle of the harbour unable to get off. But the other people laughed, and he felt relief because she was laughing too.

'Well said, laddie,' the guide chuckled. 'What about a round of applause for the young man from Gundagai?'

After they clapped him, a voice spoke out from the crowd.

'You forgot to answer his question,' Belle said.

Oh no, Teddy thought. If she starts to put on a turn, I can't dive off, 'cos there are sharks in the harbour. But the man was answering, and Belle was not putting on a turn.

'You're quite right, Ma'am. And if you're his mum, I'd say you've got a fine lad here. And he's lucky, too.'

'Why is that?' Belle asked.

'Because he has a good-looking mother – if you don't mind my saying so. As to the question, yes, I'm afraid there have been a few accidents. No doubt some of you remember reports in the papers. But that, as I'm sure we all know, is the price of progress.'

'Quite a nice type of man, really,' Belle said, after they had finished the short cruise and found a spot to sit in Macquarie Place Park under the shade of a Moreton Bay fig tree. 'He was most informative. I'm glad we went on that little trip,' she decided.

'He said you were good-looking, Mum.'

'Did he?' She cast this aside, as if she had already forgotten it, and began to unwrap a packet of chips bought from the fish shop at Circular Quay. She spread them on the newspaper so they could share. An identical-sized packet remained unopened.

'Yum,' Teddy said.

'Nice?'

'Beaut.'

'Beaut-tiful,' she corrected, then smiled. 'All right, beaut then, just for today. Teddy, the important thing to remember about chips is this: never buy sixpence worth in one go. Always ask for two threepenny portions.'

'Why, Mum?'

'Because you get more that way.'

'Truly?'

'Believe me. It's a useful tip gathered from long experience of making the pennies stretch further.'

'Are we very poor?'

'No, darling, of course not. I wouldn't say *poor*. We just don't happen to have much money. Not many families do these days. There's a thing called the Depression.'

'I know about that. They told us at school. Lots of people's dads don't have jobs, but ours does, so we're lucky.'

'Yes,' Belle said, after a moment, 'we're lucky.' She was about to unwrap the second packet when her eye was caught by a tiny heading just visible among the grease stains in the newspaper. She snatched at it, scattering most of the remaining chips on the ground, and pigeons swooped to capture this unexpected bounty.

'Mum, you spilt them . . . the birds are grabbing our chips.'

'Never mind. Here, eat these.' She thrust the second package at him while she carefully studied the news item. She read it with incredulity and started to laugh.

'What is it?' Teddy asked, offering her a fresh chip, but her eyes were fixed on the story.

'Measles,' she said gleefully, 'he's got the measles! Listen to this. "The head of United Pictures, Mr Daniel Hardacre, has announced a delay of the film due to start at the White City film studios, because the young American co-star, ten-year-old Andy Colvin, has contracted measles. The ship on which he was travelling to Australia was obliged to leave him in Honolulu for hospital treatment. It may mean an indefinite delay, Mr Hardacre said, as no steamer on which Andy could travel is expected in Hawaii before the end of the month."'

She dropped the soiled newspaper, grabbed her handbag and searched it hurriedly for coins. She found two pennies.

'Stay here,' she said, then thought about it and changed her mind. 'No, come with me —'

'Mum, I ain't finished,' Teddy complained.

'Darling, "ain't" is not a word. You *haven't* finished.'

'Well, I haven't.'

'Then hang onto them. Eat as we go.'

'Where are we going?'

'To find a public telephone. There may be a God after all.'

The same guard at the studio gate made a formal pretence of appraising them, taking his time, checking their names on a list, and eventually told them to go in. He would telephone Mr Hardacre, who was expecting them.

'I know he is.' Belle relished the brief moment, but knew her triumph was premature. The guard knew it too.

'Four other boys've already been seen by the Yankee director,' he said by way of retaliation.

She felt her stomach knot with tension as they entered the main building. At least this time Dan's secretary met them, and they were taken through a labyrinth of corridors to his private office. He greeted them, looking harassed.

'I didn't know where to contact you,' he said as he sat them down. 'I thought you must've gone home. How did you find out?'

'I saw it in the newspaper,' Belle said.

'With the chips we bought,' Teddy added for Mr Hardacre's benefit, but a stern look from Belle silenced him.

'Are we too late, Dan?'

'I'm not sure,' he shrugged. 'They're seeing others.'

'So I heard.'

'We may have to screen-test.'

'Then it'll be an Australian boy?'

'Maybe.' He sat beside them. 'I honestly don't know. I can tell you, there's one hell of a row going on. The American producer is performing like a bloody banshee. He wants to sue the steamship company. He says they could've put Andy into isolation on board ship —'

'Nasty contagious thing, measles.'

'Come off it,' Dan said. 'That's what should've happened, but apparently some of the other passengers insisted their kids were at risk. Complete crap, but one parent happened to be a director of the shipping line. As a result we can't get him here for four weeks.'

'Four weeks? Goodness,' Belle said, trying to conceal her delight. Dan Hardacre gave her a sharp look.

'The studio tried to find a pilot with a plane, but the kid's family won't let him fly – they say aeroplanes are far too dangerous.'

'They are,' Belle agreed.

'Stop interrupting,' he retorted bad-temperedly. 'Meanwhile, our female star has to leave the country in exactly three weeks. She's due to start another film in Hollywood, a big epic that can't be rescheduled. The whole thing's an utter shambles. The producer's a main-chancer, he's all for cancelling our production and going for litigation instead. Less risk, he says. To hell with making motion pictures if you can make money in court.'

'Haven't you got any say?'

He looked at her with ill-concealed impatience. 'You know my position, Belle. I told you the way things are, and how little my authority counts in this place. I just hang onto my well-paid job and try not to make waves.'

'At least get Teddy an interview. And a screen test.'

'I'm not sure if I can.'

'For old times' sake,' Belle pleaded. '*Please* try.'

Teddy sat watching them, trying to fathom what old times' sake meant. He recalled the peculiar, secret looks between them when Mr Hardacre had come to their house and George had been angry. A part of him hoped they were going home, but on the other hand, Belle was so excited when she read the story in the newspaper. He remembered how she had laughed. People in the park had looked around, because it was such a lovely sound, her laughter. But now she seemed upset and angry, and Mr Hardacre wasn't really pleased to see them, and looked as if he wished they'd go away.

'Who in the name of Christ is this?' a loud American voice said behind him. Teddy turned and saw a large bald man at the door. 'Jesus, dammit, the one thing we don't need is any more kids, Daniel. We've got four already. We're not trying to stock a goddamn kindergarten.'

'Hector —' Dan started, but Belle interrupted.

'If you don't mind, whoever you are, I'd prefer you don't use such profanity in front of my son.'

'Whoever I am, Ma'am?' The bald man gave her a withering glance. 'I'm Hector Hume, the producer of this damn movie that's falling flat on its ass, that's who I am.'

'Well, I'm Belle Carson, the mother of this boy who can act better than any child you may be testing. And if your film is really falling on that part of its anatomy, perhaps you'd condescend to test him. He might even save your "ass".'

Teddy couldn't help it; he grinned.

'Well, he's got a good face. Great smile,' Hector Hume declared.

'He can cry, too. Dan has some photographs,' Belle said.

The sound stage was huge, cavernous and dark. It seemed empty, except for a camera and its operator. Teddy felt very nervous in front of the camera. When the bank of lights came on and dazzled him, he felt as though the lens was peering into his face, trying to read his thoughts; if he moved or turned his head, the camera seemed to follow. It would not let him escape.

Somewhere in the gloom was Belle. He knew she was there, and wanted to call out to her, to say 'Let's go home, Mum. I'm scared. It's not like real acting; there are no people out there to clap or laugh.' If they would let him talk to her he would try to explain how he felt about the camera. It was just a machine on top of a tripod and it couldn't laugh at jokes or applaud.

A man appeared from out of the gloom. Teddy thought at first it was the producer, but when he came into the lit area he was younger. An American, like Hector Hume.

'You okay, kid?' He had a different sort of voice. Quieter.

'I'm not sure,' Teddy said.

'Nobody's ever sure the first time. Is it your first time in front of a movie camera?'

'Yes, sir,' Teddy replied.

'I'm Lawrence Andrews. My friends call me Larry. You can call me Larry.'

'Yes, sir.'

'You've learnt your lines?'

'Yes, sir . . . I mean Larry. It's easy to learn lines, 'specially when there's not many of them.'

'Good. There's always less lines in a movie, because your face helps tell the story. Like sometimes you have to look happy, or afraid or even sad – and if you can do that, it's better than words. Follow?'

'Sort of.'

It seemed easier to talk to him than the producer, who grumbled so loudly. And easier than Dan Hardacre, who Teddy didn't trust.

'Well, let's run through the scene, just you and me,' Larry Andrews said. 'Forget that lens. But I think you should know, Gus the cameraman says it likes you.'

'Likes me? How?'

'It's a kind-of audience. Did audiences like you?'

'Yes, sir,' Teddy said, 'they seemed to.'

'Well, the camera is gonna make you look good on the screen. Gus says that, and he's never wrong. So read the lines and forget the camera. Imagine we're on stage, but you don't have to speak as loudly. You're talking quietly to the front stalls, not trying to reach the back of the circle. Got it?'

'Yes, sir . . . Yes, Larry.'

'He's very nervous,' Belle whispered to Dan as they watched with Henry Hume by the sound-stage door. 'So stiff and not a bit at ease. He's frightened sick, I can tell. Let me go and talk to him.'

'You stay right here, Belle,' Dan tried to hush her.

'But I could help rehearse him through his screen test. I know the best way to handle him.'

'Just shut up and relax, Mrs Carson,' Hume said. 'No stage mother takes over *my* goddamn set. If anyone's making him nervous, you are. Matter of fact, lady, you're making us *all* nervous.'

They ran through the short scene, in which Teddy was a boy in hospital being told by his father he had to have an operation and he must be brave. Teddy felt stiff and anxious, because he knew how much Belle wanted him to get this role. She had said it didn't matter, but he could tell that wasn't true. It had made her cry, when she thought he was asleep. He knew you earned money acting in films, and if he did earn any money it would help her, and even help George, too. But he didn't think he'd done the scene well enough to be chosen.

'We'll try it again in a few minutes, Ted,' the friendly director told him. 'But first of all, why don't you take a few deep breaths, loosen up, and try to remember it's all make-believe.'

'Yes, sir. I mean, Larry.'

'Can you ride a bike?'

'You bet. Do I have to . . . I mean, in this?'

'No. Just asking. Shooting the breeze, we call it, while we wait for the camera to reload. Can you swim?'

'I swim in the river at home. But I'm not very good yet. Once, early this year, I nearly drowned.'

'What happened?'

'My dad rescued me. He dived in and saved me.'

'That was brave of him.'

'Yes, real brave. I tried to swim right across the river, but it was too far.'

'What's this river called?'

'The Murrumbidgee.'

'Murr-um-bid-gee,' Larry said, making it sound like four small words. 'We got a big river in the States which is called the Mississippi. I wouldn't like to try swimming across that, either.'

'Miss-is-sip-pi.' Teddy copied his way of pronouncing it. The director nodded and smiled.

'Good kid. Helps you to remember, breaking names into parts like that. Okay, so you're lying in bed in hospital, and I'm your pa, telling you the news. Let's you and me just relax, and do it again.'

Half an hour later, they left the studio building. Belle walked briskly, so rapidly Teddy had to almost run to keep up with her. The guard on the gate gave a curt nod, not bothering to speak to them. Belle ignored him as they went past.

'Surly brute,' she muttered, but only Teddy heard it. He did not know what had happened, or why they had left so abruptly. He did know his feet hurt, and to his relief when they reached the bottom of the hill there was a tram approaching.

'We'll walk,' Belle said. 'We'd have to change twice, and it means extra fares. We can't afford to keep spending money.'

'I'm tired,' he said. 'And look at my shoes, Mum.'

He raised one leg so she could see underneath the sole. There was a hole in the leather.

Belle sighed and took his hand as they stood at the tram stop. Teddy was unsure what had gone wrong. Larry, the nice director, had had a long talk with Mr Hume, the nasty producer, then Mr Hardacre had taken Belle aside to explain something, and the next thing they were leaving. He managed to contain his curiosity until they were on board and she had paid the conductor.

'Why did we have to leave, Mum? Didn't I get it?'

'I don't know,' she said helplessly. 'Even *they* don't know. Bunch of hopeless amateurs.'

'What do you mean?'

'It seems that if Dan Hardacre can't make any decisions by himself, neither can Hume. What a creep! Calls himself a producer, all he can produce is large gusts of hot air. He's not sure if they are going to make the film or cancel it. He doesn't know which boy he likes for the role, even if they do proceed. He has to send a wire – I suppose that means a telegraph message in plain English – to the coast.'

'What's the coast?'

'You may well ask, darling. Apparently it's the head office in Hollywood, where someone more important makes the decisions, then sends a "wire" back to creepy old Hume, telling him what to do.'

'But what do *we* do?'

'Wait, they said. Come back tomorrow, to see if there's any news. I would've thought that Dan, who is hardly a stranger – hardly that – might've done a bit better for me than this. But no, we must come back tomorrow.'

'But tomorrow —'

'That's what they said, sweetie. Those were the very words.'

'What about the other four boys?'

'Two of them have to come back tomorrow as well.'

'Mum . . . tomorrow . . . weren't we going home?'

'That director,' Belle said thoughtfully, as if he hadn't spoken, 'he liked you. He didn't say so, but I'm sure he thought you were the best. It's frog-face Hume who's the worry. As for Dan, he just sits there on both sides of the fence. Been doing that kind of thing all his life. It's a wonder he hasn't got a serious case of piles.'

'Mum,' Teddy persisted, 'won't Dad be expecting us tomorrow?'

She hesitated, and he knew they weren't going home yet. 'I'll write to him,' Belle said.

No, not home tomorrow. Or even perhaps the next day, Teddy realised.

When Dan asked her to sit down, offering her the comfortable chair, and Henry Hume and the director came to join them from the next office, their faces confirmed her worst fears. It had been three days. Three awful days of waiting while their precious money ebbed away.

The first day they had reported back at the White City studio they were told 'the coast' had not yet made a decision; they were not able to say if they intended to proceed, as Hume put it, to green-light the picture or shut it down. The second day word had finally come that as sets were built and artists contracted it was more expedient to proceed. That day one of the boys had been told he was not required, so it was down to two of them. Both eight-year-olds, which was the real age for the part. Teddy and another boy, who had blond curly hair.

'Please understand, Mrs Carson.' Hume for once moderated his tone. 'We think your young guy is great, but we've decided to go with the other kid.'

'We're sorry, Belle,' Dan added, looking stressed and upset, 'but we felt you deserved to be told in private like this.'

'Deserved to be?' Belle said, feeling such bitter disappointment she had difficulty remaining rational. 'Why "deserved"? A strange choice of words, Dan. As for understanding, Mr Hume, no, I don't understand at all. Is the other one, the fair-haired boy, Frank – if that's his name – is he so much better than Teddy?'

'On the contrary,' Hume began to answer, then he hesitated.

'On the contrary, what?'

While she waited for a reply that seemed as though it might not be forthcoming, both men looked at the hitherto silent director. Belle turned to him.

'Mr Andrews . . . or Larry, as you told my son to call you, they haven't answered my question. Can you?'

'They don't want to answer, Mrs Carson, because the truth is we're all as mad as hell.'

'Mad as hell? Why? Will one of you please speak in terms that I can understand? What's the truth, Mr Andrews?'

'The plain truth is . . . Frank's not better than young Ted. He's nowhere near as good. But the cable from the coast said the character should be blond, because Andy Colvin's blond. This other boy has the same kind of blond curls. And even though Teddy has perfectly acceptable light-brown hair, the studio's audience research apparently shows that blond kids have more appeal to the public.'

As Belle opened her mouth to protest, he forestalled her. 'I don't agree either, Mrs Carson. That's why we're all so angry.'

'But . . . can't you do anything?'

'I tried. I sent a wire to say we were casting the second-best actor just because of his hair colour and their dubious research. I was told to start shooting or ship out.'

'You see now, Belle?' Dan asked.

'Yes,' she said, 'provided this isn't just a tale to make me feel better.'

'Of course it's not.'

'So – what you're saying is this. If Teddy was blond, he'd have got it.'

'That's right,' Dan replied.

'I agree, Mrs Carson.' Hume was clearly anxious to terminate the meeting as quickly as possible. 'But unfortunately, he's not.'

'Don't you believe it, Mr Hume.' She was on her feet and already halfway to the door as she turned for a parting request. 'Just give me two hours.'

Teddy looked at himself in the mirror with astonishment. It wasn't him at all, the boy who looked back. He had curly blond hair. He had been scrubbed and rinsed – eyes stinging and nose running from the horrible stuff that bubbled and stank – and had his hair put in women's curlers, after which it was dried in front of the radiator as Belle fed coins into a slot every few minutes while continually calling the landlady a robbing old bitch who rigged the meter.

After this they had rushed downstairs to hail a taxi, with Teddy asking how they could afford it, and being told 'Sod the expense!'

The guard was eating his lunch when the cab pulled up outside the studio gates. He nearly choked on a ham sandwich as they swept by, the waft of peroxide trailing Belle and the transformed child beside her.

They went past the reception desk without challenge, Belle's gaze defying anyone to stop her. She barely knocked before pushing open the door to Dan's office and entering with Teddy. The three men were in deep conference. Before the other two had a chance to comment or protest, Larry Andrews was on his feet with an amazed smile, clearly delighted. He turned to Hume.

'Well, they wanted a blond star, Henry. I think you can wire the coast that we've got him.'

Chapter nine

George hoed the garden and planted rows of marrow and tomatoes, covering the seeds with rich soil sieved from the compost heap. He had little enthusiasm for the job – not since returning from work to find another letter from Belle in the mailbox – but while the daylight lasted he felt he should work in the garden, or there'd be no vegies in the patch when they came home. *If* they come home, he had begun to think lately. It had now been almost a month.

The letter had enclosed ten pounds to be repaid to Mr Burwood at the bank. She hoped George was well, and said she was not yet sure if the filming would be over by Christmas. She knew he would be disappointed, but they must think of Teddy's future. Meanwhile they had moved from the awful residential to a better boarding house, where Teddy had his own small room; this was a great improvement, for he needed his sleep because films were so demanding, and they had to get an early tram to the studio each morning to be on the sound stage at seven o'clock.

Percy Bates was riding past, sweating in his uniform. Seeing George he dismounted and wheeled his bike to the front gate.

'G'day, George.'

'How're you, Perce?'

'Bit hot. Gotta newspaper for you. Some bloke left it at the railway station, so I snaffled it. City paper. Young Teddy's in it.'

'Oh yeah?' George said.

'Getting famous, George. Good on you, mate.'

'I didn't do anything.'

'You're his dad. Must've done somethin', mate.' He laughed, and George managed a smile and said yes, he saw what Percy meant.

The policeman took a crumpled copy of the *Sydney Sun* from his jacket and handed it across the fence. George nodded his thanks, wondering if he should ask him in for a beer, then remembered he had only one bottle of home brew in the house. Sensing that no offer was forthcoming, Percy wiped the moisture off his face, waved and rode away.

An inside page of the newspaper had a photo. Teddy looked quite different, with blond curly hair.

'Strewth,' George said.

He took the newspaper into the house. He found his spectacles and read it by the window where the last of the daylight shone through the gauze curtains.

THE MURRUMBIDGEE KID – A STAR OF TOMORROW

That will be the future of Teddy Carson, from the Riverina district, according to American film director Lawrence Andrews. Teddy, aged eight, is the boy chosen from hundreds to feature in *Dispossessed*, now filming in Sydney. 'Today Australia,' said Mr Andrews, 'perhaps Hollywood tomorrow.' His mother, the former Belle Baker, herself a well-known actress prior to marriage, agreed. 'His great talent could take him almost anywhere in the world,' she said.

George sat there, the words rotating unhappily in his mind, until long after the sun had set and the room was dark.

Henry Hume watched from the door of the sound stage. In the far corner of the set they were doing a final run-through of a hospital scene. He fumed as he saw Belle hovering near the camera, mouthing dialogue as the kid said it in the rehearsal. He was about to intervene, but the clapper boy moved into shot, the bell clanged and the red light warned everyone on the lot that the doors were locked and the camera was turning for a take.

They did the brief scene. Andrews pronounced it a good one and ordered a print, but Belle differed. With incredulity the producer saw her insist Teddy could do it better, and before he could intervene they began to shoot the scene again. Too late to prevent this, Hume went back to his office in a towering rage.

'That fucking interfering bitch is getting us behind schedule!' he yelled at Dan. 'Who the hell cares if the kid didn't blink his eyelash in the right place, for Christ's sake?'

'He's giving a great performance, Henry.'

'That wasn't what I said, Daniel, so try listening for a change. Sure, he's good, but don't get carried away. Who cares in Los Angeles about his great performance if it means we run a week late and go over budget? Do you hear me?'

'I hear you, Henry.'

'I want her ordered to stay off the set. I want a meeting here tonight after we wrap – you, me and our piss-weak director. Got it?'

'Got it,' Dan said, trying not to show his resentment.

'Somebody should take that mama away and screw her while we finish the picture. If I find out she's asked for one more retake, I'm gonna nominate you as a volunteer. So you've got two choices – both difficult: either fuck her or make her shut up.'

At the shabby end of George Street, on the fringe of Chinatown and around the corner from the Capitol Theatre, was a narrow doorway fitted with a brass plate. Peeling paint and graffiti tarnished the door, but the plate was polished daily and glittered like an invitation to another universe. It seemed a far remove from the mean streets where homeless derelicts scrabbled for food in the litter bins of Belmore Park and Central Station. On the plate was engraved: FLORIAN MACARTHUR-BAILEY. THEATRICAL AGENT.

While she waited, Belle inspected the photographs that papered his office walls. Most were devotedly inscribed to him by other actors; a few were framed studies of Florian in younger days (cloaked for Restoration or Shakespearian roles) before he gained weight and realised a better living could be made beyond the proscenium by selling the talent of his peers. He greeted Belle with an acquired effusion, kissing each cheek before seating her, then barely fitting himself into a commodious swivel chair behind a substantial oak desk. He apologised that there was no morning tea or biscuits; he was on a diet.

'You've been on a diet since I was sixteen,' Belle said, refraining from an observation that it had clearly been a failure. He still had a thick mane of hair that he wore like a coronet and a fine aquiline nose, but his body was twice the size it had been in the youthful photos.

'And an astonishingly pretty sixteen you were. Lusted over by half the actors in town – and at least one agent,' he added with a sly immoderation.

'Settle down, Florian,' Belle replied. 'I'm here to talk about my son, not reminisce on your libido.'

'Ah, yes. The young Antipodean Jackie Coogan.'

'He could be.'

'No doubt the boy has talent, Belle. But film production . . . in this country? My dear girl, there's no continuity of work. And, let's face it, roles for kids his age are rare. This was a lucky break.'

'The measles were an act of divine intervention. Yes, it was luck, and I want to capitalise on it. Teddy will be well known once the film comes out.'

'Provided it gets a decent release. Most local pictures are put out like the garbage. Dumped for a brief inglorious run in some suburban fleapit, then never heard of again.'

'This one won't be. It has American stars in it.'

He laughed uproariously at the thought of it. 'Darling, do me a favour. Stars? B-picture actors, second-raters. A couple of has-beens, if they ever were.'

'Florian, I think I made a mistake in coming here,' she said, trying to control her annoyance at his attitude. 'Are you interested in being his agent or not?'

'Boys grow up. Their voices break.'

'I asked if you're interested.'

'Juveniles, sadly, are quite notoriously difficult. They have a short career span. They become singers, or lawyers, or truck drivers.'

'How about Jackie Coogan, then? He's made a fortune.'

'America, Belle. That's an entirely different kettle of fish.'

She stood up to leave. She gripped her handbag, wishing she could hit him with it.

'Florian, you were a rotten actor and it looks like you're now a rotten agent. What's more, you're not on a diet. You're as fat as ever, and too bloody mean to lash out on morning tea for visitors.'

'Since most of my visitors are clients who come here to complain that I get them no work, why should I provide sustenance? If I did, they'd be calling in daily for a feed. There'd be a queue outside my door, all the way to the Tivoli.'

'You are a miserable bugger,' Belle said. 'I can't for the life of me think why I even bothered to come and see you.'

'Because, my dear girl,' Florian replied, seemingly unperturbed by the insults, 'you've seen all the other agents in town. And no one was the least bit interested. I have my sources of information,' he added, with a fleeting smile at her reaction to this, 'so here you are, on the bones of your extremely attractive arse.'

'You leave my arse out of this.'

'Gladly,' he said. 'The one thing that stopped me leaping on you when you were a lusty young soubrette was your youth. Dangerously close, I always thought in those days, to jail-bait.'

'Well, I always thought you were long past it,' Belle retorted as she headed for the door.

Florian waited until she was about to open it. 'Before you rush off in a temper back to your shack in Bullamakanka or whatever that one-horse place is called,' he said, 'what's required first is to get him known. That's the trick. Make sure he gets in the newspapers.'

'He's *been* in the newspapers.'

'Studio publicity handouts,' he shrugged dismissively. '"The Murrumbidgee Kid" as they call him. I saw the piece.'

'I hate that name,' Belle said vehemently.

Florian nodded at this. 'I thought you might.'

'It seems to embody everything I'm trying to get him away from.'

'It regionalises him,' he said, surprising her with this perception. 'Puts him in a little box from a little town.' She could only nod agreement. 'Whereas I'm talking about creating a different image,' Florian continued expansively. 'Making the general public, the great unwashed, become aware of him. How do we do that, you may ask? It's really quite simple.'

'Is it?'

'Of course.'

Belle looked at him. 'You want me to trust you?'

'I want you to sit down again and listen. I'm the last name on your list because you think I'm a bit of a joke. A lecherous old goat who's past it. Well, that may be almost true – but you need me.'

'Do I?'

'I think so. You have this small person whom you love, and you're driven by a need to see him reach the top, to be above the titles, to – well, what's wrong with a bit of dreaming? – to touch the stars.' He smiled at her, his voice gentler now. 'Like you never could; nor, to be honest, could I. So I understand your aspiration, and it begins to tempt me. I'll make sure people will hear about him, and we'll go from there. Does that tempt you?'

Belle sat down. She gazed carefully at him. 'It might. Will it cost?'

'Not unless I get him work, then I take my usual ten per cent.'

'You said people will hear about him. How will they hear?'

'Christmas is coming,' he said. 'Filming will be finished soon after. What I have in mind will warm everyone's heart. They'll love it.'

'Love what?'

'Trust me, my darling. I know people think I'm sneaky and conniving. I know behind my back they call me Uriah Heep. But I can be quite enterprising, as you'll find out.'

George sent a Christmas card. A letter came with it, saying it would be a different sort of Christmas without them, but he had been invited next door to Mr and Mrs Miranda's, so it wouldn't be like spending the day alone. But nor would it be like other years, when they had all enjoyed Christmas together.

He wanted Teddy to know there was a present waiting – not something he could send or anything he'd need down in the city, because it was a new carrier basket to go on his bike – and it would be waiting when they came home at New Year after the film was over. George walked home from the post office, wishing he had the money to join them in Sydney, and dreading the prospect of Christmas dinner with Mr and Mrs Miranda.

On the sound stage filming had wrapped early for the Christmas Eve party. The cast and crew, well oiled with beer and wine, watched with amusement as Santa Claus came in. He was accompanied by stage hands, and on his instructions a decorated tree was moved in and set up with a mound of toys piled beneath it. An assistant director was dispatched, returning soon afterwards with Belle and Teddy. They stood at the door, startled at the sight.

'Merry Christmas, my boy.' Florian was convincingly clad in a red cloak and white beard, greeting him with a chuckle. 'Santa's come to call.'

Teddy's eyes were like saucers as he gazed at the tree and was led by the jolly Santa to the pile of presents. 'Gee,' he said. 'Golly Moses! A scooter.'

Unwrapped and occupying pride of place was a brand-new scooter. He stood on it, waving to Belle, who remained staring in amazement. Florian had sent her a message to say there'd be a small event, telling her the exact time they should arrive at the sound stage, but this . . . this was not what she expected.

She suddenly realised the gantry lights had clicked on, and a great many things were happening simultaneously. Santa Claus seemed to be orchestrating it; bloody Florian was carrying on like a pantomime dame, she thought, while he gave signals to the cast and crew, who came to surround Teddy and wish him a merry Christmas. Then other people came in, some with cameras, and flashlights began to flicker. Notebooks appeared as Florian put an avuncular arm around Teddy and addressed them.

'Ladies and gentlemen of the press,' he said, 'in this season of goodwill, I have a tender tale to tell. Some of our cast and crew have spent their hard-earned money on gifts for their young friend, our new star Teddy Carson. Such generosity in these troubled times. Is that a story to touch your hearts, or isn't it?' He beamed at them all.

'Yes, my fellow Australians, there *is* a Santa Claus,' he continued. 'Look at this boy, this talented little lad who will make us all proud of him. Look at the joy in his eyes. A joy hopefully reflected by other children in our land, despite the hard times we live in. But never mind that. This boy, and this moment – through your pictures and newspaper stories – will spread the word that faith is alive, that hope and charity survive. This, surely, is the true meaning of Christmas.'

Teddy was dazzled by the flashlights and the big arcs that had been switched on for Santa's speech. Only he didn't sound like Santa any more. He was no longer saying ho-ho-ho and talking about his reindeer and the North Pole. He bowed and thanked them for their attendance. The moment this happened, the reporters all began to shout questions. The newsreel cameraman called for a big smile from Teddy, and others told him to hold up his presents. They piled them in his arms and took more shots. Teddy was confused by the commotion; he wanted Belle, but she was busy across the studio talking to Santa.

'You see it, my beauty?' Florian was delighted with the result. 'You just cannot buy publicity like this, Belle.'

'But where did all these things come from?'

'Never mind. It worked, poppet. I told you to leave it to your Uncle Flory.'

Her initial bewilderment was turning to suspicion. This was altogether too neat, too contrived. 'What the hell is going on, Florian?'

'Relax, Belle. Just stay calm and don't get your knickers in a twist or you'll ruin it. Wait here while I see off the motley press gang.'

Belle watched him hurry to usher out the journalists and photographers. At the same time she was aware of some odd glances from the crew and the actors as they headed back to what was left of their party. She knew something was wrong, sensed it as she watched her son examine his toys. Now that the arc lights had been dimmed and the press invasion was over, he was sitting there like any lucky child, shaking wrapped boxes in delight, peering into packages, and she allowed herself a moment to believe it was a real-life fairy tale.

Then the stagehands came in. They removed the Christmas tree and started to gather the presents. At first Teddy seemed unable to conceive what was happening. Belle saw him try to hold the scooter as a stagehand firmly shook his head and took it from him. A truck was backed up to the access doors of the sound stage. Belle saw it being filled with the recovered gifts as she went looking for Florian.

'You lousy bastard,' she said, 'they were hired!'

Before he could reply Teddy ran to them, confused and distressed. 'Mum, what's happening? Aren't they my toys? Why are they taking them away?'

'It was a game, Teddy,' Florian said, 'a pretend game for the newspapers. Which did work,' he added quietly to Belle.

He pulled off his beard and stepped out of the voluminous Santa suit. He deliberately neglected to remove the red-and-white cone on his head. If he hoped to soften her anger by looking comical, she was in no mood for any such antics. She wanted to slap his face. Instead, she knelt to wrap her arms around Teddy.

'I didn't know, darling,' she said, trying to contain her outrage as she saw the last of the toys being taken away.

'I'm really sorry, Belle,' the lighting cameraman said. 'We never twigged what he was up to. He told us it was a publicity stunt, so we all thought you were in on it. You . . . and the kid.'

'Neither me nor the kid,' she said bitterly, wondering how on earth they could imagine such a thing. 'I'm all for getting him known, but I'd never have allowed a crappy trick like that.'

The rest of the crew looked sheepish. No one was prepared to admit it, but they secretly thought Belle would go to any lengths to push the poor little bloke. Some had even believed the whole thing had been her idea.

Florian arrived at their boarding house with a bunch of flowers on Boxing Day. From the window of her first-floor room, Belle looked down and icily asked what garden he'd stolen them from – and would he please go to buggery. He was littering the neighbourhood, making the street look untidy.

'You must admit,' he said, ignoring this, 'the story was a triumph. It featured this morning in every newspaper, and is sure to make the Sundays. Colossal coverage. And although I did have some minor costs and hiring charges, I suggest we forget about them. I want you to regard my expenses as a gift.'

'Expenses? You're a lying old swine. What expenses, you bastard? That Christmas tree and all the toys were props on another film. I found out that you arranged to borrow them for an hour.'

'I warned you I was enterprising,' he replied, unfazed.

'You warned me about being called Uriah Heep, and it's the perfect name for a conniving chiseller like you. I can't think of any name that suits you better. So shove the flowers up your arse and sod off,' Belle said, slamming the window shut before he could reply. The glass rattled, and she thought for an anxious moment it was going to break.

She heard him ring the bell downstairs again, and then the sound of voices below. His voice was importuning the landlady. If he tries to come up here, I'm going to kick him in the balls, even if I'm not in favour of violence, she thought, but then remembered the landlady's strict rules did not allow visitors, especially males, over the threshold. She eventually saw him cross the street to a battered old tourer. He climbed in, pausing to glance up at the window, but she had anticipated this and moved out of sight. She heard the clatter of the engine and the sound of grinding gears as he drove off.

Teddy was in his own room, no doubt trying to muster interest in the cheap toy she had bought him. This Christmas break could not have come at a worse time. Filming would not resume until the day after tomorrow, and with him so disconsolate, the brief holiday period was beginning to seem like an eternity. She wondered what George was doing, how the lunch had turned out at the Miranda house, and whether it would prove to be as dreadful as she imagined. She also wondered if she'd dare show him the array of cuttings she had already collected from the day's newspapers. For the first time in weeks, she thought about what it would be like to go home.

Later, the landlady came up to say there had been complaints from the family next door about the shouting and her language. She pointed out this was a respectable street, and such behaviour lowered the tone. Also, the gentleman caller had left the flowers and written a note for her.

Belle asked if the landlady would kindly accept her apologies and please take the flowers for her own use. As for the note, she would dispose of it herself in the time-honoured way. But after the woman had gone downstairs, she could not resist reading it. Before flushing it down the lav, she reasoned, she might as well see what he had to say for himself.

Dear Belle,

It was an unkind but effective trick. I've had two offers of work for him already. That is, if you're not too liverish to call me after the holidays and discuss it.

With festive greetings,
Uriah

Chapter ten

The train headed its way south, leaving George alone with them on the platform, except for the porter loading the mail trolley and collecting their tickets. He tipped his cap to Belle.

''Ow yer going, Mrs Carson? Been down in the big smoke, I 'eard. Glad to be safe home again, I betcha. No place like it, is there? Bet you're sick of all them mobs of people and the traffic jams, eh?'

She was saved by Teddy's intervention. 'We saw the Harbour Bridge, Mr Miller.'

'Did you, son? Probably got there just in time. They reckon it won't last, that whatever they call it? The coathanger, yeah, that's right.' He laughed. 'That's the name. Looks just like one.'

'Won't last?' Belle was already tiring of this harbinger of doom. 'It looked sturdy enough to us, and to thousands of other people.'

'Wear and tear, Mrs Carson. Nuts and bolts rust, they get loose. Once all them heavy buses and trains get on it, lotsa people round here reckon it'll be certain to fall down.'

'They'd be experts,' she said, and George, who was trying to handle their suitcases and escort them off the platform, heard her irritation. He took her arm.

'Let's go, Belle.'

They started towards the steps. But the porter wasn't to be dismissed so easily.

'Hey, young Ted, I heard you was in a fillum?'

'Yes,' Teddy said.

'Is that a fact? I ain't seen it at the local picture show.'

'It could hardly be there yet,' Belle said, knowing with a sinking heart that nothing here would ever change, 'because it's just finished shooting, and now they have to edit it. It will be released later in the year.'

'Peculiar that.'

'What is, Mr Miller?'

'Taking all them months like that, when fillums only run about an hour.'

'Well, I'm afraid I haven't time to explain,' she said, giving up. If she'd had doubts about the future, this arrival home confirmed all her fears. Leaving the porter grumbling about the post office being late as usual to collect the mail, George carried their suitcases to a waiting Model T Ford.

'Hop in,' he said, and they both looked at him with surprise.

'Have you bought a motor car, Dad?' Teddy asked.

Not exactly, it appeared. The car belonged to a friend who worked with him at Gable's; George had persuaded him to loan it for the day because it was special, he said, their coming home after all these weeks. The neighbours were aware they were arriving, and so he'd decided they weren't going to walk – he would drive them in style. It wouldn't seem right, having to walk home in the heat lugging suitcases. People knew Teddy had been in a film with overseas stars and had got his name and photograph in the Sydney newspapers, and nobody else around here had ever done that.

'Good on you, Dad.'

'I'm proud of you, Ted. So I had a few practice drives, got a temporary licence from old Percy Bates, and here we are. It's really beaut to have you both home again.'

Oh God, Belle thought, dismayed. How am I going to tell him?

Early in the new year the town grapevine had done its work, and most people knew there was trouble in the air; something odd was going on at the Carson place out on Brewinda Road, something personal between George and Belle. Everyone was certain she was leaving. There was talk from those who claimed to be in the know that they were getting a divorce; others proffered the lesser rumour it was just a temporary separation. Whatever the truth, the town clearly felt sympathy for poor old George, and could barely conceal their dislike for his hoity-toity fancy wife. They had suffered her now for nine years, and relished the day when they might see the back of her.

Teddy, sensing something amiss, was unsure what that something might be. He was glad to be home, although a few things bothered him; Norm and Ginger, for instance, were a bit distant, a bit abrupt and peculiar, and he could hardly say the rest of the gang made him feel welcome. He was not yet aware of the volume of the talk that had been circulating around the schoolyard while he was away. It had become common knowledge in the playground that Teddy Carson had done a bunk from school, aided by his mother who had told the headmistress he was not well and she was taking him to the city to see a special sort of doctor. Of course, everyone soon knew this was a lie; that he'd somehow got a part in a film and was being an actor in Sydney, and supposed to be famous.

Ginger and Norm were unsure if it was good for the image of

their gang, having a member who ponced about in front of a movie camera. There was also the discomfort of a subordinate achieving such prominence. Teddy had been their recruit; they were not certain they liked the idea of him outshining them and everyone else with his name and his picture all over the place.

When they heard of the Christmas photographs and front-page stories of all the gifts he'd been given, Ginger and Norm decided that was enough. They held a meeting after Teddy arrived home, to which he was not a party, where they canvassed the opinions of the others about the situation. Ginger put it succinctly: Teddy was now an actor who seemed to get his mug in the papers all the time, and was given dozens of free presents. This had been in the newspapers, so it must be true. Therefore, was he really the same person they'd carefully chosen to join them in the early days of their gang? Or was he some spoiled poofter-looking kid who dyed his hair blond and thought himself a lot better than them? What did everyone think?

'Got tickets on 'imself,' Herbie Bates said scathingly, 'just like his silly old chook of a mother.'

'Be talking like her next, all la-di-da,' Bill Burwood added, sure his father would approve of this remark.

Others were quick to agree that this would definitely lower the status of their group.

'Always told youse he was stuck-up – thinks hisself too flamin' good for us,' Pig Morgan insisted, seeing an opportunity for the restoration of his own prestige.

There was virtually no dissent, and when the call came for a show of hands the decision was unanimous. Teddy was requested to appear so the result could be read to him. The shock of rejection was twofold; he had thought the invitation to meet the whole gang presaged a welcome home, but instead he was greeted with a demand to face them and hear the verdict.

'What do you mean, verdict?' He had begun to realise this was not a celebration of his return.

'The verdict of us all,' Ginger said formally, and proceeded to announce it. Teddy was to be demoted from the rank of sergeant and put on probation in order to see if he was fit to remain a member of their mob. This meant he was now the lowliest of the low with the standing of a raw recruit – a new category they had just created – and as a result would have to obey orders given to him by anyone else. The period of probation would last for a minimum of six months, and could be longer if they were not satisfied.

After this was announced they all stared at him with anticipation, eager to see what would happen next. They'd had a lively debate on how he might take the news of relegation. Ginger reckoned he would probably beg to be reinstated, others were certain he'd cry. Turn on the waterworks, they reckoned, and they waited for it to happen. To their surprise Teddy was silent, his face almost thoughtful as though considering the matter, then he gave an elaborate shrug and began to laugh.

It was the last thing they expected.

In fact, he'd had a moment of complete dismay that had turned into angry determination. Nothing on God's earth would let him allow them to see what a kick in the teeth it was. It was vital to put on a face that would leave them puzzled and disappointed. So he laughed again, thinking his acting would never be put to a sterner test than this. He laughed as if it was an enormous joke.

What was so funny? Ginger wanted to know.

Teddy said Ginger was funny, carrying on like a dill as if he was important. He said if that was how they felt, he didn't want to belong to anyone's silly childish gang. What's more, he wasn't going to stand in front of them like some criminal on trial. He was quitting, and they could forget about probation or whatever they called it because he'd had a gutful of their pathetic crap. Relishing their startled faces and invoking his mother's rich vocabulary, he told Ginger they could all go to buggery. Gangs were bullshit, and only for dumb kids.

But the moment he said this, he knew it was a blunder.

'We'll see who's dumb,' Ginger said, lashing out with his fist and knocking him down. Teddy tasted blood on his lip. He got up slowly. When he was barely upright it was Norm's turn to throw a punch and send him sprawling.

'*You're* the dummy,' Norm said, 'so you better say you're sorry for that, or else stay down there in the dirt. Which is it gonna be?'

'Neither' was the silent answer. Inured to punishment, he would not give them the triumph of surrender. He kept doggedly rising while refusing to apologise, and they kept on hitting him, for there was no one within sight to prevent them.

Luckily, it was the long summer holidays and they would not be back at school until the first week in February. By then, he felt sure, the bruises that had made Belle so angry when she saw them would be gone, and even if he was no longer part of the gang, at least by then he might be able to renew friendships with some of the kids again. Quite a few had not liked the way Norm in particular had kept knocking him down and kicking him while he was on the ground. He'd glimpsed some trying to remonstrate, but they were all a bit scared of Norm, so nobody interfered until Teddy could no longer get up.

Even then he was acting, pretending to be unconscious while they began to look scared. He could hear Ginger swearing them all to secrecy, saying if anyone was to ask questions none of them knew a thing. He waited until they were gone, then sat up. That was when he decided he wasn't really acting after all; the pain in his side was like a knife thrust. It took over an hour to limp his way home.

Belle had cried and tried to hug him, which hurt alarmingly. George had wanted to take him to the hospital to see if any ribs were broken, and had told his friend Percy Bates that this was downright thuggery, it was criminal and a matter for the police. And if Perce wouldn't do anything, then George would report it to the local paper and write to the district inspector in Goulburn.

When Constable Bates came to question him and asked for the names of the young hooligans involved, Teddy said they were from another school and he couldn't give names because he'd never seen them before. Neither Bates nor George believed this, but he persisted with the story. Teddy knew Herbie would hear about it from his dad, and Herbie had always been his best friend. Not that there was any way Herbie could be his friend again – but at least he might realise Teddy had not dobbed him in, and thus saved him from big trouble with his dad. Herbie knowing this might even help the awkward situation when they had to start school again. He hoped so, for the new term in February was only two weeks away.

The mere thought of school kept him awake at night, visualising other problems. Teddy could imagine the kind of mockery he'd face in the playground if his blonded hair hadn't returned to its proper colour by then or, worse still, if the film of *Dispossessed* was shown at the Magnet Picture Palace in town, where the kids would all be sure to make fun of it even if they secretly liked it, because that's how the kids around here were. They'd roar with laughter in the sentimental scenes, roll Jaffas down the aisles and create such an uproar that none of the dialogue would be heard. The girls would all complain, and the boys would shout at them to shut up and, worst of all, if the film was shown in town, his mother would insist that she and his dad both attend.

In addition to this, he had no illusions that going back to school would be easy. There'd be the same old taunts about Belle that he always stubbornly refused to ignore. But that was the future, and not his major worry. There was something far more unsettling. It was not even the incessant gossip by people in the town; this did not bother him unduly, for it had always been like that.

It was the atmosphere at home that disturbed him. Since the day of their return from Sydney it had been strange, and growing steadily more alarming. He felt tension in the house – sometimes a stony silence seemed to pervade the hot January days and nights. Even worse were the quiet but ferocious exchanges between George and Belle that always abruptly ended when he was near them. George seemed sad at times; on other days he was upset and refused to talk to her. As a result Belle ignored him; she talked to Teddy, sang songs to herself, wrote letters to friends in Sydney and seemed to treat George as someone she had to cook for and call to dinner, but when they sat down at the table there was silence and the atmosphere was icy. Teddy dreaded meal times. He wanted to ask what was wrong, but could not bring himself to do so, for he was afraid of what he might be told.

As the summer days went by, he rode his bike and felt alone, uneasily aware that something in his life was changing.

PART *Two*

Chapter eleven

The tram clattered out of the bridge tunnel into bright sunlight. It was always a moment of wonder to Teddy, being able to look down and see the harbour below, and to think back to the day on the ferry last year gazing up at the unfinished steel giant while the guide told them all about it, and how it would soon be opened officially by the State Premier. And now, nearly a year older, he felt the excitement of being able to travel across this bridge in a tram with Belle on their way to the Paragon film studio at North Sydney.

He had some lines to learn for his role in a new picture, but his mind was diverted watching the ships. Ferries were converging on Circular Quay, and there were splashes of white sail as a fleet of eighteen-footers assembled for a yacht race. Out towards the arm of South Head a huge freighter was making its way into the harbour. Perhaps from Africa or China, he surmised, as a tug steamed out to meet it, and he tried to speculate what it would be like to be a sailor on board. His imagination took flight, picturing a violent storm with the vessel heading for a dangerous reef in dire peril, the captain lost overboard, the mate injured, himself roped to the helm as he calmly brought the ship and its crew to safety. It made him think of a poem that Belle had taught him as an audition piece.

Now the great winds shorewards blow;
Now the salt tides seawards flow:
Now the wild white horses play,
To champ and chafe and toss in spray . . .

Not entirely sure what it was supposed to mean, he liked the thought of the wild white horses, but decided it might be best if he concentrated on his lines. There were not many; it was a small part, a lousy spit and a cough, Belle had called it, but Mr MacArthur-Bailey said times were tough and it was work; what's more, he told her he'd forced the producer to raise his original offer to an improved fee of one pound a day.

Belle had not been impressed. She said it was typical of the empty promises he spouted and not to hold his breath if he expected applause for negotiating this fee. It was pathetic – if this was an improvement, she dreaded to think how insulting the first offer must have been. Three scheduled days of filming for the sum of three pounds was hardly a princely price for a rising young star, especially after Uriah reduced it by extracting his ten per cent.

'Not,' she had said, 'that I begrudge you your commission. We all have to make a living.'

'How benevolent of you,' he said, 'to allow me to make a living.'

'No need to be sarcastic, Uriah. I just wish you were smart enough to take on these robbing crooks with their tightfisted budgets. This would never happen in Hollywood.'

'Then give the rest of us a break and go there,' he snapped back at her.

They were always in some sort of dispute, his mother and his agent; they argued over everything. They had daily disagreements about Teddy not getting enough work, or not the right kind of work:

about the parts being too small, the billing too low, or the money too miserly. The money was the most frequent cause of combat. Once, in a noisy quarrel, Florian had said that Belle should take over the job of being her son's agent. Nobody else could possibly come up to her expectations. No one else could be as tough, bitchy or bloody-minded as her.

A train sped noisily past the open tram, startling Teddy out of his reverie. On the roadway a steady stream of cars queued at the toll gates. The toll was sixpence. There were complaints that this was too expensive, but the government said millions of pounds had been borrowed from Britain for the construction and the interest had to be paid. Teddy noticed that many of the cars looked like the Model T Ford George had borrowed that day to drive them home. Remembering it made him feel down in the dumps, for he sorely missed his dad. George wrote regular letters: in one of them, a few months ago, he told Teddy how everyone had packed the local cinema to see *Dispossessed*, and how they applauded when he first appeared on the screen, and clapped him again at the end when his name was listed on the final credits.

A pretty sad sort of film, George had written, but the manager of the Magnet Picture Palace had told him that business was good all the week; most nights had been fairly crowded, and the Saturday matinee was a full house. Teddy could clearly imagine that matinee, with Herbie, Ginger and Norm jeering and pretending they were being sick at all the sentimental scenes. In order to avoid thinking about the treachery of these former friends, he gazed up at the great steel arch and thought about what had happened on the bridge instead.

It had been opened in front of a huge crowd as the guide had predicted, but it was not the opening he or anyone expected. Just a few moments before the ceremony, while the State Premier was speaking, a man on horseback had ridden past him to slash the ribbon with his sword. His name was Francis de Groot, and he was arrested and later appeared in the Magistrate's Court where he was fined five pounds. Some people claimed it was too much, and he should've been given a medal; others declared he deserved jail for an outrageous political stunt. In court he had insisted on calling himself *Captain* de Groot, because he had formerly been an officer in the army and was now a member of the organisation known as the New Guard.

Teddy had seen it on the Cinesound newsreel at the State Theatre. Some of the cinema audience had applauded while others booed as de Groot was pulled off his horse. Belle said loudly that it showed how fascists like the New Guard had polarised the country. Before Teddy could ask her what polarised meant, a woman in front had turned around and told her to shut up; that if she hadn't anything sensible to say, then to keep her silly trap shut, or was she a communist, a dirty red, trying to poison this young boy's mind with her stupid commo lies? Belle, of course, had let fly back at her and soon everyone in the nearby seats had started to yell at them both to shut up, and Teddy felt relieved the place was dark so that nobody could see his embarrassed face.

He had learnt a lot about the New Guard. It was a frequent topic in Kellett Street, where large town houses were now divided into tiny rooms called flatettes. Kellett Street was only a brief walk from the centre of Kings Cross, which Belle loved as a neighbourhood to live in; she said 'the Cross' was like a village, an exciting bohemian village that felt as if it belonged to another part of the world, far removed from the boring Australia of dull country towns or the monotony of the suburbs.

Belle had made some new friends and renewed acquaintance with lots of old ones: painters and actors, a few writers and a poet. Most lived in the district, and their room had become a popular meeting place. The door was never locked and people began dropping in, and when they could afford it, came with a bottle of what was called plonk or four-penny dark. They talked and argued while drinking it, sitting on the floor because there was no room for chairs, discussing theatre and how lousy things were in the business, or else politics and their despair at the way the country was going to the dogs, being ruined by idiots in parliament. Teddy often fell asleep while they talked late into the night, for none of them ever seemed anxious to leave and go home.

It was during these evenings he heard their opinions about the New Guard. They were all vehemently opposed to it, declaring it a clandestine organisation and the enemy of ordinary people. Teddy had a receptive memory: he later asked Belle what clandestine meant and was told. He heard how the Guard professed undying loyalty to the King and the British Empire; how they held military training, for the protection of that empire, they said; and saluted in the same way as the fascists in Italy and the new Nazi party in Germany. He learnt how members of the Guard despised Jews and foreigners; their policy was to keep out refugees fleeing from persecution in Europe. While America offered thousands of such people asylum, Australia did its best to reject them.

'But where do they go?' Teddy had asked, and was told most of the poor buggers were shunted back where they'd come from. He often thought about this, and wondered if they hated these places as much as Belle hated their own town of Gundagai. He was now aware how much she did hate it. He was adept at picking it up from scraps of conversation late at night – often her friends spoke openly, imagining they were talking in a code he couldn't comprehend; they sighed and said it was just impossible, way out beyond the black stump. They talked of her being stifled there, snared like a butterfly among beetles, or said she was caged in an alien landscape, an outsider in a redneck culture. Not always sure of what the words meant, Teddy knew what they presaged. Recalling the fights at school, the scornful names the kids had called her, the way their parents had always seemed to be gossiping about her, he had long ago begun to realise it was unlikely Belle would ever go back to live there. At least not willingly. But what did that mean for him? And what about George? When would he ever see his dad again? These were questions nobody wanted to hear, let alone answer.

'Daydreamer,' Belle said, and he realised the tram had left the bridge and was approaching their stop in North Sydney. They got off and walked past the church in Blues Point Road to the film studio.

'G'day, young Ted,' the gatekeeper greeted him, and said to Belle it was a real beaut day, wasn't it, a bottler of a day, and he wouldn't be dead for quids.

The gatekeeper met them with this statement almost every morning, even on days when it was cold and wet. Belle agreed it was a fine lovely day, then exchanged a wink and a quick smile at Teddy. It was their private joke that he'd probably say the same words if there was a flood or an electric storm. Hoping her smile was an omen, he reached out and took her hand as they walked towards the sound stages, deciding to ask the question.

'Mum . . .'

'What, darling?'

'When am I going to see Dad again?'

After a pause Belle said, 'It depends.'

'You always say that.' He felt disappointed, but this time was determined to pursue it. 'Depends on what?'

'Well, he did come down to see us when he had his holidays.'

'But he couldn't stay with us. It wasn't like a real visit,' Teddy protested.

'He couldn't stay because we had that awful room in Crown Street then, and the landlady wouldn't allow visitors. At least we met him every day.'

'It was only for a week.'

'Darling, he had to go back to his job.'

'But you promised he might leave his job soon, and come to live with us.'

She stopped for a moment, and squatted alongside him. 'We hoped it was possible. But jobs are hard to find, Teddy. And, after all, he already has a good one at home in Gundagai, as assistant manager of the kitchenware department at Gable's Emporium.'

'You used to say it was a lousy job.'

'Did I?' she asked, brow furrowed as if doubting this.

'You did, Mum, you know you did.'

'I shouldn't have said that.' She brushed a tuft of his unruly hair into place before they resumed walking. 'If I did, I must've been in a bad mood. He can't possibly give up a good position like that to take up menial work.'

'What's menial work?'

'Well . . . on the roads, or driving a truck —'

'I wouldn't mind if he did that, not if we were all together again.'

'But *he'd* mind,' Belle said firmly, trying to put an end to this. 'Your dad's a proud man. As a department executive he's what's called a white-collar worker. He wouldn't enjoy being a labourer. And, on top of that, there's the house in Gundagai to consider . . . that can't be left empty.'

'But I thought you said he was going to sell it?'

'I said he was going to *try*. The local estate agent has it on his books, but he's not very optimistic. It's not easy to sell a place like that.'

'Why? It's a nice house, Mum. Dad and I like it, even if you don't.' He was impelled to boldness by her evasion.

'Teddy, dear, are you trying to pick a fight with me? I was telling you what the agent said. He meant not many people have the money to buy houses these days, the way things are. And the banks are being stingy about lending. Try to understand, your dad can't just shut the door and walk away, even if he'd like to. He has to repay the mortgage. If he just shot through he might end up in jail.' They stopped outside a squat building that housed make-up and wardrobe. 'Now, do you know your lines?'

'Yes, Mum,' he said gloomily, taking out the pages of script he'd folded in his pocket.

'Of course you do. After all, just five lines and a few reaction shots.' She stooped to adjust his shirt collar and smooth down his hair again. 'Cheer up, darling. I'm going to have a serious talk to Florian. He has to do better than this, or we'll find another agent.'

'I don't care about an agent, or how many lines I've got,' Teddy said with sudden heat. 'Am I ever going to see my dad again?'

'What a question!' Belle expressed her amazement with a gesture of her hands and elevated eyebrows. 'What a very peculiar question.'

'Am I?' he demanded.

'Of course you are.'

'Is he going to live with us the same as he used to?'

'Teddy, we haven't time to talk about it now.'

'You always say that, Mum.'

'But we haven't time, truly. You're in the first scene, and one thing Ted Carson never does is keep a film unit waiting. It's the sign of a true professional, and that's what you are.' She tried to hug him, but he evaded her embrace. 'Listen to me, darling . . . please try to understand . . . people sometimes make plans that don't work out. It's not their fault, it's not anyone's fault, it's just the way things happen. We'll talk about it another time soon.'

'You always say that too,' he told her, and hurried into the building before she could reply.

The whole day stretched before her. For the uninvolved, film sets are tedious places, with their endless delays for lighting changes and the many rehearsals before a director is prepared to shoot a scene. Belle believed actors were often wearied by this repetition, that performances lost their edge with over-rehearsal and became automatic. But she had learnt not to voice this opinion, or any opinion other than to profess approval of the day's work. Her change in attitude, which most film crews found surprising, was entirely due to the advice rendered by Florian MacArthur-Bailey. Despite his maddening air of superiority and their constant bickering, the agent had managed to explain to her what could otherwise happen.

'My dear girl, if you continue to give advice to the cameraman about where to put his lights – or tell the director which angle to shoot and what the dialogue really means – you're going to be chucked off the set and more than likely banned from all the studios.'

'They can't do that,' Belle had retorted, 'because every child actor must be accompanied by his parent or a guardian.'

'That's the law,' Florian said, 'but there's a simple remedy.'

'Really? Since you're so full of yourself, Uriah, what's the remedy?'

'Cast another child actor.'

'They can't! There's no one else with his ability.'

'True,' Florian had assented, 'but there's also no one else with his mother, which is what people are starting to say. So unless you get smart and learn to shut up, you're going to lose him any chance of future work.'

'Don't talk garbage.'

He had assured her it was not garbage. Keep it up, he told her, and she'd make Teddy unemployable. She and her unstoppable mouth was about to deal herself and, more importantly, her talented son a mortal blow.

'I don't care if this upsets you, Belle, but since it also affects me as his agent, you're going to listen for once. The word I hear around town is that producers will soon prefer kids who may have a bit less talent, provided they don't have such a difficult and meddlesome mum.'

It had upset her deeply; she and Florian had another of their incessant rows, but the change that so surprised people in the industry had occurred from that day. Belle was not a slow learner. Since then she kept away from the set and invariably brought a newspaper with the crossword puzzle to help pass the time. It was not easy to sit in an empty dressing-room cut off from what was happening on the sound stage, but she had begun to realise it was vital. If Teddy could no longer get work, it would be the end of this new life. It could mean a humiliating return to Gundagai, facing the knowing glances of the people who disliked her as much as she despised them. When Belle had calmed down after Florian's warning, she recalled her conflicts with Henry Hume and disputes with others since then, and had seen the danger for herself.

But today she was restless, unable to concentrate on crosswords. Teddy's questions had been disturbing. She wrote him a note to say she'd be back later, put it with his belongings in the dressing-room shared by most of the cast, then left the studio and walked down to Milson's Point and the park beneath the bridge.

She sat on a bench in the sunshine. A nearby magpie studied her with shiny combative eyes, then flew away, annoyed at his loss of territory. An old man sat eating a sandwich, spilling crumbs as pigeons scavenged around him. A pair of lovers lay entwined on the grass, oblivious to the disapproval of a stout lady walking her dog nearby. The couple were equally unaware of the dog, a friendly labrador, sniffing around them until its wet nose intruded on their rising passion. Belle smiled as the dog eagerly licked their faces; for a moment the pair was unaware of anything but each other, then realising there was a third tongue involved in their fervour, they sprang apart and sat up.

'Fuck off, Fido,' the young man said, while the girl laughed and hugged the labrador.

'Disgraceful,' the owner remarked as she paused beside Belle. She clearly hoped for some agreement; not receiving this, she called the labrador, who took no notice. He was enjoying being fondled by the girl. Belle was amused to see him showing signs of an erection. The woman began to notice it too.

'Come here, Jasper,' she called impatiently, twisting the lead in her hands. 'Here at once, you *bad* boy! Bad, bad boy.'

'Bye-bye, Jasper,' the girl said, kissing him on the nose, 'off you go, back to Mummy.'

The couple watched as the dog returned reluctantly to his mistress, who immediately clipped the lead to his collar. Then they resumed their activity on the grass. The girl, as though aware of an audience now, opened her legs and wrapped them around the boy's body, displaying the tops of her stockings and a suspender belt as well as a glimpse of bare flesh and panties.

'How disgusting.' The labrador's owner eyed Belle again, as if daring her to disagree about this scandalous exhibition of public lust.

Belle shrugged. 'They're young,' she said.

'That's no excuse.' The woman wore a flowered hat that seemed more suitable for church or a garden party. 'Both are quite old enough to know better.'

'The young very rarely know better. I'm sure I didn't. Or weren't you ever young and foolish?'

'Don't be impertinent,' the other said. 'I've a mind to report their behaviour. They should be arrested for indecency. This used to be a pleasant park where one could walk without being offended.'

'It used to be a park where one could sit in peace without being bothered,' Belle said, tiring of the intrusion. 'Call the police, go ahead. Dob them in. I'll warn those children to be off before the weight of the law ruins their day.'

'Come, Jasper, we've had more than enough.' Her face was flushed, her lips thin with disapproval. She tugged on the lead as if anxious to be somewhere else, but her timing was astray as the labrador refused to budge. Instead he squatted to deliver a large pungent turd between them. This did nothing to help his owner's disposition.

'Phew,' Belle said, rising from the bench to escape the odour, 'so much for your pleasant park – I'd hate to tread in that. Someone will, some dark night. Jasper, old darling, you'd better be careful of the dog catcher.'

When they had gone, the dog most unwillingly, Belle moved across to sit on the sandstone wall where she could look down at the tide lapping against the rock wall. The expression on that woman's face, she thought, has restored my day. I needed a laugh. Now I've got to decide what on earth to do about Teddy.

She had begun to realise how deeply he missed George, and for once she did not know how to deal with it.

Chapter twelve

George Carson locked the kitchenware department, left his keys on the desk of Mr Gable's secretary as usual, and began his fifteen-minute walk home to Brewinda Road. He no longer hurried so he might share the last of the daylight in the garden, playing cricket with Teddy, or watching him ride his bike, pretending to be Australia's famous cyclist Hubert Opperman, who had won a great race in France and become almost as big a hero to his son as Don Bradman.

A son who was not really his, George thought sadly. Belle had never tried to deceive him about that: he often wished she had. It would have been possible to believe a baby born a little under six months after their marriage was premature and belonged to that miraculous night – the first time he had gone to bed with and made love to Belle Baker. He could easily have persuaded himself. But she had been adamant he know the truth: pregnancy was the only dowry she brought to their modest nuptials. Dazzled by her, disbelieving his good fortune, he'd agreed he need never know the identity of the father, and promised he would bring the child up as their own. In return for this she had become his wife.

He still wondered if Teddy's father was that conceited show pony Dan Hardacre. Belle had denied it, insisted she'd swear to it on a stack of Bibles, and while not the least religious and often derogatory about wealthy land-owning churches, she had a strange respect for the Bible. Which was odd, but she had always been a mass of contradictions. So many diverse characters; for ten years he'd woken unsure which one he'd be wed to that day. Variety, people liked to say, is the spice of life, but it had been the bane of his. Yet he felt utterly lost without the excitement, the erratic roller-coaster ride that had been his marriage. And lost without the child who was someone else's, the one he'd held in his arms and loved ever since he was a few hours old.

The daylight was almost gone when George reached Brewinda Road. In his garden Mr Miranda was packing up his tools after mending the front fence, and George could see Mrs Miranda at her sink in the lighted kitchen as she prepared a meal. He was no longer on close terms with these kindly neighbours who had invited him so regularly for Sunday lunch. At first they were content to accept the tale he and Belle had embroidered before her departure, the fiction of a brief but friendly separation which was necessary for the sake of Teddy's future. Mother and son would soon be back, everyone was assured, but in the meantime film producers were queuing up to employ him. It was only sensible to cash in on his lucky break and make good use of this transient fame.

Most people seemed to accept that. But as weeks became months and then a year, the invented excuse became so transparent he could no longer bring himself to continue the deception. Admitting the truth to Mr and Mrs Miranda one Sunday, he was swamped by their sympathy, to such an extent that the regular lunches became an ordeal. Suggestions were constantly offered on how he might tempt Belle back, or even invoke the letter of the law to force her back, but George said that was not his style, not his style at all, and he'd prefer not to talk about it. Just leave it be and talk of something else. Truly, if they didn't mind.

Mrs Miranda declared of course she didn't mind, not if that was George's wish. She wouldn't utter another single word on the matter – but really, it was a crying shame, and what kind of a wife was she to leave a nice home the way she did, to walk out on a decent man, a good husband and a fine father, and go off with that poor child, taking him to live in a slum room like a gypsy?

George realised the subject would never be allowed to lapse; as a result he began to refuse their invitations, and soon they stopped asking him.

He paused at his own gate, where it was not yet dark enough to hide the wreckage of the garden. Weeds had proliferated, they ran unchecked across the once-neat lawn, now unsightly with bindi and paspalum. Most of the vegetables in the patch he had lovingly cared for had been eaten by slugs; what remained had gone to seed. He kept promising himself he must do something: clear it up, have a burn-off, start again. The question that kept preventing him was why? Why bother?

He heard the sound of shouting from the Lucas house next door and shrugged. Nothing ever changed around here, he thought, at least not on Fridays. Every Friday afternoon Harry Lucas spent half his wages in the pub near the council chambers where he worked, and afterwards staggered home to pick a row with Essie. Sometimes she would appear the next morning with bruises on her face, always proclaiming she'd had an accident with a door. Once, two years ago, when Percy Bates had been called to intercede after a particularly violent night, Essie had vehemently denied that her husband battered her.

'Of course he does,' Belle had declared after the couple went back inside their house. 'You don't get black eyes and those kinds of bruises from bumping into the dunny door.'

Perce had insisted nothing could be done about it unless Harry's missus made a proper complaint. That sort of trouble – between a husband and wife – was best left to the parties themselves to sort out, he'd stated, which was when Belle had shaken her head and said there was none so blind as a copper who couldn't be bothered to see what was going on under his nose, and their neighbour was a nasty and dangerous neanderthal allowed to bash his wife while Percy did nothing. His attitude was the typical parochial view of a bloody backwoods walloper.

George remembered it vividly. It had caused a frosty few days with his mate Perce, but he'd risk that and a lot more to have Belle and Teddy back here waiting for him. Instead, he'd accepted her plea that she could no longer live here, and the anger between them had cooled into a tacit acceptance. A defeat for him, he knew, but trying to restrain her would not have been a victory. So they had remained civil, and played the roles Belle devised for them. As a result the house was now empty, devoid of life, George felt, and lacking warmth and laughter it was merely a dump like she'd always said. It was dark and smelt from being locked up all day, and sometimes he hated coming home to it.

The gate squeaked, and as he pushed it shut the small dog across the road began its habitual high-pitched bark.

'That fucking dog!' he yelled in a moment of futile rage at the predictability of it all. 'Does it always have to yap like that? Can't it just for fucking once, for one time in its fucking life, fucking shut up?'

Miss Limmington, who was in her late seventies and always refused to admit she was deaf, opened her front window and stared out at him.

'What did you say, George?'

He began to spread his arms in what he intended as a conciliatory gesture of apology, then realised she had not heard a word. He walked across the street.

'I said he's a good watchdog, Miss Limmington.'

'Just as well he is,' she said, 'because I was waiting for you to come home. That new young postie put this in my box by mistake.' She leant out her front window and handed him a letter, with an air of shared excitement. 'I couldn't help recognising the handwriting, George. It's from *her*.'

He noticed the envelope was not sealed as securely as it should be. She was watching carefully, her faded violet eyes intent on him as he held the letter, and he remembered she was an incorrigible stickybeak. Miss Limmington spent a great deal of her time viewing the activities of the street from her front window; to be left alone all day with this, knowing who had sent it, he was almost tempted to ask her what Belle had written.

Instead he took the letter home, eager to find out.

The alarm clock beside the bed ticked like a metronome, the hands said it was almost three-thirty. The neighbourhood was dark, Miss Limmington's dog and drunken Harry Lucas asleep and oblivious to the distant lilt of reedwarblers down by the creek, a sound as liquid and melodic as the song of a nightingale. It was interrupted as the municipal garbage truck rumbled past on its weekly collection, and a disturbed rooster, seeing the bright headlights, decided it was dawn.

George heard every sound. He looked at the clock once more; it was a full ten minutes since he had last checked the time. Finally acknowledging that sleep was impossible, he switched on the bedroom light, wrapped himself in his dressing-gown and went to the kitchen to warm some milk. Then he sat down to read the letter again.

Dear George,

I'm writing this late at night with Teddy fast asleep, as I don't want him to read it and expect too much. He's been very busy doing lots of work, quite often small parts, but it all helps to make him known. It's part of a process that I know you find hard to understand, but I believe it will lead to great things, and on this you must try to trust me.

But here's the real reason for this letter. He works so hard and he's such a darling that I'd love to give him a special treat, a real surprise. He does miss you, and it would be wonderful if we could plan this together. The best possible treat would be you turning up out of the blue, so to speak, coming here to visit and spending a week or two with us. I don't mean like the last time, when you had to stay in a boarding house and we could only meet to have meals and go on train trips or walk around the Botanical Gardens. I know you hated that, and so did I. I hope this time will be different as we no longer live in that frightful room with the bossy landlady's restrictions.

Now, I can just imagine you frowning, asking yourself the usual questions, like how can we afford this, and what possible excuse can you offer Henry Gable to be absent from work, and all sorts of George-like worries that I have no doubt are already occurring to you. I suggest you simply tell misery-guts Gable the truth. Tell him your son is doing well in his career, but he's missing you and we both feel he needs a spell of family life. Tell him you'll take

unpaid leave. I'll arrange for Florian to buy your train ticket.
You remember Florian, the one I call Uriah Heep. He looks after
everything, even invests Teddy's earnings for us, and to my surprise
he seems good at it. So don't worry about money. Obviously you
will stay with us in the flat at Kings Cross and will be welcome, I
assure you. Please try to arrange it, and write as soon as you can to
tell me when to expect you.
  With love,
  Belle

━━━━◆━━━━

They were late reaching Central Station. Their tram had been delayed
by the holiday traffic, and they hurried through the colonnades to
the platforms where the country trains arrived. The concourse was
packed with visitors descending on the city for the Royal Easter
Show.

Belle had not yet told Teddy who they were meeting, inventing
a friend from her past, for she was still uncertain if George would
actually arrive. The weeks of delay and their exchange of letters had
clearly revealed his timidity at the prospect of confronting Henry
Gable with a demand for unpaid leave.

You say it should be easy, but you should remember that he's not
an easy man and these are not easy times, George had written. *He*
takes advantage of the way things are and he's just as likely to refuse
me. He fancies himself as the leading citizen here, which I suppose
he is, and if you fall out with Gable the chances of any other decent
jobs around here are nil.

I know what he fancies himself as, Belle felt tempted to reply,
remembering the rich town councillor and emporium-owner whose
speculative eyes had so often undressed her, and who, at a gathering

to welcome a touring theatrical troupe, had made a thinly veiled proposition that her husband's employment prospects might very well benefit if she cared to be more friendly. Perhaps a promotion, or a slight increase in salary, although she must be sure not to misunderstand what he was suggesting; he was merely expressing the hope they might meet on less crowded occasions, so they could get to know each other better.

For the sake of George's job she had withheld the scathing retort this inept overture deserved. But from that day on she made certain she was never alone with Gable if they happened to attend the same function.

Surely, she wrote to George in response, *he must know how loyal you've been all these years – working five-and-a-half-days each week, eight till five. A bit of unpaid leave is not unreasonable, and you should request it in this spirit. Be confident. Remember, you're not asking for any special favour – just for fair treatment which is not going to cost him a penny.*

I can't believe you're so afraid of this man, she wanted to add, but decided not to, as his prevarication proved otherwise. Besides, detachment had made her more understanding of George's situation; to him the job was a guarantee of safety in precarious times. There was no real assistance for the unemployed, no welfare and precious little sympathy either. And with a mortgage on the house, and the house itself now worth less than when they bought it, such insecurity created a fear that was easily exploited by men like Henry Gable.

During the month of March letters passed between them without anything being resolved. Just when it seemed as if the proposal had become bogged down and there would be no convergence until George's annual holidays next summer, he had written to suggest the approaching Easter week. His letter said little about Gable's reaction; it simply relayed the news he would catch the Southern Express – hardly an express at all, more like a milk train – which left Gundagai after midnight on Thursday, and should arrive around eight on the morning of Good Friday. Belle had dashed off a letter containing a postal order to pay for the ticket after a hurried visit to Florian MacArthur-Bailey's office in Lower George Street.

'Reconciled, are we?' Florian had been his usual intrusive self.

'Actually, Uriah, I don't think it's any of your bloody business.'

'I think it's very much my business if the young client might do a vanishing act. I need to know if your expectations include a return to the nuptial nest beyond the black stump.'

'They certainly do not,' Belle told him firmly, 'so get cracking and find him some real work for a change. No more lousy walk-ons. A decent role that'll get him back in the public eye again and higher on the billing. But no work during the Easter week.'

'In which time your ex will be among us, I take it?'

'He's not my ex. We just happen to live at slightly different addresses.'

'Oh, that's good,' Florian smirked. 'I like that. I must remember it.'

'Do me a favour and remember something else. If you should happen to meet George while he's here, try to remember that he's Teddy's father.'

'Come, come, duckie. Don't be ridiculous. You were well and truly in the pudding club when you met him. We all know it isn't him.'

'Teddy doesn't,' Belle replied fiercely, 'and he's not going to. As far as he's concerned, George will always be his dad.'

'What about the real genitor? The actual pater?'

'Cut it out. Besides, you haven't the remotest idea who that is.'

'Oh, yes, I do,' Florian replied. 'With my propensity for gossip, who would find out quicker? I've known his name for years. Rest easy, petal, it's the best-kept secret of my life – probably the *only* one.'

Belle had gazed at him stunned, uncertain how to deal with the revelation.

'Do any others know?' she asked eventually.

'I doubt it. Certainly not from me,' he promised.

She had left the office soon afterwards, believing him because she so badly wanted to. *Had to*, she realised. But it came as a shock, Florian knowing. Only one other person had ever been entrusted with that knowledge, and Nuncie, a close friend she had lost touch with, would never have confided it to a man, let alone the garrulous and unreliable Florian.

The station clock showed they were fifteen minutes late as she and Teddy crossed the crowded terminus.

'Excuse me.' Belle tried to steer her way through a cluster of arrivals, a group of country women just off a train, one of whom gave a gasp and pointed directly at Teddy.

'Look, it's him! It's the boy who was in that film. I'll swear it is.'

That was the moment when Belle saw George in the distance, waiting beside the barrier gate where the Southern Express had disgorged its passengers. He was scanning the crowds in search of them, looking anxious and out of place.

'It is, isn't it?' the woman insisted, and without waiting for a reply she knelt down to Teddy's level. 'You were blond in it, weren't you?'

'Peroxide,' Teddy replied.

'Peroxide? But you have such nice brown hair.'

'They wanted it blond. Mum did it for me.'

'Goodness! Did you hear, girls?' she said to the others. 'It *is* him, the little darling. We loved that film. I saw it twice. Madeleine saw it three times. Didn't you, Madeleine?'

'Yes, three times. Lovely picture. You were sweet in it,' the woman called Madeleine said to Teddy, as they gathered around him like a trophy they'd cleverly acquired during their first moments in the city.

'Excuse me, ladies,' Belle tried to rescue him, 'but we're running late —'

'You'd be his mother,' another of the group decided.

'We have to meet someone,' she started to tell them, but nobody listened. They were much too intrigued with Teddy. One took a box brownie from her handbag and asked him to say 'Cheese' as she took his picture.

'You must be very proud,' one of them said to Belle.

'Very proud,' several of the others echoed.

'Of course I am,' Belle replied hastily, 'but if you don't mind, we are late —'

'Why "of course"?' The one on her knees turned waspish. 'All we want to do is congratulate your son. He's a talented boy, and you're a lucky woman. You don't seem to realise that.'

At a less ill-timed moment, Belle might have been flattered. 'I realise it,' she replied brusquely, 'but his father has just arrived from the country to see us, and he's over there wondering where on earth we are.'

'Is he?' Teddy's eyes were wide with surprise. 'Where, Mum? Why didn't you tell me?'

'It's an Easter treat, darling. So say thank you to these ladies, because we have to go and meet him. Look, he's seen us —'

'Whacko!' Teddy shouted, abandoning his admirers without another word as he waved frantically and raced across the terminus to hug George. Belle, who felt no obligation to apologise for this behaviour, ran after him.

'Amazing,' one of the women declared, watching them. 'What on earth did audiences see in that pallid child? Off the screen he looks quite ordinary.'

'She peroxided his hair, did you hear him say that?' The woman who had first recognised Teddy felt aggrieved at their abrupt discard. 'The kid will be bald by the time he's thirty.'

Madeleine agreed. 'I'd say the father doesn't live with them. Just arrived to see them,' she said. 'Sounds like the dad got left behind by Her Ladyship.'

'Forget them,' another member of the group who had been quiet until now said. 'We're staying at the CWA tonight, and off to the show tomorrow. All those big boys with big muscles chopping wood, it never fails to get me a bit fruity.'

'You're awful, Deanna,' Madeleine said. 'Isn't she awful?'

They all agreed she was awful.

'It's very nice,' George said, thinking it was hideous and quite tiny, really – poky and dark – just one room with what looked like a double bed, a gas ring and a sink, and beyond this a cubicle barely able to contain a small bed with Teddy's pyjamas folded on the pillow. The only real window looked out onto an adjacent brick wall, the buildings so close together that no natural light could penetrate, which was why Belle had switched on the unshaded globe that hung like a flytrap from the ceiling.

'This is my place in here.' Teddy was intent on a guided tour as he pulled aside a frayed curtain that screened the cubicle. There was a louvred casement in there, but the same brick wall and years of what looked like bird droppings on the glass prevented the entry of discernible daylight.

'And here's where you and Mum sleep.' He bounced up and down on the main bed, which was not a double, George now realised – hardly a three-quarter – and with only the curtain between beds, there would be little chance of anything happening here. Least of all the sort of happening he'd visualised in wakeful moments of last night, while fantasising to the rhythm of the train.

'Very nice,' he said again, and glimpsed Belle's fleeting reaction, a rueful smile that seemed to read his mind and recognise his disappointment.

'It's small,' she said, 'but inexpensive. Fits the budget.'

'That's good,' George nodded, hardly able to take his eyes off her.

'The Cross is mainly like this. Rabbit warrens. The landlords don't like to give us too much space. After all, we might spread our wings and fly away.'

He was unsure how to reply to that.

'I'll make some coffee,' Belle suggested. 'Or would you rather tea? I expect you would.'

Tea was what he liked best, he agreed.

She switched on a jug and took his suitcase, unpacking the clothes he had brought and putting them on a shelf, then storing the suitcase beneath the bed.

'One good thing about a pigeonhole like this, you have to be tidy. Not possible to be anything else.'

He nodded. She looks somehow different, he thought. Like a stranger, a rather exciting stranger. He had felt it at the station, his first glimpse of them both with Teddy running towards him, Belle running behind. Waving and animated, like a young girl, had been his first impression. Young and . . .

'Did you hear me, Dad?'

'What? Oh, sorry, Ted. What did you say?'

144

'Were you dreaming? Daydreaming like Mum says I do?'

'No, just . . . just looking out the window.'

'You can't see out the window.'

'That's right, that's what I was thinking. You can't. What a pity they built these places so close together. So go on with what were you telling me, old son.'

'About our friends.'

'Oh yes . . . friends . . . ?'

'How they often drop in, and Mum cooks spaghetti. They all bring a bottle of four-penny dark, only some people call it plonk, and everybody argues about the government making a mess of the country, and the fascists in the New Guard.'

'Goodness. And do you take part in these arguments?'

'No, I mostly listen till I go to sleep. But I know the Guard are a bunch of right-wing dingoes. Aren't they, Mum?'

'Dingoes and drongos,' she replied. 'Reactionaries, the lot of them. They think Mussolini's all right because he makes the trains run on time. And they like Hitler because he hates the Jews.'

'Some people at home reckon Hitler's not as bad as they make out.'

'People like who? Percy Bates?'

'Perce . . . and a few others.'

'I can imagine.' She clattered cups. He wished he hadn't spoken.

'You ought to meet our friends, Dad. Some of them are painters. And actors. One's a poet. You'd like them.'

'I'm sure I would,' George said, doubting this.

'You should see this place when everyone drops in. Sometimes, golly, we have ten or twelve people in here.'

'Do you really? Where do they all fit?'

'On the floor,' Teddy told him. 'Or the bed. Delia and Frederick are lovers, so they like to lie on the bed.'

'Oh.' If his wife seemed much younger, his inherited son seemed to have grown older than his age. While Teddy kept talking George responded, but his mind was drifting. He was acutely aware Belle was wearing a simple cotton dress. Deep blue, matches her eyes, he thought. A cotton dress and not much else. As she moved he could see the outline of her buttocks, the motion of her firm breasts. Knowing exactly how she looked naked, he felt surprised at how strongly her fully clothed body heightened his desire.

'There,' she said. 'Milk, no sugar.'

'Remembered that.' He was oddly pleased.

'Of course. Why wouldn't I?'

Of course she'd remember, he told himself. Ten years of making his tea. How many cups of tea do you make in ten years? He wished he didn't feel as if they were meeting for the first time, with all the nervousness it entailed.

The room contained only one chair. He carried his cup and saucer to the bed and sat there. Belle took the chair, indicating her awareness of his gesture with a faint nod of acknowledgement and a smile. He felt an anxiety verging on shyness and tried to think of what to say. Nothing about the town, or people back home. Nor her new friends, whom he didn't know or want to. Somehow in the rush of meeting, they'd exhausted small talk, avoided awkward subjects and now, feeling the gulf of the past year between them, he was tongue-tied.

It had not been at all like this in any of his conjecturing, ever since Belle's letter had been handed to him by old Miss Limmington. In imagined dreams of this day he had been thoroughly at his ease, lively and talkative, impressing her, arranging to take Teddy out for treats later. Teddy had been the perfect child, understanding the situation, running off to play with his friends, while he had returned to Belle, who was waiting so eagerly for him, undressing her and then himself, feeling the rapid beat of her heart and the heat of her body as he entered her . . .

'How's the tea?'

'Oh . . . good. You always made a good cuppa.'

In the afternoon they went for a walk to show George their local neighbourhood, the Cross. Or the dirty half-mile, as the newspapers called it, because of its racy reputation. Actors and artists abounded here, as did many recent arrivals from Europe; they liked its freedom, the *laissez faire* of a bohemian atmosphere that was almost unknown in rigid suburbia. Apart from its inhabitants, Kings Cross drew a constant stream of visitors, among them the prurient who came to view the vice and see for themselves if the district was as decadent as reported.

The centre of the Cross was only minutes away from the squalor of Kellett Street, a garish new world to George. He could not believe the babble of so many different foreign languages, or the waft of strong and rather peculiar smells from small shops that were called delicatessens. Garlic, Belle told him, when he asked what the stink was. The other pungent aromas were Port-salut or camembert; these were her favourite French cheeses, she told him, which she loved but could not afford. He was glad he preferred good old plain cheddar, which didn't pong like this froggy muck. But he refrained from saying so.

In Darlinghurst Road, electric trolley buses attached to overhead cables slid silently by. He found himself astonished, for this was Good Friday and at home nothing would be open, whereas here hardly anything was shut. Flower sellers were doing a thriving business; at the street kiosks queues of people were buying cigarettes and glossy magazines; all the coffee shops were crowded and across the street a Salvation Army band was playing 'Onward Christian Soldiers' in front of the Picture Palace, where posters advertised a torrid romance with Norma Shearer and Frederic March.

He became aware of some women who stood loitering in the shadowed doorways. Since he was curious enough to stare at them, he received a variety of invitations: a raised eyebrow, a gesture of the head, a beckoning finger, deep and meaningful sultry gazes, and even – despite the presence of Belle and Teddy – a shapely lipsticked mouth pursed in a kiss of sexual promise. By then he realised this was not city friendliness but ladies of the night trawling for daytime custom. He was shocked it could happen so blatantly, with no one in the least concerned. He thought it was hardly an atmosphere in which to bring up a child, but debated whether to voice this. Belle clearly liked the place; she seemed to know lots of people, and they seemed to know and like her. George felt totally out of his depth, and the hopes he had arrived with for some kind of permanent accord began to dissipate.

At the corner of Orwell Street was an accordionist balanced on crutches, an ex-service badge in the lapel of his ragged coat and an empty trouser leg tied above his right knee. He saw them approaching and switched from a mournful rendition of 'The Rose of Tralee' to a stylish and rhythmic Latin number from the new musical *Flying Down to Rio*. Teddy smiled as he heard the first chords, his feet began to tap and he hurried to join the busker. By the time they reached the pair George realised that people were actually pausing to watch Teddy perform.

'That's my young Fred,' the accordionist encouraged him. 'Now, let it rip, Master Astaire, show us peasants how to dance.'

Teddy followed him as he swung into the fast beat of 'The

Carioca', the main dance routine of the hit show. More people gathered to watch, those who had seen the film recognising the Astaire style and the skilful impersonation. They started to applaud as the tempo increased, and even some of the traffic slowed to watch the impromptu street theatre.

'Belle, don't you think —' George started to say, feeling acute embarrassment at how they were the centre of attention, but before he could suggest they move on she thrust her handbag at him, and began to dance herself.

'Well, look at her now, the darling girl,' the accordionist called out, his voice resonant like an actor's and easily heard over the music. 'If it isn't our Ginger, come to dance with our Fred.'

The crowd had grown. They formed a ring and started to beat their hands in time to the steps and the music while Belle sang the words and danced with Teddy as though they were in a ballroom. Astaire and Rogers stepping out in the middle of the road, where the cars had now come to a halt. Horns were tooting in chorus, a token of approval, not frustration, as the two voices blended in melody until the concluding lines:

> The Carioca, Carioca,
> Rio's dance of love.

Finally, and mercifully for the discomforted George left clutching her handbag, it was over. The crowd applauded; some threw pennies and even a few silver coins into the street musician's hat. They smiled their approval at Teddy and Belle for the unexpected entertainment, and gradually moved away. The traffic resumed.

'Great, Mum,' Teddy said, hugging her.

'She's too young and good-looking to be a mum,' the accordionist declared. 'Ginger Rogers come to the Cross, that's who she is. A vision from off the silver screen.'

'Flatterer,' Belle said, flushed and pleased.

'Dominic, this is my dad,' Teddy introduced them. 'Dad, this is Dominic.' The musician surveyed him for a moment, then nodded a brief greeting.

'He's a good kid,' he said, 'a natural. He'll be a name some day.'

'Why do you think that?' George asked him.

'He stopped the traffic,' Dominic replied. 'Ain't that good enough for you? Never stopped the traffic before, have you kiddo?'

'Never,' Teddy said.

'Besides, it's a matter of instinct. I might only have one leg, but I've got instinct.' Dominic smiled and turned to Belle. 'Thanks, darl. We made at least ten bob. Half of it's yours.'

'Get off,' Belle said. 'You keep it. We're all right this week.'

'Suits me.' He put down the accordion. 'So this is George from beyond the black stump?'

'Yes,' Belle replied. 'But he doesn't like that expression. Nobody in the country does.'

'They get their own back by calling us a mob of city slickers,' Dominic said. 'How long you staying, George?'

'I don't know,' George said, feeling embarrassed by the whole incident, his wife and Teddy dancing publicly in the street and apparently sharing money with the busker. Although he knew full well how long he'd be staying, he had no wish to discuss it with Dominic. He had not yet managed to explain to Belle he had to be back at work in less than three days from now, when the Easter weekend was over.

If not, there'd be no job waiting when he returned.

Chapter thirteen

The night was hot, the room airless and the less-than-three-quarter-size bed made for single comfort, not for two bodies doing their utmost to avoid each other. It was much too cramped, and despite his best efforts he kept encountering the bare flesh of her arms and legs, and wondered if she could feel his growing erection. He tried to edge carefully away from contact with her body so it would not be so apparent, but felt it might be too late.

Teddy was asleep, only a few feet away, behind the curtain. Belle was breathing softly, giving an impression of sleep, but doubtless feeling equally uncomfortable. George realised her nightdress had ridden up as his hand encountered bare buttocks and lingered there. He heard her hold a breath in reaction to this, then began to run his fingers provocatively across the curves of her bottom. After a moment she turned to face him, and he gently stroked her breasts.

'We can't,' she whispered.

'Please?' he murmured in her ear.

He could feel the shake of her head in the dark, but ignored it. He pulled her close, and had an erotic memory of the woman with the bright-red lips who had been standing in the doorway of a private hotel: the way she had pouted them at him in a kiss full of lewd suggestion. He kissed Belle and felt her responding. Her hand crept beneath his pyjamas and held his erection, but while gently caressing it she whispered words that seemed to be saying it was impossible.

'Please, Belle.'

'Not now.'

'When?'

'He's too close . . .'

'He's asleep.'

'Can't tell.'

'I'm *sure* he's asleep.'

'We can't be certain.'

'Belle, I'm randy . . .'

'I know.'

'Randy as hell.'

'I do know. It's not your pyjama cord I'm holding.' He heard a muffled giggle from her.

'That cock's been so bloody lonely.'

'Poor old cock.' She gave it a gentle squeeze. He took it as an invitation.

'Belle, darling. I'm dying for it. Sex-starved.'

'Me too,' she whispered. 'Me too.'

'I think about you – about doing it with you – all the time. All kinds of different ways. Half the time at work all I think about is us doing it.'

'Stop it, George.'

'Why?'

'You're getting me excited.'

'Well, then?'

'Not when he's so close. We couldn't relax.'

'I don't *want* to relax.'

'I have to,' Belle said.

'We'll be quiet.'

'We can't be *that* quiet.'

'Let's try.'

'No.'

'It's impossible to be in bed like this with you . . . and not want to —'

'I know. You're not the only one who's been sleeping alone.'

'Then let's stop talking and do it.' George's voice thickened, and he tried to remember he should whisper. 'I need you. I wanted to see Teddy, but most of all I wanted to make love to you. When I read your letter, that's what I thought about. I've been thinking about it ever since. About fucking you. Nothing else but that. Every day since. At work, at home, in the train on the way here last night. Fucking you. Belle —'

There was a murmur and a movement from close beside them.

'Now you've done it,' Belle hissed fiercely. 'You've woken him up.'

'Oh shit,' George hardly bothered to whisper as Teddy got out of bed. Making his way through the darkened room to the door, he opened it and went out into the dimly lit hallway to the communal lavatory.

'You see what would've happened?'

'I'm sorry, Belle. But I can't be wedged up against you like this and just go to sleep. Not after so long. It would've been better to stay somewhere else, in a boarding house. I think I'll go crazy.'

'We'll find other times.'

'When?'

'I don't know. When it's safe.'

'He might go straight back to sleep,' George said with desperate optimism.

'We can't risk it. Put your best friend back in your pyjamas.'

'Oh God . . .'

'I promise I'll work something out.'

'How?'

'I don't know, but I will.'

'But when?' he tried to whisper insistently, as he heard the chain flush and knew Teddy was coming back.

'Soon.'

Soon, he wanted to tell her, wasn't good enough. Soon he had to go home to Brewinda Road and his job at Gable's. There could only be these few Easter nights, for he had asked Henry Gable for unpaid leave beyond the Easter break and Gable had told him to go to buggery. Had frightened the life out of him. Told him if it was so important, taking time off to try mending his hopeless marriage, then there were twenty other people eager and able to fill his job.

And when George had attempted to say it was crucial, really imperative, Gable had become abusive and said the only one who decided what was imperative was the man who owned the store. No bloody employee on wages was going to hold him to ransom. And if George was thick enough to run after his tarty and ridiculous wife, who couldn't wait to dump him and get out of this town according to all the rumours (and who probably was shacked up with someone else by this time, almost certainly saddled and ridden by some city slicker), if he was going to be that dimwitted, then he couldn't count on holding his job for much longer.

'Soon,' Belle whispered the promise to him again, as they heard Teddy make his way back to his bed in the dark. He stopped close by them.

'Did you say something, Mum?' he whispered.

'What's the matter, Teddy?' she muttered drowsily, as if he had woken her.

'Sorry, I thought you were awake.'

'Go to sleep,' she said, and turned in the bed as though resuming her own sleep. Her mostly naked back was wedged against George. His erection, which had so rapidly subsided with impending defeat, now began to betray him and grow again in response to the heat of her body.

Belle shifted a few inches away from him, which was as much of a retreat as the bed would allow, and gradually her breathing became soft and regular. Long after she was asleep – and Teddy too – George lay awake in discomfort, his genitals aching, suffering from what in his school days had been the subject of comedy and widely ridiculed as 'lover's balls'. Sometime in the hours between this pain and the blessed oblivion of sleep he heard again the venom of Henry Gable's threat, with his acidic and contemptuous dismissal of Belle.

It had been unfair and quite extreme, and the memory of it even now made him feel uneasy. Because he knew he should've stood up to Gable, should've said his comments were offensive and untrue. But nobody spoke back to the owner of the store, not when jobs were so hard to find. Least of all, George had to concede, people like himself.

It was Easter Saturday, and Belle went downstairs to the corner shop because the petite French woman who owned it had saved her some leftover hot cross buns. When she came back, it appeared that more than buns had been acquired; some hurried arrangements had been made. George was sitting in the chair finishing a cup of tea. Belle gave the semblance of a nod, and his eyes lit up.

'Chrissie wants to take you to the pictures,' she said to Teddy.

Chrissie, she explained to George, was Christine LaRue, the shop owner's daughter. She was seventeen, studying shorthand and typing, and despite the difference in their ages she and Teddy were good friends.

'Sometimes, when the film is suitable, she takes Teddy and they get in for free, because her boyfriend is the projectionist. So, the matinee this afternoon – what do you say, darling?' she asked her son.

'But Dad's here. Can't he come too?'

'I don't think it's his sort of film,' Belle said swiftly.

'*Bulldog Drummond*, Dad. It's beaut, honest.'

'He means beautiful, don't you, darling.' Belle ruffled his hair affectionately.

'All right, it's extra grouse. Drummond's a famous English agent. He fights spies and crooks and protects people.'

'Sounds pretty exciting, Ted . . .' George agreed, but tried not to show too much enthusiasm.

'It is, you'll like it. Ronald Coleman's in it. He's a really famous actor. And there's a kids' serial, too. A real ripper serial, and we all cheer the villain and hiss the hero.'

'I'm sure it's good fun, but I'm not a great one for picture shows.' He could see Belle's oblique glance, her eyes focused on him. 'Besides, I'd rather take you to the Easter Show, or on the Manly ferry. Or both, if we have time.'

'You beaut! The Easter Show! Honest, Dad?'

'Honest.'

'But can we afford it?' Teddy asked, and George felt a moment of dismay that he should ask such a question. He patted Teddy on the shoulder reassuringly.

'This is a special treat. We can always afford special treats,' he promised.

'When will we go?'

'How does tomorrow sound? Easter Sunday?'

'Beaut!'

'So run downstairs and tell Christine,' Belle suggested, 'that you'll be at the shop at two o'clock. Ready to escort her.'

'Righto,' he said, but at the door he stopped and frowned. 'But that means I'll be gone all afternoon. What'll you two do?'

'Oh, we'll think of something,' Belle assured him.

'Of course we will,' George said. 'And, before we know it, it'll be teatime. You'll be back in time for tea.'

'Mum calls it dinner.'

'Well, there you are. You'll be back in time for dinner.'

'Whacko!' Teddy said. '*Bulldog Drummond* today, Easter Show tomorrow and Manly on Monday. A beaut weekend. It's so beaut it's almost beautiful,' he said with a cheeky grin at Belle, and heard their laughter as he ran down the stairs.

They lay in the tousled bed. George felt numb with disappointment and close to angry tears that threatened to disgrace him. 'I'm sorry,' he said, over and over. 'I was too tense . . . it all felt wrong. And it was worse, you pretending.'

'Then it was my fault?'

'God, no.'

'I was trying to help . . .'

'I know.'

'Never mind.'

'But I do,' he said. 'I mind terribly. It was the waiting . . . it would've been all right last night.'

'We couldn't then. You know that.'

'I'm only saying it felt natural then. We wanted each other, and that was the right moment.'

'You mean while my son listened? Or else he could've put on the light and watched?'

'Stop it, Belle. You know what I'm trying to say. The waiting, all morning, trying to act normal, watching the time till it was two o'clock . . . Even then, getting undressed, still worrying he might forget something and come back. It wasn't natural. It was a sort of performance . . . and I couldn't perform.'

They lay in mutual dismay. There were at least two more hours to spend together, before Teddy returned from the cinema.

'Might as well get dressed,' Belle said, pushing the sheet aside as she rose and reached for her underclothes.

He watched her take her pants and put them on. Frilly scanties, they were called; the only pair she owned, sexy lacy underwear kept for special times. He felt a strange moment of heartbreak as he saw this. She had worn them to kindle a flame, but instead . . . He shied away from the memory. In all their volatile years, no day, no act, had been as distressing as this.

'I'm sorry,' he said yet again, and she had no answer except a shrug. What was there to say?

She put on the same blue dress, found her hairbrush and a mirror.

'I haven't been able to tell you,' George said, 'but I have to go back on the Monday afternoon train. To be at work on Tuesday morning.'

Belle nodded, brushing her hair and looking into the hand-held mirror. 'I did wonder,' she said. 'You didn't mention how long, and I noticed you said to Teddy "the Easter Show or the Manly ferry. Both *if we have time*".'

'I tried – I asked him for two weeks' unpaid leave. In the end I thought that three days were better than nothing.'

'Perhaps nothing might've been better,' she said gently.

'Not for me. Despite the way things have turned out.'

She thought about this, but avoided a direct answer. 'Teddy will be sorry you're not staying longer.'

'I'll try to make the most of what's left. I've been saving money, to give him a good time at the Easter Show.'

'That's nice.' She put away the mirror and smiled. Her smile had always entranced him. Even at the worst times, like now, it made him feel as if a shaft of sunlight had found its way into the drab little room.

'Did Gable just turn down the idea of unpaid leave?'

'A bit more than that. He threatened that if I insisted, there wouldn't be a job when I came back.'

'He's a bully. A rich bastard and not much of a gentleman, Henry Gable.'

'No, he's certainly not a gent,' George agreed. He thought about his unsuccessful meeting, and the spiteful way Gable had talked about Belle. Malicious and almost personal. He looked at his wife and wondered.

'What's the matter?' she asked.

'Did he ever . . . did Gable ever try anything?'

'With me?'

'Yes. Did something happen that you could never tell me about? Because you can tell me now.'

No, I can't, she thought. It would be pointless, for apart from Gable's crude attempt to blackmail her into his bed, nothing had occurred. To even mention it to George would be unnecessarily cruel. She laughed and shook her head convincingly.

'Mate, don't be bloody ridiculous. A bastard like him is only interested in making an extra quid and driving his poor bloody staff into working longer hours for less pay. You, more than anyone, should know that.'

The train moved slowly through the inner suburbs and picked up speed as it began to head for the southern tableland. The carriage was half empty. George was in a seat by the window, oblivious to the sun setting on the landscape of dairy farms. His thoughts were occupied with the past few days. So eagerly anticipated, but in the end such upsetting days. Belle was right – it might have been better had he never gone to Sydney. It was not, and would never be, his kind of city, nor would the strange hedonistic lifestyle of Kings Cross ever be his choice.

He had to forget Belle, had to let her go. They no longer had a future together. He felt distressed about the loss of Teddy, but that was now inevitable. It was out of his hands; she was his mother and there was no other person to influence the way she would shape his life. So Teddy would grow up as Belle wanted him to, among her poet and painter friends. Easter had been a truly bitter educative experience.

He would agree to a divorce if she requested it, or met someone else. George thought that more than likely, but doubted if there'd be anyone else for him. He felt as though he had had a surfeit of marriage, and more than enough of love.

'What time will Dad get home?' Teddy asked as they waited for the tram back to Kings Cross after seeing the train leave Central Station.

'Early tomorrow morning,' Belle replied, imagining him having to find his way to Brewinda Road through the dark and empty streets. There were no lights beyond the centre of town, and she had forgotten to ask if he had brought a torch. She remembered the rare occasions when they had gone out late together, trying to pick their way home along the dusty corrugated roads. She could picture it all too vividly, the front gate squeaking, Miss Limmington's unpleasant little dog woken and starting to yap. The neighbours all on watch in the morning to see George hurry off to clock in at Gable's before the store opened. Speculating. Pitying him, condemning her. Thank God, she thought, I will never see that street or those unfriendly faces again.

She wished things had been different and he could've stayed longer for Teddy's sake. The weekend had been a failure and it upset her, for even in the worst times she had no real antipathy towards George. In a different environment they might even have survived as a couple. He had been a good father for her son, better than she deserved; she was ready to admit that, if only to herself. But she also realised the illusion of his parentage could not be allowed to continue. Not indefinitely. Sometime in the foreseeable future, she would have to sit down with Teddy and confess the truth. Tell him the facts of his life.

It was something she dreaded. The truth was a problem, it was beset with complications and difficulties. To explain the past meant depriving him of the only father he'd known. Worse than that, it meant admitting that for ten years she had allowed him to live a lie, as well as informing him he had another father, a real one – still alive and living not very far away from them – who would be most unwilling to believe that this particular son existed, or to ever accept him.

A tram approached and they boarded it. Perhaps, she thought to herself on the way home, it might be best to leave things as they are for a while, and to say nothing.

Chapter fourteen

The winter that year was hard, everyone said so; it was as bad as any time since the crash on that astounding day in New York when panic engulfed the city and America erupted into chaos. Belle could still remember the headlines that tried to explain how the stock market had overheated, how the paper millionaires became paupers before nightfall, seeing fortunes lost on the ticker-tape machines they had installed in their offices as status symbols. And how, in the turbulent weeks after the crash, some of these deprived rich, inconsolable with loss, jumped despairingly from the windows of their skyscraper buildings.

In Australian cities few such high buildings existed, but the same fear spread like a pandemic. Unemployment soared and businesses closed as the Wall Street disaster of 1929 spawned a world collapse and ensuing years of hardship. But now, nearly five years later, the federal government had decided it was time for optimism. That winter Prime Minister Joseph Lyons told parliament there was a new reassuring upward curve in the economy. He predicted the Depression could soon end, and he forecast an era of affluence ahead.

'Political piss and wind,' Ross Tanner called it. 'Much ado about keeping this terminally confused rabble in power.'

His was a new face among the Kellett Street circle, those actors, artists and poets who still held court in Belle's Kings Cross habitat. A former law student who had abandoned his studies a year before graduating, his background and source of income was unknown, but he invariably arrived with a thoughtful gift for Belle or a bottle of good wine. Not the anonymous cheap plonk that was the only tipple most could afford; Ross Tanner's offerings came in elegant bottles with the name of the vineyard and the year of harvest on decorative labels.

While enjoying his wine the circle speculated on how he could afford it. Was he the son of a wealthy family? Did he have private means? Who, in fact, was he? They speculated about his age, for he was clearly younger than many of them. Some were envious of his looks; he was tall and fair-haired, with an athletic build and an easy manner. *Je ne sais quoi*, one of the artists remarked, with a trace of envy.

The circle was curious because youth and apparent financial security was a rare combination in such times: they were doubly intrigued because Ross never volunteered information about his background. Direct questions were deflected by a smile and a change of subject. When they asked Belle about him, she professed not to know or care, and pronounced it downright *bourgeois* to be so concerned about personal details. Bohemians and free spirits accepted people at their face value, she declared; he was amusing company with his political invective, and, after all, weren't they all on the same side – the *only* side to be on – against this inept conformist government?

Belle had become skilled in this kind of equivocation. She soon had them agreeing Ross could turn on a good political blue, he'd be a star on a soapbox in the Domain where orators gathered on Sundays. And, she pointed out, he was right: the devious prime minister was a wily bastard whose rallying call was bluster and hyperbole. Fat chance of a recovery with half the population out of work! Even if good times did come they'd bring inflation, so whichever way it went the country would be stuffed. As for the arts – the arts were already stuffed. Well and truly. The rotten government had brought in an unpopular tax on live theatre, and as a consequence some of the finest playhouses had been converted to cinemas showing overseas films. They all agreed Australia had become a cultural wasteland.

'The rich will get richer,' Ross Tanner said, 'as they've always done. For the rest of us, it'll be the same old battle. Getting a fair go as an artist or a writer in this country is like farting against the wind.'

While they all agreed with him, such comments set them speculating again. He spoke as if he was an artist, but nobody knew what kind of art. So was he an actor? Unlikely, since no one had met him at a rehearsal. Perhaps a writer? Not to their knowledge.

A few of Belle's coterie, members of the Communist Party, began to wonder if he might be something covert, an *agent provocateur*. Others dismissed this as Marxist paranoia. They conjectured about the expensive wine, the unfinished law degree, the educated voice and the unmistakeable panache. He had a bit of flair about him, this joker. Couldn't argue over that. It also did not go unnoticed that he was the most frequent of Belle's visitors, ever since the day the pair had met for the first time and been arrested.

Despite the proclaimed optimism, the times were bleak. Each month there were more beggars visible on the streets. People unable to pay rent or keep up their mortgages were forced from their homes; they moved into tents or had to survive in squalid shantytowns, living in packing cases or under sheets of scrap iron. Soup kitchens were unable to accommodate the increasing destitute. Factories shut down, shops were vacated, whole areas in the cities took on an air of desolation. There was a great deal of anger, much of it against the unfairness and frequency of home evictions, and demonstrations against them became widespread.

One began as a routine protest outside a house in Glebe. In the poorer inner-west suburbs close to the city people were living on the breadline, in constant fear of foreclosures. The district had been alerted by news that a family was to be removed that afternoon, the message leaked by a sympathetic filing clerk in the local magistrate's office. Belle's neighbour, Louise Blake, a member of a network to combat evictions, came to recruit her.

'We need lots of people for this one,' she said. 'The husband and wife are just kids themselves, in their early twenties, and their children are babies. The landlord says they're overdue with the rent and wants them out. Their furniture's already been tossed into the street, and they've barricaded themselves inside.'

Belle promptly agreed, as Louise knew she would. 'How do we get there?'

'We've got a utility truck. Be outside St Vinnie's in an hour. Warm coat and hat, or you'll get windblown. We're travelling steerage in the back of the ute.'

St Vincent's Hospital was a ten-minute walk away. Belle called at Helene LaRue's corner shop, where she left a message for Teddy. She had expected to be at home to help him with his homework that afternoon. The Department of Education had recently intervened in their lives, directing her that apart from those days when Teddy was properly and gainfully employed, he was required to attend Darlinghurst Public School. Wilful avoidance of her son's education could land her in serious trouble, she was warned.

'Another demo,' she told the French woman. 'I should be home before dark, but the door's always open, so he can go upstairs and start his homework. I'll be back in time to give him a hand.'

'How is he getting on at his classes?' Helene asked.

'Hates it. But he's missed so much, they put him in with the young kids. He says it makes him feel dumb, especially when the eight-year-olds laugh at him. Little brutes. Probably can't hold a note or dance a step between them.'

Helene said she would ask Christine to help Teddy with his homework when she came home. And in case she was delayed at this demo, they would give him supper. Helene LaRue liked Belle, but often felt concern for her son. Missing school for so long, he lacked playmates and had hardly any friends his own age. His companions were almost entirely his mother's crowd: actors and artists, sophisticates who lived in their own extrovert world. He was a talented boy, no doubt of that, but she wondered how it would all end, a child brought up in such an adult *milieu*.

Christine, who was also fond of him, said Teddy was like *un petit homme*, too mature for his age; a young boy who had missed out on boyhood. Helene resolved to put aside some nice sweet biscuits for when he arrived, as well as giving him something special for supper. Perhaps a meat pie. She knew Belle thought them a bit common, but Teddy loved meat pies.

Two policemen stood guard outside the house. It was a shabby semi-detached, a narrow wooden dwelling with a tiny front porch abutting the footpath. The furniture – a cheap table, two chairs, a bed and some pots and pans – had been confiscated and were stacked in front of the house. At the window the young husband was glimpsed as he nervously peered out.

'They've cut off the water and gas,' a woman in the crowd told Belle, 'and them little kids ain't had a feed since early this morning. It ain't right, not for little toddlers.'

'When are they going to try to evict them?'

'They're in no hurry. The longer the wait, the more scared it makes that couple in there. Get 'em nervous enough, the cops reckon they'll just walk out and give up. The buggers didn't count on this big a mob.'

Belle looked around her. The street was crammed. Neighbours stood watching from their porches, the women silent and grim-faced as if wondering when the same treatment might be meted out to them. All it took was a few months of being out of work and unable to pay the rent.

A police car attempting to get through with reinforcements was stopped as some of the crowd began to lie down in front of it. The driver pressed the horn, which squawked a protest. A tirade of abuse greeted this. A young man in an open-necked shirt and a thick pullover raised his hands to his mouth and created a sound like a donkey braying. The uncanny similarity to the honking of the car horn brought a great wave of laughter.

'Good on ya, mate,' a man yelled. 'Heehaw, you bloody mongrel coppers.'

'Heehaw,' the crowd chanted.

'Donkeys,' they started to jeer, 'Keystone Kops, donkey-drops.'

The young man repeated the sound, the crowd laughed again and yelled for more. A press photographer began snapping pictures of the beleaguered police constables stuck inside the vehicle, for the crush of people prevented them from opening the doors. That was when the brief display of humour ended and the scene turned violent. The police guarding the house rushed to aid their colleagues, producing their batons and swinging them wildly. Several people went down, and Belle felt a moment of alarm as she glimpsed a scalp split open.

A second squad of police appeared at the far end of the street and began a concerted drive to disperse the crowd. They pushed women roughly aside, arbitrarily kneed and punched men in their way. Reaching the photographer taking shots of the furniture outside the house, they ripped his camera from him and smashed it. They took his flashbulbs, broke a light meter, then knocked him down when he tried to reason with them. Meanwhile there was an outburst of anger as people began to realise that yet another group of police were forcing their way through the melee while protecting a process server. Wielding truncheons with indiscriminate force, they cleared a pathway for the court official, keeping him in their midst as they progressed towards the house.

In the wild scuffle that followed, Belle slipped and fell. She tried to shield her face as she was trodden on, felt a moment's panic as the sky was blotted out, then someone pushed his way through the crush of bodies, leant down and grabbed her. It was the fair-haired young man with the open shirt, and he began yelling at people to give her room, she was suffocating, while he tenaciously managed to haul her to her feet.

'It's gone crazy,' he shouted amid the clamour, 'let's get the hell out of here.'

She nodded, feeling dizzy and nauseous.

'Hang onto me.' He realised her distress, and did his best to shelter her from the crush of other bodies as they tried to push their way to safety. Then Belle heard a voice yell.

'That's him, that's the bastard.'

'Get him!' another policeman shouted, and she saw the sticks flailing and knew they were in serious trouble.

People were giving way as the uniforms converged on them. Before they could move any further a baton hit the young man hard on the side of the head and he went down in a heap, dragging Belle with him. A burly policeman stood over them as the crowd scattered and ran.

'You're the clever prick,' he said, his stick raised menacingly. Belle knew that any move by either of them would give him an excuse to use it again. And by the look on his face, he would relish it.

'The fuckin' heehaw man. Fuckin' smart-arse, let's see how smart you are in a cell. You and the woman are under arrest.'

There were only four other detainees, most of the crowd having scurried to safety as the police turned their attention to evicting the tenants. As she was pushed into the squad car, Belle saw them kick down the front door and escort the couple with their children from the house. Both babies were crying until one of the neighbours came and picked them up, trying to calm them as she took them into her house. Belle heard the cop who had arrested them tell the husband to get his shitty furniture off the street before dark or it would be burnt. He called them a pair of losers, saying if they hadn't been so stubborn, there wouldn't have been this shemozzle. People had been hurt and arrested because of them dodging their lousy rent.

The couple made no reply; Belle had a feeling they were too intimidated to speak. She watched as they went into the neighbour's house to join their children. She had been to other protests at forced evictions, but had never experienced this level of violence. The big ugly cop reminded her of Percy Bates, although she decided that was unfair to Percy. This one would certainly approve of Adolf Hitler. And from what she had seen of violence in Germany on newsreels, Hitler would approve of him.

At the Glebe police station they were placed in a communal holding cell with no access to ablutions. Those who needed to had to ask to use the bathroom, and endure the humiliation of being escorted there. They were kept waiting for almost two hours while Belle fretted about getting home. When they were brought before a duty sergeant to have their names taken for possible charges to be laid, the same burly cop was waiting there, watching the proceedings. The sergeant was an older man, less aggressive.

'This is the one who started it,' the cop advised him. 'He's the ringleader who got the crowd going, then all the shit happened.'

'Name?' the sergeant said to the young man.

'Tanner.'

'First name?'

'Ross.'

'Address?' Before there was an answer, the sergeant frowned at the name he had written, then studied the face in front of him. 'Do I know you?'

'I think so, Sergeant.'

'Ross Tanner? Law student?'

'I was, several years ago.'

'But I've seen you recently.'

'Occasionally I get part-time work.'

'Where?'

'Here in Glebe. Filing clerk in the Magistrate's Court.'

So he's the one who leaked the news, Belle thought. He's the filing clerk. She wondered if the duty sergeant realised this. He was scrutinising Ross Tanner with what seemed to be unusual care.

'Your name please, Madam?' She realised his gaze was now fixed on her.

'Carson. Mrs Carson.'

'First name?'

'Belle.'

'Just a minute,' the cop interjected, 'I don't think that's a proper name, Sarge.' He seemed disconcerted by the sergeant's more moderate manner and was determined to make trouble for them. 'I've got to say I've never heard of a name like that.'

'It's what I've always been called,' she said to the sergeant, without even a glance at the other policeman. 'If it's important, I was christened Arabella.'

'Struth!' The cop stifled a laugh. 'No wonder she wanted to change it.'

They both ignored him. Belle sensed an empathy in the older man's eyes. 'I changed it when I was aged twelve,' she said. 'Arabella didn't seem to quite belong on a theatrical poster.'

'Thank you, Mrs Carson,' the sergeant said. 'And your address?'

'Forty-nine Kellett Street, Kings Cross.'

'I shoulda guessed. She's from tart town,' the cop said, and this time the sergeant turned and stared at his younger colleague.

'I think that's enough, Bert. I have your statement, so there's no need for you to stay.'

'But they're the ringleaders. I pinched 'em, and I want it on the record.'

'May I say something, Sergeant?' Ross Tanner asked.

'If it's relevant, Mr Tanner.'

'The constable claims we're the ringleaders – as if we'd conspired together. I don't know how that can be, because I've never met this lady before today. She happened to fall on the ground, and I tried to stop the crowd treading on her. Which was just before I got this bash on the side of my head.'

'Are you accusin' me of somethin', sport?' Bert demanded.

'I have a big lump on my head to prove you hit me,' Tanner said. 'Whether it was warranted is a moot point.'

'A what?' Bert eyed him belligerently.

'Things had got slightly out of control. You may have felt it was justified.'

'Bloody oath it was,' the cop said, and turned to his sergeant. 'If you read my statement, you'll see this bloke has a lot to answer for.'

'I'll read your statement. Mr Tanner, do you feel you want to comment?'

'Yes, Sergeant. What I did was probably wrong.'

'What did you do?'

'I made the crowd laugh.'

'How?'

'The police car had an odd sort of horn. When it tooted, it sounded a bit like a donkey braying.'

'A donkey?'

Belle could sense the sergeant was trying not to smile.

'I imitated it. People thought it funny and they laughed.'

'Wait on, wait on a bit,' Bert interrupted angrily. 'It was some sort of signal to the mob. That's when they started gettin' really bolshie.'

'Can I say something?' Belle asked.

'If it's relevant, Mrs Carson.'

'I hope it is. Nobody got "bolshie". People laughed because it was funny. Until then, it was an ordinary crowd protesting peacefully. We felt bad about the young couple being thrown out of their home, but nobody was aggressive. It was when the police used batons, that's when the trouble seemed to begin. I don't know if we're to be charged, but if so will we be given bail? Because my son is at home wondering where I am.'

The sergeant studied her for a moment. 'May I say that in the future it might be better if you stayed at home so your son needn't be worried, Mrs Carson. And Mr Tanner might confine his talents of mimicry to less tense occasions. I realise it's distressing when a family is evicted. These are not easy times. They're not easy for us in the force either. We have to uphold the law, even if we sometimes have misgivings about whether it is fair.'

They all watched the rigid figure of Bert as he abruptly turned and walked from the room. The sergeant waited until the door slammed shut behind him.

'While there is no charge, the incident must be recorded. Your names will be noted. If you find that a concern, Mr Tanner is a lawyer – well, almost a lawyer, and I daresay he will know how to appeal. Now,' he looked from one to the other, 'is there anything else you'd like to say?'

'Nothing,' Ross Tanner said.

'I'd like to say thank you,' Belle told the sergeant.

They came home by tram. He lived in a boarding house in Rushcutters Bay, and insisted on getting off at her tram stop.

'Just to walk you safely through tart town,' he said.

'Wasn't he awful?'

'Appalling. But lucky for us – each time he opened his mouth he put the desk sergeant on our side.'

'You mean we could've been in trouble?'

'We could've. *Big* trouble. Why do you go to these protests?'

'Why do you pass on the word they're about to happen?'

'Conscience.' Tanner shrugged. 'I have concerns about the way our nice friendly country is heading. How can we send coppers to kick down the doors and drag families and their kids into the street?'

'Okay,' Belle said, 'I'm with you on that. Thanks for saving me from being hurt. Do you really work as a filing clerk in the Magistrate's Court?'

'Sometimes,' he said.

'Why did you give up law at university?'

'I didn't give up. My dad went bankrupt, his business went bust, and the uni threw me out because we couldn't pay the fees any longer.'

'Truly?'

'Unfortunately, yes. So I have a grudge against the law.'

'If the clerking is only sometimes, do you do anything else?'

'I'm a bookie's runner.'

'Good God!' She wondered if he was joking. 'Truly?'

'Yes, Ma'am. An SP off-course bookie.'

'You're illegal.'

'Absolutely.'

'Is it to do with having a grudge against the law?'

Ross Tanner laughed. She thought he had the whitest teeth she had ever seen. And nice eyes, although she had no intention of saying so.

'If you promise not to tell anyone else, it's to do with making ten quid each Saturday afternoon.'

'So much?' She was startled.

'My boss can afford it. Starting-price bookies are big business.'

'Is it dangerous?'

He hesitated, looking at her quizzically. 'What makes you ask that?'

'It's an awful lot for one afternoon. It sounds like risk money.'

'Not really. Once in a while there might be a raid —'

'Police?'

'No, they're on the payroll!' He laughed again at Belle's reaction. 'I meant the opposition. Now and then they try to sort us out. Occasional fisticuffs, a minor contretemps, hardly dangerous.'

'I must say you seem to live in interesting times,' she said.

'Can I tell you something?' he asked, and continued without waiting for her answer. 'You're beautiful.'

'Steady on, Ross. May I ask how old you are?'

'Twenty-six,' he said.

'I'm thirty-three.'

'So?'

'So I'm a bit older. Or, to put it another way, you're seven years younger than me.'

'So when I'm sixty-three you'll be seventy.'

'Don't be cute,' Belle said.

'I don't care how old you are. Can I come home . . . so I can "know" you? So we can know each other?' As she looked at him, puzzled by this, he added, 'I mean in the strictly biblical sense, of course. They had a rare way with words, those Old Testament scribes.'

'They did indeed. But I don't do one-night stands.'

'Nor do I. Relationships should have time to nurture and grow. We have all that time until you're seventy and I'm a lively sixty-three.'

Belle laughed and said, 'I think you're full of shit, Mr Tanner. Besides, my place is out of the question. I have a son waiting there.'

'How about my place? It's crummy, but it has a harbour view. Well, almost. Down there in romantic Rushcutters Bay – we could certainly know each other in the most marvellous biblical sense without any interruptions.'

'Not tonight.'

'Tomorrow?'

'For a young man, you're in one hell of a hurry.'

'But not only to know you. I'd like you to take your clothes off —'

'I did get the message,' Belle retorted, unsure whether to be flattered or insulted that he imagined her so instantly available.

'I mean to take them off so I can sculpt you,' he said.

'Oh!' She was discomfited and tried to regain her poise. 'You're a sculptor? As well as a magistrate's clerk and an illegal bookie's runner?'

'As well as those. But they're just jobs to help pay for my art. Two years and I haven't managed to sell a sculpture. I keep on telling myself Van Gogh never sold a single painting in his life. And you may not know it, but his brother was an art dealer.'

'Poor unhappy Van Gogh.'

'At twenty-six I still have enough time.'

His smile really was nice, she decided. Engaging. And although she might be thirty-three, people always said she didn't look her age.

'Please? Tomorrow?'

'Maybe,' Belle said. 'If you walk me down Kellett Street to my door, then you'll know where I'm to be found. That's supposing you really want to find me.'

Belle, to the surprise of some who had lusted after her, was not promiscuous. In the macho ambience of towns like Gundagai, most men nurtured a popular belief that actresses were wantons – voluptuaries with easy morals; this was the way provincial Australia regarded women in the theatre. Ripe fruit for the sideboard, Henry Gable had believed, at a cost to his ego.

Before marriage, Belle had had her share of lovers. While adroit at evading the casting couch or the groping hands of those with fake promises of stardom, her youth and looks enabled her to pick and choose her own partners, mostly of a similar age and with mutual interests. Apart from one disastrous episode she had enjoyed an uncomplicated love-life. The disaster, which had been by far the most passionate affair, had produced her only son; while she rejoiced in the result, the relationship itself had ended badly, making her desperately unhappy at the time, and the memory of how close she had come to an abortion could still trouble her with lurid images.

When she married George Carson and he had accepted Teddy as his own child without reservation, staunchly keeping their secret when they moved to Gundagai before the birth, she had resolved to be faithful to him, and had remained so during ten years of marriage. It had not been difficult. There was no one in the district who had the least physical attraction for her, and she was soon aware that any hint of an extramarital relationship – especially one that involved her – would sweep the town like a cyclone. She created enough gossip without hurting George by the folly of a local affair.

And although the marriage was over, there had been no man or sexual partner in her life since leaving Gundagai. She had begun to feel an indifference to it; nothing had truly aroused her, not until she and George were forced to share her cramped bed on the Easter weekend, his hand roving as she felt her nipples distend and her vulva grow warm and moist. It would've been the right moment, she knew that; instead it had led to the unhappy failure of the following afternoon.

After this she had retreated from the possibility of sex with anyone else. It was no more than an ephemeral release, she tried to convince herself; it meant emotional mess and endless complications. Deep down she realised it was only a season of temporary chastity; after all, she was not disposing of her Dutch cap or considering a nunnery, but life was infinitely easier without being motivated by her libido.

Which is why she was astonished at her response to Ross Tanner's rather gauche and overt advance.

He had begun to sculpt a figurine of her two days later, and at the second sitting, after a break for a cup of tea, they made love on the floor of his borrowed studio. In the tiny attic of a squalid building in Paddington, lying on a paint-stained drop sheet amid the debris of dried plaster and the smell of turpentine, she had an orgasm the like of which she had forgotten existed; she came and cried aloud, and soon afterwards repeated this in a tumult of awakened delight.

Chapter fifteen

When the school bell rang Teddy was poised, ready to escape, pushing his books into a satchel and rising to be the first out the classroom door. By the time he reached the playground fronting Liverpool Street he could see the hasty exodus preceding him, all stampeding from the daily tedium of education and obedience. He glimpsed her tangle of red hair, and caught up with her at the gates.

'Sally?'

She was with a bunch of other girls, all chattering, but Sal was chattering more than anyone and untidier than the rest, with a torn skirt, and socks that slid around her ankles, the freckles on her pale skin and the flame-coloured hair so distinct she stood out in any crowd. She turned and smiled, dismissing the others with a wave, as she linked arms with Teddy. They walked up the slope past the hospital.

'So how'd you be, me darlin' boy?' Sally Sharp asked.

'Better fer yer kindness in the askin',' Teddy replied, trying to mimic the Irish lilt she could adopt so easily. She laughed, squeezed his arm, and in broad Australian – her normal accent – said to get off himself, and not to come the raw prawn, not with her.

They were both ten years old, and friends from dancing class.

Sally lived with her mother in a large modern flat in Roslyn

Gardens, and on the days when Teddy was not working in a film and had to attend school, the pair walked home together through the back streets of Darlinghurst. Her mother, Eunice, was quoted as being unsure if she approved of Teddy Carson. On the other hand, Belle made it known that she liked Sally, but could not stand Eunice, considering her a snob and far too pushy and up-herself with her harbour-view apartment and her closets of expensive clothes. They were the result, Belle declared, of a failed marriage and a highly successful divorce.

The two women were obliged to spend most Saturday mornings together while their children had a class with Greta Torrance in her dance studio beside the Victoria Hotel in Oxford Street. From the public bar a faint waft of stale beer was a perpetual intrusion. Eunice constantly complained about it, as well as being critical of the shabby studio with its rumble of traffic. She often spoke of moving her daughter to a more amenable environment, but Belle knew this wouldn't happen. Greta Torrance had studied in London, had danced with the Royal Ballet and was considered the best teacher in the country. There was a waiting list for her school, and having a child there was a mark of distinction for the pupil and a social cachet for her parent. Sally's up-herself mum would not contemplate moving to second best.

Eunice was charged the full fee for lessons, while Teddy was on what Greta called her 'scholarship rate'. It was paid from his earnings by a cheque from Florian sent directly to the school. This, at Belle's request, was a means of keeping the arrangement private, for it would create friction if Eunice learnt of the disparity, and found out it was offered to Teddy as the studio's star pupil. In Eunice Sharp's view, the only star in any group was her daughter.

On these Saturdays Belle borrowed a copy of the show-business paper, *This Week*, immersing herself in casting news and gossip. Eunice came armed with imported magazines like *The Tatler* or *Country Life*, and when bored with photographs of English mansions, produced her knitting. This required her close attention, so conversation between them was desultory, their exchanges guarded, whereas their children shared some remarkably intimate confidences. Both mothers would have been astonished.

'What's his name?' Sally asked.

'Ross Tanner,' Teddy said, and waited mischievously, knowing she was agog with curiosity.

'Well, go on.' She nudged him. 'Is he?'

'I think so.'

'Honestly? Your mum's boyfriend?'

'I'm only guessing. But he's there most nights, and she seems happy when he turns up. The other friends are older. They're all right, but they talk all the time – mostly about themselves. Ross is different. She definitely likes him.'

'Then he must be her lover,' Sally said, pleased with this news of romance.

'Do you reckon?' He deferred to her on matters like this, which gave her an opportunity to air her knowledge of the adult world.

'A woman has needs, Ted. She can't go through life without *someone*,' Sally pointed out to him.

'S'pose not.'

'And your dad's not coming back, is he?'

'Dunno.' He hesitated. 'I wish he would, but I don't think so.'

'Is he nice? Ross?'

Teddy considered this for a moment. 'Yeah.'

'Does anyone else know?'

'Only us. Will you keep it a secret, Sal?'

'Of course.'

'From your mum as well?'

'Especially from my mum, silly. They hate each other, our mums.'

'I know.'

'Think they'll ever change?'

'Doubt it.' Teddy grinned. 'She reckons I'm a bad influence on you.'

'Eunice has some very peculiar ideas,' her daughter said.

They crossed the street, passing the fire station. One of the firemen waved. The pair of freckle-faced kids were a regular sight, the little redhead and her dancing partner.

'G'day,' he called to them, 'when are you two gettin' married?'

'On Thursday,' Sally called back, and they blew him kisses and laughed all the way to the junction of Bayswater Road. Here the traffic converged and Sally waited for her bus to Macleay Street. Teddy waited with her.

'See you tomorrow, Ted.'

'Not tomorrow. I got two days' work in a film.'

'Lucky thing,' she said enviously, 'I wish *I* did.'

'You wouldn't wish for this. It's only a spit and a cough.'

'Doesn't matter. I'd love to be in a film.'

'You're better being at school, where you come top all the time.'

'It'd be exciting to act, though.'

'It's boring,' Teddy assured her. 'Only two lines, then I'm a face in the crowd. Like an extra. Belle had another row with Florian. She says it's . . . dem . . . dem-something-or-other.'

'Demoralising?' she suggested.

'No.' He frowned. 'Not quite.'

'Demeaning?'

'Yeah, that's the word.' He looked at her admiringly. 'No wonder you're top at school.'

'Why does Belle have so many rows with your agent?' Sally wondered. 'She's always saying he's no good. But at least he gets you lots of jobs.'

'She says they're bit parts. Walk-ons. She wants me to be a star.'

'Well, you are a star . . . in a sort of way. *I* think you're a star,' she said shyly.

'I think you should stick to being good at school,' Teddy replied, although what she had said thrilled him.

'Poo to school,' she scoffed. 'Anyone can be good at school.'

'I can't.'

'If you're a star, you don't have to be.'

'I never thought of that!' Before he could add anything, the hum of electric wires signalled the arrival of her trolley bus. 'See you at Greta's, Saturday,' he called as she scrambled aboard.

'Hooroo, Ted.'

'Ta-ta, Sal.'

When the figurine was finished, Ross Tanner wrapped it in a damp cloth and took it back to his boarding-house room in Rushcutters Bay. He had a cupboard that contained his clay and plaster sculptures, as well as a shelf of bas-relief and wood carvings – his entire body of unsold work, two years of it – but the figure of Belle he placed on a table by the window where the morning light would catch it. If he tried to save money, bought less wine perhaps, he might afford to have it cast in bronze. On the other hand, if he was ever rich it would look best in polished brass.

He thought he might really be able to sell this one, but that brought with it the perennial problem. As an artist infatuated with his subject – totally in love with her, was the reality – he'd feel like a pimp selling it, trading her as an item for cash to stand naked and admired in someone else's room. The idea was anathema after the painstaking creation, trying for perfection, twice beginning all over again.

He could give the figurine to Belle – a thought that tempted him – but it would mean subjecting his work to the scrutiny and perhaps the scorn of her *salon*, her gaggle of arty mates with their bloody airs and pretensions. So far he and Belle had kept secret any disclosure of his current life, particularly his source of income as a bookie's runner, allowing them only the knowledge he'd been a law student and had not qualified. This greatly intrigued them; he had watched them puzzling over it, beavering away in an attempt to sort it out, to categorise him. Belle enjoyed it; she said they were like people trying to do a crossword puzzle without any clues.

Personally he classified them as a mob of hangers-on, wishing them to hell so he could more often be alone with her. It was part of the bliss and frustration of the past few months. They sometimes snatched precious moments in Kellett Street on days when Teddy was at school, although the landlady was awkward, forever snooping and eyeing them with disapproval. Belle said to take no notice, she was a frustrated old trout: besides, it was none of her business since they were doing it in private, not out in the street and frightening the horses. But whenever it was possible, on days when he was not working and Belle was free, they preferred the afternoons in his own room where they could make rowdy and uninhibited love, because his next-door neighbour was at work during the day, and the room on the other side was empty, lacking a tenant all year.

These were the best of times: Belle, naked in his bed, looking like a twenty-year-old, playful and vulnerable, then feverish with passion, everything outside the room forgotten and unimportant, even the relentless ambitions for her son cast aside, if temporarily – nothing in the world but the two of them. After twenty-six years and an occasional steady girlfriend, it was sometimes hard to believe that he'd discovered someone like this. It had to be love, for they found it difficult to be apart for even a day; they shared a sense of humour, laughed a lot together, and between the ache for each other's bodies and their lusting, they were good friends as well.

In flights of fantasy he sometimes wondered what might happen if he asked her to marry him. At more rational moments he knew he would never do this, for the wrong answer could be the end of it.

Now that the weather was fine George Carson spent his weekends restoring the garden for spring. He resolutely dug out the bindi and paspalum, then sharpened the blades on his mower, and soon the lawn was trimmed, the edges tidied and the whole place took on a new appearance. Encouraged by this, he weeded the beds and planted asters and petunias; then, deciding he might as well grow a few vegies to help the budget, bought packets of seeds – lettuce and cabbage – to go under a homemade glass cloche. If they all flourished, there'd be ample to give away to the neighbours.

There had been changes in Brewinda Road. Harry Lucas had at last gone too far, beating up Essie so badly she had been rushed to hospital with a suspected fractured skull, facial damage and a broken arm. When the police sent a squad to arrest Lucas he was still drunk and out of control. Appearing from the house with a loaded rifle he tried to shoot them, missing the sergeant in charge but hitting Percy Bates a glancing shot that took the helmet off his head. The next bullet was aimed straight at George, who had offered himself as a witness to testify to the regularity of the violence. It had shattered a window beside his face, but before another shot could be fired Lucas was knocked flat by Percy, minus his helmet, in a ferocious rugby head-butt that had left the neighbour unconscious.

Lucas was in now Goulburn jail facing a long sentence, Essie had left the district to live with cousins, and a new family had moved into their house next door. A quiet, middle-aged couple, the husband was a council clerk, his wife a former district nurse. They had invited George for a meal to meet the wife's sister, who had been recently widowed and was considering coming to live with them. The meal, by a nice irony, happened to take place on a peaceful Friday night; the sister, Maureen, was a pleasant woman of his own age, a few years younger than he had expected, and very eager to know all he could tell her about the town and its background. He liked her quiet manner and her alert grey eyes that showed interest when he spoke. George was listened to, he found his opinions canvassed and respected, and had enjoyed himself immensely.

In the process of this neighbourhood change he had repaired his friendship with Mr and Mrs Miranda, and the restoration of his garden brought much approving comment in the street. At times he thought even Miss Limmington's dog now seem to tolerate him; its owner, after sly enquiries about whether he had enjoyed his weekend in Sydney, had ceased her prying. People at last seemed to accept he would go on living there among them, but probably alone. Nobody mentioned Belle any longer, nor did they expect her to return. Much as he missed her, it made everything a great deal easier.

He put away the garden tools and went inside to finish his letter to Teddy. He wrote regularly, although sometimes it was difficult to find news that might still interest him. Easter had made apparent the enormous gap that existed between Brewinda Road and Kellett Street. But some continuance was necessary – after all, he was ostensibly Teddy's father, and hoped to always be regarded as such. Apart from any obligation this imposed, he did not want to lose touch. The untidy, smudged replies were always a welcome sight, even though the spelling and handwriting showed no sign of improvement, and Teddy's dislike of going to school was becoming more pronounced.

His last letter had certainly emphasised this. He, at the advanced age of ten, was being forced to attend a class with kids so much younger than himself. Even some seven and eight-year-olds! It was rotten and unfair.

George had pondered for the past two days over how to reply. He knew that being taught with beginners would be humiliating, but he could hardly write back encouraging him to rebel against education. Too often in the past he'd been concerned when Belle claimed a few weeks missing school didn't matter a hoot in hell, not if there was a good stage or screen role instead. She'd had a running battle with local teachers about his irregular attendance. George felt that condoning Teddy's complaint would be wrong, but also knew it would be a shame to moralise or distance himself by preaching.

He sighed. His pen seemed to be waiting for him to say something, the ink on the nib drying while he delayed. Whinge, George thought, that's the word. It was important to establish their old rapport, or he'd be just another grown-up dispensing unwanted adult advice.

Whinge. Yes, that was it. *Dear Teddy,* he wrote:

I commiserate with your whinge about school and being the oldest in the class, but cheer up and, whatever happens, don't you get discouraged and give up. Some day those annoying young kids might boast that they were at school with Teddy Carson. Some day when you're a star. But on the other hand, wouldn't it be a terrible shame if you became a star and weren't able to read your own press notices? Especially if they were good ones.

———•———

Sally handed the letter back to him with a smile. They were walking home from school. She was as careless of her appearance as ever, with socks around her ankles and her bright hair in its usual disarray.

'He's right, Teddy. Really! It would be a shame, when you come to think of it. Sort of funny as well, the way he says it. He sounds really nice.'

'I thought you'd like it.'

'Did you?'

'Yeah. That's why I showed you. In a way it felt just like he was speaking to me. We used to talk about all sorts of things, me and Dad. Things I couldn't talk to Mum about.'

'Like what?'

'Aw, I dunno. Like . . . pretend games. In the backyard with my cricket bat, pretending to be Don Bradman. When I told Mum she said, "Who's he?" Fancy a person not knowing about Don Bradman! Can you imagine?'

'Easily. If Bradman was in the theatre, Belle would know everything about him, even his batting average.'

Teddy laughed. He was glad he'd shown her the letter. Sally really *was* his best friend, better than anyone else, better than his last best friend Herbie Bates – definitely miles better than that turncoat cowardly Herbie, who had stood and watched while he was kicked out of the gang, with Norm and Ginger bashing him. Sal was different, he could tell her anything. His innermost secrets would be safe with her.

'I could tell Dad most things,' he said. 'Things that I never told Mum, for instance, because she wouldn't believe them.'

'Like what?'

'Like when I was in a gang, how I devised this plan and we trapped the rival gang and covered them with cow dung.'

'Phew.' Sally held her nose while she mimed pulling a chain.

'Phew is right, they really stank. They all had to dive in the river to get clean, the whole lot of 'em.'

'What did George say when you told him that?'

'Laughed, and said they were pretty fierce battle tactics. I told him that all's fair in love and war, and he said he s'posed I was right.'

'He sounds almost normal – for a parent. Honestly, were you really in a gang of boys doing horrible things like that?'

'Yes. I was the sergeant, third in command.'

'I can't imagine it. What did you do? Break windows?'

'Sometimes. Only the windows of people we didn't like.'

'And tie front doors together, then ring all the doorbells?'

Teddy knew that one; all the neighbours trying to open their doors at the exact same moment. He grinned at the thought of it, but shook his head. 'You can't do that in the country, Sal. The houses are too far apart for the front-door trick to work. But we had battles with other gangs, and on Empire Day we put fireworks in people's letterboxes.'

'What happened?'

'They blew up. Lots of letterbox explosions all over town.'

'Golly,' she said, 'you were lucky the police didn't catch you.'

'They were always trying.' Teddy's imagination started to take wing and enhance the story. 'We suspected they had a spy in our gang. I worked out it was Herbert Bates, the local copper's son.'

'Keeping an eye on you for his dad?'

'We could never prove it. But Herbie looked a real turncoat to me. Like father, like son, that's what I thought.'

'Don't you sometimes miss those days?' Sally asked. When Teddy shook his head she said, 'Do you keep in touch with anyone from back there? The friends in the gang, for instance?'

'No.' He made it sound positive. 'It was just mucking-around kids' stuff. I was only eight in those days, don't forget.'

'I bet they were all sorry when you left.'

'Yeah, they called a special meeting,' Teddy said, 'and told me it'd never be the same. They reckoned the gang mightn't last long without me.'

The moment it was said he wanted to recant. But it was already too late. She believed him, so it was not possible to apologise and say it didn't happen that way at all. It was equally impossible to explain the cruel way it had really happened.

They crossed the traffic intersection to Sally's bus stop. Instead of waiting as usual, he said a hurried goodbye and walked on alone past the Picture Palace and the Californian coffee shop. Some actors he knew were gathered at a table in there. Behind him he heard the traffic, the electric hum of her bus as he saw its shape mirrored on the coffee-shop window when it went past. He turned to glimpse her hand waving, and was not sure if she could see him wave back. He went slowly home, feeling sad and unhappy. He had thought he could tell Sally all his secrets – anything at all – but had just discovered the uncomfortable truth.

There was really no one in the world to whom you could tell everything.

Chapter
sixteen

Florian MacArthur-Bailey sat in his swivel chair behind his oak desk and listened to Belle Carson cataloguing her complaints. He folded his hands over his mammoth stomach and gazed towards the ceiling, trying to count the number of flies fornicating on the stained frieze above him while he waited for her to finish. At the same time he speculated on the surprise he had in store, a bombshell she could not expect but thoroughly deserved, and not for the first time he wondered how a gorgeous and sexy young soubrette could have metamorphosed into this virago, this scold, this inflexible shrew of a stage mother.

'Are you even listening to me?' she asked.

'Every word,' Florian said, 'I hear every wounding word. To sum up, you are not well pleased. Work is extremely spasmodic and becoming more difficult to find. Since I represent him this is clearly my fault.'

'I didn't say that.'

'It was implied. You should try listening to yourself, Belle. You've been bitching away for the past twenty minutes, non-stop. Each gripe, each spiteful criticism causing me grievous bodily harm and dyspepsia. If I had ulcers they'd be bleeding.'

'If I had a violin it'd be playing hearts-and-flowers,' she said.

'There you go. No attempt to understand the problems. Never mind the ill-health of the nation, no matter that the economy is under stress and the pound in peril – all this is irrelevant, because young Master Carson is not being gainfully employed, and you want someone to blame.'

'That sounds like a well-rehearsed spiel for your other clients. This is me, remember? The point is, it's been two months since he had any work at all. It seems to have come to a full stop. You're supposed to be his agent, so I want to know why. It doesn't seem unreasonable to ask what the hell has gone wrong!'

'Indeed,' Florian replied, 'you may well ask. There's no use in us not facing the facts, because clearly things will not improve. On the contrary, things are going to get decidedly worse.'

'Are you trying to cheer me up, Uriah?'

'If you'd manage to be quiet and give me half a chance, I'll tell you how things have deteriorated while you've been otherwise engaged – enjoying a new love affair with your young man,' he said acidly.

'Who told you —'

'Will you please shut up, Belle? For once in your life, button your lip and let me explain.' He fixed her with a look. 'Would that be possible?'

'Right,' she said, 'explain.'

'It's a show-business cliché that in hard times people turn to entertainment as a release from reality, and consequently it thrives. But the truth is, only the pictures churned out by Hollywood have thrived here lately. Our own film production has almost ceased, so local actors have little employment. Also, two vaudeville theatres have closed – one sold as a factory – which means less stage work. But there's something else of concern, which you're well aware of – or should be. He's ten years old.'

'What's that got to do with it?'

'Everything. He was a star when he was eight. Played support roles when he was nine. Since then he's grown a few inches. He's not the tiny Murrumbidgee Kid who enchanted audiences with his precocious talent any more.'

'That is utter bullshit!' She felt enraged; he was attacking her unfairly, even stooping to flourish that stupid newspaper tag that she hated.

'Just listen to me, Belle. Until recently, if a row of child actors were lined up for a part, he was the natural choice. Lately, that's changed.'

'How?'

'A month ago I tried to get him a cameo role. The director said no – he felt the public might be getting a bit sick of Master Carson. It's happened again, a few times. Nobody is rushing to employ him any more.'

'If that's true, why didn't you tell me this, Florian?'

'Because I knew you'd blame me and we'd have a blazing row. But I'm telling you now. The halcyon days are finished, Belle – the gravy train has moved on. He's a talented boy whose time is very possibly over.'

'That's ridiculous.'

Florian spread his arms with a theatrical sigh. 'I predicted that's what you'd say.'

'It's sheer bloody defeatism!' she snapped angrily. 'The last thing he needs is a pessimist who doesn't believe in him any more.'

'I entirely agree with you,' Florian said unexpectedly, 'which is the reason why I've decided that I should no longer be his agent.'

Belle opened her mouth to retort, then realised what had been said. She stared numbly at him.

'Did you hear me?' he asked. 'I've had enough. More than enough. A gutful and then some, to be exact.'

'Florian, you can't do this —'

'Of course I can. What's more, I *am* doing it, so spare me the protests and forget any use of the tear ducts. You'll only spoil your make-up.'

She felt in disarray; it was totally unexpected. But apparently not to him. Even in shock she realised that.

'You bastard. You didn't just decide this, did you?'

'No, I've been considering it for some time. But today, when you turned up with your diatribe, no smile, no time for even a friendly chat, just straight at the jugular with complaints about how inept I am, how I was a lousy actor and now I'm an even worse agent – somewhere in the middle of that, Belle, I thought, Fuck this. Life's too short to put up with you any longer.'

Lying awake that night, still in shock, Belle thought of all the things she should have said. It was always easy in hindsight, but disbelief at what was happening had made her tongue-tied, while Florian seemed to relish continuing his venomous insults.

'I've met some obsessive stage mums, but you're far and away the most ferocious. You're positively feral. I always said you'd be his best agent. Nobody else could be as bitchy, biased or bloody-minded as you. So now comes your big chance to show us all.'

She should have been calm, should've tried to thank him for the past two years, for looking after their finances and investing Teddy's earnings wisely. Instead she had sat there stunned and mute while he calculated the sums of money due and wrote out a statement. On the credit side, the amount earned plus bank interest: deducted from this his agency commission, payments to Greta Torrance for dancing classes, and the weekly rent sent to the landlady in Kellet Street.

'I'll give you a cheque. As well – I'd almost forgotten – he's to audition for a stage role tomorrow. If you don't make too many stupid demands and scare the management, he might even get it.'

She wanted to ask why he hadn't bothered to tell her sooner. Instead she remained in a daze until he gave her the cheque, then she left his office, making her way downstairs, past the street door with its brass plate, and found herself in the Chinese quarter walking in the wrong direction to catch her tram. By the time she reached Kings Cross she was in a state of burning resentment, ready to do battle, but it was all far too late.

When Teddy had gone to bed she tried to sleep, consoling herself that in the morning after taking him to his audition she would go to the bank and cash Florian's cheque. One hundred and five pounds, ten shillings and sixpence. She lay there trying to calculate how long the money would last before sleep at last rescued her and the figures merged into oblivion. In the haze of early morning she worked out that if she was careful and they lived on less than three pounds a week, it was enough to see them through the next eight months.

By then she'd have found him work, so that would be all right.

The next day began badly. Mrs Burch, the landlady, came knocking on the door, and when Belle called out that it was inconvenient, that she was trying to get dressed and Teddy was due at the Castlereagh Street rehearsal rooms for an audition, she was told there was an important matter that couldn't wait.

'Well, it'll have to,' Belle said, opening the door a fraction, 'we've got to catch a tram in ten minutes.'

'You listen to me before you take trams to anywhere.' The landlady was a combative woman, her eyes magnified behind thick glasses. 'We need a talk, you and me, about a few things. One of 'em is your behaviour in this house.'

'What are you talking about?'

'You and yer fancy man. It ain't decent.'

'What?' Belle stepped outside in her underclothes, shutting the door behind her as she confronted the landlady. 'What did you say?'

'You heard. A woman with a kid and a husband – even if he ain't here – shouldn't carry on like you do. Them arty friends are one thing, even if they do make a racket when people are trying to sleep, but this Tanner joker's another thing entirely. Nippin' in and out at all hours like he's a tenant.'

'What the hell business is that of yours?'

'I happen to own the place, remember? The next thing we'll have private detectives raiding the joint to get divorce evidence for your poor dill of a husband. Be on the front page of *Truth* one Sunday. Give us a bad name, it will.'

'Mrs Burch, if you have something private to discuss with me, we'll discuss it in private. But not now. Tonight when I'm able to talk freely.'

'We'll talk about it now. That – and the other matter.'

'What other matter?'

'The rent. It's overdue.'

'Don't be ridiculous.'

'Overdue, I repeat, and got to be settled. I suppose you've been too busy playing tootsy with your boyfriend to remember ordinary things like the rent.'

'It can't be overdue.'

'It'll be three weeks on Friday, Mrs Carson.'

'But Mr MacArthur-Bailey takes care of all —' She stopped in a moment of uncertainty, assailed by an uneasy thought. 'I mean, he sends you a cheque each week for the rent. That's been the arrangement ever since we came here.'

'It has. But sometimes he's late. This time he's too late. Three weeks too late. So you pay up now, before we discuss the other business any further. When what's owed is paid, I'll decide whether to let you stay or not.'

'Of course I'll pay,' Belle said, shaken. 'There's no need to threaten. After I go to the bank I'll give you your money, then you can apologise for your malicious slander. Or I'll find a more suitable place to live than this.'

'Don't get on your high horse with me, Missus. And don't try to do a bunk, or I'll sool the law onto yer. People who attempt that end up in big shit.'

Belle shut the door in her face. She was angered by the intrusion, but more than that, perplexed about Florian. On the statement he had given her, the rent to this week was deducted as having been paid. Someone's playing silly buggers, she thought, and began to feel the first onset of alarm.

The bank manager was polite but his words brought a chill of verification. The cheque she had presented could not be cashed because there were insufficient funds in the account. When she became agitated and tried to explain that this was surely impossible, the manager asked her to please sit down.

'I'm very sorry, Mrs Carson. I don't want to labour the point and distress you unduly. But the simple truth is the cheque has bounced.'

'But how could it? He's a reputable theatrical agent who runs a well-known business – he's been running it for years. His office is in George Street. You could pick up the phone and ring him right now. That'd be the best thing.'

'I doubt if that would help.'

'Surely, it must. Please . . . it's extremely important.'

'Mrs Carson, I'm sorry, but —'

'*Please* ring him up. There's been some terrible mistake. He gave me this cheque yesterday afternoon.'

'What time yesterday?'

'About . . . I'm not sure . . . about four o'clock.'

'After the bank shut, Mrs Carson. I'm afraid that's very often the case with cheques like this one.'

'But how could he do such a thing? How is it possible? I even have a final account he gave me. Everything is detailed.' She fumbled in her handbag and gave it to him. 'You'll see from that he collected my son's earnings and paid our bills —' Even as she said it, her memory of the morning's clash with the landlady was like a moment of razor-sharp clarity.

'You mean he managed your money?' The manager frowned and seemed astonished. 'Not a very safe practice, surely?'

'I never thought of it as unsafe. I mean, it's often done; he did it with other people he represents. Our profession is not very good with money. A lot of actors spend it as soon as they earn it, and forget things like rent and income tax. It was a service that Florian used to say he only provided for his very closest friends, free of charge.'

Suddenly, without any warning, she felt an uncontrolled rush of emotional anger and began to cry. These were not simple tears, this was a noisy and protracted sobbing she could not restrain, alarming the manager and making her look a dishevelled mess.

'I'm sorry,' she stammered, aghast at the spectacle she was creating but unable to prevent herself. 'But truly, I can't believe this. I really can't.' She tried to wipe her eyes, but couldn't find a handkerchief. She realised the bank manager was offering her one.

'Thank you,' she said, and wiped her eyes, apologising for making such a mess of his clean linen handkerchief. He insisted that it didn't matter.

'Have you known him very long?' he asked.

'Since I was sixteen years old – that's why it seems so impossible. I've always thought I could trust him. He was a bit of a rogue in his way, but that was just Florian – he was a sort-of showbiz character. Larger than life,' she added, and thinking of the often jovial figure, began to cry again. 'We had rows, lots of rows – that never seemed serious till yesterday. But to do something like this – I find it impossible to imagine. I just can't believe he's cheated me.'

'I'm afraid he has, Mrs Carson. And what seems worse, in view of the long time you've known him, it was a calculated fraud.'

'What do you mean?'

'When I said there was insufficient money, I should've been more specific. In fact, there is *no* money. None at all. Before he gave you the cheque yesterday afternoon, he had already been here in the morning and drawn out all his money, yours and no doubt other people's. A large sum, over four thousand pounds. If you care to look at this statement, you'll see that Mr MacArthur-Bailey now has a nil balance. He left instructions the account was to be closed.'

'So there's nothing I can do.' Belle was too dazed to properly study the document he showed her. It seemed unreal that Florian could possess so much money. The fact he had decamped with it all left her feeling drained and helpless. Clearly, she had been a gullible fool.

'There's the police, if you wish to bring charges.'

'Would it help get our money back?'

'Mrs Carson, it amounts to criminal deception against you. And I feel sure there'll be more cheques and distressed people in here before the week is over.'

'That doesn't answer my question. Would it help me recover one hundred and five pounds, ten and sixpence?'

'I rather doubt it.'

'Then it's pointless.'

'I'm awfully sorry,' the bank manager said.

Teddy felt mystified. It had been the strangest day. Early that morning he and Belle had gone to the audition at the Castlereagh rehearsal rooms. He was one of three boys being considered for a small part in a stage play to be produced by J. C. Williamson, Australia's biggest theatre management, with seasons in Sydney and Melbourne, then other capital cities. Which meant it was important, Belle had said; the role might be small but it could lead to months of work.

After their evening meal she had spent a long time rehearsing him, explaining the plot of the play and the motives of the character. He had gone to sleep with it churning through his mind. Then, in the morning, they had been in a rush to dress and catch the tram, which was when the landlady knocked on the door and Belle had had some sort of a row with her, but when he asked what it was about she wouldn't tell him.

All morning she seemed to be peculiar. He did his audition but knew it wasn't right, he felt sure he hadn't concentrated properly and this was confirmed when they said he hadn't got it. The strange thing was Belle didn't get upset like she normally did, her thoughts seemed to be somewhere else. But he didn't know where, or why.

It was afterwards that they went to the Commonwealth Bank at the bottom of Martin Place, the big building that looked like a church – a cathedral, Belle had called it, a monstrous monument erected for the worship of money – and Teddy had waited in the downstairs banking chamber while she went to see a manager. When she came down she was upset, he could tell that, but she said there was nothing to worry about, he was to go to school for the rest of the day, and she had things to attend to. They'd taken the tram to Darlinghurst, and he'd been picked on by the teacher for not concentrating, which was true, because all afternoon he was trying to work out what was bothering his mum.

When the bell rang there was a note left for him, saying that if she was not at home he was to go to Mrs LaRue's shop after school. He walked there with Sally Sharp. Since they had no secrets, he told her about the day. She did her best to help decipher what might be wrong with Belle.

'Would it be anything to do with your dad?' Sally wondered. She had been intrigued by his distant father, ever since reading the letter.

'Don't think so.'

'Was she crying?'

'No . . .' he said dubiously, 'but I think she had been. And it looked like she might start up again any time.'

'Not concentrating much?' Sally probed. 'Lost in her own thoughts?'

'Yeah.'

'You had to say things twice, before she heard?'

'That's right,' Teddy agreed. 'What do you think's wrong?'

'Well, my mum was peculiar like that, before Dad and her had their biggest row and got divorced. Could yours be going through the same thing?'

'A divorce? Dunno. I don't see why she'd want a divorce.'

'She might want to get married again. To you-know-who.'

'Shut up, Sal. That's supposed to be a secret.'

'It *is* a secret. Nobody can hear us, dopey. Do you think Belle might want to marry him?'

'Hmm. Might.'

'You don't sound too keen. I thought you liked him?'

'I do, sort of. But . . . *marrying?*'

'It happens,' Sally advised him.

'How would you feel if Eunice got married again?'

'Not sure,' she said after a moment's thought. 'I suppose it depends who it was. At least it'd be different.'

'That's the trouble,' Teddy said. 'I don't like things being different.'

Now it was nearly six o'clock and growing dark. Chrissie LaRue was home from her job, telling Teddy it'd be best if he stayed the night with them; she was sure his mum would explain in the morning. Despite their kindness, he found it difficult to sleep on the sofa in their flat above the shop. He had begun to suspect that whatever the problem was, it would mean change. Life had been almost stable for a year and a half now, and change was the unknown that always made him nervous.

The brass plate was already gone from the front door, so she knew what to expect upstairs. The door was open, the office like an empty stage stripped of its set. The oak desk and armchair were gone, the walls looked naked without the playbills and photographs of Florian in his prime. A man wearing a suit and a hat stood writing notes on a clipboard.

'If you're looking for him,' he said tersely to Belle, 'he's shot through.'

'Do you know where?' she asked.

'If I knew that I'd be out after him, not here making notes of the mess he's left behind. The rotten bugger owed me on his rent, plus other things, and gawd only knows what it'll cost to fix up this place for a new tenant.'

'When did you find out?'

'Today. When I tried to ring this morning to give him a hurry-up about the rent, as well as the money he'd borrowed, and found the phone was disconnected.'

'He borrowed money – from you?' Belle gazed at him in sheer astonishment, as if the secret life of Florian was unravelling beyond her capacity to imagine.

'Last week, five hundred quid. Needed it for "expansion" – said I could buy into the business and become a partner. I musta been mad – a real bunny – but he was a persuasive old coot. Plausible, that's the word – a plausible bloody crook.'

Clearly, she thought, a better actor off the stage than on.

'You a friend of his?'

'Not any longer,' Belle said. 'I'm starting to think I never was a proper friend. Just one of his bunnies, but not smart enough to realise it.'

Greta Torrance still had the slim figure and graceful movements of a ballerina, although it had been thirty years since her last season at Sadler's Wells. She suggested Belle sit down and have a cup of tea. The studio was empty, her next class not due for another hour. This was the time she liked to take off her pumps, put her feet up and relax.

'I can't relax,' Belle said, 'not until I talk to you about the fees. I just know he hasn't paid them.'

'You must have a nice cup of char, and some sinful fattening cream biscuits,' Greta said firmly. 'You could do with a rest and some nourishment. It's obviously been a thoroughly unpleasant day.'

'A real bastard of a day,' Belle agreed.

They had their tea, then they talked about the fees for Teddy's classes, or, rather, the lack of them.

'I feel so awful, with you giving us a special scholarship rate. Why didn't you mention there'd been no cheque for . . . how long is it?'

'A couple of months,' Greta said, trying to dismiss it with a shrug.

'Greta, how long exactly? Please.'

'Three months. He paid regularly for a long time, but then it stopped.'

'You should've spoken to me about it!'

'I was going to, eventually. There was no panic.'

'I wish you had. God, you must've thought me a real cow, taking advantage of being given a special rate, then not even paying it.'

'I thought things might be a bit tight, that's all. I didn't want to push it.' She could see Belle was still in a state of bewilderment at the shock. 'I've told you before, I'd rather teach one real talent like Teddy for nothing than twenty of these socialite kids whose mums pay whatever daft fees I like to ask.'

'I know, but —'

'Belle, this school does well financially, so relax. Have another cuppa, and let's talk about something else.'

'I feel humiliated.'

'By me?'

'Certainly not by you. Humiliated and made to look a dumb Dora by that counterfeit old phoney Florian. I'm grateful to you.'

'Good, then let's change the subject.' She smiled. 'I just had a letter from a friend in England. Do you know the latest scandal doing the rounds there? His Highness the Prince of Wales has a new American mistress, a divorcee named Mrs Wallis Simpson.'

But Belle had no interest in royal rumours. 'Greta, I'm very grateful and flattered by your opinion of Teddy's talent, but I can't let him come to any more lessons until I've saved enough to pay you back.'

'That's unnecessarily stubborn, Belle.'

'I suppose it is, but that's how it has to be.'

'Why?'

'It's been a strange experience, today has. I kept thinking that old bugger has stolen my money, but it wasn't mine, of course – it was Teddy's, and he's been keeping us ever since we left Gundagai. It wasn't meant to be that way, but at first there was a lot of work for him, and my son could earn more in one day than I'd earn in a week as a barmaid. Only now that work is drying up.' She paused, and Greta Torrance watched her. She liked Belle. There were many who didn't, who thought her too assertive, too manipulative of her son and his talent. Greta had always felt there was far more to her than the impression she seemed to convey of a ruthlessly ambitious stage mum.

'At least Florian was not lying about that,' Belle said. 'The work is a definite problem. Things are tighter. So tomorrow I look for a job, and find somewhere cheaper to live. After that I want to pay off what I owe my landlady and you.'

'I keep trying to tell you, I don't need it.'

'But *I* need it, Greta. I really do. I need to put my life in some sort of order. Which means paying debts, getting a job and looking after Teddy as best I can.'

'If that's what you want.' Greta nodded awareness of it. 'But you do realise this pride of yours is going to deprive my elite class of their best dancer.'

'Not for long, I hope.'

'I'll raise my teacup to that. He and Sally are my stars. They're so good together. She's a hardworking, clever girl, while he's an absolute natural.'

'That's nice to hear. Be careful you don't say it in front of Eunice Sharp.'

They both laughed, and for the first time that day Belle began to feel that if everyone was as charitable as Greta Torrance, the future might not be as dreadful as she feared.

It was dark when she approached the house where Ross Tanner lived. The street lamps were few in this part of Rushcutters Bay, but the lights ringed around the tennis courts shed a reflected glow across the park, and spilt onto the houses that flanked it. As she hurried past she could hear the clunk of tennis balls and occasional voices of the players raised in cries of celebration or lament. The steady rhythm of gut on ball seemed to keep time with her anxious footsteps. She had been wearing high heels throughout the day, and her feet were beginning to hurt.

The boarding house had been the home of a wealthy merchant when it was built in the 1850s, and was now a prized lodging in this locality. Adjacent to the carnival gaiety of Kings Cross, it could enjoy the proximity without the frenetic nightlife, the neons or tourist traffic. At the front door was a speaker system enabling tenants to admit visitors; Ross had told her it was a novelty in Sydney, and quite rare anywhere outside New York City. He lived on the first floor, but after pressing twice and receiving no answer Belle stepped back to get a view of his window and realised it was dark.

She knew that a caretaker lived at the back of the house. A light was on inside, and she rapped on the door.

'Who's that?' a voice asked, and the caretaker's elderly wife looked out.

'I'm sorry to trouble you,' Belle said, 'but do you know if Mr Tanner has gone away?'

'No idea, luv,' the woman answered. 'He didn't say nothing, but he don't have to.'

'I need to see him urgently. He's usually home by this time.'

'Can't help you. We just put out the rubbish and clean the stairs and hall.'

She was tempted to ask if she could wait on the stairs outside his room, but thought better of it. The answer could only be an apologetic rejection. She contemplated the idea of sitting in the park opposite until he returned, but decided this was dangerous and unwise. Besides, he could've gone to a theatre, or be working on prices for tomorrow's races with his illegal bookie.

Was there anyone else? she wondered, but it was already too late. There were very few people who could help in an emergency. She momentarily thought of George, but rejected this as impractical. What little he could spare would take several days to reach her by mail, and tonight was what mattered. It was more feasible to humble herself and seek a few days' amnesty from the landlady, so she reluctantly began the steep walk up the Bayswater Road hill in the direction of the Cross.

———•———

Edith Burch said the story reeked of fantasy, and she didn't need fairy-tales; what she wanted, without further delay or any more excuses, was the money owed to her for the past three weeks. She lived in a gloomy ground-floor flat where Belle did her best to explain the circumstances and again pleaded for time to pay.

But even when Mrs Burch was shown the dishonoured cheque and the bogus statement she displayed no sympathy. This place, she said doggedly, was her sole means of support, and had been ever since her hubby died. So if Belle couldn't cough up, that was her tough luck. If she cared to look upstairs she'd find the lock on her door had been changed. All her belongings would stay there until the debt was settled, and she'd have to find somewhere else to doss down for tonight: tonight and every night till she stumped up the overdue rent.

'Yer boyfriend might share his bed. But I dunno what you'll do about the kid,' Mrs Burch said.

'You can't treat us like this,' Belle protested.

'Watch me,' the landlady replied. 'I know the law, and it's on my side.'

Belle hurried upstairs to check the veracity of the threat. Her door was securely locked. The key she possessed no longer worked.

'The old bat had a bloke come to change it,' a voice spoke, and she turned to see her elderly neighbour at his door opposite. 'She wouldn't tell me why. I thought you musta up and done a moonlight,' he said.

'No, Mr Randall.' Belle tried not to reveal the desperation she felt. 'But I owe her and she's locked me out. All our clothes, everything we own, is in there.'

They heard footsteps on the stairs. Mr Randall looked alarmed, gave her a hurried smile and fled to the safety of his room.

'Satisfied?' the landlady asked.

'I promise I'll pay you tomorrow,' Belle vowed, 'somehow I'll borrow the money. But it's too late to find anyone to help me now. I have tried. But truly, first thing tomorrow —'

'I deal in cash, not promises. Thirty bob a week is four pound ten shillings you owe me. You get the new key when I get that dough in my hand. Not before.'

'This is unfair. Teddy's got to sleep somewhere tonight —'

'Your problem.'

'You're a nasty, cold-hearted bitch,' Belle said, knowing it was futile even as she spoke.

'It's a nasty, cold-hearted world,' Mrs Burch replied, and stood on the stairs watching vigilantly until Belle went out the front door and into the winter night.

Chapter seventeen

Donald Ferrier drove home more carefully than usual. It had been a convivial and important night in the private dining room at Usher's Hotel, and he had no wish to ruin it by a traffic infringement because of those extra glasses of the vintage port. Drinking it had been imprudent after the wines served throughout the meal. But old Judge Fulton had brought the port from his family vineyard in the Hunter Valley, a treasured remnant of the fabled 1905 crop, and while eulogising on its virtues, he had also been generous in his speech of welcome to Donald.

'The notion we might make a decent port in Australia caused hilarity at the time. My contemporaries, all pundit *vignerons*, called it "Fulton's Folly", but the folly matured well. Tonight it is my privilege to offer this port to toast our newest member, who has shown his own maturity in the practice of law, and has had a fine career. I congratulate him on his election to this singular and elite club.'

The tones of those words, by the State's senior judge, were still a comforting resonance in his ears. The Foundation Club was certainly elite, its singularity deriving from the limited membership. Since its establishment in the volatile wartime days of 1916, with the country torn apart by the issue of conscription, there had always been exactly fifty members. Fifty, it had been decided by the founders, was not spreading the net too wide or the quality too thin. It allowed for a select group of like minds, without risking unknowns who might be undesirables. It was formed to combat the resistance to compulsory military service, which had been twice voted down in referendums, and because this vocal opposition was mainly led by Irish Catholics, the cardinal rule of the Foundation Club was that all prospective members must be Protestants.

For the past twenty years it had remained something of an enigma: while its existence was known, rigid rules ensured it remained a shadowy and clandestine society. No one could be invited to join until an original member died. The club register was a protected list, but included conservative politicians from state and federal spheres, industrialists, businessmen, army and naval officers, a university vice-chancellor, church dignitaries, and some leaders from the medical and legal professions. There were a disproportionate number who also belonged to the New Guard. The club had no written constitution, but its charter was concerned with the preservation of Empire ties, the retention of the monarchy, and a carefully muted antipathy to Catholics.

Donald Ferrier had no strong opinions on these matters. He assumed a loyalty to the King and the mother country, and believed most Australians felt the same, although rows over interest payments demanded by the City of London bankers and Britain's reluctance to provide financial investment in Australia during the Depression had spawned friction. An element had begun a subversive flirtation with communism, and even started a movement to encourage the concept of a republic. There was dissent that governors of all states and the Commonwealth were British, most of them retired military men, mockingly described by rags like *Smith's Weekly* and *Truth* as 'Chelsea Pensioners put out to grass in the colonies'.

He had a fleeting sympathy for the more moderate of these views, but kept such thoughts strictly to himself. He had gladly accepted the invitation to join the Foundation Club, not for its inflexible agenda, but because it indicated a sign of distinction, a personal and prestigious accolade from a group of eminent people. It marked a final step on the ladder he had begun to climb as a junior solicitor in the Magistrate's Court a long time ago. A gauche young idealist he'd been then, who had since shed a few of those ideals on the way to a barrister's gown and recognition as one of the most eminent silks in the city. Dining monthly with his new colleagues, forty-nine of the town's illustrious citizens, might mean discarding a few more ethics, but it would certainly cement an image of his accomplishment.

As he drove through Kings Cross, past the Mansions Hotel, a brewery truck came abruptly out of Kellett Street. He just had time to slam on the brakes. The truck, which had only one working headlight, crossed the road in front of him, ignoring the clanging alarm bell of a tram approaching in the other direction, and headed recklessly down the hill towards William Street.

'Stupid bastard,' Ferrier said, but he felt a moment of concern. The accident would not have been his fault, but it might have resulted in an awkward and embarrassing end to what had been one of the most significant nights of his life. Besides which, his car – an imported Daimler – was barely a month old, still with the agreeable smell of brand-new leather greeting him each time he drove it, like a flattering reminder of his status. His wife said she hated the smell, calling the frisson it created a *nouveau riche* reaction, but Caroline could afford to be blasé and occasionally snobbish. She had been born to wealthy parents and was indulged throughout her comfortable childhood, whereas he had fought for this security and prosperity all his life.

The traffic on New South Head Road was heavy, and it was with a feeling of relief that he reached Edgecliff and headed towards the quiet streets of Woollahra. As he turned into the driveway of his house in Marlow Road, lights were ablaze in the mansion opposite, where a party was taking place. If it had not been for this, he might have missed seeing the figure of a woman leaving the vicinity of his home, a woman who seemed to be loitering there. He managed only a brief glimpse as she quickly moved into shadows cast by trees in the street.

For one strange moment he felt as if he recognised her, but that was surely impossible. Either he was imagining things, or it was a surfeit of the judge's port. When he fumbled twice with his door key he blamed the port. It could not have been the woman he'd thought it was, even if she did seem oddly familiar.

After all, he had not seen Belle Baker for eleven years.

Overhead wires hummed as a tram approached from the direction of Double Bay. She stood waiting for it. On the skyline in the distance loomed the bulky shape of White City Studios, looking more than ever like an abandoned warehouse. The building was in darkness, the gates locked; the near shutdown of the local film industry meant there were no night shoots or late shifts any longer. Belle gazed at it with a feeling of nostalgia that almost brought tears; life had been so uncomplicated and full of promise then, she thought, conveniently forgetting the battle she'd fought to secure the role for Teddy, and her many subsequent conflicts with the American producer.

Her shoes were crippling her. The high heels were a mistake, but they had been chosen for escorting Teddy to his audition, not for the ensuing events of this terrible day. By the time she walked all the way back from Marlow Road, she knew it had been an irrational and futile idea, imagining she could call so abruptly on Donald to help her – but after the confrontation with Mrs Burch, and with Ross not there, Donald's was the only name that occurred to her. Leaving Kellett Street without money or any clean clothes, in a state akin to panic, she had barely enough coins in her purse for a tram that would take her within walking distance of his house in Woollahra. She had confirmed the address from the phone book, but telephoning was not really an option.

He had not been home. After bracing herself to face him or, even worse, his wife, the door had been answered by a stranger. The middle-aged woman said she was the housekeeper and explained Mr Ferrier was attending a dinner, and Mrs Ferrier was interstate, visiting her parents in Adelaide with the children. It was the first time Belle knew that Donald had children. But she also realised that with Caroline away, she at least had a chance to beg him for help.

'Do you know what time Mr Ferrier will be home?' she asked.

The housekeeper was not disposed to hazard a guess. It was a private engagement, and she had been told she need not wait up for his return. Was there any message?

Belle thanked her, and declined to leave a message or her name. She said she was a client who needed some urgent legal advice, and would therefore phone Mr Ferrier in the morning. She could tell the woman did not believe her.

Unsure what to do, but deciding that having come this far she should try to wait for his return, she took shelter away from the streetlights in case the housekeeper was inquisitive, doing her best to be inconspicuous while watching the gaiety of the party opposite. The first hour seemed endless. By the second the cold had thoroughly chilled her feet, cramped her legs and eroded her resolution. She began to face the stupidity of her impulse.

After all these years, to think she could unexpectedly ambush Donald when he reached home, to beg for a few pounds, perhaps a fiver . . . A fiver would pay the rent and stop the landlady's spiteful game so she could obtain the key and at least recover their belongings. They would then have a roof over their heads for two days, until the next rent was due. Surely enough time to find somewhere else to live. But rehearsing this scenario over and over again in her mind, trying to imagine what to say, it began to feel like supreme effrontery. Even worse, how could she give Donald Ferrier – of all people – the opportunity to see her in a state like this?

She was on the point of leaving when the headlights of his car almost blinded her as he turned into the driveway. While he parked she fled into the shadow of a camphor-laurel tree and after that limped her way back to the tram stop. She had only tuppence left, one short tram fare, but enough to return her to Rushcutters Bay and Ross Tanner, who was now her only hope. At least she would not feel mortified asking *him* for a loan.

A fiver. That was all she needed; it would give her those two vital days, time to think, to gather her wits and sort something out. A fiver was the difference between assurance and despair.

But Ross was still not home. There was no answer when she rang his bell, and the window on the first floor remained dark. It was much too late to seek out the caretaker's wife again. This time she hobbled across the road to the park, found a bench and sat down, undaunted by the thought of being accosted. She took off her shoes, despite the grass being wet with dew and the night growing colder. While she sat there she tried to think of an alternative to Ross, perhaps one of the coterie of friends who had long enjoyed her hospitality, but she faced the probability she would not be welcomed by any of them, not if she arrived at this late hour asking for a loan. It brought a wry concession that they were not actually friends at all, those bright and breezy guests who had so readily made her room their habitat.

Belle was uncertain how long she stayed there. The lights over the tennis courts had been switched off, the players gone. It seemed hours since she had heard their cheerful shouts, the sound of car doors slamming, engines revving and driving away. Later a well-dressed couple arrived in a taxi; she heard them telling the driver they needed the walk across the park after a big night out. They had strolled past her in the direction of the lavish homes on the Darling Point peninsula. She had been conscious of their appraisal, the instant and hostile assessment of her as a tart who should be up the road in Kings Cross, parading along the dirty half-mile where she properly belonged, not loitering here for clients. If there were many like her – she could read in their judgemental faces – it could ruin the neighbourhood, make it as raffish as the Cross, and bring down property values. In a fit of childish pique at this spurious assumption she had wanted to confront them or throw something, but had no available missile except her shoes.

The incident made her realise it was futile to remain any longer. She forced her feet into the shoes and stood up, walking gingerly on the soft grass, which was when she finally saw Ross. He was on the other side of the road, passing beneath one of the few street lights. There was no likelihood he could see her as she instantly froze, protected by the dark overhang of a Moreton Bay fig tree.

He was not alone. The girl walking with him seemed youthful. It was difficult to see her face for they were intent on each other, strolling in step and arm in arm, her head against his shoulder and their bodies bonded like lovers. He murmured something to her and she laughed in reply. To Belle that easy laughter contained all the vibrancy of someone both young and confident.

She could follow their progress by the lights when they entered the boarding house opposite. First the hall, then the stair lights came on and after that it was the tiffany lamp in his room. She briefly glimpsed his figure outlined at the window before he drew the curtains. For a reckless moment she contemplated going to the door, ringing the bell and pleading for help. Instead she limped her way back to the main road, and stood there trying to decide how to endure the rest of the night.

It was the final setback of an awful day, but she could feel no anger at him or jealousy towards the unknown girl. Envy, perhaps; despair certainly. She had invested all her hopes in Ross on the rash assumption he would be there for her unplanned arrival, as if he had no other life outside his jobs, his sculpting and her. It had been stupidly egotistical, for what they had was an affair, an intense affair of friendship and lust, but it could never be more than that. She had always known it must be ephemeral; likable but ambitious Ross Tanner was not really going to tie himself to a woman with a ten-year-old child, no matter how much he enjoyed their rapturous afternoons in bed.

She wished, with the benefit of hindsight, she had been more practical and asked Helene LaRue for shelter – an armchair, a blanket on the floor, anything would have done – but it was far too late to disturb them. She consoled herself that at least Teddy was safe there. As she contemplated the long hours ahead of her a taxi approached. It slowed and seemed about to stop, but she had no money to pay for it, and no other place to go where help would be available. She shook her head and the cabbie picked up speed, heading past the dark outline of the boxing stadium, up towards Paddington.

While she stood there, a late tram turned into the depot adjoining the park. She watched it stop alongside others stationed there, and saw the driver and conductor sign off their shift at a counter deep inside the building. Soon afterwards they emerged, voicing a hope they might still get a drink at a sly grog club in William Street. She felt their speculative glances as they went past her, and waited until they were out of sight.

Except for the brightly lit counter the rest of the cavernous tram depot was in virtual darkness, which was when she started to realise there was no security patrol. Apart from the distant figure of a man who appeared to be a supervisor engrossed in paperwork, no one else was visible. She waited until certain of this, then moved carefully inside. She chose one of the Bondi trams, the 'toast racks' they were called, because of their slatted wooden seats across the width of the carriage. Unfortunately the slats were unyieldingly rigid; by the morning her back was stiff from the discomfort of lying down on them, and she had hardly slept because of the intense cold.

Much of the night had been spent in troubled speculation that somewhere her life had gone astray, that she had mortgaged the future for a vain conceit and a foolish illusion.

Towards dawn, when sleep finally came – far too late for her to feel rested – an inspector on his early rounds shone his torch in her face and woke her, ordering her to clear out of State Government property before she was charged with trespass. Belle, who had so often lived precariously in her past and even relished the romantic days of being dangerously indigent, found out for the first time in her life what it was like to feel helpless and afraid.

PART Three

Chapter eighteen

The shop was the same as she remembered – just as cluttered, the window filled with an eclectic display that ranged from a pair of ivory tusks to a trombone, from a cylindrical phonograph able to reproduce the voice of Nellie Melba to an original crystal set. There were paintings, Persian rugs, coin and stamp collections, used clothes called 'previously loved' garments, and shabby secondhand furniture elevated to 'items of antiquity'. On the window she read the same familiar sign.

CASH FOR YOUR OLD CLOBBER

FAIR PRICES – FAIR DEALS
CAN'T BE FAIRER THAN THAT!
H. W. 'NUNCIE' BILLINGSWORTH. Prop.

Above the door lintel, beside a flamboyant pawnbroker's sign, was the name of the shop that had originally caused uproar at the local council and scandalised the sedate North Shore neighbourhood: NUNCIE'S THREE BALLS.

Belle stood for a moment, watching the chaos within. A very

large man and another who barely reached to his shoulder were struggling to move an upright piano without breaking the delicate objects that surrounded it. A glass cabinet full of crockery trembled as the small man brushed against it, and the third person in the shop, a thick-set woman wearing a beret and smoking a midget cigar, removed it from her mouth long enough to shout at him.

'For Christ's sake, Clarence, get a grip on yourself.'

'I'd love to, old dear, but both hands are fully occupied,' he replied, and when the other man began to laugh the weight became too much for them and they let the piano down with a heavy thud.

'Useless pair of queens,' the woman said. 'Come on, boys, try to get your act together.'

The 'boys', who were well into middle age like their employer, resumed the struggle with their burden towards a loading bay at the back of the shop, while she made the job more hazardous by trying to direct their progress through the clutter.

'Careful. Down a bit your side, Charles, now up yours, Clarence . . . and if you damage that antique commode it will definitely be up yours.'

'Such promises,' Clarence said, pursing his lips at her.

'With a large blunt instrument,' she added.

'Oh, you know how to tease, you do,' he sighed, and while the pair made ribald comments about this Belle entered the shop. The woman turned, opened her mouth and the cigar literally fell out of it.

'Jesus! God Almighty,' she exclaimed. 'It can't be, but it bloody well is!'

'Hello, Nuncie,' Belle said. When the other held out her arms Belle felt a moment of uncertainty, then ran to be enclosed by them. They hugged each other, then Nuncie stood back, still holding both Belle's hands, gazing at her.

'About time you turned up. Let me look at you. Lovely Belle Baker —'

'Belle Carson.'

'As if I could forget that. Broke a heap of bloody hearts, that did. Half the male population of this city . . . and me.'

Belle smiled and carefully detached hands. 'Same old Nuncie.'

'Older, dear.' She lifted her beret to disclose traces of grey in her cropped hair. 'But not necessarily wiser. Where's the boy?'

'At school.'

'Not working?'

'Not at the moment. It's gone a bit quiet.'

'I saw him in his first film. Took myself off to the flicks for a look at him. I thought he was good . . . in a precocious kind of way.'

They heard the piano bump into a metal object and send it crashing. 'Bleeding hopeless!' Nuncie shouted at them.

'It's only an imitation fire scuttle,' the larger of the two said.

'Imitation my arse. That's Georgian, that is. Worth fifteen quid.'

'Yesterday it was worth five,' the other man replied.

'Well, now you've put a dent in it, it's distressed. Makes it a genuine antique. This is my very good friend Belle. The large poof is Charles, and the small one with the big mouth answers to the name of Clarence.'

'Bell,' the large one said, 'as in Tinkerbell?'

'No,' Nuncie said, 'as in belle of the ball. She was christened Arabella, but changed it.'

'Very wise,' Clarence said. 'I had a maiden aunt named Arabella. A ferocious woman, built like a battleship, with a voice like a Dogger Bank foghorn.'

'Well, thank you for that frightening glimpse of the family tree,'

Nuncie retorted. 'Now be a good boy and shut your gob before you catch a fly.'

They went back to struggling with the piano while Nuncie led the way to a tiny office. It contained two upright chairs and a desk that was almost obscured by paperwork. Burrowing beneath this clutter, she found an ancient electric jug and plugged it in, then opened a cupboard and produced a tin marked 'tax receipts' that contained biscuits and a packet of tea.

'Where do you keep the tax receipts?' Belle asked.

'Don't believe in that sort of thing, pet. All transactions strictly cash. I'm a shopkeeper, not a bloody bookkeeper, which is what I'll tell the mongrels if they ever try to audit me. I can show a loss on everything.' She lit another small cigar. 'Now, tell me about you, while we're talking of losses. I have an impression things are not brilliant.'

'Not as brilliant as they were,' Belle said. 'I've honestly been meaning to come and see you, but . . . you know . . . good intentions and all that.' She felt uneasy about the deception, but Nuncie smiled away any discomfiture.

'I know. I hear the road to hell is paved with them. I also heard you've permanently shed the country town.'

'How?'

'The font of all gossip, darl. Fatter than ever and twice as patronising.'

'Florian?'

'Who else fits that bill? He strolled in here a few months ago with a pair of crummy plated candlesticks he was trying to flog. Wanted fifty quid each for 'em. Antique and genuine silver, he said, looking down his great beak at me. Reckoned he was doing me a favour by giving me first option. I told him to fuck off.'

'And now he's done so,' Belle said. 'Departed, well and truly.'

'You mean he's dead?'

'Nothing so simple. Emptied his bank account, even borrowed money from his landlord, and skipped town.'

'Where?'

'If we knew, we'd all be after him. With shotguns.'

'Oh shit,' Nuncie said, catching on at last. 'He owes you.'

'Not me. He owes my son most of what he earned in the past year.'

'Strewth, Belle,' she exclaimed, 'you didn't, you *couldn't* have let him handle . . .' She shook her head in despair. 'Oh, God almighty, you're a dill.'

'I know that now,' Belle said ruefully.

'If you'd come to visit me months ago like you promised, I'd have warned you not to be so trusting.'

'Water under the bridge.' Belle took a deep breath and braced herself for what had to be said. 'The truth is, because of Florian I'm a bit strapped for money, and although I'm ashamed to say it, Nuncie, I'm afraid that's one of the reasons why I'm here.'

'Why not? That's what friends are for.'

'Stop being nice. It makes me feel bloody awful.'

She took an aquamarine ring from her pocket. It was all that George could afford at the time, and had served as an engagement ring. Nuncie assessed it, then reached for a jeweller's glass and fitted it to her eye. She examined the blue stone with the same concentration she would bestow on a more valuable gem.

'So work's a bit quiet for Teddy?'

'So quiet that I've got myself a job as a barmaid. Starting tomorrow.'

'The theatre . . . a bastard of a business, ducky, no matter how

227

much you love it. Always was.' She removed the eye glass. 'Sell or loan?'

'Loan. Just for a few weeks, till I get sorted out.'

'I'll lend you ten quid on it,' Nuncie said.

'Don't be mad!' Belle was startled. 'It's not worth even half that.'

'Don't tell me how to run my shop, Belle. I said ten quid for a couple of months, renewable. Take it or leave it.'

'Thank you.' Belle felt grateful but uncomfortable with what she knew was charity. It was one of the reasons she had not come for help sooner. Nuncie's generosity could at times create an awkward emotional indebtedness. But in the end there had been no one else she could turn to.

'No thanks required,' Nuncie replied briskly, her leathered face impassive. 'It's a business deal. A loan at five per cent per annum. Right? Divided by a couple of months means that after repayment of the original, you'll owe me two and sixpence interest. Right?'

'If you say so.' Belle had no head for figures, especially when computed so swiftly, but felt sure the interest should be more than that. Before she could voice this feeling the telephone rang, and Nuncie was immediately engrossed in a lively haggle with someone about the price of an Ottoman rug. Belle hardly heard the exchange. Her mind was so full of the past forty-eight hours ever since she had left Kellett Street; especially being woken by the tram inspector, his nose wrinkling with disgust – the second time in one night that she had been mistaken for a prostitute, she thought – and the desperate need to find clean clothes and a hot shower. There was only one way to do this, which was to walk up the hill to the Cross once again. Since her feet were rubbed raw, she carried her shoes and walked barefoot.

Helene LaRue had been shocked and expressed herself in voluble

French when she opened the door of the shop. It was just after five-thirty, and the sun had not yet risen to warm the day. Belle was shivering after waiting for almost an hour outside the hotel across the street until a light had appeared in the flat over the corner store. She knew Helene always rose early in order to take a tram to the markets, where she bought the day's fresh fruit and vegetables.

'*Mon dieu!*' Helene stared at her and switched into her strongly accented English, 'But what has happened? Where have you been? Look at your poor feet, they are bleeding!'

'Please, can you lend me five pounds?' Belle asked urgently.

'*Comment?*'

'Five quid,' she repeated desperately.

'But for what purpose, Belle? First of all, perhaps you do not wish for me to speak like this, but I think I should be truthful and say you look awful.'

'I *feel* awful. I slept in a tram down at the depot.'

'Tram,' she repeated, startled. '*Pourquoi?* For what strange reason do you go to sleep in a tram?'

'The old bag locked me out of the flat because I owe rent.'

'Then why didn't you come here?'

'I would've – but by then it was far too late.'

'You should have woken us!' the Frenchwoman scolded.

'Helene, please, tell me if you can help.'

'You ask for five pounds? But I cannot. I do not have five.'

'Never mind,' Belle said, 'if you'd lend me the tram fare to Neutral Bay, I might be able to borrow the money from a friend there.'

'*Non*, you cannot travel anywhere looking like that,' Helene told her severely. 'You need to bathe and put on clean clothes. You could bathe upstairs here, only I do not think it is good for your son to see you like this.'

'I agree. Trouble is, I can't get hold of any clean clothes. Not unless I get into my room. Don't you understand what's happened? The bitch has changed the lock on our room.'

Helene LaRue said that of course she understood, and to please wait. She opened the till and counted the money in it. 'I have four pounds, but I need one for the market. And also I must pay the baker. So I can loan you two. Do you think it will be enough to help?'

'I hope so.' Belle felt a great wave of relief. She had been broke before, but never like this, not with the responsibility of Teddy, or with such a feeling of insecurity. 'Bless you, Helene. It's only for a few days, I promise.'

Both women looked up as they heard the sound of someone stirring in the living quarters above. Helene warned her to be silent with a finger to her lips, in case it was Teddy. She took two pound notes from the till, gave them to Belle and gestured her towards the door.

At first Edith Burch had refused to consider the payment of a measly two quid. She insisted she had the law firmly on her side, and for all she cared Belle Carson could sleep in the street, the park or another tram – whichever she preferred. No stuck-up lodger was going to get the better of her. Especially one with such airs and graces. The room would remain locked until the full rent was paid.

In that case, Belle had told her, she was prepared to abandon the belongings in there because they had no real value, and Ma Burch could whistle for her lousy money. So the question seemed to be, did she want two quid now and the rest when she could pay, or would she prefer nothing – absolute fuck-all, Belle had said, because she'd had a gutful of her landlady. Or would Mrs Burch prefer to go to court, which meant that a few months from now the case might be scheduled for hearing. The magistrate would be cranky because such a small debt should be settled without wasting his valuable time, and the only winners would be the people who always won in court – the lawyers.

Edith Burch took a few moments to consider this, then decided to accept the two pounds, insisting the balance be paid within a week or it would be handed over to a debt collector. She gave Belle the new key on condition she vacate the room by the following day.

'Bloody Ottoman rugs, the silly cow.' Nuncie finished her phone call and leapt to switch off the jug before water boiled over her desk. 'It is completely impossible to comprehend the stinking rich. This absurd woman, she lives at Beauty Point in a great ostentatious palace, and she's trying to sell me a threadbare Ottoman. *Sell me one!* I said I've got four in stock, so why not chuck her rug in the garbage tip and buy a new one from me? The batty old bitch wants a trade-in.' She looked carefully at Belle. 'You were deep in thought, my love, or you might've turned off the jug.'

'Sorry,' Belle said.

'So bring me up-to-date with the rest of your life. Have you dumped the husband – what was his name?'

'George. We saw him at Easter, but he's gone back to live in Gundagai.'

'How does Teddy feel? Does he know the truth?'

'No. He still thinks George is his dad.'

'Are you going to go on letting him believe that?'

'If I can.'

'Never heard from the real one?'

'No.' Belle decided not to mention her fruitless pilgrimage the previous night. 'And never want to.'

'I see his picture in the papers sometimes. The social pages. Him and his wife at the races, or attending some charity dinner. No doubt stuffing his face for a good cause, like all that mob.'

'Has he put on weight and gone bald?'

'No such luck.' Nuncie shook her head and smiled. 'The bugger's hardly changed, still looks quite young, though he must be nudging forty.'

'Thirty-six,' Belle said, then wished she hadn't.

'You keep tabs.'

'Not really. I don't even want to talk or think about him. Except . . . I did hear he's become a silk. Is that true?'

'Absolutely true. One of our top barristers. But since you hate his guts, don't waste time on him. What have you been doing since George? Found a new lover? I'll make the tea while you tell all and make me laugh.'

'Not too many laughs lately, Nuncie.'

'No laughs? Are you going to tell me no lovers, either?'

'Only one.'

'And? Details, please.'

'No details. I think I can say it's all over. He was too young for me. It was fun and he was rather nice,' she said reminiscently, 'but I always knew he was too young.' She watched Nuncie making the tea in a china pot. 'If Donald is a King's Counsel now, I suppose he has to wear a wig and gown in court?'

'Ducky, for a bloke you'd rather not talk or think about, he occupies a lot of your time. As far as I'm concerned, he's a great big shit, but I'm told he does wear a wig and looks splendid. If you really want to, you can find out the next time he performs in a trial. Sit at the back of the court and see for yourself.'

'Don't be ridiculous,' Belle replied and promptly changed the subject. She began to recount the events of the past days, the shock of being left penniless, and her plans for a more secure future.

The landlord said his name was 'Erbert, but everyone called him plain 'Erb, so they might as well call him 'Erb too. Belle and Teddy followed him to the top landing where the stairs became steeper and quite narrow. He was a huge man, almost as wide as the final flight that led towards the garret, and Belle tried to suppress a comic image of him being stuck halfway up there. She believed at first he had paused on the landing to regain his breath, but when he gestured to them she realised he intended to wait there while they went the rest of the way to view what was offered.

'Lovely little top-floor room,' he wheezed. 'Jest wot youse are looking for, cheap as chips for this 'ighly regarded part of town. Gotta view, real close to everything, only ten bob rent a week. Better be quick, she'll be snapped up real smart, this will. Youse get free 'ot showers on Frideys. Extra ones charged for.'

They left their suitcases with him and climbed up to where the frayed stair carpet ended to inspect their new home. Not a lovely room at all, Belle could see that at once. A little room certainly, cheap most assuredly, but as for this being a highly regarded part of town she already knew the neighbourhood was a dismal suburb, much of it wasteland surrounded by industrial chimneys belching smoke. Planes regularly flew overhead to the new aerodrome at Mascot. There was an incessant noise of traffic rumbling past. The houses here were all in a state of disrepair, gaunt places, some with windows boarded up, the whole neighbourhood creating an impression that it was only surviving until there was sufficient money to knock it down and begin again.

The room was in fact an attic, a makeshift renovation that had been built against the slope of the roof, which meant only half of it had adequate headroom. It contained two iron-frame beds with horsehair mattresses. They were set together because there was insufficient space for them to be apart. The only other item of furniture was a clothes cupboard with a broken latch that would barely accommodate half their belongings. Mahogany veneer was peeling off the sides, exposing flimsy plywood. Inside it she saw insects, the petrified remains of long-dead moths and flies, and a litter of tiny black pellets that could only be mouse or rat droppings.

At the lowest point in the attic where the ceiling and the floor met was a grate with scraps of charred timber in it, which Belle realised was a fireplace with a rudimentary tin chimney cut through the iron roof. It looked dangerous, but 'Erb insisted it was necessary in the cold weather and worked a treat. He showed them what he called 'the ablutions'. The sole lavatory in the house was a long way downstairs. It contained a stained bath and a shower fuelled by a chip heater. Belle felt too tired to register her disgust. She wished she could resume the search, find somewhere if not better, then at least half decent, but there was no time; they had to vacate Kellett Street that day or owe more rent to the landlady.

She looked at Teddy with a silent apology. 'We'll take it,' she said.

'Botany?' Nuncie pronounced the name of the suburb with a slight shudder, as if it might be akin to somewhere obnoxious in outer

Siberia. 'But that's an industrial area, darling. I know that people work in Botany, but surely no one actually *lives* there.'

'We do now,' Belle said.

'You can't bring up a kid in that neighbourhood, Belle.'

'I've paid a month's rent, and we've moved in.'

'Such a rush! I could've found you something better.'

'Not at this price. When I pay back Mrs LaRue and get settled with that bloody landlady, then I start to repay you and Greta Torrance. Meanwhile my wages have to keep us. So a cheap room, no matter how awful, will do until we get on our feet again.'

'And how,' her friend asked carefully, 'do you think that's going to happen?'

'Teddy will eventually get work. After all, everyone knows him; he's talented. Things are bound to change.'

'Of course,' Nuncie said, wondering if things ever would.

Chapter nineteen

Teddy thought it strange; they had moved only a few miles away in the same city, but life was so different. In the first weeks he walked along bleak streets that were almost deserted until sirens sounded to end the working day, after which they were briefly swamped with men from the factories hurrying to their homes in other places. Hardly anyone seemed to live in the district. There were no shops. No electric trolley buses or neon signs, no cheerful crowds or the familiar smell of garlic or coffee that drifted out from doorways along Darlinghurst Road.

He missed his previous life dreadfully.

There was no one here like his friend Dominic, the accordionist, who had lost his leg in the war at a place he called bleeding Mesopotamia; none of the painted street ladies, who always made a fuss of him and called him darl; and no matinees on Saturday arvo at the Picture Palace, where Chrissie would hold his hand in the scary films, which was why he always elected to see them, because he liked holding hands in the darkened cinema with her. He missed the nightly clamour of what Belle had called the Kellett Street circle, their rowdy debates and political arguments, and at times he secretly wondered what had happened to Ross.

More than anything else, he felt the loss of Sally.

He had tried to see her. The day before they'd moved he'd waited at the school gates when the bell rang, but she was not there and one of her friends said she was away sick with flu. The trouble was, apart from knowing she lived in a flat in Roslyn Gardens, he didn't know her actual address because he'd never been asked to her home. She sometimes made feeble excuses about this, but they both knew the reason; her mother didn't like him, and disapproved of their friendship. Belle said it was typical of a stuck-up cow who had hit the jackpot in her divorce settlement: there was no snootier snob in town, so he shouldn't let it bother him. It never had, until he realised there would be no more dancing lessons and he would not be able to keep in touch with Sally.

He made an attempt to find out where she lived, running through the maze of streets that led past St Luke's Hospital and into Roslyn Gardens, down the hill towards Elizabeth Bay, ringing doorbells in the large blocks of flats, asking if they knew the address of a Mrs Sharp and her daughter, but nobody could help. An elderly lady said she thought she'd heard the name, but felt sure they didn't live in this district. Or perhaps they did, and she was thinking of someone else. At the grocery shop on the corner an assistant said to come back another time when they weren't so busy. When Teddy replied there wouldn't be another time because he was moving from the district, he was told the assistant was far too busy to listen to other people's troubles – he had enough of his own.

Worse than this, he was confronted by a janitor of a block of flats who said he'd been watching him ringing doorbells, causing a nuisance and wasting decent people's time. Teddy tried to explain, but the man had him categorised as a street larrikin, and warned he'd report him as a truant playing hooky from school. When he ran from this threat, legs beginning to ache as he tackled the steep return hill to Darlinghurst, his one remaining hope was the Kings Cross post office. There, on asking for their home address, he was informed they were forbidden to give out private information.

As time passed after they moved to Botany, he began to wonder if he'd ever see Sally again. Facing the daunting experience of a new school, new classes and the same old humiliation of being put with younger kids all eager to show up his ineptitude, he felt it more keenly because he lacked a friend. Sally had been his confidante, his companion and best mate, and school had been tolerable because of her presence. Now there was no one with whom he could share his secrets or confess his loneliness. Each afternoon when school was over he returned to an empty room, for Belle was working six days a week, serving in the saloon bar of the Joseph Banks Hotel. She was rarely home before seven, having to help clean up after the rush hour.

Being lonely was a new experience, a disturbing one that made Teddy feel moody and introspective. Back in Gundagai there'd been the mateship of the gang, at least until his final weeks, and he'd had his dad as well; while in Kellett Street he'd never lacked for company. He had not wanted to leave either place. Certainly not Brewinda Road because he missed the old house, the games he could play in the yard, even the Murrumbidgee River itself. He missed George, who had been left behind, although at that time he had thought it just a temporary separation.

Often awake at night in his new room, his bed joined with Belle's because of the lack of space, he could still recollect the day they left Gundagai. The long walk to the station – no car this time – carrying their luggage in the January heat, the platform empty except for them and Mr Miller the station porter in his shabby State Rail uniform. All of it still so clear in his mind.

Mr Miller, staring at Belle perspiring in her best clothes, asking if the town wasn't smart enough for them. Was that why she and the boy were off again so soon, heading for the big smoke? Belle ignoring him. Looking through him as if he didn't exist. Then George taking Mr Miller aside, saying there was no reason to be so discourteous, no need to be rude, because it was none of his business, and any more remarks like that there'd be a complaint to the stationmaster. George telling the porter his wife was not leaving the town – insisting on this as if it were important, saying she was going to the city as chaperone for their son, because there was such a demand for him to appear in films and on the stage that it'd be bloody stupid not to take advantage of it, and in due course they'd both be back again.

All of this Teddy believed at the time, but discovered afterwards that it was a lie. It was play-acting, the way Belle and George had kissed and exchanged a hug as the train came in, how they'd sworn they would miss each other, and soon be back together as a family. The whole day was a lie. He supposed they'd felt it was necessary, but whenever he thought about it, which was often, he wished his dad and mum could've trusted him with the truth. Although he was only nine years old at the time, he felt sure he could've handled it.

Leaving Kellett Street was very different. It was so sudden, all happening in two days without the slightest warning, no chance to say goodbye to anyone. Until later he didn't have the faintest idea *why* they were leaving, except that Belle and the landlady had had an enormous row, and after they'd packed and taken the suitcase downstairs, Mrs Burch had been waiting there as if she was on guard, saying she was glad to see the back of them. Belle had said the feeling was mutual – the rent was exorbitant and the bedbugs were a plague; there should be a warning on the front door: beware of fleas, lice and a parasite.

The landlady had gone bright red, held out her hand and demanded the key of the room. This was when Belle had told him to wait outside, and although he was not supposed to listen, he heard her call Ma Burch a string of names; there were so many that he could only remember 'a bloodsucking avaricious leech' and 'a nasty rapacious old tart'. Afterwards, while waiting for the tram, about to ask her what rapacious meant, she'd told him instead how she'd given back the key. She'd opened the lavatory door, dropped it in the pan and pulled the chain.

'Good on you, Mum,' Teddy said, momentarily cheered out of his dejection. Belle could always be relied upon to do something a bit weird and unpredictable.

'Pity it wasn't an Outback dunny,' she'd said, making him grin most of the way across the Harbour Bridge to Neutral Bay, where they had left the tram and walked to a strange shop that seemed to be full of almost everything, and where he had his first sight of Nuncie Billingsworth.

'So you're the darling boy!' she said, and years afterwards he could still remember the baggy cord trousers, the beret, cigar and a voice ripened on years of whisky and tobacco. 'I'm sure your mum has told you who I am. I'm her oldest friend, and apart from that, petal, I'm the only woman you'll ever meet with three balls.'

When Teddy looked startled she had pointed at the pawnbroker sign and the name of the shop inscribed above it. They had both laughed, then she picked him up and hugged him. He had tried not to mind the smell of the cigar or the smoke that made his eyes water.

'We'll be good mates, you and me, ducky,' she said. 'It's a very special day, this is. The first time I've seen you since . . . well, to be exact, you weren't yet with us, not in the flesh, still a bun in the oven, as the saying goes. Never thought I'd see you grown up into a fine young chap like this, and that's the truth.' She put him down and smiled as she quickly brushed a sleeve across her eyes.

'Wasn't I born?' Teddy asked, puzzled by what she was saying.

'Not when I first knew you, pet. More than ten years ago. Talk about time's winged chariot,' she said. 'Lord love us, it doesn't half belt along. Seems such a short while since I heard the news . . .' She had sniffed, feeling in the pocket of her trousers for a hankie to dab at her eyes this time. Teddy, who thought it had been caused by the cigar smoke, began to realise these were tears.

That night he asked Belle why Nuncie had been crying. 'Was she?' Belle had assumed a look of surprise. 'I didn't notice it.'

'She said the last time she saw you, I was a bun in the oven.'

'Well, you were, darling. That's just Nuncie's way of putting it.'

'I know what it means. But why would that make her cry?'

'I think you must've been mistaken,' Belle said, and changed the subject.

Long after winter had officially ended, the cold persisted. The westerly winds that came off the Blue Mountains brought with them extreme heat in summer and bitter temperatures now. Although Belle disliked the improvised fireplace and worried it might be unsafe, there was little option. Their garret, perched like a bird's nest at the top of the house, had no protection from the cold. When the wind blew and the galvanised-iron roof clattered, they shivered in their warmest clothes.

After school Teddy went to collect kindling and pine cones in the woodland area near the bay. He took with him a woven basket that Nuncie had lent them, one made of palm fronds, she said, brought back from a trip she had once taken on an ocean liner to Fiji. It was meant to be for shopping, but he used it to carry the twigs and cones, then slung it over his shoulder to take them home. Belle insisted he must always be safely indoors before dark, and he was not to dally there talking to people he didn't know.

Sometimes he was distracted by ships that came into the bay to discharge cargo, ships with foreign names, some with strange and different sort of writing that he couldn't read. Wog boats, he heard someone say, and when he asked Belle what it meant, she said it meant the person was pig-ignorant and the phrase was vulgar and he was not to use it. She told him the vessels might be from Japan or China, or else Arabia, but since he couldn't tell this from the weird lettering on the bow, they remained categorised in his mind as wog boats.

One afternoon, tired of gathering wood, he walked down to the sea wall to watch one unloading its cargo. A floating crane was alongside, hoisting crates from the deck, swinging them high in the air and safely onto the dock. Suddenly one of the biggest crates fell and crashed to the ground. Even from where he stood, Teddy could see it splinter apart. All the goods spilled out as wharfies on the dock converged on it and started grabbing the contents. Dark-skinned people on the ship were shouting in alarm.

Alongside him a man laughed softly. 'Serve 'em right. Bloody heathens.'

Teddy was startled. He hadn't been aware anyone was there. The man looked skinny; he wore sandshoes and had on shabby trousers, a woollen open-necked shirt and a cardigan. He grinned and took a half-smoked cigarette from his mouth, pinched it out with his fingers and put it behind his ear. Teddy avoided his gaze

242

as he picked up his basket and went back into the bush, towards the pine trees. The cones burnt so quickly that he still needed more for that night's fire. After a while he began to feel uneasy. He tried not to look, but from the corner of his eye he realised the man was still watching him. He'd moved from the sea wall – again, Teddy hadn't heard him – and was not far away, leaning against a tree. Just watching at first. Staring at him.

Then the man opened the buttons at the front of his trousers. He put his hand inside there and smiled. It was a smile that gave Teddy the creeps. A smile that seemed to say, 'Come and look at what I'm doing.' He was rubbing himself with one hand and he beckoned to Teddy with the other.

'Give yer two shillings,' the man said, 'two bob, if yer come here.'

Teddy tried to be calm. He picked up the basket. It was nowhere near full yet, but he slung it on his shoulder without another glance at the man. He started to walk away, not attempting to look back, walking firmly and steadily as if he was unafraid, but the moment he reached a thicket of native shrubs and felt out of sight he began to run. A short cut through this stretch of scrub led back to the main park; people would be picnicking and walking dogs there, it would be safe.

It was difficult to run with the bundle of cones jolting against his side. The bush was dense. Sharp grevillea branches slapped at his arms and face, thick morning glory vines amid a jungle of lantana threatened to trip him. Unsure of his bearings he changed direction, then choked back a terrified scream as he became entangled in what felt like an impenetrable spider's web. Suddenly the only thing that seemed to matter was fighting to free himself of the cobweb, and moments later he came into a clearing to discover he'd gone the wrong way.

With a feeling of horror he saw the man there waiting for him. In his panic he'd run almost in a circle, and his pursuer had heard and tracked his flight, hardly having to move at all to block his escape. There were no people here, no dogs, no safety. Just the same creepy man. Still smiling. The same scary smile. Teddy had never felt such fear.

'Silly boy,' the man said, and reached into his open trousers and brought out his cock. It was red and stiff. He slid his hand up and down it, like a caress. 'Y' see? That's all you have to do. Two bob . . . easy money.'

They were face to face, only about ten paces apart. Teddy moved slightly forward. He could see the man's intent eyes fixed on him, bright and eager, his head nodding encouragement, his tongue starting to roll across his lips, as if to moisten them. 'Buy lots of ice-cream with two bob, kid.'

Teddy moved another pace, then in desperation ran at him, swinging the half-filled basket with all his strength. He had never felt so strong, nor so sure of where he meant to hit. The man gave a shout of pain and doubled up, falling to the ground in agony.

'You fuckin' little bastard!' he cried, and Teddy swung and hit him again, then jumped out of reach as the man tried to grasp his ankle. There was no chance to retrieve the basket as he turned and ran. The voice was yelling at him to come back or he'd be sorry, and when it seemed to be distant enough, he risked a quick glance behind. The man was getting painfully to his feet, and trying to button his trousers.

Teddy ran for the safety of the park, and it was only when he reached there and gratefully recovered his breath that he remembered the basket with the pine cones had been left behind.

———◆———

They had no fire in their tiny grate that night. Belle was huddled in a blanket. She had brought home a half-bottle of sherry, and refilled her glass while Teddy sat and looked at the empty grate and tried not to tremble. It wasn't the cold, even though the wind was biting; it was the man's smile that made him shiver.

'What do you mean, you lost the basket? How could you lose it?'

'I just did. I forgot where I left it.'

'That sounds a bit like a fib, my darling . . . a little white lie.'

'I *did* lose it. I won't be able to find it.'

'It was a loan from Nuncie. It wasn't ours to lose.'

He retreated into stubborn silence. There was no way he could tell her.

'Never mind,' she said, 'I'll just have to save up and buy her a new one.' She poured herself another sherry, and put the bottle in the cupboard.

He felt guilty about Nuncie's basket. He remembered the creepy man's smile with a feeling of terror. 'Mum . . . I don't like it here.'

'Nor do I, my love. But when things are better, we'll move.'

'When will they be better?'

'Soon. As long as we don't get gloomy and down in the dumps, like a pair of woebegone wombats.' She looked for a smile, but there was none. 'Things will get better, they have to get better.'

'Why can't we go home?'

'That's not possible,' she said, 'and I think you know it's not.'

'But why?'

'So many questions, darling. It's time for bed.'

'Aren't you ever going back there?' Teddy asked, but he knew the answer to that before she shook her head.

Later, when he was in bed and she had switched off the light, he tried to ask her why she didn't like Gundagai.

'I spent nine years there, Teddy. I tried to like it.'

'Why couldn't you? It's a nice town.'

'There's nothing wrong with the town, darling. I was the wrong one, out of my element, a Promethean in that sterile landscape . . .'

'A *what*, Mum?'

'A bit of an odd-ball, darling. Different. People didn't like that . . . or me.'

'Dad likes you.'

'Yes,' she said, 'your dad's a good man. I like him, too.'

'Then why —'

'Time for sleep, I think.'

'Mum —'

'Last question,' she said.

'Will we be able to save up and buy Nuncie a new basket?'

'We must. Of course, it won't be the same. Not as nice. We can't go to Fiji and buy one like that.'

Teddy heard the school bell as he hurried past the asphalt playground and saw some boys from his class going into the brick building that he always thought looked like a prison. At least it looked like the prisons he'd seen in films, when he used to go to the Picture Palace with Chrissie LaRue. He hadn't been to a film since then, because there wasn't a picture show anywhere near where they lived now, and he knew they couldn't afford it. Wanting what they couldn't afford only made Belle unhappy, so it was best not to ask. Best to believe things would get better soon, and he'd be able to see films again. There had to be a cinema somewhere near; it wasn't civilised not to have one.

Nobody at school saw him run past. He knew he'd be late but it couldn't be helped. He'd invent an excuse. When he reached the park there were people walking their dogs, which made it feel safer. But he had to go into the thick bushland to find the basket. *If* it was there. The man might've pinched it. Or else he might even still be there, waiting. Thinking about that almost made Teddy change his mind. But he'd decided, lying awake last night, it had to be done.

He was frightened the whole time he spent searching. It was hard to remember exactly where it had happened. The bushland was far bigger than he'd realised. If he needed to shout for help nobody would be able to hear. A blackberry scratched his leg; he felt it was probably bleeding, but he didn't want to stop to check. Memory of the thick spider's web kept him on edge, while he began to wonder if there might be snakes. He heard a rustle and turned in terror, but it wasn't the man, it was a small furry creature that scuttled away, and he felt his heart pound even as he recognised it was a rabbit.

When at last he found the right clearing the woven basket was intact on the ground. Some of the twigs and pine cones were still inside, the rest scattered nearby. He swiftly gathered them up, then, clutching it to his chest, ran all the way back to school. He was made to stand in the corner, and the eight-year-olds in the class giggled and whispered about him, but he didn't care. He felt as if he'd made a journey; in his vivid imagination he'd fought a battle and won it, or, better still, had climbed a mountain and reached the top.

In his solitary hours after school, before Belle finished work at the hotel, Teddy carefully composed a letter to George. He wanted this one to be a real letter, full of news about their change of address and all that had happened: at least two pages of running writing which he'd been practising so that George would see he'd taken to heart the advice about working hard at his lessons.

In order to impress his dad, the letter had taken a long time. He confessed he didn't like their new room, and the neighbourhood was different and not as nice. But Nuncie was nice, he said; did he know Nuncie Billingsworth? She had given him a present, a book of poems all about places in Sydney, written by her friend Kenneth Slessor. He was trying to read one of the poems each night, and when Belle got back from work she helped him to spell and understand the big words. Did he know the news that Belle was working at a hotel behind the bar, and rotten old Florian had blown through with their money? He decided to cross this out, then had to rewrite the whole page, remembering Belle had asked him not to tell his dad about that. It was spilt milk and it would only worry George who could not help them, she said, so it was best to say nothing.

The letter-writing was often interrupted by his moments of introspection, and at times he wondered why they never heard from all the poets, actors and artists who used to visit their Kings Cross room so often . . . the many friends with their gossip and arguments over bottles of four-penny dark. It was strange the way they had vanished, and at night now there was just him and Belle after she came home. All the time they lived at Kellett Street the circle had met there regularly, and he could not understand what had happened to them. After all, it was only a short tram ride away. Once he had raised the subject with Belle, who had shrugged and said it showed they weren't actual friends at all, just a bunch of people happy to grog-on at someone else's expense. Fair-weather friends was one name for them, she added, although bludgers was a word that seemed quite apt. She said it was just as well they could not be bothered to seek her out, because she could no longer afford pointless little luxuries like that.

She sounded angry. He was unsure if her criticism included Ross Tanner, but as she didn't mention his name Teddy felt it was unwise to ask, and decided that if Ross was also considered a bludger, then he and Sally must have been mistaken about them being lovers. It was another reminder of Sal, making him wish he could see her again so they could discuss this. He missed her more with each passing week, far more than he thought possible. In bed at night he held silent imaginary conversations with her, and sometimes it felt so vivid and real as if she was actually there with him, the two of them chatting and laughing together, her mop of red hair spread across the pillow beside him.

There was so much to tell her. About the way he'd tried to find her home address when they had to leave Kellett Street. How he'd gradually learnt that Florian had shot through with all their dough. Imagine it! Rotten old Uriah, doing a bunk! And just to make it worse, there was no work at present – it was what they called a slump – so he was trapped into going to school every day. Sally knew how he disliked change, but this time he kept wishing there could be one big change in his life, to leave Botany behind, to come back to live in the Cross so he could find her again.

He had a thousand things to say. He wanted to tell her about Nuncie, the funny lady with three balls. About the book of poems she'd given him. How he could now read every poem without help. In time he might even talk to her about the creepy man in the park, although he was not sure about that.

He knew one thing. He'd like to tell Sal that he missed her so much he felt certain he must be in love with her, even though they were only ten years old.

If he could pluck up enough courage, he'd really like to tell her that.

Sometimes on a Sunday, when the hotel was shut and Belle did not have to work, they would walk to Mascot and watch the planes taking off. The aerodrome, as it was called, was a large, treeless field with a concrete strip for the planes to land, and a corrugated-iron building called the air terminal. Not many years ago, he was told by one of the pilots, the place had been a dairy farm.

On many of these days Nuncie would join them, arriving there on her sturdy pushbike with complaints about the crazy fools driving motor cars – all of them men – who had nearly run her down. Nuncie, wearing familiar baggy cords, a floppy pullover and her trademark beret, invariably lit up a small cigar the moment she finished airing her views on those irresponsible idiots who should be barred from the roads. A bunch of raving dingalings, she called them.

'I hear the blokes are complaining about this madwoman on a pushbike,' Belle teased her one Sunday. 'They want her chained up so the roads are safe for them. Or was it the bike they wanted chained up? No, it was the rider.'

'I know which part of their anatomy I'd put a chain on,' Nuncie said with a grin, then turned to gaze at Teddy. 'Well, young sir, I may be the only woman you know with three balls, ducky, but don't I get my usual Sunday kiss?'

Teddy liked it when Nuncie joined them to watch the planes, for she could always make Belle laugh. These were the best Sundays. When his mum laughed like that he had this strange feeling of happiness, because of the way her face lit up; she looked younger and really beautiful, and Teddy liked it when other people seemed to notice and admire her.

On days like this they would stand behind the perimeter fence near the air terminal building and watch passengers climb steps that were wheeled alongside the planes so they could go aboard. The engines would be started and warmed up until both propellers were at full speed, throttling so loudly it was impossible to hear themselves speak, then the plane would taxi across the one-time dairy farm to become airborne and climb out to sea over Botany Bay, until it was a tiny speck in the sky. It was a source of wonder to Teddy how the same plane a few hours later could land its passengers in distant cities such as Melbourne, Brisbane or Perth – even places overseas. When he learnt that Singapore could be reached in three days, and it took just two more overnight stops to India, his imagination began to take wing, visualising great adventures – sometimes as a passenger, or in more daring dreams as the pilot – crossing oceans, cruising over exotic foreign lands, arriving in New York or London to the applause of cheering crowds.

Charles Kingsford-Smith became his new hero; mere land-locked mortals like Don Bradman and Hubert Opperman could not compete with a man who rode the skies on such a magic carpet.

Chapter twenty

In the months that had passed since the night of his induction into the Foundation Club, Donald Ferrier often thought about the woman he had glimpsed on his arrival home. It was irrational, he knew, but he kept wondering. Exactly why he should imagine it was Belle Baker puzzled him. She belonged to the past – eleven years past – and a lucky escape it had been. On reflection, this was perhaps unfair; there were some fond memories, some tender and rather loving times if he cared to recall, memories that were best left as history for the sake of his marriage and its current difficulties.

It could have been the judge's port, or the stimulus of his initiation, but he had not slept well that night. In the morning as she served breakfast, the housekeeper had told him about the caller; how the woman requested to see him, claiming she was a client needing urgent advice, but refusing to leave a message or even her name. Mrs Abbott clearly thought it extremely odd, and by implication her attitude seemed to suggest he might know a bit more about this than he was prepared to admit. 'No smoke without fire,' she would doubtless confide to her friend the gardener next door, or anyone else in the street who enjoyed a gossip.

'What time was this?' Donald asked.

'Shortly after nine.'

He shrugged as if it was of no real importance, buttered his toast and turned to the news pages of the *Sydney Morning Herald*. He did his best to appear engrossed in the paper when she returned with the tea, although his mind was busily absorbing what she had said.

Nine o'clock? In that case, he estimated she – whoever it was – must have waited outside the house for almost another two hours, which was more than odd, it was downright bloody peculiar. He could think of no one who would linger for so long in the cold, then scuttle off when his car turned into the driveway. Nobody except . . . but it was surely unlikely. Ridiculous.

He shook his head as if to clear it, and tried to focus on the newspaper. In Berlin, Adolf Hitler's new Nazi party was burning books, while communists were running riot in Madrid. The world was going crazy. Another headline announced Prohibition had officially ended in America after thirteen dry years. Sanity in some degree seemed to have returned there, he thought. Adults could again drink booze without it being a criminal offence.

Why on earth should it be Belle? Why was he even considering it? Just because of a fleeting look, an instant when he seemed to catch a glimpse of . . .

'Mrs Abbott,' he said, as she returned with the early morning mail, 'this woman last night, your mysterious visitor —'

'Not *my* visitor, Mr Ferrier,' she said quickly.

'No, of course not.' He smiled. 'Just a manner of speaking.' He knew he had to be careful with her. Mrs Abbott had been Caroline's choice, and over the past year had become her confidante. The housekeeper knew a great deal more than she should about the state of their relationship, which was why he found her presence uncomfortable. But he needed to ask one more question, and try to make it seem casual.

'Call her *our* mysterious visitor, by all means. Probably, if the truth is known, someone trying to sell encyclopaedias.' He hurried on before she could dispute this. 'What sort of age was she? An elderly lady?'

'No, quite the contrary. I'd say she was in her thirties. Let me see, yes, I'd say mid-thirties. A bit taller than average, quite slim, dark hair. She was rather good-looking, in fact . . . yes, quite good-looking, though she appeared to be in something of a state and, I would have to say, looked somewhat dishevelled. So it was difficult to tell . . .'

Mrs Abbott, who was well known for her verbosity, looked ready to continue discussing the matter at length, but he thanked her and said he had an early appointment at his chambers. If his wife called, he would be in court until four, but he'd telephone her tonight about the date she and the children intended to return from Adelaide.

'But I thought you knew,' the housekeeper remarked.

'Knew what, Mrs Abbott?'

'She's due back a week Friday, on the fourteenth. Spending two days with the kiddies in Melbourne, and then they're all taking the Thursday-night train.'

'I see,' he said. 'Well, as long as that's settled.'

He went out to the car in a hurry, before he was tempted to wrap the *Herald* into a club and hit her with it, thus making the sort of headlines any newspaper would relish.

Belle asked for an extra shift at the hotel, to help her save money. Popular with the exclusively male clientele who packed the saloon bar in the late afternoons, she was careful to look after her favoured regulars in the rush against closing time, the notorious six-o'clock swill. Amid the haze of cigarette smoke and the clamour of orders for final drinks – a din in which it was difficult to distinguish a word – Belle learnt to be adept at reading customers' signals. The fastest gun in the pub they called her, a tribute to the speed with which she could handle several beer taps at once and fill their schooners, ignoring the rigid legality of the clock until the landlord forced closure by turning off the kegs. Then the place rapidly emptied and she could draw breath, gathering the coins that lay soaked on the bar in front of her, the small change left there as a token of approval.

The pennies accumulated. Occasionally there would be a threepenny coin; once a silver sixpence to be rescued and dried. Generosity peaked during the afternoon shift on Fridays, when the men from the factories were paid and a weekend of sport or the beach lay ahead. But despite her share of the beer money and the cheap rent, it was proving difficult to save. There were the debts to be settled. After three months she was able to repay Greta Torrance for the dancing lessons. Greta protested it was not necessary, but Belle was adamant, or else she would feel unable to bring Teddy back to the class again.

When will that be? Greta had asked, pleased at the prospect.

In a few months, Belle had replied. Soon.

She could not risk even a small outlay like the dancing lessons yet. No matter how much she wanted Teddy to resume, it would have to wait a while. When she was free of all encumbrance, she would start to rebuild her life. Find work for Teddy. Move from their appalling room. But first she must accrue enough to feel a measure of security. The terrifying experience of being so totally without money had shaken her. Her despair during the freezing night in the tram was never likely to be forgotten. The former landlady and Helene LaRue's loan were both repaid, but there was still Nuncie.

'Keep the damn money,' Nuncie insisted.

They were drinking wine in the flat above her pawnshop. It was a Sunday evening and Nuncie had made a cottage pie for dinner, and bought ice-cream as a surprise treat for Teddy. Now he was in the shop premises below, experimentally picking out notes on a piano.

'I mean that,' she repeated. 'Keep it for a rainy day.'

'I can't.'

'Why in hell not?'

'Because I owe you,' Belle argued, 'and I want to settle up.'

It seemed decidedly ironic that no one appeared to want the money she had so carefully scrimped and saved to return to them. It was difficult to make Nuncie realise this was something she *must* do, but until she cleared this debt in particular she'd never feel at ease. Beholden to a friend's compassion. Or worse, her charity.

'It's only a bloody tenner.'

It makes me a hostage, Belle thought, but she couldn't say that. Nuncie seemed visibly upset, refilling her own glass and instantly drinking half of it. 'No strings, Belle. God almighty, I've been working like a dog since I left school, and for what? I'm going to be fifty any minute. If I can't give you a few lousy quid, what's the point of me busting a gut to earn it? Who else is there, for Christ's sake?'

Belle could hear the sound of the piano below, Teddy picking out the melody of a favourite Irish song, 'Danny Boy'. She wished she could join him and escape this increasingly uncomfortable conversation.

'I could make things so much easier for you.' Nuncie swilled down the rest of her wine as if to bolster her nerve. 'You know I could. You don't have to go on scraping a living in that shitty room —'

'Nuncie, please —'

'Bugger it, I've been wanting to say this for months, ever since you walked into the shop and back into my life again.'

'Nuncie —' Belle knew this was why she'd kept away for so long. She wondered how to prevent her continuing and possibly ruining their friendship.

'For God's sake, will you listen? Please, darling, listen . . . let me say this. Why not move in here, you and Teddy. There's stacks of space for all of us. He'd have his own room. I could get the boys to lug that piano upstairs and put it in there. He could take music lessons —'

'Stop it.'

'Don't try to run away from this,' she said reproachfully. 'I want to help you. Just to share digs, that's all I mean – nothing else. I know there can't be anything else. I wouldn't dream of asking, because I know the answer. Share a home, have a sort of life together, be friends. Isn't that possible?'

'We *are* friends,' Belle said, unable to extricate herself from this situation without causing pain. She was vaguely aware the sound of the piano had stopped. She wanted to say it was getting late – time to take Teddy back to their shitty room. But that would sound like trying to escape. 'We'll always be friends, Nuncie.'

'What's the fucking use?' Nuncie declared bitterly. She picked up her glass, and finding there was no wine in it, suddenly flung it against the wall, where it smashed and scarred the wallpaper. Tears began to disfigure her face.

'We both know it's hopeless,' she wept. 'We know you'd rather not move in with a lesbian ratbag like me.'

'That's a bloody stupid thing to say,' Belle answered, and began to pick up the broken pieces of glass.

'I'm a bloody stupid old tart,' came the embittered reply, 'who happens to love you.'

Don't, Belle wanted to plead, please don't, or you'll make it impossible for us from now on. She had always known Nuncie had these feelings for her; it was one of the reasons she'd been loath to approach her for help. In the past, on the rare times Nuncie's sexual attachment had surfaced, it was always raised in fun and dismissed with a laugh or a shrug of self-mockery. Not this time.

'I can't hide it. I don't see why I should. It's no crime to love someone.'

Neither of them was aware of Teddy at the open door. 'Who do you love, Nuncie?' They both turned, disconcerted by a pair of puzzled brown eyes regarding them.

'Why, you of course, my ducky,' Nuncie responded instinctively.

'How could you mean me,' he said, 'when you were talking to Mum?'

'So I was, my small friend with big ears. You're quite right. I was telling your mum how I love her – just like a sister.'

'If you were her sister,' he said, solemnly considering the ramifications of this, 'you'd be my auntie.'

'I wish I was,' Nuncie said, 'since I love you both. But that's not to be, my darling, so let's all stay the way we are – the best of best friends. And between us, we'll look after your mum. She needs a bit of looking after, don't you agree?'

Teddy thought Nuncie's eyes looked suspiciously moist. He knew she cried easily, and looked as if she might start again at any minute. So he agreed they would both look after his mum.

In the Supreme Court the Crown rested its case with an air of complacency. The accused, Karel Janacek, was a known foreign subversive. The Attorney-General, Robert Menzies, had ordered his arrest as an illegal immigrant after Janacek had failed the dictation test. His Honour Justice Fulton, known for his strong views on dissidents, would certainly find him guilty. He would be imprisoned and then deported back to Prague in Czechoslovakia. Everyone knew it was a formality. All those in court suspected his barrister, Donald Ferrier KC, felt the same.

'Mr Ferrier.' The judge looked down at him. 'I suggest this is a suitable time to adjourn for lunch. Are you calling defence witnesses this afternoon?'

'No, Your Honour. I merely wish to address the court on my client's behalf.'

The Crown felt celebratory. Their success was guaranteed. His Honour was quietly content; this surely meant there would be time for a round of golf later. Ferrier declined lunch with his junior counsel or the advising solicitor, preferring to have sandwiches in his chambers while reviewing the tactics of the afternoon.

In fact, over the sandwiches his thoughts were more occupied with the personal subject that had perplexed him for so long. Even more lately, he found himself puzzling about whether it had really been her, and if so, what had she wanted? Why seek him out after all these years? And why did she flee after such a wait? There was the crux of it – that two-hour wait. It could hardly have been a stranger. Nor a contemporary friend, who would surely have left her name. And if it really was Belle, there was another conundrum: how in the hell could he find her?

Damn the woman, he almost said aloud, trying to dismiss her from his mind and concentrate on the case. His client was a Czech writer, invited to Australia to speak at anti-fascist rallies, who had barely landed before he was declared *persona non grata* by the conservative Lyons Government. The case bristled with high-handed tactics by the Attorney-General, which might not stand scrutiny in more generous times. But freedom of speech seemed to depend upon who the speaker was and Judge Fulton, as stern on the bench as he was jovial in the secrecy of the Foundation Club, would have no difficulty with this one.

Unless . . .

Somewhere Donald felt sure there was a precedent. The walls of his chambers were lined with law books, the dry-as-dust legalese contained in bound volumes like Hennessy's law reports. Though it would hardly be dry if he could find what he sought, if he was able to dig out a particular precedent, a High Court judgement on a dictation test, which, if memory served him, was surely in the 1925 folio edition. He took it down from the shelf, and as he opened the pages a photograph fell out.

A snapshot of Belle taken on a ferry ride. She was perched on the bow rail, no doubt in defiance of marine regulations, smiling directly at the camera, her long dark hair framing her animated face. He stared at the photo as his memories of the day flooded back. They were on board a Manly ferry, after an afternoon spent in a harbourside private hotel making love. A long and passionate afternoon, during which the rather shabby room had seemed like an enchanted honeymoon suite.

It was the day that he'd promised to marry her.

Belle watched Teddy fondly, absorbed and gripping the pencil as he tried to write a reply to the letter from George that had arrived the previous day. The letter had pleased him, for while it was spare on news, it was complimentary about the way Teddy's writing and spelling showed an improvement.

Obviously it's a better school, and your teacher must be satisfied with your progress, he had written, after devoting much of the letter to town events and how he had attended the Musical Society with the new neighbours Jim and Betty Nelson who'd taken the Lucas house, and Betty's younger sister Maureen, a widow who had now come to live permanently with them. The show they'd seen was the local production of *Rio Rita*, and he told Teddy that lots of people at the performance had stopped him to say what a pity Belle wasn't still here because she could've starred in it.

'No, thank you,' she'd replied when Teddy read this aloud.

'But you could have, Mum. You were in that show when it was on at the Theatre Royal.'

I was in the chorus, she thought, but merely shook her head and said it was different, and she might be a bit old for the part now. Frankly, she doubted if anyone had even mentioned her name, and was certain the amateurs at the Gundagai School of Arts would never cast her in anything, but it was considerate of George, and Teddy believed it, which was the main thing.

She wondered about Maureen, whose name had appeared in two recent letters, both times mentioned as being widowed. She hoped Maureen was nice, not too tied by convention. Perhaps even liberated enough to sneak next door for an occasional cuddle after dark, when the vigilant eyes of Miss Limmington could no longer monitor the street. The idea made Belle smile. Without having met the widow she'd neatly paired them off together. But, after all, why not? There seemed to be a hint of a message in his letters – and George deserved someone to keep him warm at nights.

Imagining this, while trying to repair Teddy's school trousers, concerned that they were now slightly small for him and soon there'd be the expense of a new pair, made her reflect again about

George and the crisis she'd have to resolve one day. The prospect of having to confess he was not really Teddy's dad was daunting; it filled her with a sense of dread. She hardly knew how she'd manage to explain, or how he'd take it. Next month he would be eleven. Each time she prevaricated, every week that passed, was making this decision more difficult.

But, on the other hand, must she really confess? After all, George could be relied upon to support the facade. He had done so all these years, and he relished his role as Teddy's father.

So why tell her son the truth, if the truth would be so painful?

Caroline had a bridge four in the living room when Donald Ferrier reached home, and the children were playing on the swing in the garden. It was the opportunity he needed to talk to Mrs Abbott. He went into the kitchen, where she was preparing dinner. While he poured himself a gin, she brought him a bottle of tonic from the refrigerator.

'I heard on the wireless, sir, you got that communist off.'

The housekeeper was an avid listener, ever since Caroline had bought her a mantel set. No scrap of news or information escaped Mrs Abbott.

'He's not actually a communist,' Donald said, attempting to be amicable.

'Mr Menzies said he is.'

'Mr Menzies sometimes uses it as a pejorative term. All those who aren't with us are obviously against us, and therefore Marxists.'

'Commos,' she said, reducing it to her terms.

He allowed her the small victory, and sipped his drink, reliving the day's triumph while she cleaned the vegetables. When he felt properly relaxed he took the photograph from his pocket.

'By the way, Mrs Abbott, I was clearing out some files in my chambers and found this. It's a photo of a former client, used as evidence in a law case some years ago. Could you identify it?'

He watched her as the housekeeper gazed at the photograph of Belle with an instant recognition. 'It's her,' Mrs Abbott said. 'A bit younger in this, but it's definitely her. No doubt about it.'

'Well, that seems to solve our mystery,' he said. 'Just as well I wasn't home that night; she was an impulsive and difficult client.'

She handed it back, with a raised eyebrow that betrayed her cynicism. Found it in his files, her look seemed to say. How very convenient.

The bridge players stayed late; when the children were called in for their dinner Donald remained sitting in the garden. It had been an extraordinary day: first of all finding the photo of Belle hidden in the pages of Hennessy, proof at last of his nocturnal visitor. He could recall how the undeveloped film had remained in his camera for so long, and by the time it was processed he was engaged to Caroline. Clearly he had chosen a safe hiding place, then forgotten about it.

How strange the Hennessy folio had disclosed not only Belle but the ruling he needed: the precedent of 1925. And what a moment to savour: the court half empty, most of those remaining convinced the case was over, Fulton anxious to pass sentence and be off to the golf course. The old bugger had thought it would be a formality, Donald remembered, thinking of the judge's attitude as he spoke.

'Your Honour, the accused is charged as an illegal immigrant, yet he holds a valid passport. He was invited here by an anti-war group to speak, and whatever we might think of such groups, they are not yet illegal in this country. He intended to return to Europe when his speaking tour was over. Instead he finds himself faced with a term in prison and then deportation, all because of a technicality in the Immigration Restriction Bill. Because he failed our dictation test. It is a device used almost nowhere else in the world, acknowledged as a means of preserving the White Australia Policy, and in this case applied quite unlawfully to discredit a person whom the Federal Government dislikes for his political views —'

'Mr Ferrier.' Judge Fulton had looked down with unmistakeable frostiness. 'If this is to be a tirade against government policy, I don't think I can allow it or you to continue.'

'I apologise, Your Honour, but the point I wish to make concerns a rush to judgement by the federal authorities, indeed a rush so hasty that in their anxiety to prosecute they made a serious error in law.'

'Please explain that to the court, since none of us appears to have noticed.'

'Thank you, Your Honour.' He proceeded as though oblivious to the judge's sarcasm. 'The dictation test is often used on Asian and African people, who are tested in European languages, selecting one they cannot speak in order to exclude them as illiterate. But my client, Mr Janacek, is fluent in German, French, English, of course, also Italian, Russian, Greek, Swedish and Dutch. I have a list of other tongues and dialects he is competent in, if Your Honour would like it read.'

'I think we can assume the accused is exceptionally multilingual, Mr Ferrier. Where exactly are you taking us, in this recitation of his accomplishments?'

'To what I might call the heart of the matter, Your Honour. To the dictation test. Since it was apparent he might pass any normal test in any of the languages usually chosen, the test was conducted in Scottish Gaelic.'

'A difficult language, you're suggesting, are you, Mr Ferrier?'

There had been some smirks at the prosecution table. His Honour was having a bit of fun at counsel's expense.

'Not only difficult. An *illegal language*, Judge,' Donald Ferrier had replied, and noticed how the sly glee in court turned to sudden disquiet. 'If Your Honour pleases, I offer a precedent for your consideration. On appeal in the High Court, the Commonwealth against Carlos Antonio, 1924.' He read from the judgement. '"We find that Scottish Gaelic is not a listed language within the meaning of the Act, and its use in a dictation test is therefore unlawful."'

He could still see Justice Fulton's annoyance as he tersely allowed the accused his freedom. He doubted if the old boy would be quite so cordial at the next meeting of the Foundation Club.

'You look pleased with yourself,' Caroline said, joining him in the garden as her friends drove away. 'Mrs Abbott says you got your "commo" off.'

'A trenchant foe of all foreigners, that woman.'

'I won at bridge.'

'Well done.'

'Makes a change. Mrs A says you showed her a photograph.'

He nodded, knowing this would happen. He took it from his pocket and handed it to her. She gazed at it, then shrugged as if unsurprised.

'She was beautiful in those days. What exactly was Belle doing here, while I was in Adelaide?'

'I haven't the faintest, Caro.'

'Have you been seeing her?'

'Don't be ridiculous. Your source in the kitchen must've told you

I was out that night. I didn't even know who it was, until I happened to find this.'

'Happened to find it?'

'For Christ's sake, it fell out of a law book.'

'And how did it get in the law book? It's interesting to know that all these years you kept a photo of her.'

'I can't discuss this, if you're going to be so fucking stupid,' he said.

'Don't use that language around our house, Donald. It'd be a fine thing if the children heard you.'

She gave him back the photo. He tore it in half, walked to the incinerator and dropped it in there.

'She wouldn't like that,' Caroline said.

Chapter twenty-one

It was an impulse that made Belle leave the tram at Kings Cross one day and call at the shop to see Helene LaRue again. Which was how she heard that Ross Tanner had come there asking about her. Not just once, but almost every time he was in the vicinity. Soon after Belle and Teddy had left Kellett Street, she learnt from Helene, Ross had gone there unsuspectingly, and received an acid reception from the landlady. She told him she hadn't the faintest idea of Mrs Carson's whereabouts, nor did she wish to know. Possibly she'd returned to the country to be reconciled with her husband like any decent woman should, was the terse message before the front door was shut in his face.

'Heavens,' Belle said, 'nothing ever changes with that sour old prune, does it? Why does she hate me so much?'

'You were happy. Madame Burch, she don't like it when people have a big *amour* like you and Ross. Many times since then he comes here asking for you.'

'But you didn't tell him where to find me?'

'I think to discuss with you first. In case it's over. So I tell him you haven't left any address yet. Each time I tell him the same. Was it wrong?'

'No,' Belle said, 'not wrong, Helene.'

'*C'est la vie*,' Helene said with a little shrug, and they both smiled. 'Now sit down, have a coffee and tell me all about Teddy. Any more films for him to make? Or is he at school?'

They spent a companionable hour together between customers, during which Belle realised how much she missed the ambience of Kings Cross. If it had bitches like Ma Burch, it also had friends like Helene and Chrissie LaRue.

That night she thought carefully about Ross, and the following morning before work she went to the boarding house opposite the courts in Rushcutters Bay. After she pressed the doorbell, she had a moment of unreasoning panic and wanted to flee. But before she could decide whether to announce herself or run, she heard his voice on the speaker.

'Miranda?'

'No, sorry about that. I'm not Miranda,' Belle said, and wondered what to do as a barely stifled reaction was followed by the sound of the buzzer unlocking the front door. She went up the familiar winding staircase to the first floor, and he was there on the landing waiting for her. She felt the warmth of his embrace. When they went into his room, she could not help contemplating the bed that had been their playground.

'Belle, for Christ's sake, where have you been?'

'Running away, darling,' she said.

'Why?'

'Because I discovered I'm definitely too old for you.'

'When did that happen?' he asked, and she had an answer rehearsed, one that she hoped would allow them both to retain their dignity.

'When I met someone my own age,' she replied.

'You what? Truly?'

She nodded and managed a smile, trying not to feel upset by the fleeting glimpse of relief he had been unable to suppress. It was replaced by a frown, as though to imply disappointment. He put his arms around her again, but this time kissed her chastely on the cheek. 'All a bit sudden, Belle.'

'That's how it sometimes is, Ross.' She leant against him to hide from his scrutiny. 'And when you get to my advanced age, if it's the real thing you grab it.'

'Your advanced age . . . that's ridiculous. Besides, I thought we were the real thing.'

'Very nearly, darling. I'll always remember you fondly, I promise.'

'Is . . . whoever it is . . . is he anyone I know?' When she shook her head, he added, 'Well, I'm glad it's not one of those phoney old goats from Kellett Street.'

She stepped back from his embrace and laughed at this. 'Fair go, my love. I can do a bit better than that.'

'I'm sure you can,' he said.

'And you'll find someone else.'

'Maybe.' He shrugged, as if doubtful of this.

'You certainly will,' Belle assured him, 'or perhaps you already have, if her name's Miranda,' she added, and laughed at his expression.

'Miranda's a nice girl,' he said, 'but it's not permanent.'

'Well, there'll be someone. No doubt of that.' She hesitated. 'As for us, I hope we'll both remember our good times together. Because what I want to say is, I'm awfully glad I met you.'

'I'll never forget you,' he said, and indicated the nude figurine of her. 'As if I could. You're there on the table to remind me every day. In fact I think Miranda is sometimes jealous.'

He wanted to walk her to the tram, but she declined. Belle was eager to leave before she made a complete fool of herself. He insisted on at least seeing her down the stairs.

'That bitch of a landlady tried to say she kicked you out for refusing to pay the rent, which I knew had to be a lie. Then Mrs LaRue explained you'd been cheated by Teddy's agent.'

'Yes, he did a moonlight. It was a bit awkward,' Belle told him, 'but it's all sorted out.'

'Are you sure?'

'Of course, darling.'

'Why the hell didn't you come and ask me for a loan?'

'I would've, but I believe in the old rule,' she said, 'never borrow from relatives or lovers. Especially lovers.'

She kissed him, a brief kiss as chaste as his had been, and hurried off. When she was about to turn the corner, she glanced back. He was still at the door watching her; he raised a hand in farewell, and when she returned the wave he went back inside.

The letter in the mail came the following day. It was waiting when she came home from work. Teddy had brought it upstairs after school. The writing on the envelope was neat but unfamiliar.

My dear Belle,

It may be arrogance, but I did not believe your older lover story. I think things have been much tougher than you admitted, but you're not given to complaining so I'll never know how bad it's been. Now don't you dare be upset about this. I don't trust letters not to be opened by scruffy landlords, so I've sent twenty pounds to the post office at Mascot for your collection. All you need to do is identify yourself and it's there waiting.

Now before you blow a gasket, if you don't collect it then the post office is twenty quid richer, which would seriously upset me. And upset you, if you think carefully about it! The money is in payment for modelling. I didn't tell you yesterday, but I was

*offered FIFTY POUNDS for you in the nude. But I'll never part
with it. (With you, is what I mean.) If you won't take the money
for yourself, then it's for Teddy, because I went around to Helene's
shop yesterday after you left, and found out the film business is
in bad shape. She thinks, and I agree, that you're having a hell of
a battle to survive, so this comes with my affection and respect,
as well as my love. And before you start thinking it's charity, just
remember it's only the ill-gotten gains from two Saturday arvos'
illegal work for my SP bookie. Now stop complaining, my darling,
and get thee to the post office.*

God bless and much love,
Ross

Late that night when Teddy was asleep, Belle sat in bed and
penned a reply.

Dearest Ross,

*You are a bugger. Not for this mad, generous, ridiculous gesture,
but for making me cry. I shed bucketfuls, which is my custom when
I'm moved and happy. All those months we had together was a
lovely time in my life – it is difficult to think of one better – and for
that and what awaits me at the post office, thank you. Take care.
Find someone really nice, and have a wonderful life.*

With all my love,
Belle

Chapter twenty-two

The dance studio in Oxford Street alongside the Victoria Hotel was just the same. The slight smell of stale beer, the comfortably shabby building and continuous rumble of traffic all held the same excitement for Teddy as they arrived and Greta Torrance was there to meet them, giving him a hug and introducing him and Belle to new pupils as if she were displaying a trophy. Only Sally was missing from this day he'd been awaiting so eagerly, so it was not really the same. The thought of a reunion with Sally was what had kept him awake at nights, ever since Belle had told him things had changed for the better and he would be going back to Miss Torrance's Saturday dance classes.

But where is she, he wondered? None of the other students seemed to be sure, no one had seen Sally Sharp lately. Not for weeks. One thought she was ill, another claimed she'd given up dancing. Broke her ankle, so that was the end of her, a girl who had always been her fiercest rival said without sympathy. When the session was over he braced himself to ask Miss Torrance.

It was none of those things. It was worse. Her mother had remarried, and moved away from Roslyn Gardens to a different sphere altogether, across the harbour to Mosman. Miss Torrance didn't know if Sally was attending another dance studio. And no, she didn't know the new address either. She and Eunice Sharp, who by now would have a new name, had not parted on friendly terms.

Teddy silently wondered if Sally had a new name as well.

Dan Hardacre heard the phone ringing in the adjoining office, but he knew there was no one there to answer it. His secretary had been paid-off the previous day. She was one of the last to leave, except for the girl on the switchboard, who had been told to put all incoming calls through to him. After all, who else remained in the place to answer the telephone? It was almost the sole responsibility still left to him, he thought ironically as he picked up the receiver. He had started in the film business as a messenger boy who helped answer phones, and his career with its few prestigious and well-paid years as a producer appeared now to have come full circle and back to square one.

'United Films,' he said.

'I've already been told that.' The male voice sounded thoroughly impatient. 'I've been told it several times. I want to speak with Mr Hardacre, and I seem to be having the greatest difficulty in doing that.'

'Well, you've got him.'

'Got who? What do you mean? Is that Dan?'

'It is,' he said brusquely, 'so the next question is, who are you?'

'A voice from the past,' the other said. 'Donald Ferrier.'

'Christ, you can say that again,' Dan replied, startled a man he had known years ago and read about in newspapers only recently should be phoning him after so long. 'You seem to have been making a name for yourself in a wig and gown these days.'

'Trying to,' Donald Ferrier said.

'Got some Czech agitator out of bother, against the wishes of Bob Menzies. Surprised me, that. I thought you and the Attorney-General would be in the same rowboat, politically speaking. What do you want, Donald?'

'I was going to ask you to lunch today.'

'Me? Lunch?'

'If you can make it. I hope I haven't interrupted a meeting. I gather it's one of the functions of your game, meetings. Or maybe you're busy with whatever else you do there – casting a starlet on the couch, perhaps?' His slight chuckle at this irritated Dan immensely.

'I should be so lucky! The couches have been repossessed by the liquidators, and the starlets have all gone back to Central Casting or their sugar daddies. I'm afraid we're deprived of the rather mythical producer shack-up. You did say lunch?'

'If it's convenient.'

'Just a moment and I'll check.' Dan was determined it would not be *that* convenient. 'Let's see,' he murmured, as though there was a full diary at his side which had to be consulted, 'yes, I could manage that. I assume there's some particular purpose to this lunch?'

'Apart from anything else, it'd be rather nice to have a chat about old times. I thought that fish restaurant down on the harbour at Double Bay. That's in your neighbourhood. How does twelve-thirty sound?'

It sounds, Dan thought to himself as he hung up, extremely odd. Old times? We have no old times to talk about. You were a bastard then, and I imagine nothing's changed.

Donald Ferrier waited by his Daimler and watched his guest arrive, taking his time to lock his gaudy Italian sports tourer. It seemed to fit the Hardacre image that he remembered: all style and little else. He had often wondered how a woman like Belle could have seen anything attractive in such a shallow creature. A pretty ordinary actor; he had a recollection of an awful evening at the new North Sydney theatre, the Independent, taken there by Belle against his better judgement. Her former lover's performance had been an acute embarrassment. After that it was hardly surprising Dan had given up acting and diverted his modest talents to the film world.

'Good to see you again,' Donald said heartily, as they shook hands.

'Likewise,' Dan said, 'an unexpected pleasure.'

They went up the gangway to the restaurant, a moored ferry now doing duty as a select eatery for those able to afford it. After enquiring about each other's health, they ordered drinks. The refurbished ferry had become fashionable, known for its French chef and prominent clientele. Dan could not help but be impressed and envious at the warmth of welcome from the *maître d* when he greeted Donald and showed them to an upper-deck table with a view across the harbour towards Taronga Park. Yachts were sailing leisurely past, others lay at anchor along the shore, the sun was warm, the imported wine expensive, and for an agreeable moment it was almost possible to forget how much he disliked the barrister.

'So how's the film business?' Donald asked after they raised glasses, each repeating what a pleasure it was to meet up again like this, and sipped their drinks.

'Stuffed,' Dan replied. 'Our studio gates are locked, and the audit team is in residence to calculate what's left over for the creditors. It's a wonder the phones weren't disconnected.'

'That bad?' Donald showed his surprise.

'Worse. Empty offices and vacant sound stages, with all the lights and equipment stripped out. It's like a shipwreck, and I'm the only man left on deck. Captain of the *Titanic*.'

'But what's happened? Local films have done well, haven't they? I mean, *Dad and Dave* and *The Sentimental Bloke*, surely they were big hits.'

'Moderate hits,' Dan said. 'Popular here, but not promoted in America.'

'Even so. How can a complete industry take a dive like this?'

'Easily – if you're up against a giant that wants to crush the competition. The distributors, *our* local distributors, prefer to book Hollywood pictures. Their stars are bigger, their publicity is vast, American films are launched here with trumpets blaring, and the truth is, we can't compete with the fanfare. Our movies get second-rate releases, they get talked down by the newspaper critics, some of whom are following orders of their proprietors who have overseas interests. We're all quite pleased, but slightly abashed when one of our good old home movies actually does well.'

Donald listened intently. Listening was good tactics at this stage; he would get to his reason for the invitation later.

'Meanwhile, down in Canberra,' Dan continued, 'the dummies we elect as politicians talk of helping the film industry, but there's always something more important to spend our taxes on, like farm subsidies or a war.' He drank his wine and shrugged. 'Don't get me started. We had a good industry, and it's been allowed to go down the drain by a mixture of shady practice and indifference.'

'What about your job?'

'I'm a call away from unemployment. United Pictures wants to sell the whole shebang for development. When they ring from California to say they have a buyer for the land and buildings, that's when I go. I daresay that's why the lines are not disconnected yet.

"Will the last man to leave the studio please hang up the phone.'"

The waiter came and silently refilled their glasses. They studied the glossy menu and ordered. On Dan's copy the prices were diplomatically omitted. He drank more wine and pronounced it delicious.

'The vineyard's in Dordogne,' Donald said. 'My father-in-law imports this, so my wife and I visited there last year. Great spot.'

Of course, Dan remembered, the once-lowly lawyer had married money. Caroline had been rich, although none of them had known it at the time. She had been briefly on the stage, but mostly on the fringe of the theatrical scene, always at first nights, a regular in the city pubs and cafés where actors gathered. She had gravitated into their circle and had even for a time, he recalled, been a close friend of Belle's. He supposed that was how Ferrier had first met Caroline. Belle might have introduced them. A good-looking young woman, especially one who was wealthy, would have been the ideal answer to this prick's lofty ambitions. As gorgeous as Belle had been, she would have been well and truly outflanked in his push for a luxurious future.

'Did you hear what I said?'

'Sorry, I was remembering old times.'

'It's because of old times I need to talk to you,' Donald said. 'A very odd thing happened a few months ago, and I think I should tell you about it.'

He gave Dan only the essential details, the momentary glimpse he'd had, his housekeeper's statement on the visitor to his home. How he felt sure it was Belle, but there was no proof of it until the photograph. Now it was certain, he'd decided he ought to find her. There had to be a reason for her unexpected visit that night; something had driven her to seek him out, just as some other thing must've made her run away. He felt it incumbent on himself to discover what it had been about.

'Which is why I got in touch with you,' Donald concluded, 'because I thought you might help me.'

'How?'

'You may know where she is.'

Dan stared at him. 'You mean you want to meet up again with Belle, and you're buying me lunch in case I can put you on the right track?'

'Come off it, Dan. She hung around my house all that time, then skipped. That was pretty irrational behaviour, and I'm concerned about her. You're the only person I could think of who might still be in touch. And if you are, what's the problem? It's not such a big ask.'

'It's a very big ask, Donald. Too fucking big.'

'Are you saying you're not going to tell me? That's childish.'

'I'm saying I don't know where the hell she is nowadays. But if I did, I'd take a childish pleasure in sending you in the opposite direction.'

The waiter arrived with their lunch before Donald could reply. His anger was suspended while the meal was served, the waiter carving their salmon from a platter, offering them a choice of hot vegetables from a trolley or a salade niçoise or both. Then he took care to replenish their wine. By the time he retreated, trusting they would enjoy their meal, the anger had ebbed.

'Carrying an old grudge after all these years?' Donald commented. 'I don't see the reason. I didn't pinch your girl.'

'No, you didn't.'

'You and she were already breaking up. So why the resentment?'

'I wasn't Robinson Crusoe on this,' Dan said as he speared a grape tomato on his fork, 'all her friends resented you.'

'Because I wasn't an actor . . . wasn't one of them.'

'No. Because she fell in love with you – I mean properly in love – and you took everything she had to offer until someone else came along, someone who was social register and rich, then you dumped Belle. Left her flat. The silly girl thought it was forever, but she should've known better, shouldn't she?'

'I never promised to marry her.' He hoped the lie would pass unchallenged, which it did.

'Why should you? She was just a showgirl.'

'Christ,' Donald said, made more uncomfortable because he had been so easily believed, 'you make me sound like a real shit.'

'We all thought so at the time. It was unanimous.'

'Ouch! It wasn't entirely my fault, Dan.'

'Of course not. Belle could be a right pain in the arse at times.'

'There were other things involved. Things I'd rather not talk about.'

'So let's agree it's ancient history. Enjoy our meal.'

'Agreed. *Bon appétit.*'

The food was delicious. The first wine bottle was emptied and replaced so subtly they barely noticed. There was a dessert wine with the fruit and cheese, after which coffee was accompanied by a liqueur. When they left the restaurant somewhat later than planned, Dan Hardacre felt he might have been a bit severe in his former judgement. Old Donald was not so bad after all. Certainly knew some of the best restaurants, and chose a pretty decent drop of *vino*.

'You're not such an arsehole,' Dan said as they reached their cars. 'I mean, it takes a real ponce to drive a dreary English car like this, but apart from that . . .'

'Better a staid English car than a gaudy Italian job with a back seat that's extra wide for shagging,' Donald said.

'How did you guess?' Dan replied. 'It's well-known in Rome as a fuckmobile.'

'Excellent.' Donald started to laugh, 'And I have to tell you, I thought *you* were a prick, but I've reconsidered. There are a great many bigger pricks around the place than you.'

'You mean size doesn't matter? I'll take it as a compliment.'

Donald kept laughing and wondered why he had never liked Dan Hardacre. The fellow was quite pleasant when you got to know him. Amusing, and very entertaining with his scandalous gossip about various film stars he'd worked with. It had certainly been a most convivial lunch. 'We ought to do this again,' he said.

'My shout next time,' Dan said, 'unless I get a call from God on the west coast, and they fire me.'

'Then *I'll* buy lunch. We'll get pissed and drink damnation to the west-coast God and all his acolytes.'

They shook hands like old friends. Dan felt an impulse to make amends for his earlier hostility. 'Mate, forget what I said before. If I knew where to find Belle I'd tell you. But it's about six months since I last saw her – since then she's moved and never left an address —'

Donald, unlocking his car, turned and stared at him. 'You saw her? Where?'

'At the studio. She just turned up one day. But things were already going pear-shaped, and I told her there was no work —'

'Hang on, Dan, you mean she's been working? Acting?'

'No, not Belle. She hasn't been in anything for years. I mean the boy.'

'What boy?'

'Her son.'

'She has a kid?'

'I assumed you knew.'

'Not me. Not the faintest idea.'

'Young Teddy. Teddy Carson. He was in a film of ours – one of our better ones, *Dispossessed*.'

'I saw that picture.' Donald's face revealed his growing bewilderment. 'I took my children to see it. You mean that was Belle's son?'

'That was him. He's been in quite a few movies since then, but far smaller roles. Belle insists it keeps him in the public eye. She sees him as an Aussie Jackie Coogan. If you want my honest opinion, she's hanging rocks around that kid's head. He has to be a success because she never was. Has to be a star, poor little bugger, because she needs it. I don't know what's happened to them, but for the kid's sake I sometimes hope she's given up and taken him back home.'

'Where's home?'

'Gundagai. Her husband lives there . . . only I heard she'd left him.'

'How old is the boy?'

'I reckon he's close to eleven by now.'

Jesus Christ, Donald Ferrier thought. But he prided himself on his control, and all he did was nod and express his thanks for this extra information. He watched as Dan went to his flashy car and drove off with a wave.

Close to eleven! God almighty!

He sat there, feeling drained, unable to start the engine. He did his best to recall the boy's face from the screen, but all he could summon up was a cheeky grin, lots of appealing freckles and a mop of blond hair. Belle's son, close to eleven years old. He tried to calculate the timing, but his mind was befuddled with the wine from lunch and this seismic tremor from the past.

Chapter twenty-three

There were candles on the cake, and the living room above the shop was festive with balloons and paper chains. Teddy was dressed in the smart new trousers that Nuncie had bought him as a birthday present and a shirt Belle had purchased on lay-by. The assistants, Charles and Clarence – 'the boys', as Nuncie called them – were there and had put up the decorations. They all combined to sing 'Happy Birthday' as Belle lit the candles.

'Make a wish,' she said as Teddy blew them out and everyone applauded.

'I wish Dad was here. I wish he hadn't forgotten my birthday.'

'You're not supposed to tell us your wish, darling, or it mightn't come true.'

'It can't come true,' Teddy said.

'Part of it can.' She handed him an envelope. He saw at once it was addressed in George's handwriting. They all watched while he excitedly took out a card. It was clearly homemade, with a pastel drawing on the front of it.

'It's a picture of our place at home! Look!' Teddy showed them all the sketch of the house in Brewinda Road. 'Dad says Maureen who lives next door did it.'

'Good old Maureen.' Nuncie gave a sly glance at Belle. 'What else does it say, my duck? Read it out.'

'Dear Ted, lots of love on your eleventh birthday. It hardly seems any time since I was holding you soon after you were born, while your mum was saying "Be careful, don't drop him". I hear there's a party tonight, so if you go downstairs and out the back door, you might find something waiting that you'll recognise.'

He gave the card to Belle and ran down the stairs, through the shop. He opened the back door and stared in amazement. There was his bike from home, the wheels and pedals wrapped and the handlebars labelled for its train journey.

'Golly.' A sudden rush of love filled his throat and made him almost cry. 'Golly Moses. Whacko,' he said, and felt speechless.

Charlie and Clarence helped him unwrap the bike. They switched on the lights in the small backyard while Teddy rode it in the space available, just to show them he had not forgotten how. He said he was going to write to George as soon as he got up in the morning and tell him it was the bestest present ever. 'The boys' smiled at this and felt quite sentimental.

'There you are, my poppet,' Nuncie said, 'and you thought he'd forgotten.'

'It's a beaut surprise, and he's the world's beautest Dad. I can't wait to tell him.' He sped around the tiny space on his bike while Belle looked on and made no attempt to correct this joyous ineloquence.

Later they went inside the cluttered shop and she played one of the pianos for sale while they all sang old musical hall songs. Teddy made them laugh with 'Burlington Bertie', and they all joined in a rousing chorus of a familiar favourite:

I do like to be beside the seaside,
Oh, I do like to be beside the sea!

I do like to stroll along the prom, prom, prom,
While the brass band plays tiddleyyompompom!
Oh, just let me be beside the seaside,
I'll be beside myself with glee.
There are lots of girls, besides,
That I'd like to be beside,
Beside the seaside, beside the sea.

Nuncie sang with robust happiness. It was like a dispensation. In the past weeks she had begun to fear her long friendship with Belle had been irreparably damaged. Meetings had become infrequent and when they did meet conversation was stilted; they kept to safe subjects like Teddy's return to dancing lessons, and Belle's decision to shorten her hours at the hotel so she could spend time trying to find work for him. It was a waste to let his childhood go by, she declared, his talent stifled when all it would take was one small lucky break. Nuncie dared not suggest lucky breaks were not that easily come by, that perhaps education was of equal importance. All their exchanges were imbued with caution; there was a wariness on both sides, as if the wrong word could fracture everything. There were no hugs, none of the warm spontaneity that had always marked their relationship. Ever since that night – when flushed with wine she'd opened her big mouth – it had been like walking on eggshells.

Until a week ago, when Belle had rung from a public phone in Botany, saying it was the only box that hadn't been smashed by the bunch of little thugs in the district who masqueraded as children.

'Nuncie, he's going to be eleven and I want to give him a small party. When I say small, I mean just us. He wants you there, and so do I. But our room's a dump, and the landlord's an awful creep who'd probably complain if we wanted to sing, so I thought it'd be nice if we could do it at your place.'

'It'd be *very* nice!' She'd been elated, unable to conceal her eagerness. 'But I want to be allowed to pay for the party. And I want to buy him a pair of new trousers, because those duds are getting far too small. That's all I want, and I'm praying you won't give me any shit, Belle.'

There'd been a moment's silence on the line, then her laughter. 'I won't give you any shit,' Belle had promised.

Nuncie smiled, thinking of it. Paying for the party indeed! It was purely symbolic, for the only cost was the cake, the candles, a few sandwiches and the decorations. But the symbolism had harvested a reward worth far more than the money. They could be friends again. As if in celebration she sang loudly, slightly out of tune, she realised, but it didn't matter. Happiness was what mattered. Belle hit the keys harder, harmonising with her to blend their voices and Nuncie saw her smile, looking just like she did when she was everyone's darling and only twenty years old.

> I do like to stroll along the prom, prom, prom,
> While the brass band plays tiddleyyompompom!

When it was almost time to go home Teddy climbed on one of the tables to gain their attention.

'I just want to say thanks to Nuncie. It's been a corker night – and this is for her. It's a verse from the book she gave me written by her friend Ken Slessor, about Kings Cross, which is a place my mum likes best in the whole world. And I quite like it too.'

They smiled indulgently as he cleared his throat, bowed and began:

Where the black Marias clatter
And peculiar ladies nod,
And the flats are rather flatter,
And the lodgers rather odd,
Where the night is full of dangers,
And the darkness full of fear,
And eleven hundred strangers
Live on Aspirin and beer.

'Wait on!' he said hurriedly as they began to clap. 'Here's another beaut one by Mr Slessor. It's about the Cross too.'

Where the stars are lit by neon,
Where the fried potato fumes,
And the ghost of Mr Villon
Still inhabits single rooms.
Where the girls lean out from heaven
Over light wells, thumping mops
While the gent in fifty-seven
Cooks his pound of mutton chops.

Clarence and Charles applauded heartily, and Nuncie hugged him and shed a few joyful tears.

Belle sent a note to Teddy's school saying he had to stay home because of a sore throat, and they caught a tram into the city. For the past month since his birthday there had been a series of such excuses while they attended theatrical auditions, though without any success. After each failure Belle kept repeating her mantra that they mustn't be downhearted, but Teddy sometimes thought it was difficult not to be.

He knew – it had been ingrained in him since he was eight – that he must be animated and optimistic at interviews; no job was ever gained, no role ever won by being what Belle called 'tentative'. But how would he get another job? Nearly all his work had been in films and many of the studios had closed down or turned to making newsreels. Theatre and vaudeville was different, unfamiliar territory, and although he tried his best he began to lose heart, feeling as if they were wasting days and tram fares in a vain pursuit of something that was beyond him.

The audition room, part of a disused warehouse in Sussex Street, was full of hopefuls. Belle knew how to deal with this; she took a firm grip of Teddy's hand and began to carefully edge her way, promoting them closer to the front before a queue started to form. She glanced about her to see if there were others of his age, doing what she called 'her homework on the opposition', while he looked in vain for any sign of Sally. It was the first thing he did at all the auditions they attended, but without a real expectation of seeing her. She had a new stepfather, which meant she had a new name, and now lived in a place called Mosman that seemed so remote it felt like another country.

Belle collected news of auditions at the studio on Saturday mornings, where Greta always had a copy of the entertainment paper *This Week*. While Teddy danced, she scrutinised the advertisements. RICKY M was a name she recognised; CASTING A NEW REVUE was the information in a boxed classified on the back page.

Ricky M was Ricardo Mendoza, an immigrant from South America. Nobody quite knew which part. Peru, some said. Or Bolivia. Or one of those places. Rumours abounded that he chose never to deny: he'd been a dancer in a whorehouse, served a prison term in Rio, worked as a deckhand on a Chilean freighter and as a gigolo in Paris. Whatever the truth, it was known that after arriving in Australia he had found a job as a sparring partner in a tent show, and when the promoter struck financial trouble he'd borrowed the money to buy it. Now he had a house in Vaucluse with harbour views, where he lived in apparent harmony with his wife and a young Filipina mistress. He was known in the business as a tightwad who paid his performers peanuts, but his credit was good and his cheques had never bounced.

'Bella!' He caught her eye and greeted them, taking her hands. '*Cara* Bella, and the boy, the *chico*. How fast he grows up, the young *muchacho*, eh? Getting older.'

She was unsure how to respond to this. Whenever the subject of Teddy's age was raised, she could hear Florian's voice: 'He's ten. A star when he was eight. Support roles when he was nine. He's a talented kid whose time may possibly be over.' She knew there was a grain of truth in his warning. Each added year, she was uneasily aware, took him that bit further away from the freckle-faced Murrumbidgee Kid who had enchanted audiences and captured so many hearts. Growing up, she admitted reluctantly to herself, was not necessarily an advantage.

'Not that much older, Ricky. He's only ten.'

She felt Teddy tug at her skirt and wished she could tell him to be quiet. 'Eleven, Mum!'

Ricky Mendoza laughed, and affectionately ruffled Teddy's hair. 'You see, *cara*? Even if you wish it, you can't keep him in the cradle. Soon he has long trousers and starts to shave.'

'That's a fair distance off.' She tried to be casual, knowing he had an eye for her, indeed for any woman, and flirting a little would hold his attention while she made her pitch. 'I happened to hear about your new show. Big news as always, another spectacular by Ricky M. As we were coming to town, I thought we should drop in.

Besides, it's always nice to catch up with you.'

He smiled as if in accord with this. He had a strong face, with dark intense eyes and a mane of hair that was always perfectly groomed and turning silver. A handsome man, who had been lucky and become powerful. She could well believe the stories about him enjoying a *ménage à trois* with his Australian wife and the Filipina girlfriend. Plus a few liaisons on the side, no doubt.

'Always good to see you, *mi querida*.'

His assistants were waiting for him, he was about to move away. Belle felt herself forced to ask the question. 'This new show – anything in it for him, Rick?'

'Not this one, *cara*. Maybe next time . . . but, hey —' He stopped as if some important detail had just occurred to him.

'What?'

'Make sure you keep in touch.'

'Of course,' she said, swallowing the disappointment.

'What I mean is, you could call me. Any time you feel like it. Why not?' He gave her a visiting card from his wallet. She knew the number on it was a very private line, but not his home number.

'*Hasta la vista, chico*.' He ruffled Teddy's hair again, smiled at Belle with a sly conspiracy and returned to where the assistants were organising interviews. Belle almost pushed her way out of the crowded room. It was a small humiliation, but she felt angry about the affront. Ricky Mendoza was notorious for his cards and this tactic; calling him on this private phone number would indicate her availability as well as her consent. He never had to risk a possible rejection. If the phone didn't ring, there was always another card, another caller. She tore it up and flung it in the gutter.

———•◦•———

Donald Ferrier waited while the French woman served customers, wondering if his car was safe where he had parked it. It seemed to him the Cross was no longer the same as he remembered it. He had come to know it through meeting Belle, when she shared a room with a bunch of other girls from the chorus, and then it had seemed wonderfully outrageous, both romantic and stimulating. But the best-known artists and poets had moved from cheap bedsitters to the sanctuary of apartments in Macleay Street. Underworld figures from interstate had moved into the network of streets that surrounded Darlinghurst Road, hard men who carried guns but preferred razors, recruited by two rival women gang leaders.

Donald had a close acquaintance with both these ferocious ladies, having appeared in court for Tilly Devine, the vice queen who ran the district's brothels, defending her on a charge of maliciously wounding a lover. Despite her record of dozens of criminal charges for assault, consorting and prostitution, he managed to convince the jury there was insufficient evidence and she was acquitted. Apart from paying his fee she wanted to reward him: she suggested a week in a luxury hotel suite, as well as providing her youngest and prettiest girls to indulge his every whim.

When he declined on the grounds that his wife might maliciously wound him, she had roared with laughter, and sent him a card and a massive hamper for Christmas. But there was no hamper or even a card the following year after he defended her *bête noire*, the sly grog queen Kate Leigh, on a murder charge. The two women loathed each other, and Tilly was livid when Kate was found not guilty. Donald heard Tilly had thrown a lavish party at her house in Palmer Street, the invitation reading 'Anyone invited except the bitch and her counsel, that turncoat bastard Ferrier'.

Helene LaRue finished with her last customer and apologised for keeping him waiting. He apologised for bothering her, but he was hoping to get in touch with a friend, Belle Carson.

Mrs LaRue apologised again. No doubt the awful landlady from number forty-two had sent him to her, but she'd wasted the gentleman's time. Her friend Belle had failed to leave a forwarding address. But could she have his name, just in case Belle should get in touch again?

Donald drove across the bridge. He didn't believe her, but there was little he could do about it. Dan Hardacre would be disappointed that his first suggestion had proved fruitless. He had telephoned to say the dreaded phone call had come from Hollywood. They'd actually sold the studio to another film company, instead of a developer, but his services were no longer required.

He asked if Donald had made any progress in finding Belle, because if not, Dan had been lucky enough to come across her former address when clearing out his office, and while he'd like to help Donald for old times' and friendship's sake, he was actually in a spot of bother with his bank. And also with his rent, because his penthouse in Elizabeth Bay cost an arm and a leg, which had been fine while the salary was coming in, but was rather a problem now that things were so different. Would Donald be able to assist him, if he assisted Donald?

Donald, who halfway through this peroration had got the picture, offered to pay a hundred quid if the information led him to locate her. He had begun to realise his new friend Dan was on very thin financial ice.

Dan had replied that he was thinking of a higher figure. 'A far higher figure, old mate,' he added.

'One hundred is the *only* figure – and only payable if it helps me find her.'

So Dan had given in and suggested if she wasn't traceable through the address at the Cross, then he should try a woman called Nuncie Billingsworth who ran a hock shop at Neutral Bay.

After leaving the audition room they walked along Sussex Street in the direction of The Rocks, past the old cottages that had once been homes for sea captains, and went down the steps by Argyle Cut towards Circular Quay.

'Do I have to go back to school today?' Teddy asked.

The harbour was spread below them like a Conrad Martens canvas. Ferries, small and large, were arriving and departing from the busy wharves at the quay. Belle held his hand while they paused to watch the activity for a moment. It had always been a restorative sight, this lively maritime gateway. If she felt the morning wasted, and Ricky Mendoza's overture an insult to her, she realised that for Teddy it was another disturbing disappointment. There'd been a plethora of them, one wretched let-down after another. A regular mare's nest of them. He tried not to complain, but she knew it was having an affect. The fear of failure was like a darkening shadow that went with them each time they made the long tram ride home after a day like this.

'Let's go to the zoo,' Belle suggested.

'Mum, can we afford it?'

She looked down at his anxious face. It was a shock to realise a child – her own child – had to ask questions like that. He'd once asked George the same thing. Some things, she thought, we bloody well have to afford.

'Don't you want to see the lions and tigers? As well as the

monkeys. And what about the giraffes, and the aquarium where the sharks are fed?'

'You bet, but —'

'But nothing. We're going.'

'Truly?'

'On the ferry, what's more. Such a beautiful day, we should forget about trams and take the ferry.'

'Can we sit outside, up the front end?'

'Wherever you like, my love.'

'Do you think we could have some chips to eat?'

'We'll definitely have chips. Chips for lunch on the ferry ride. Now, do you think you can remember what happens when we buy them?'

'We ask for two threepenny packets. We get more than way.'

'That's my smart boy,' she said, and as they walked they began to match the tempo of each other's steps, swinging their clasped hands in lively expectation.

'Do they have elephants at the zoo?'

'They certainly do. You want to have a ride on one?'

'Can I, Mum? Truly?'

'Truly, darling. But I'll just watch from the ground, if you don't mind.'

'A ride on a real elephant. You bottler! Whacko-the-diddly-oh!' he said, his eyes sparkling in anticipation of the treat ahead.

It was a slow afternoon, no customers, not even the usual local bowerbirds who pestered her trying to flog bits of rubbish they'd scrounged. Earlier the boys had brought in a truckload of furniture from a deceased estate. Clarence was out in the back shed using a studded belt to distress the tables. She could hear the thud as he rhythmically thwacked the wood. It was quite an art, distressing. Had to be done carefully. For instance, if you belted timber like mahogany excessively it became too obvious, whereas oak needed a good smack. Little Clarrie was a real professional at it, having learnt all the tricks in an East End auction room.

Charles was polishing silver inside the shop, humming to himself. Nuncie looked hopeful as she saw a car stop outside. A posh car, it appeared promising. Hardly one of her usual mob coming to pawn or redeem something. Then she saw the driver get out, and almost choked on her cigar.

Donald studied the shop. A bit of a dump, he thought, and saw the name above the door. NUNCIE'S THREE BALLS – he imagined how that must have raised a few eyebrows in the neighbourhood. He went inside. The shop was more substantial than it appeared from the street, but so crowded with articles it was difficult to move freely. Most of it seemed like junk, a mishmash of chaotic disorder. In a corner a large man was polishing bric-a-brac.

A strange-looking woman smoking a midget cigar and wearing cords and a beret approached him. As butch as a mallee bull, he thought, while politely enquiring if she was Miss Billingsworth. When he introduced himself Nuncie instantly realised he did not remember her. They'd met only once briefly, almost twelve years ago. She decided not to enlighten him.

'What can I do for you?' she asked, knowing there was only one reason he could be there. Hardly to hock his watch, or anything else.

'I'm trying to find a friend of mine, someone I haven't seen for a long time. I was told you might be able to help,' he explained politely.

'What's the friend's name, Mr Ferrier?' she asked.

'Belle Carson. Or Belle Baker, as she was when I knew her. Does that name mean anything to you?'

'Of course.'

'Then I've come to the right place,' he said gratefully. 'You do know her?'

'I know her quite well.' The woman stubbed out her cigar in a spittoon. He watched this, saw her gaze as her eyes coldly raked him, feeling for the first time as if there might be something amiss.

'So can you tell me where to find her?'

'I didn't say that, Mr Ferrier.'

'Just her address – that's all I need.' He remained resolutely polite. 'I feel sure you know her address.'

'Naturally.'

'Then, please, if you'd be so kind?'

'Why do you want it?' she asked bluntly.

'I beg your pardon. *Why?*'

'That was my question. Why?'

'Obviously to get in touch.'

'With exactly what in mind?'

There was no doubting her attitude now. She was downright aggressive. 'I feel that's entirely my business, Miss Billingsworth.' He felt angry at her equivocation.

'If I reveal her whereabouts, then it also happens to be mine,' she said with no pretence at civility.

Her reply riled him. 'I don't understand this. What exactly are you? A sentinel? Some kind of private Praetorian Guard? What gives you the right to refuse a simple request, as if you're trying to stop me contacting Belle again?'

Nuncie saw Charles watching, attracted by the visitor's raised voice. When he gestured to ask if he should intervene, she shook her head.

'I'm sorry.' Having glimpsed their exchange, Donald was more conciliatory. 'Please excuse those remarks. But I really would like to see her.'

'My question still remains on the table, Mr Ferrier. Why?'

'Because several months ago she was most anxious to see *me*,' he replied. 'She came to my house one night when I was out, asking for me. Not only that, but she waited there for several hours. Unfortunately, not quite long enough for us to meet again.'

'Then she obviously thought better of it,' Nuncie said, trying to conceal her astonishment at this revelation.

'I think she needed help. I've been told she and her husband have parted. There's a child. The boy's been in lots of movies, but not lately because the film business is in a bad way.'

'Who told you all this?'

'It doesn't matter. He's someone who would certainly know the situation. Look, can we start again, Miss Billingsworth? I want to assure you I have no ulterior purpose. I mean no harm. So will you please give me her address?'

'No, I don't think I will, Mr Ferrier.' She saw his eyes tighten with anger. 'You obviously don't remember, but we met years ago – in the days when you were fucking her. You've forgotten me, but I sure as hell haven't forgotten you.'

They came back on the ferry. Teddy felt happily exhausted. Belle wished she had worn her comfortable walking shoes, but it had been worth it. The man in charge of the elephant had even recognised Teddy from several of his films, and given him an extra ride for free. It had been a wonderful afternoon. They'd bought peanuts for the monkeys, talked to cockatoos, tossed crumbs to brilliant coloured lorikeets, gazed at cruising sharks through aquarium glass and watched the lions and tigers being fed.

For an entire afternoon they had forgotten everything else: auditions, sleazy producers, the daily grind of school, the tedium of her job, even the hovel in which they lived. For those few hours they had been like any small family having a rare day in the sun. The ferry began to pass the tram sheds on Bennelong Point as its engines slowed for docking. In the distance behind them all traces of the zoo had now vanished into a hillside of flowering gum trees.

If only, Belle thought, there could be more days like this.

Donald drove home feeling angry and frustrated, wondering what he could do to circumvent these people who seemed to have formed a protective ring around Belle. First, the French woman, clearly lying. Then the belligerent and ridiculous lesbian shop-owner who'd given him the bum's rush. No chance of a rational discussion there. It was infuriating. For God's sake, all he wanted was to find out the truth. At least to meet the boy, so he could form his own conclusions.

When he arrived home the removalist van stood in the driveway, blocking his entry. He leant on the horn until one of the men appeared, gesticulating at the needless row.

'Move the bloody thing,' he shouted, 'so I can get into my own garage!'

It took five minutes – a tedious wait while the van reversed and attempted to make space. He drove in, very nearly grazing the other vehicle, and slammed the garage doors.

'No need to do your block, sport,' one of the removalists said. 'All you had to do was ask.'

He didn't bother to reply. It was what he'd been doing all day, asking and getting a bland denial or an aggressive rebuff.

Mrs Abbott was cleaning the kitchen stove, her head deep inside the oven. No successor would dare deny she had kept an immaculate house, that was her unmistakeable purpose.

'The removalists are here, Mr Ferrier.'

'I noticed,' he said. The housekeeper made an art form out of stating the obvious. He would assuredly not miss her.

'I gave them a list and put labels on Mrs Ferrier's furniture. But you better see that they haven't taken anything belonging to you.'

He felt like saying that what had belonged to him was now in Adelaide. Not just for a visit this time. He didn't care about Caroline; that had been over for ages. He'd been the complaisant husband far too long, and she was welcome to her lover in the city of churches. But the kids. He should have fought her for the kids.

Teddy fell asleep and dreamt of elephants. First of all he was climbing the ladder to sit with other children on the seat fitted to Jessie's back. Jessie, that's what her trainer called her when they went along the pathways in Taronga Zoo, but in the dream that swiftly changed. His elephant had an Indian name, and Teddy rode it wearing a brightly coloured tunic and a turban decorated with jewels and garlanded with flowers like all the other Indian princes. People came out to welcome him as he rode through their villages. Some bowed. He reached a huge temple that he felt sure he'd seen in a film at the Kings Cross Picture Palace with Chrissie, and a moment later he was shaking hands with someone who looked like Ronald Coleman, when a noise woke him and spoilt it.

It was 'Erb the landlord, complaining bitterly. He was puffing heavily when he reached the landing, shouting up at their attic that he did not allow phone calls; his private number was not for tenants, and this was the third time the persistent bleedin' woman had rung. Twice when they were out yesterday, and now refusin' to hang up till he agreed to give a message, which meant he'd had to climb the stairs. He didn't let his rooms to spend his time chasin' up the bleedin' stairs, not unless it was urgent, like someone failin' to cough up their rent.

'Yer to ring this pest of a woman, her name's Nancy,' he wheezed.

'Nuncie, that's her name. What did she say?'

'She wants ter talk. So find a public phone. I said yer ain't using mine.'

They could hear him grumbling all the way down the stairs.

Belle was stunned. Who could've told Donald where to look for her? She felt uneasy and disturbed. Nuncie, on the other hand, was manifestly upset because she'd not been told of her impulsive visit to Donald's house. It was a stupid thing to have done, she said, and Belle could only agree, but it had not been a rational night. In her defence she pointed out that Nuncie had never known what it was like to be without shelter or clean clothes, with only a couple of pennies left in the world.

She didn't dare say she'd considered going to Donald because she feared the emotional dependence that might result in seeking aid from Nuncie. That she was afraid of putting herself in the position of a supplicant, which was why she had kept her distance for so long. She couldn't say it because it would hurt a loyal friend. And with Donald blundering around, trying to find her, she might need friends.

Chapter twenty-four

Teddy thought many lessons at school were boring, but easily the worst was arithmetic. Feeling uninterested and fed up, he was gazing out of the classroom window when he should have been doing multiplication. He sat up with a start, because he saw someone who looked just like Belle crossing the school yard. It was the moment when the teacher, Miss Singleton, called his name. She told him to stand at once, demanding to know if he was paying attention. Miss Singleton had been picking on him lately, and the rest of the class exchanged knowing looks and giggles. They were ready for a bit of fun; Teddy Carson was about to get whacked with the cane again.

When he said yes, he was paying attention, she walked slowly down the length of the room. She paused by his desk and stared at him. 'You were paying attention, were you?'

'Yes, Miss.'

'What were we doing? Addition?'

Versed in the devious methods of teachers, Teddy hesitated. From long experience he knew there would be an alternative.

'Or subtraction?'

'Subtraction.' He realised it was a grievous error when the class laughed.

'Bad guess,' the teacher said.

'I meant addition, Miss.'

'An even worse guess. What were you looking at outside the window?'

'My mother,' Teddy said.

The class, who thought it was a joke, fell about with laughter this time. Miss Singleton was livid. She silenced them with a shout. She took hold of Teddy's ear, twisted it painfully and marched him towards the back of the room. It was there she kept a number of canes in a cupboard, along with the blackboard chalk and her textbooks. While they all watched she selected the slimmest bamboo, which everyone knew hurt the most. Bending it to test the flexibility, then tapping it on her hand, she told him this was his last chance.

'We were doing multiplication, Edward. Since you were expert enough not to bother taking part, please tell me the solution to the following sum. What is the answer to nine times thirteen?'

Teddy stared at her, his mind in a turmoil. Nine times thirteen? He knew she had deliberately chosen the most awkward number. Ten times thirteen would be . . . well, he wasn't quite sure, but it would be easier than nine times. As for thirteen, she had chosen it because they had only learnt up to their twelve times table, and anything after that was unfamiliar territory.

'It's more than a hundred,' he said, and the giggles of the class were stilled as he held out his hand. But Miss Singleton shook her head, and gestured for him to bend over.

They all watched spellbound, some slightly frightened, others excited, as he bent and the teacher laid the cane against his bottom, assessing and measuring her target. It was her custom to delay the punishment as long as possible to cause the maximum stress, so she kept him bending while she made preparatory swishes through the air, creating sound effects that he and everyone else could hear.

'It will hurt me more than it hurts you,' she said sanctimoniously, 'but we are trying to teach you, and sometimes this is the only way.'

She swung the cane and it lashed against his legs, just below where his short trousers gave protection. He flinched with the pain, and she hit him again, then a third and a fourth time across the buttocks, and after that was so obsessed with punishing him she was unaware the classroom door had opened and the headmaster was standing there with Belle.

'So this is what you call an education for my son!' Belle had no need to perform the role of furious parent, she had rarely been so enraged. 'I ought to go to the police and make a complaint. That woman was enjoying herself, she was salivating, *relishing* it. I'll take him to Prince Alfred Hospital to have the whip marks treated, and after that I think my only recourse is to go to the newspapers. Fortunately a number of our friends are journalists on both the morning and evening papers.'

'Mrs Carson —' the headmaster tried to interrupt the flow, but Belle was having none of it. She stood aggressively in front of his desk, hands firmly planted on it as she fixed him with her gaze.

'The public ought to know what happens when we entrust our young to the care of people like you. We hope for an education, for a decent start to their lives, and instead we discover you employ sadists.' The headmaster flinched. He was sure Belle's angry voice would carry to anyone listening outside his door. 'That's exactly what she is. You can't deny it, I saw that creature lashing my child with what seemed like the utmost pleasure —'

'Mrs Carson, the teacher will be disciplined —'

'That's *your* business. Mine is to take my son to have his injuries treated, then decide if further action is required. He won't be returning to school today.'

'I imagine not,' the headmaster replied, managing to get in a word at last and sensing her threat was mostly rhetorical, 'after all, you did come to collect him for a family funeral.'

'His Aunt Penelope.' Belle was reminded of her excuse for plucking him from classes. 'Poor Penelope would certainly have been most upset about this. He was her favourite nephew.'

'Doubtless he'll be well enough to attend her last rites,' the headmaster said, making little attempt to hide his disbelief.

'Who's Aunt Penelope?' Teddy asked her as they left the school. Following Belle's instructions he limped until they were out of sight, even though he insisted it had hurt his bum and there was nothing wrong with his legs.

'Keep limping, but don't overact,' she warned, aware of the beak watching from his window as they crossed the playground. Cynical old chalkie. No doubt he'd heard all the excuses since becoming headmaster, and funerals would have rated fairly highly among them. But it had been a matter of urgency.

'Who is she, Mum?'

'She was a character I played on stage once,' Belle said, 'and you're supposed to be going to her funeral, because I couldn't think of anything else. I had to get you out of school in a hurry.'

'Good-o. But why?'

'There's a call for juveniles and younger kids to audition for a new variety show. A friend rang to tell me, but we nearly missed out because that oaf 'Erb kicked up an almighty fuss about another phone call. He's the pits, that man. But this one's a chance, Teddy. A real chance that we can't afford to miss.'

Not another audition, Teddy thought despondently, debating whether to risk saying he didn't feel like it, because his bum was really quite sore.

But when they arrived he thanked his stars he hadn't. For among those there, the first face he saw was Sally's.

The phone call was from Dan Hardacre. Donald was abrupt with him. He felt no necessity for them to meet. He was due in court shortly, and both suggestions Dan had offered several weeks ago had led absolutely nowhere.

'I think we should talk,' Dan said.

'I don't see the point.'

'I'm sure you will after we've met and spoken.'

Reluctantly Donald agreed his court appearance was a summary matter, and he was leaving his chambers early. He should be home by two, but told Dan not to be surprised if the house was half empty.

It had been a miserable few weeks since the furniture had followed Caroline and the children to Adelaide. Mrs Abbott had departed, to his considerable relief; he would have liked the pleasure of sacking her, but even there his wife had scored a victory. She was paid a handsome redundancy by Caro and taken over by one of her friends who apparently needed a treasure like Mrs A to run her new mansion in Bellevue Hill. The housekeeper had bade him goodbye with a self-satisfied smile, as if Bellevue Hill was an undeniable elevation. It was a smile so smug it had annoyed him intensely.

Dan Hardacre arrived promptly at two o'clock. The flash Italian car looked incongruous in Donald's sedate driveway. 'I see they didn't repossess the shagging wagon.'

'The old fuckmobile . . . It's about the only thing I own outright now.'

They went into the house. There were vacant spaces in the main rooms where furniture had stood. Indentations marked the carpet, and the wallpaper revealed where bookcases and a sideboard had been removed.

'Looks like you've had the bailiffs in,' Dan said.

'Worse than that. By now it's all in Adelaide, with my wife.'

'Is she coming back?'

'I wouldn't think so.'

'And the kids – also in Adelaide?'

'Yes, living there now. I'll see them here at Christmas, and on their birthdays.'

Dan shook his head, surprised. 'For a smart lawyer you seem to have got shafted with the rough end of the pineapple.'

'Sarah's eight, young Donald's six. I was trying to be considerate and not turn their lives into an arm wrestle. Moderation in a marriage bust-up is a bit of a misnomer. I was shafted by a smart woman – now let's forget it and have a drink. And tell me what was so important that we had to meet.'

Donald poured drinks and they took them out onto the side verandah.

'I've been working things out, Donald.'

'What things?'

'A time line. Twelve years ago, you and Belle were lovers until the big bust-up. Pretty quickly after that she married. She hinted a few times . . . well, more than hinted to me, but I'd lost interest. So she married George Carson. Met him when she went to spend a few weeks with her aunt who lived at Greenwich. Sort of seeking sanctuary there, I felt, after the break-up. Odd choice, George. Not her sort of bloke. Or her kind of life, in the backblocks of a country town.'

'Just a minute.' Donald had listened to this with growing unease. 'What on earth has Belle's marriage to do with me?'

'As far as I can work out,' Dan ignored the interruption, 'about six months later she had a child. My guess is that was your child.'

Donald, anticipating it, was nevertheless shaken to hear it spelt out so precisely. 'You have a vivid imagination, Dan.'

'The timing seems to fit.'

'You may think so. I'm afraid it's fantasy.'

'Perhaps. And yet all these years later you want to find her —'

'I told you, she turned up at this house one night. I wanted to find her because I was concerned. My former housekeeper said she seemed in distress.'

'You wanted to find her a hell of a lot more after I dropped the news she had a kid. An eleven-year-old.'

'I suppose I was curious.'

'Why not? Anyone would be. You want to see what he looks like – see if he looks like you.'

'Cut it out, Dan,' he retorted, not wanting to acknowledge the accuracy of that remark. 'If this is what you came to say, you're wasting my time.'

His visitor smiled knowingly, sipping his drink with no intention of leaving. 'To be honest, I'm not sure he does look like you, but that's for you to judge. There are photos, but they don't tell much and are no substitute. You need to meet, to talk to him. What I suggest is, this time I'll do the legwork and I'll find Belle for you.'

Donald was cautious. He hesitated. 'How?'

'We'll come to that. In the meantime I'm on the bones of my arse, and there are no jobs in view. The price has gone up, Donald. I'll find her, but I want five hundred quid. And two hundred for expenses, up-front.'

'Are we talking about a reward? Because it sounds more like blackmail.'

'That's pretty insulting, Donald. It's a fee – for my time and services. The money is probably less than you earn for a few days in court. It may take me a little time, but I will find her. And the boy.'

There was a silence. Donald gazed out at the side lawn, where the sandpit remained, but the children's swing had been dismantled. It was no doubt by now erected at Caroline's parents' home in Adelaide, or in storage for when she moved in with the lover. He should have fought for the kids, he knew that now.

'Have another drink,' he said to Dan. 'Let me think about it.'

Teddy saw her the moment they came into the building, at almost the same time as she saw him. She stood up, murmured something to her mother, who was sitting beside her, and ran to meet him. They faced each other, wondering what to do, whether to kiss or hug or what, and in the end they just held hands and grinned at each other.

'I was trying to find you!' Sally said.

'Me, too . . . I was trying everywhere. Golly, Sal . . .' He felt tongue-tied. So many things he'd saved up to tell her, and now he couldn't think of a single one.

'We live in Mosman,' she said.

'I heard that.'

'Mum's got a new boyfriend.'

'I thought she'd got married again.'

'No, she tells everyone she's married, but he's just a boyfriend. His name's Sylvester Polkington and we live with him.'

'Fancy name,' was all Teddy could think of to say, as Mrs Sharp rose.

'Silly name and a horrible man,' Sally whispered, while their mothers met each other with fixed smiles.

'Eunice, I heard you've married again. Congratulations.'

'Thank you, Belle. You've moved house, I'm told?'

'Yes, we felt it was time for a change.'

'Somewhere nicer, I hope?'

Belle appeared not to hear this. 'I suppose marriage means a new name. What do we call you now?'

'I've decided to remain Eunice Sharp. It's more modern, I think, and I'm used to it. We women should keep our own identities.'

Not by the flicker of an eyelash did Teddy betray his desire to laugh at this exchange. First he directly gazed at Sally, whose lips began to twitch. Remaining straight-faced was proving difficult. So he looked at the floor, then sideways at some of the other hopefuls who'd turned up – mostly young, but he and Sal seemed by far the youngest – he looked anywhere except at her. He knew they'd both collapse with laughter if their eyes met. Meanwhile Eunice, who hadn't bothered to acknowledge Teddy at all, appeared totally oblivious to this.

'They want young singers and dancers. It's a two-week guarantee, that's all,' she told Belle before returning to her seat. She beckoned her daughter. 'Sally, sit here and relax.'

'She's as bossy as ever,' Sally said in a whisper.

'Why not tell her you want to talk to me?'

'*You* tell her.'

'Righto,' Teddy agreed and moved to confront her mother, who had already taken out her knitting.

'If you don't mind, Mrs Sharp, Sally wants to talk to me. And I want to talk to her. So we'll wait outside together until one of us is called.'

Eunice opened her mouth to remonstrate, then realised he had spoken loud enough for others to hear and all their eyes were on her. So she smiled a frigid smile and said not to go too far.

Sally had a multitude of questions for him. Where had they gone to, and why in such a rush, not even a message? Was his mum still sweet on Ross Tanner? Had he been in any more films? What was the name of his new school? Was it better than their old one? With so much to explain he was no longer tongue-tied; he was overwhelmed, not only by her cross-examination, but by the knowledge she had missed him and been as dejected as he had.

He told her everything. Shocked her with the news of Florian's venality, told her about their awful attic room and how bad things had been, and still were. No hope of film work, just unsuccessful auditions – like this one today. Although today, he said, could hardly be called unsuccessful whatever the result, because they'd met again, and not even her bossy mum was going to keep them from seeing each other.

But how will we do that? she wanted to know. Mosman and Botany were too far apart. Teddy had to agree. Eunice would never allow Sally to venture into his neighbourhood, her up-herself mum would throw a fit at the thought. As for visiting their new place in Mosman, first they had to be invited. Fat chance of that!

They glumly contemplated the possibilities. In the end all they could do was assure each other they'd swap addresses and somehow keep in touch.

Belle came out to warn Teddy he was on next. The call was in alphabetical order, she said, and it was an utter shambles. If he wanted to skip the audition she could hardly blame him, but since they'd come all this way he might as well go through the motions. She'd just heard the producer wanted a song-and-dance number, which was surprising, because until now what he'd wanted was a comedy sketch. So 'Burlington Bertie', which would've gone over a treat, had to be junked, and they had about five minutes to think up a suitable song.

'What were you going to do, Sal?' Teddy asked.

'Eunice has a few song sheets with her, but I don't like any of them much.'

'I'm sorry, Sally.' Belle was trying not to sound impatient. 'But nice as it is to see you again, we have to sort this out. So you'd better go inside now.'

'Wait a minute —' Teddy started to say.

'We haven't got time to waste, darling —'

'*Hang on* a minute, Mum – just hold your horses,' Teddy insisted, and began whispering to Sally. If Belle was startled at being told to shut up, she was equally astonished to see the way Sally smiled, nodding at whatever was being said, nodding again and then laughing out loud. As they stood up to face her they were clutching hands.

'We'll do a piece together,' he said.

'You can't. It's a solo audition. Besides, you have no routines, you've never rehearsed, and they won't allow it. The idea is just ridiculous.'

'Then I won't bother, Mum. We'll go home, like you said.'

Belle paused. 'What on earth can you do together?'

'Lots of things, Mrs Carson,' Sally begged. 'We used to try out ideas after school, and at dance class. I promise you it'll be all right. Please, won't you trust us?'

As Belle hesitated, the producer's assistant came out. 'Young Ted, you're on.'

'We're both on.' Teddy hardly paused before saying it. 'We're a double act.'

'Nobody told *me*.' He frowned and referred to his clipboard, then looked at Belle. 'Did you know about this, Mrs Carson?'

'It should be down on your list,' Belle said, 'but if it isn't then someone has forgotten to tell you. Let's go, kids.' She followed them inside, trying to anticipate what Eunice was going to say.

Eunice glanced up from her knitting, relieved to see Sally coming back. More than enough time had been spent with that boy. She supposed he was talented, but far too much attention was paid to him, as if he was some sort of star, which was absurd. One big role in a film and nothing much since, just lots of bit parts, driven by that obsessive and difficult mother. A pity they had to meet again like this. Sally was at last getting over her moods, the complaints about missing him, and now this had to happen.

'Sally, dear —'

'Sorry, can't talk now. We're on, Mum,' her daughter said, walking past. She and Teddy, hand in hand, with Belle and the assistant, all headed for the room where the auditions were being held. Eunice hastily put her knitting away and went after them, managing to reach Belle just before the door was shut.

'What's happening?' she asked.

'Settle down, Eunice. Wait and see.'

'I want to know what's going on! What is all this?'

'If you ladies wish to stay,' the producer addressed them from a long table where he sat with a number of his acolytes, 'you should be aware I insist on total silence. No talking whatsoever, and if you find that difficult you have to leave.'

Eunice sat down. She looked furious. Belle sat with her fingers crossed, praying this would not be a colossal blunder. She had no idea what they intended. It had not been Teddy who swayed her; Sally's plea had done that. She'd always liked Sal. The mop of bright red hair, the friendly grin, the tousled appearance; such a natural kid, so unlike her mother, who was never less than immaculate – like a dummy in a shop window and with about as much animation.

The producer was talking to Teddy and Sal. She didn't know him; he was a newcomer, a businessman who'd rented the small Crown Theatre in Bathurst Street. Hardly a prime venue, and with just two weeks to make the show work or everyone would be paid off and sent home. The producer – she tried to think of his name without having to ask Eunice: Hugh something or other . . . Hugh Bellamy, that was it – had imported a well-known Scots comedian, and was casting locals to build a show around him. This explained why the request for a comic sketch had been changed. No overseas star would allow some local player to do a comedy spot in case he pinched the laughs, which Teddy might easily have done, she reflected.

Mr Bellamy seemed agreeable enough. He sat with the kids, listening and letting them do most of the talking, then took them across to the pianist. He left them with an encouraging pat on each of their shoulders and returned to his chair. They went on talking to the pianist, explaining what they wanted. It seemed an unconscionably long delay. Eunice was fidgeting; Belle felt a mounting tension. Her chest grew tight, as if all the breath in her body was compacted into a ball there. She thought she might be physically sick, might have to run from the room, then thankfully the pianist hit a chord and they began to sing. Belle recognised it instantly, one of the romantic songs Dominic the accordionist used to play:

> Being young is complex, people say,
> Life should be a careful matinee.
> It's far too soon to seek the moon,
> And early love can often go astray.
> But we confess – we've said yes,
> Yes to love, and yesterday.
> It's true we've always felt this way,
> Yes to love, and to tomorrow,
> Yes to dreams, no chance of sorrow,
> We'll never fight, never grieve,
> This lovely moment we believe
> Will last for always, every day,
> And life's a dazzling matinee.

Their voices blended in tuneful harmony. They sang the second verse, then began to dance. Belle leant forward, feeling a catch in her throat. She knew it at once; the Astaire and Rogers style, everyone in the room recognised it with a unified gasp that felt strangely like applause. Belle no longer had any tension, she was smiling, tapping to their rhythm, wanting to cheer. Especially to cheer Sally, who was electric: she spun and pivoted and danced with him in such perfection it seemed as if they'd been performing together all their lives.

Then, as if deciding to leave their audience asking for more of this, they came forward with arms linked and began to sing again. But this time they were toying with the song, acting it out, having fun taking alternate lyric lines, like actors improvising or children enjoying themselves in a playground. Then, returning to the simple words of the verse, they danced a waltz together, moving with perfect fluidity, their eyes linked, captivated with each other as if they were entirely alone, making Belle want to cry at the emotion they engendered.

The song ended, the pianist played the final chords and they stood facing each other for what seemed an extended moment. Then Teddy bowed to Sally, and she curtsied to him. The silence in the room was absolute.

'Jesus Christ,' Hugh Bellamy said, and started to applaud.

Dan Hardacre drove back to his apartment in Elizabeth Bay. It was down on the edge of the waterfront, select, expensive and, with luck, sustainable. It seemed possible now that he could survive here until conditions in the industry improved, at least enough for him to find a new job. All he had to do was locate Belle and the kid, which six months ago would have been easy; she was forever ringing him from public phones, or coming to the studio to find out if there was anything, a small part, if not then a walk-on, even a background extra, any scrap that could keep Teddy employed and his mother living off his earnings.

He had no real affection for Belle, despite long ago being lovers. In those days it was different, she was a twenty-year-old prize. Even now she was an attractive woman; he could imagine taking her to bed, undressing and arousing her. Once aroused, Belle had no emotional boundaries, no restrictions on bed behaviour; he could still remember a glorious night when they had reached home drunk and rampaged with sexual abandon until they were exhausted.

But now she was his lifeline. He had two hundred pounds in cash for his expenses, and a promise of five hundred more when he found them. It seemed the French woman who ran the shop in

Kellett Street would be no help, and paunchy old Nuncie was a rampant foe. He expected that; Nuncie had been lusting after Belle since she was a young soubrette, although there was never a chance she'd acquiesce to a cigar-puffing lesbian. Why they'd stayed friends baffled Dan, but the longer he lived the less he understood people. Nuncie was the key to this because she knew where Belle was living. Her refusal to reveal the address was a minor irritation that was going to cost him fifty quid. Fifty of his two hundred advance would hire a private detective to monitor Nuncie Billingsworth, and in time this would lead to Belle.

It was a fair enough pursuit; the kid was almost certainly Donald's, and it would be up to him what might happen then. He'd lost his wife and the other two children, maybe he'd attempt a deal to gain custody of Teddy. Tricky lawyer's stuff. But even with legal finagling, he'd surely find it impossible – Belle would never agree – unless Donald had something more in mind. Unless he had some other aspirations.

Dan sipped a drink on his balcony and thought about that.

Donald and Belle, after all this time? It was an interesting speculation. They'd certainly been a red-hot item once, and most of their friends had been surprised when he'd ditched her, even for Caroline and her money. So, perhaps? Life was full of twists and amusing turns.

Whatever the outcome, Dan was confident of his payment. With luck there might even be a little more.

They waited outside the audition room, still elated by their reception, but becoming anxious over the long delay while their future was discussed. The building was at the lower end of George Street, an unlovely part of town, full of cheap hotels and gun shops.

A tram clanged past on its way to Central Station. There were more derelicts than ever making shanty homes in the park, and across the square Teddy could see the entrance of what had been Florian MacArthur-Bailey's office. He pointed it out to Sally.

A lousy crook, he told her, although at times he'd quite liked the agent and found it easy to laugh at his jokes. But the same fat funny man had tricked Teddy over Christmas presents when he was only eight, and had shot through months ago, leaving them without a bean. Uriah was a bastard, as Belle had always said. And now he'd escaped, sailed on a ship for England. When Belle heard it she said there was no justice. Bastards always escaped and prospered.

'I can hear her saying it.' Sally smiled, then was thoughtful. 'He might have been our agent talking to Mr Bellamy right now, if he hadn't been a crook.'

'You mean instead of our mums?'

She nodded. They were both nervous about that. After their performance the applause had startled them. Teddy, a veteran of more auditions than her – almost more than anyone – said it was an historic first. Nobody ever applauded at auditions like this.

'It really felt good, every minute, everything we did. You were great, Sal.'

'So were you. Even before they clapped, I could tell they liked us.'

'They did. I hope they still do – after our mums have finished negotiating.'

'Yes,' replied Sally, 'it's taking an awful long time.'

They sat across the table from Hugh Bellamy, who had a draft contract in front of him. One assistant remained to take notes, the rest of the production team had departed. Belle and Eunice had spent several hours waiting for the remaining auditions to conclude, and this delay had given them more than enough time to adopt entrenched positions.

'They were extremely good,' Belle commented, 'but of course it was an off-the-cuff performance and they will be even better.'

'Naturally,' Eunice added.

'I don't want them better,' Bellamy said. 'I want them just like they were today. People are going to love them.'

'They're bound to be better, Mr Bellamy, with more rehearsal.' Belle felt he was a newcomer who needed advice. 'Wait till they're in their right costumes, and, by the way, I have some ideas on that. And the lighting needs to be soft focus. I thought Sally was splendid, she kept up very well —'

'What do you mean *kept up?*' Eunice interrupted.

'I'm not criticising, Eunice, I'm complimenting her.'

'By suggesting that she *managed* to keep up? You call that a compliment?'

'Ladies, please. Can we get on with the contractual details?'

'Certainly,' Belle answered promptly. 'Top billing for Teddy. I'm sure that goes without saying.'

'What do you mean? Why does it go without saying, Belle?'

'Because it's obvious, Eunice. He's a star.'

'Star my arse.'

'You know he is.'

'I know nothing of the kind. He might've been a star when he was smaller, but that was for one film. What's he done since? Bit parts, a few lines here or there, absolutely nothing that matters.'

'Ladies, *please* —'

They took no notice of him. Belle was infuriated by the way Eunice was so determinedly undermining Teddy, her anger sparked by the grain of truth that lay in the accusation. She realised it was dangerous stupidity, this quarrel, but could no longer help herself.

'Let's face it, who has ever heard of Sally Sharp? You tell me, Eunice. Go on, tell me. Has she ever been in pictures? Toured? Been on a stage? No. She's a very lucky girl because my son has taken such a shine to her. Talented – but lucky.'

'*Ladies!*' Hugh Bellamy said again, vainly trying to restore peace.

'They said you were a nasty, impossible cow, Belle – and I said you could hardly be as bad as people made out. But my God, they were right.'

'I think you should stop insulting me, Eunice, and let's try to at least agree on something. Top billing and a sixty–forty split of the fee our way.'

'Go to buggery,' Eunice said.

'Right, that does it.' Hugh Bellamy rose from his chair, took the contract and ripped it in half. He gave a half to each of the startled mothers. 'I wanted those kids. But you can tell them you've seen to that. With you as their agents, I'm not having them in the show.'

'Why?' Eunice almost whispered, as if she'd lost her voice.

'Because I couldn't risk you pair coming to the theatre and putting on a turn like this.'

Belle stood in shock, holding her half of the contract and staring numbly at him. After so long, so many months of hopes and disappointment, and after such a superb audition . . . All she could think of was a warning long ago – from bloody Florian, of all people – that one day she would talk her son out of a job. It seemed as if she just had. She wanted to weep or shout at the producer to wait and listen, but instead she just watched him starting to gather his papers. She felt frozen with the enormity of what they had done.

'Mr Bellamy . . .'

He paid no attention to her. The assistant switched off an overhead fan, while he closed his attaché case. Both men were waiting for them to leave.

'They were wonderful,' she said slowly, trying to choose the right words, 'and we were awful. Like a pair of fishwives – at least I was the fishwife – I admit I started it. But the kids, they were so very good, and it seems ridiculously unfair, to them and to you, Mr Bellamy, that you no longer want them because of our bad behaviour. It's probably far too late, but even so I'd like to apologise.'

Hugh Bellamy remained quiet. After a moment he looked towards Eunice. 'How do you feel, Mrs Sharp?'

'Better for hearing that,' Eunice said, then realising it appeared like scoring a cheap point, felt obliged to add, 'I apologise as well.'

They went home by tram. It was late in the afternoon, the traffic was banked up on South Dowling Street, and the tram was packed. Teddy sat squashed against Belle, wanting to talk but this was impossible. She knew he was relieved there was only another two days of school before rehearsals. Tomorrow she would go with him and make that plain to the headmaster; while she had the beak on the back foot over the caning she'd lay down a few conditions about the times he'd be absent. A week rehearsing, and then a minimum two weeks away from school because of matinees and late nights. Perhaps longer if the show ran.

What a relief! She felt contrite and thankful Hugh Bellamy had ultimately forgiven them, but that was because he wanted the act, not for the pleasure of their company. He'd taken another contract from his case – a duplicate copy – telling them to sit down while he read out the proposed offer.

'This is not negotiable. So I don't want any interruptions or comments. The billing will be in small type, like everyone else except our star. It will read: Teddy Carson with Sally Sharp.' He'd looked up as Eunice gave a slight murmur which subsided as he stared at her. 'I pay fares and four shillings a day during rehearsals, then two pounds a week when we open. If the show runs beyond the guaranteed two weeks, the salary increases to three pounds. If that's agreeable, you sign as their guardians. But before you do, because of what took place earlier, I have some other conditions.'

He'd laid down the law, and that bitch Eunice hadn't liked it one scrap. Belle hadn't been too thrilled herself. They were barred from all rehearsals, including the dress: they were not allowed backstage until the end of each show, and were prohibited from giving any advice to any person in the company – especially the wardrobe lady and the lighting supervisor. He gazed intently at Belle while stating this, and she had nodded obediently. For a moment she thought she'd glimpsed a hint of a smile on his face, but rather than risk such an assumption had decided to treat it as a nervous tic.

She slept soundly that night for the first time in weeks. Alongside her in his own bed, Teddy lay awake. It was far too exciting to sleep. When he did, it was close to midnight. He was dancing with Sally, but they were grown up, with their names in big letters above the title. A full orchestra played their music. The audience was immense, there were rows of people in their hundreds, even in their thousands, overflowing and stretching as far as it was possible to see beyond the footlights, as though they went on forever.

Chapter twenty–five

Nuncie Billingsworth looked out the window and saw the same man. This time he was leaning against the lamppost across the street, as if absorbed in the view, which was odd because the view was a brick wall. Two days ago he walked past her shop at least five times. She stepped away from the glass so he could not see her, and studied him more carefully. In his thirties, a nondescript sort of bloke, medium height, thinning hair, slim build. An open-neck shirt, fawn trousers and sandals. He looked harmless, so why was she concerned?

She knew people were often cautious before approaching a pawnbroker, second thoughts were a regular occurrence; she'd seen enough of them debating with themselves, studying the window, questioning whether they really needed the money before taking the plunge. She was used to customers loitering while trying to come to a decision – but this one didn't seem like that kind of a customer. So what did that leave?

'Boys,' she called, and Charles and Clarence gratefully lowered the heavy bookcase they were trying to shift through the clutter, and came to join her. 'Over there by the lamppost. Now he's going to have a look in the real-estate window. It's the fourth time he's done that.'

They all studied him. 'Same geezer as last time,' Clarence said promptly. 'And I thought I seen him hanging around the back lane yesterday as well.'

'So what do you reckon, Clarrie?'

'Dodgy,' the small man replied. 'He certainly don't look like a punter to me.'

'That's what I thought,' Nuncie agreed. 'What would you do?'

'Set the bleedin' dog on him – if we had a dog.'

'Well, we haven't.'

'No, but if you cast your mind back, I always said it'd be a good idea. Not one of these soppy animals, a bloody big frightener like a Rottweiler or an Alsatian, something to make a tea-leaf shit himself.'

'So you reckon he's a thief?' she asked, ignoring his sly reminder about keeping a watchdog.

'Well, what else is he hanging around for?'

Nuncie turned to the larger of the two. 'What about you, Charles? Any suggestions?'

'Got one, Miss B.'

'Good. Would you care to share it with us?'

He picked up the phone and handed it to her. 'Call the coppers.'

'Why?'

'You're a bit worried. So call 'em. It's your right as a citizen. After all, what do you pay taxes for?'

'Who said I pay taxes?' Nuncie replied, but she rang the police station anyway.

Dan decided it was better not to tell Donald Ferrier the private detective he'd hired had been arrested. Talk about a Keystone Kops scenario! The hopeless dill-brain had made himself so obvious that

Billingsworth had been alerted and called the North Sydney rozzers. In Neutral Bay of all places, with its shops and constant shift of people, this peeper, this supposed sleuth, had managed to lurk so visibly that he'd stood out like dogs' balls. In the resulting fiasco the drongo had tried to avoid arrest by escaping; a wild chase ensued down Ben Boyd Road and through the back streets of Cremorne, and after a long pursuit he'd been taken into custody for questioning. To avoid summary charges and the prospect of a night in the cells, he had identified himself as a private eye.

'But I didn't tell 'em who hired me, or what it was all about,' he faithfully promised Dan. 'I invoked client confidentiality.'

'Fucking brilliant,' Dan said.

By now she'd have been told the assumed thief was not what he seemed; he was a legally registered investigator on the job – *keeping observation* – on a certain matter in the area, details of which he refused to disclose. Nuncie was no idiot, it wouldn't take her ten seconds to put that little set of circumstances together. Just weeks ago Donald had come there in his attempt to track down Belle, and all of a sudden there was a hired bloodhound on her doorstep.

Dan told the man he was fired, and tried to work out what to do next. For a start Nuncie was forewarned, so any kind of future surveillance was out. There had to be some other way, or else the promised five-hundred-pound bounty was at risk, and so was his bank overdraft and the occupancy of his apartment.

The Crown Theatre in Bathurst Street had once been a Presbyterian Church hall. Its entrance was down a narrow lane, which precluded the likelihood of passing ticket sales, and the reviews that Hugh Bellamy hoped would bring the public to fill the small theatre had been less than fulsome. Only two critics bothered to attend the first night; one said the Glaswegian brogue was unintelligible, the other could interpret the words but found the jokes obscure. By the second week the rows of empty seats were indicators of disaster, and the imported leading man and local cast could hear the echo of their failure in a stony and relentless silence from the other side of the footlights. At the mid-week matinee there were more people on stage than in the audience.

The Scottish comic blamed it on the management. The former church hall was a bleak venue, he told everyone, a crappy wee space better suited for sermons than slapstick. In this crypt, this burial chamber of his career, there was as much chance of getting a laugh as obtaining a decent meal of haggis in the antipodes. Since the cast had no idea what he meant by this, it was greeted with the same leaden reception as his jokes.

When closure was inevitable, the visiting comedian became angrier. After condemning Bellamy's administration, he impugned the people of Sydney for not knowing of his triumphs at Blackpool, Morecambe and other British seaside towns where he was a household name. He then became derogatory about the supporting cast. They were utterly useless; the show would've been better as a solo vehicle without any of them. It was when he dismissed Teddy and Sally as mere childish amateurs that Belle and Eunice found themselves united in outrage.

'How dare he!' Eunice exclaimed, for news of his latest fulmination was travelling around the company like wildfire. 'The egotistical little turd. What do you think?'

'I think he's a bastard,' Belle said, 'as well as an egotistical little turd.'

'It's unfair.'

'It's the last gasp of a has-been who never got past the Blackpool pier. We should do something about it, Eunice.'

Forbidden by contract to go into the theatre except to collect their children after each show, one engaged the stage doorman in conversation while the other left a cutting on the cast noticeboard. It was the most virulent of the opening-night reviews, which concluded:

---

the local cast did their best, but sadly the dead weight of weak and incomprehensible Celtic jokes sand-bagged them. The entire show was no more than a dreary waste of time, with the exception of the youngest couple, a charming singing and dancing duet that enlivened the second act.

Belle and Eunice, who had shared indignation at the critic's neglect to name their progeny when it was published, now underlined the passage and pinned it up with a mood of what felt surprisingly like camaraderie.

Dan Hardacre picked his time carefully, late in the day just before the shop closed. He introduced himself to Helene LaRue. In the background a girl was stacking the shelves. He remembered vaguely the French woman had a daughter.

'I'm from United Films.' He gave her one of the cards he'd taken before his departure from the company. 'I need help. I've lost touch with Belle Carson, and it looks like we might have a nice little role in a new film for Teddy.'

Helene took the card and the bait, as he felt sure she would. '*Très bon*,' she said, 'that's good news for them.'

'It certainly is. Can you give me their new address?'

She took a scrap of paper and a pencil from beside the cash register. She was about to write it down for him, when the girl came and looked at the card. 'United Films?'

'That's right,' he replied, smiling at her while waiting for the mother to finish writing.

'Mama, wait a moment,' she said, then spoke in French. The exchange that followed was too quick for Dan to grasp, but he knew from their expressions that something had upset them.

'What's the matter, Mrs LaRue?'

It was her daughter who answered. 'I heard United has closed down.'

'A rumour.' Dan smiled. 'Don't believe all you read in the papers.'

'I didn't read it,' Chrissie LaRue said, 'my boyfriend works in the film business. He was trying to get a job there, but he told me they've closed.'

'Only temporarily. I'm putting together a new movie for them. If you look at the card, I was the executive producer who got Teddy his first starring role.'

'I know you did, Mr Hardacre. So leave the card. We'll give it to Belle and she can get in touch with you.'

'For goodness' sake, young lady, I'm only asking for an address. What's the problem with that? Do you want to lose him this job?'

'Certainly not. But let me get this straight – so that I can ask my boyfriend. It's a film for United, which hasn't really closed after all? Is that right?'

'Not exactly.' Dan tried to regain his smile, which was usually so effective with the opposite sex. 'I'm actually working more as an independent now.'

'Not with United? Just using one of their old cards to introduce yourself?'

'You're being ridiculous.' He turned to her mother. 'Mrs LaRue, this is a simple request. Can you please help me?'

'*Non*,' Helene said firmly. 'I begin to think what you say is untrue. I think it is like the *merde* from the *taureau*.'

'She means it's bullshit,' Chrissie said.

There was no reprieve, and Belle did not expect one. The show closed after the Saturday-night performance, and on the Monday Teddy went unwillingly back to school. For a brief moment it had seemed as if their lives might change; she had hoped they could afford to move from their attic, but for that to be possible the revue had to succeed. Which, sadly, was out of the question.

At least the final few days had provided their own hilarity. The noticeboard incident had created glee among the cast, and put the visiting comic in a ferocious rage culminating in an outbreak of hives. Armed with a doctor's certificate citing a stress-created allergy, he had refused to appear at the matinee. As there were only six in the audience, the performance was cancelled without difficulty.

Poor Mr Bellamy, she thought, his first production was undoubtedly going to be his last. He was really an accountant, the stage manager had told her, with ambitions to be an entrepreneur. This experience would've cured him, she surmised, hoping he could afford his losses; after their first prickly encounter she had come to like him, only wishing he had been a better producer, for it was a unique opportunity squandered.

She returned to work, back to the tedious chore of filling schooners of beer as she contended with the unappealing banter of flirtatious drunks. There was also what she called the eye-play: the meaningful stares, sidelong glances, winks and lifted eyebrows that were all intended messages, each one implicitly sexual. The worst offenders were those who seemed to consider themselves irresistible. From her side of the bar she went through the daily burden of being an uncomplaining recipient of their lust.

The mechanical nature of the job, its sheer monotony except in the turmoil of the rush hour, made it possible to reflect on other matters. Nuncie had come to bring her news of the private detective. While they laughed about his arrest, it was a disturbing escalation. Belle assumed he'd been hired by Donald, and she contemplated a phone call to warn him off – better still, a call to Caroline, who had once been her friend, and might be surprised to hear of her husband's current activities. But before she could come to a decision on this, she saw a newspaper paragraph headed 'BARRISTER AND WIFE TO DIVORCE'.

Then came an unexpected letter from Helene LaRue, revealing Dan's visit and his clumsy attempt to find her whereabouts. It seemed unlikely they would be seeking her for different purposes, so they must be acting jointly. Dan was out of a job, she knew this from the weekly trade paper that had reported the shutdown of the studio and United closing its Australian office. She also knew he had an expensive lifestyle. He must be working for Donald, she reasoned. Knowing Dan, he would hardly associate with the man who'd replaced him in her affections, unless it was for money.

Belle felt dismayed. The idea that two former lovers – men she had once cared for – would unite in an ugly intrigue to stalk her, to track her down as if she were a kind of prey, was abhorrent. She was uneasily aware Teddy was certainly the objective of this and must be protected. While she tried to think of what to do and how to deal with it, the telegram arrived.

That she should receive a telegram was the first big surprise; the next was its content, which was so astounding it lifted her spirits and made her laugh.

She and Eunice Sharp were invited to afternoon tea.

Hugh Bellamy's office in Macquarie Street was another surprise. It had one of Sydney's best panoramic views that included the harbour, the Conservatorium of Music and the Botanic Gardens. The building itself was luxurious, his own office spacious. A series of impressive company names were gold-lettered in the foyer where they waited for the lift. It was a galaxy away from the squalid rehearsal room and the theatre. For the first time it occurred to Belle that their former producer, for whom she'd felt such concern about his financial loss, might be a wealthy man.

They were both mystified by the invitation. Eunice was concerned by it. She could not imagine he'd have anything to say to them, apart from a rebuke. After all, they had upset the star who'd threatened to sue. Perhaps that was it, a pending lawsuit, with them in the witness box. Belle had reminded her that was weeks ago, all forgotten, and told her not to be so cretinous.

'What are you talking about? Who's cretinous? What's it mean?'

'Dumb,' Belle said, wishing she hadn't opened her mouth. A new outbreak of hostility was never more than a word away.

'Who's dumb? Why else would he want to see us? If you believe it's for afternoon tea, then you're dopey enough to believe anything.'

They managed to summon smiles to meet Hugh Bellamy, who said he was expecting another visitor, but asked his secretary to bring in the tea. Good bone china, Belle noticed, and plates of cakes and fresh sandwiches. Eunice was a fool; they were clearly here as guests, not prospective witnesses or penitents.

'I'm sorry we had such a flop,' he said when they were settled, 'but I made a mistake. I should've stuck to my trade, fundraising for other productions. I'm an enthusiastic supporter of the theatre, but not a producer. Certainly not again.'

Neither saw any reason to disagree with this. They sipped their tea and tried to work out why they were here.

'I'm afraid the comedian didn't transplant. Jokes that were a riot in the north of England fell as flat as the Nullarbor here. The one good thing in this fiasco was your kids. They're a class act. You were right, Belle, they did improve – with each performance. A great pity it had to end.'

You can say that again, Belle thought. The chance of a long run and an opportunity to make their names on stage . . . it was just too good to be true. Yet it could've been true, with a decent comic and a better show. She realised Hugh, as he'd asked them to call him, had changed the subject.

'I trust you ladies have sorted out your disagreements amicably?'

'We have,' Eunice assured him, and Belle nodded assent. Mutual umbrage against the Scot had bonded them into an alliance, even if it was a bit precarious.

'Good. I hate to see talent squandered. If they were unable to appear together again, it would be an awful waste. So that's why we're here.'

Belle felt confused but hopeful, until his secretary knocked and showed in a visitor. Hugh rose to greet the man who entered and they shook hands cordially. With a sense of shock she saw it was Ricky Mendoza.

'You know these ladies, Rick?'

'I know the lovely Bella. *Buenas tardes, cara.*'

Oh God, Belle thought, not you. 'This is an unexpected surprise,' she said, as he raised her hand and she felt his wet lips on it.

'Surprise or shock, *mi* Bella?' He smiled knowingly at her, as if reading her mind, then preened as he was introduced to Eunice. 'A delight to meet you, Madame. If I may call you Eunice, I would consider it a favour.'

'Of course you may.'

It was immediately apparent Eunice was impressed. This was, after all, the man of legends, the famous and notorious Ricky M, the most successful producer of vaudeville in the country. He chose a seat beside her. The secretary brought his tea and offered sandwiches. Ricky took a large handful and chuckled at their reactions.

'I never have lunch when I come to see Hugh. The delicatessen downstairs, which he happens to own, makes the best sandwiches in town. So, my *amigo*, have you told them everything?'

'Not quite, Ricky. I was halfway through the preamble.'

'Ha! Now we cut to the chase, yes?' He smiled at Eunice, and at the same time managed a sneaky glance at Belle's legs. 'Last month Hugh takes me to a show. Not a good show, but in it are two young people, two little gems. Hugh is an *aficionado*, also the broker who supplies moneybag investors for me. He says in my next revue I must include his gems, or no moneybags. So – I come to take tea, and talk to the *señoras* about this.'

'I might add,' Hugh said, 'Ricky agrees with my opinion of their talent.'

'I might agree,' Ricky rebuked him, 'but I never express such sentiments before negotiation. All compliments can come later. Now, details of my new show. Roy Rene and Patricia Lamont are the stars. It opens at the Tivoli. Rehearsals next week. I want your little gems to have a six-minute song and dance duet ready by then.'

Despite her growing excitement at what was being said, Belle noticed the change in him. The Latin persona had been replaced by a hardnosed theatrical.

'I plan to bill them as Carson & Sharp. Teddy and Sally does nothing for me, it makes them sound like a pair of kids.'

'But they *are* a pair of kids,' Eunice said.

Ricky took her hand and smiled benignly. 'This is showbiz, darling. I want the audience to expect an adult act, then we surprise them by bringing out two small figures in spotlights. Individual spots, one from each side of the stage until they meet and begin to sing. It's an instant impact. Carson & Sharp. Any other comments?'

Clever, Belle thought, liking the idea of the spotlights. She also preferred him without his South American masquerade.

'Belle, no comments?'

'You forgot to mention salary.'

'I knew you'd remind me,' he said. 'Three pounds a week, an eight-week guarantee.'

'No wonder you forgot to mention it. Try doubling it to six pounds a week.'

'You try to remember this isn't the movies, *cara*.'

'It isn't child labour, either. Five pounds, with a ten-week guarantee, or we walk. Right, Eunice?'

Eunice looked stricken, as if the magical daydream she'd just been listening to was about to drift beyond reach and become a nightmare. She knew they could not possibly walk, and secretly believed Belle was stupid enough to carry out the threat and ruin everything.

'I'll pay four,' Ricky said with a sigh that suggested impending ruin.

'Four pounds ten shillings, rising to five after the guarantee, if we're still running. And a boxed credit on all the posters – "With Carson & Sharp".'

'Sure you don't want them above the title?'

'At the bottom will be fine for now,' Belle smiled, 'from there they can work their way up.'

Ricky capitulated with a characteristic shrug and a warning. 'Goddamn it, Belle, don't you spread rumours about this. I'm not used to haggling – I never bargain with performers, as everyone in the business knows.'

'Relax. I'll say you're as stingy and tight-fisted as ever. Is that suitable?'

'I don't want anyone thinking that I might be getting soft or generous.'

'Oh, I'll make sure of that,' Belle promised.

They signed the contracts that afternoon. Before he left, Ricky produced his wallet and gave Eunice one of his cards – just in case, he said, she might wish to get in touch with him.

The room was on the ground floor, and had access to a garden. There was even a shed where Teddy could keep his bike, instead of having to cart it down from the attic as he'd been doing ever since his birthday. Nuncie and the boys came in a utility truck to help them move, bringing an upright piano as a gift for the new lodgings. They said goodbye to 'Erb and his house in Botany without regret.

'Youse never gave me no proper notice,' he shouted as Belle climbed into the front seat, and Teddy joined Charles and Clarence in the back of the ute.

'So sue them, you great ponce,' Nuncie shouted back, and drove off with a jerk and a strident clash of gears.

'Anywhere there will do,' Clarence said loudly, hearing yet another piercing noise as she tried to change into top gear.

'Does Nuncie drive the truck often?' Teddy asked them.

'Not if we can help it,' Charles said.

'She's good on a pushbike, but,' Clarence added.

Apart from a close encounter with a bus in Randwick, they reached the new house in Glenmore Road safely.

'Bit more space in here,' they observed carrying in the piano.

It was a modest room with twin beds. There was a small table, as well as two chairs and a sofa. A gas ring for boiling a kettle, and cups and plates. It felt like luxury after the months in their tiny garret beneath the iron roof.

'I don't know how you stood that dogbox for so long.' Nuncie spread herself on the sofa with approval at the way the soft springs received her bulk. 'Practically needed a bloody shoehorn to get in and out of there.'

Dear Dad, Teddy wrote once their new life had settled down:

> *a lots happened. I'm in a new show, me and my friend Sally, and we got six minites singing wile we do a dance in the first act and then another number in the second act. People seem to like us, they stood up and clapped last night, then gave us a big cheer when we came on agen. We've moved to Glenmore Road, its near the tram that goes into town, because our show is on at the Tivoli and it only takes about 15 minutes to get there. And the room is much bigger. I keep my bike in the shed and can ride it near here as its safe and nicer than our last place. I thort we might go back to Kings Cross, but Mum said here was better becose I can ride*

*the bike even tho she likes the Cross. I have to go to school in the
mornings, and Mum helps me with the homework so I cant write
much more as I have to do a lot of homework now. Or else I'll get
into truble at school.*

   Love from me and Mum,
   Teddy

It was waiting in the letterbox when he came home from work,
and he read it at once, then later read it aloud to Maureen – without
a mention of the spelling mistakes – when she came in from next
door with a flask of hot cocoa to share with him. She did this every
night after having dinner with her sister and brother-in-law, except
on Fridays when Jim and Betty invited George over to share their
meal. Maureen's visits had begun as an impulsive gesture, and over
the past few months had become a welcome routine.

'He sounds much happier, George.'

'He does.'

'Do you think he ever misses home?'

'It's hard to tell. Different sort of life down there.' He thought
about it, recalling Kellett Street with all its cramped deficiencies,
and shrugged. 'He liked that little dump they had in Kings Cross.
Poky, hardly any daylight, it was a real mystery to me.'

'Bet he misses his dad, though,' she said gently. 'Like you miss
him.'

'That's no secret,' George said, but the word itself had a
connotation that made him uncomfortable.

For it *was* a secret, and one he could never tell her. Or anyone.
He and Belle were the only two in the world who knew it, not even
the real father had the faintest notion; Belle had assured him of that
and he believed her. While he trusted Maureen and there had been

many times he had wanted to confess to her, it somehow remained a part of his life he could share with no one else. Revealing it to a third party would be like relinquishing Teddy himself, after eleven years of what had been a deep parental love.

It was difficult to articulate how desperately he missed him. He had never been good at communicating his innermost thoughts.

'I miss coming home from work and seeing him there, riding down the road to meet me,' he said, and Maureen felt the pain he could not express. She leant forward and kissed him. The same way that she'd kissed him so gently and spontaneously the first night she'd brought him cocoa, appearing apologetically at the back door after dark, the night he'd been unable to prevent himself putting his arms around her, and when he did had felt her body trembling, and they'd sat on the settee touching and fondling until it was no longer possible to resist, and they'd begun to remove their clothes without the need of a word spoken.

She had been a widow without a man in her life for two years, and he was starved for affection. If she was middle-aged and homely, so was he, and the warmth she generated was emotional and overwhelming.

On that first night they had gone into the bedroom to make love – as they had been doing many nights since then, and as they did now. George sometimes wondered how many of the neighbours knew about him and Maureen. Jim and Betty Nelson, for certain. Mr and Mrs Miranda on the other side? He hoped not. Miss Limmington? They'd done their level best to outwit her, because if she found out half the town would soon know. They wanted to keep it private, this autumnal joy they had found with each other.

It seemed as if nothing could go wrong that year, and for a long time nothing did. Carson & Sharp – the name caught on brilliantly, and Belle had to admire Ricky M's insight and expertise in this, grateful the 'Murrumbidgee Kid' label had been left behind at last; Carson & Sharp were accepted and loved by their audiences. In an otherwise grown-up show, full of leading comedians, well-known singers and a very professional dance troupe, they gradually began to be the main attraction, the word-of-mouth magnet that brought crowds to the revue. These packed audiences took away an abiding memory of the diminutive figures as they sang popular new songs and old-time music-hall favourites, while dancing with great panache, the pair of them creating constant waves of approval and applause. The admiring crowds spread the word that this was something different, something a bit special, and other people came to see for themselves. Once their ascent began it was rapid.

Ricky Mendoza not only extended the current show, he had plans for the future and wanted a contract before his competitors tried to white-ant him and lure them away. He went to work on Eunice, silkily persuasive that he could secure their future. All she must do was convince Belle to sign an exclusive two-year deal with him.

'Sorry, we're not interested in being tied up for two years.' Belle was rock solid about it. 'We'll sign for six months – on condition their salaries go up to ten quid a week.'

Ricky, who had expected a demand for more than this, hastily agreed on condition the contract gave him first option when the six months was up. Belle, who knew options could easily be broken, signalled her agreement. Eunice, who by now was in awe of Belle, could hardly credit the way fortune was smiling on them. Her daughter had become a celebrity. At times when she was out with Sally strangers would stop them in the street asking for an autograph.

It was such a startlingly different and thrilling existence.

She invited Belle home to Mosman as her new best friend and there she confided her secrets. She confessed that her current status was not conjugal at all but temporary, and even more temporary since she and Ricky had begun to have occasional afternoons in his office, or rather in the cosy room behind it. Belle must promise not to tell a soul.

Belle promised, deciding it best not to reveal to Eunice that everyone would know by now anyway, for one of the most obnoxious traits of Ricky's character was his liking to boast of his conquests. Nor did she tell Eunice that he still tried to grope her whenever he had the slightest opportunity. Which was why she had been making some discreet approaches to the Fullers and the J.C. Williamson company about what might happen when Mendoza's tenure expired.

But if Ricky's concupiscence was an aggravation, Belle could find no fault with his managerial skill and enthusiasm. When the revue closed he put Teddy and Sally into a Christmas pantomime called *Beyond the Black Stump*, a locally written farce that mixed iconic names like Ben Hall and Ned Kelly with fictional favourites Ginger Mick and the Sentimental Bloke. The pair were cast as Outback characters, a larrikin brother and sister from a hayseed family. It was a riotous romp; they loved it, and encouraged at rehearsals by Ricky they began to over-act outrageously. Belle was alarmed and protested vehemently.

'You'll ruin them,' she complained.

'Settle down, Belle,' he retorted, 'wait till you see the show, and read the notices.'

'That's what I'm worried about, you idiot. The critics will hate them.'

'Don't forget, you're here at my invitation. So shut up or leave.'

'You'll destroy their image, letting them ham it up like this. The public knows them as sweet young kids, not bloody little monsters. Make them tone it down.'

'Belle, dear.' Eunice invariably sat with her at rehearsals, ever since they'd become united by success. 'I hardly ever disagree with you, but Rick might be right this time. People might like them being little monsters – just for a change.'

Which proved prophetic. Belle had to admit it, sitting beside them both on opening night, collapsing with laughter like the rest of the audience at the wildly extravagant nonsense on stage. *Beyond the Black Stump* received good reviews as a piece of festive fun, and Carson & Sharp were singled out for a series of glowing comments, citing their versatility, comedic ability and the clear message they'd conveyed across the footlights that here were a pair of talented youngsters able to take on virtually any kind of roles, who were on the road to stardom.

After the holiday season Mendoza put them straight into another revue. He resisted the calls to give them more time on stage; he wanted them kept fresh and innovative by one brief appearance in each act. Make the audience want more of them, was his rationale. This time their billing was in bigger lettering, a boxed credit just below the title and the stars. They had more glamorous costumes and their own group of dancers. They became a topic, and people were curious to know more about them.

When the popular new magazine *Women's Weekly* published their photographs with the caption 'EXCITING YOUNG NEWCOMERS', the instant increase at the box office did not go unnoticed by Ricky M. He quickly arranged for an interview on one of the new commercial radio stations, this one transmitting under the call sign 2GB from premises above the Savoy Theatre in Bligh Street.

The studio was just a small room without windows. Alongside it was a glass partition and a booth full of strange machines, where a gramophone record was playing. Behind the desk in the studio sat a young man who, to Teddy and Sally's surprise, was wearing a dinner suit and a bow tie. The assistant who ushered them in whispered reverentially that he was the announcer. They were ignored for a few moments until the music finished, when he invited them to sit on chairs facing his desk, and asked if they had ever done radio before. At the same time he flicked a switch, and a light appeared on the peculiar apparatus in front of him. Teddy supposed something had been turned on, but was unsure about this as they hadn't been told. He wanted to ask, but felt tongue-tied and nervous until Sally nudged him and gripped his hand reassuringly.

'Ever done it before?' The announcer repeated the question, with a sideways glance at his control operator in the adjacent glass booth, a look that encapsulated his cynicism about this interview. A couple of juvenile actors, stage kids with nothing real to say; who the hell needed it? Certainly not him, Bobby Parkin, better known to the listening world as King Bobby.

'Have we done what before?' Teddy asked, puzzled by the undercurrent of what felt like antagonism.

'An interview on the air. To put it in simple terms, have you ever spoken to our faithful audience out there, via the wonderful world of the wireless?'

Parkin had a deep mellifluous voice despite his youth, and seemed to be very sure of himself. Teddy felt at a disadvantage, uncertain what to answer, mesmerised by the contraption that stood between them on the desk. He was trying to recollect what it was called, then remembered Ricky saying it was a microphone, and explaining that once the light was turned on, anything they said would be heard by hundreds, even thousands of people. Recalling that, he realised the man had switched it on without bothering to warn them. It was then he decided what to do, and hoped Sally would catch the drift. He tried to communicate his intention with a glance at her.

'The wonderful world of the wireless,' he repeated. 'No, I've never spoken on that. I've never even *seen* a wireless. Have you, Sally?'

'I've seen pictures of them,' she responded, keeping a tight hold of his hand. 'My mum was talking of buying one.'

'Was she? What happened?'

'She decided it wasn't worth bothering.'

'Why was that, Sal?'

'She said there's an awful lot of rubbish talked on it.'

You beauty, Teddy wanted to say to her, you absolute beaut, and wished he could hug her. He glimpsed the announcer with his mouth open. The man in the booth seemed to be laughing, but they could not hear it because of the glass.

'What sort of rubbish, Sally?'

'Gasbag stuff, she said.'

'Gasbag?'

'Yes.'

'What's she mean by gasbag?'

'She means a lot of hot air comes through it.'

'Hot air, eh? Not worth having one then, Sal?'

'Ted, she says if you want hot air go down to speakers' corner in the Domain. You can hear it there for free every Sunday.'

Her voice was a perfect mimicry of Eunice. They were still holding hands. Teddy squeezed hers and an answering response told him she was enjoying this. On the other side of the microphone, the announcer was gazing at them like a rabbit caught in a spotlight. Now he tried to intervene and end this damaging duologue.

'Excuse me, Teddy and Sally —'

'Carson & Sharp,' Sally interrupted him, 'that's what we're called. What are you called?'

'I'm the Chief Announcer, Robert Parkin,' he declared tersely, unused to losing control of interviews like this, 'and my public like to call me King Bobby.'

'What do we call you? Your Majesty, or just King?'

'Or Mr King?' Teddy suggested.

'That can't be right,' Sally corrected him, "cos his wife couldn't be Mrs King. Is she called the Queen?' she asked with such wide-eyed innocence that the control operator almost wet himself with glee. He'd never seen any of the guests take the piss like this; most were usually bullied into being docile and agreeing with whatever question they were asked. But these two were doing such a lovely deadpan job on the bombastic and conceited Bobby Parkin, who so relished his self-bestowed title of King Bobby, Emperor of the Wireless Waves.

'You kids!' Parkin forced a chuckle. 'Good on the ad lib, eh? Having a bit of fun at King Bobby's expense.'

'We're just getting used to the microphone.' Teddy smiled at him disarmingly. 'When are you going to switch it on?'

'It's been on all the time, son.'

'You mean we've actually been speaking to the magical world of the wireless and we didn't even know? Wow! Jeepers! Do you realise that, Sal?'

'Golly, Ted. All those people. Do you think they heard us?' She turned to the near-apoplectic announcer. 'What do you think, Your Maj?'

Before he could speak, Teddy anticipated him. 'Tell you what I think, Sal. We'd better tell them about our show, *Galaxy Galore* at the Criterion Theatre, before the King gets cross with us and orders us to leave his palace.'

The interview was widely heard. Bobby Parkin commanded a large audience, but in reality King Bobby, the so-called Emperor of the Wireless Waves, was not widely loved. The following Sunday's newspapers relished his discomfort at the hands of the youthful Carson & Sharp, and made much of it on their show-business pages. The publicity was immense. Ricky M, who had been disappointed at their shenanigans, pointing out he had paid a hefty sum to Parkin on the side and there was no real promotion for the show because of their tomfoolery, was delighted by the eventual result. The revue had packed houses with bookings until Easter.

Belle had a fleeting concern at the increasing amount of exposure, in case it brought unwelcome attention, but recalled that when she knew him Donald Ferrier never attended vaudeville shows, nor did he bother with anything in the papers except the news and the law reports. He had no interest in the entertainment pages. If he ever saw the names Carson & Sharp on a poster or a billboard they would mean nothing to him. But in her concern about one former lover she had entirely forgotten the other.

Dan Hardacre read every show-business section of every paper, with the intensity of a man still searching for a job. He had been in Melbourne for the past three months, in a vain attempt to secure a position with J. C. Williamson Theatres. If not, he would've been aware far sooner.

A few days after their radio interview Dan gave up his search for employment and returned to Sydney. He drove back through Queanbeyan and Canberra, reaching his flat late on Saturday night.

The next morning he bought all the newspapers and went to his favourite coffee shop The Arabian to read them over a leisurely breakfast. An hour later he had made a phone call and was on his way to Donald Ferrier's home, confident he would be able to pay his debts at last.

Chapter twenty-six

Until the interval it was just like any other normal night at the Criterion. Another packed house, the same huge applause for the pair of them, making Belle feel all those hard years she had battled for Teddy were at last being rewarded. When Eunice went backstage to their dressing-room to enthuse about how well the show had gone so far, Belle sat among the audience in the stalls feeling a weary but satisfying sense of achievement. It had not been easy, never easy, but she – and her son, she could hardly forget *him* – had managed to succeed beyond her or anyone else's most extravagant dreams. Where it went from here she could not yet imagine. Other venues of course, interstate perhaps, even overseas. She had an aspiration of England and the London Palladium; in her mind they had come so far, all the way from distant Brewinda Road to this, that anything and anywhere was now possible.

She felt a slight lethargy, and attributed it to the heat generated by people so tightly crammed into the theatre. Not that she minded the crush. She knew the precise number of people the Criterion held, especially now that Teddy and Sal were on a percentage. It had been a ferocious fight with Ricky M, but with the contract about to expire she had bluffed him into believing they'd go elsewhere. Eunice had been petrified, but she'd won. It was a tiny proportion, just ten shillings for every hundred tickets sold, but already she knew tonight's full house was worth an extra four pounds. Translated into each week's six nightly performances and two matinees, it meant they shared an additional thirty pounds after their salaries.

It felt like riches, and with the basic working wage barely a tenth of that, it was. Belle had given up the bar job with relief. They could even afford to move; an apartment with a view in Macleay Street was not out of reach if they wanted, but she was unsure. It was better to be careful; there'd been enough reversals and poverty. No one could predict tomorrow; she'd learnt that lesson. Besides, she liked the room in Glenmore Road. It was convenient, safe for Teddy to ride his bike in the street, and the landlady was amicable. So they would stay there, at least for a while.

She glanced at her watch, wondering if there was time to shake the feeling of fatigue by a brief walk outside in the fresh air. But with only a few minutes left before the curtain rose for the last act, she decided to remain. It was when she turned to look across the aisle, expecting Eunice's return from backstage, that she caught sight of Donald Ferrier sitting in the stalls with a rather self-satisfied Dan Hardacre.

The second half of the show had always been her favourite. It was faster and funnier, but tonight it seemed turgid and endless. She fidgeted until Eunice gave her a puzzled glance, and in answer Belle touched her brow to indicate a sudden headache. She knew both the men had seen her, despite her immediate attempt to look away and study the program to avoid eye contact. They must have seen her when they first entered the theatre before the opening curtain. All through the first act she'd been blissfully unaware; they would have realised this and no doubt enjoyed her state of incognisance.

There was no longer need to feign a headache. She felt as if she was on the verge of something awful like a migraine. Or a catastrophe.

Donald had no interest in the rest of the show. He sat impatiently while a comedian made the audience around him laugh; he endured songs and dances while waiting for another glimpse, and it was not until quite late in the second half that they returned. The empty stage, the instrumental theme of their song and the expectation the music aroused in the theatre signalled it.

People began to applaud before they appeared, then the spotlights caught them as they emerged from opposite corners upstage – he seemed to recall that upstage was the professional term – so the impression of distance accentuated their figures into looking even smaller, while the lighting threw long shadows as they converged. It was clever, he thought, but was quite unprepared for the burst of cheering that greeted them, a reception so loud and so long that they could not begin the song, and went into a routine that appeared impromptu, but surely was rehearsed, where Teddy nervously tried to kiss Sally's hand, which she kept snatching away, until finally she allowed him to kiss it continental fashion, after which he tried to eat it. Following this he gave an elaborate bow and the girl curtsied in reply, and when the applause continued he parodied a curtsy and she gave a masculine bow as the laughter enveloped them.

When they sang Donald watched intently, searching for some trace of a familiar gesture or a look, something of himself in the figure on stage, which was hardly possible. But it gave him the opportunity to appreciate their style and realise why they were so popular. It was the simplicity: they were like kids next door, like his own children and their friends, except they could dance to every kind of music, their rhythm matched by the hands of the crowd keeping time to the beat. Backed by a group they high-kicked, then danced a prolonged and popular charleston, after that the bolero, and finally a waltz so tranquil that the change of tempo seemed unachievable. Yet they managed it with ease. And all the while there seemed to be this affection, this magnetism between them – almost like lovers, he thought, if they had not been eleven years old.

Then the music stopped. Their accompanying dancers froze like statuettes. The pair were silhouetted by a single spotlight and went into a sketch. The instant laughter of the dialogue signalled recognition, though Donald had no idea why. The girl was calling Teddy His Highness Prince Boobie, the Wonderful Wizard of the Wireless Waves. The applause when they did a reprise of the charleston and danced off the stage brought them back again and again, until finally the little redhead pretended to be exhausted.

She started to sway to her left. Halfway to the floor, with her feet firmly anchored, she recovered her equilibrium, then swayed alarmingly to her right, while Teddy scratched his head and gazed at the audience inviting them to share his concern. It was extraordinary how far she could sway on either side without falling. At last he lifted her up, slung her across his shoulder, pretended to go weak at the knees under her weight, then staggered off while she laughed and waved as she was carried into the wings.

'Well?' Dan Hardacre could hardly be heard amid the deafening ovation.

'Bloody good,' Donald found himself saying enthusiastically.

'I mean, he has a smidgen of you, don't you reckon?'

'Impossible to say that, Dan.'

'I think so. By the way, I'm sure Belle knows we're here. Still a bloody good-looking woman, eh?'

Someone in front hushed them as a conjurer came on. Belle was certainly that, Donald silently agreed, as he spent the rest of the program thinking about what tactics to adopt when meeting her after the show. For a start, he thought it might be easier if he got rid of Dan.

Belle spent most of the second half puzzling what to do for the best. She even contemplated asking Eunice to drive her and Teddy home because of her splitting headache, but decided that was a non-starter. Or she could spin a story that she had to hide from a former boyfriend and needed help, but that would mean inviting Eunice into a conspiracy, and while they had become companions – almost friends – she was not quite ready to trust her private life to her.

Unfortunately there was no escape, no way she could avoid meeting him; before the curtain fell she had come to accept that. Donald had no interest in this kind of theatre; he would never have come to a vaudeville show, unless . . .

So he'd worked things out. She realised it was bound to happen eventually. She resolved to be firm, to remember he had no claim, while at the same time she would remain calm and polite – except to Dan, who'd tried to deceive Helene LaRue with a lie. Dan was a cheap conniver who deserved a good kick in the balls.

She picked a spot near the stage door and sent a message to Teddy to take his time dressing, as she had to meet two unexpected guests. But to her relief only one arrived. She nodded to the doorman to let him through.

Dammit, she thought, he really doesn't look any older. The same rugged good looks, tall figure, neat brown hair without a trace of grey. A girl in the chorus passed with a glance at his profile, a reminder of how women were attracted to him, but she brushed the thought from her memory. She'd steeled herself to be courteous and calm – it was the only way to handle this – until she saw his rather overconfident smile, which was when all her best intentions fled.

'Where's your tame bloodhound?'

'Can we start by saying hello, Belle?'

'It would make a change from your last words to me – "Sorry, but it's goodbye, Belle". Or have you forgotten?'

'I just wanted to meet. I hope you're not going to give me a hard time.'

'I don't want to give you any time at all, Donald, but here you are. Looking a bit longer in the tooth, a bit wrinkled and weather-beaten, but aren't we all?'

'You're not, actually.'

'Skip the flannel,' she said. 'Where's the parasite?'

'If we're speaking of Dan, I paid him off and told him to get lost.'

'What a pity. I had a few words to say to him.'

'I can imagine.'

'No, I doubt if you can,' Belle said. 'Trying to find me, he lied to a friend of mine, saying he wanted to cast Teddy in a film. What's cruel about that is there were a dozen times he could've cast him in the past few years. Times when we were broke and badly needed help.'

'Like the night you came searching for me?'

She did not respond to this, refusing to be diverted. 'Dan is a low-life. Stalking me for money. Hiring a detective to watch Nuncie, after you tried to bully my address out of her. I find it very distasteful that you actually paid him to do whatever it took to hunt me down. As a lawyer, Donald, wouldn't you say that constitutes harassment?'

'I'd say we need to talk of this another time, because your son is about to join us,' he said, and Belle turned swiftly to look behind her. Teddy, along with Eunice and Sally, was coming from the direction of the dressing-rooms.

'Be with you in a tick,' she called to Eunice.

'We'll be in the green room,' Eunice said, her gaze lingering on Donald as they walked towards the stairs. Teddy gave her a quick wave.

'Let me meet him,' Donald said.

'No.'

'I only want to tell both the kids how much I enjoyed their part of the show.'

'I'll pass the message on.'

'Belle, I think you should know, I'm not going to be shoved away like this,' he said, his voice betraying a quiet tenacity.

'I can't imagine what you mean, Donald.'

'I'd like to do this in a decent, friendly way. Or else we can play rough.'

'There's no way in the world you can frighten me,' she said, determined to wipe the optimistic smile from his face: a smile that seemed to convey he was in no doubt of the outcome.

'Frighten you? For God's sake, that's the last thing I want. I hurt you enough years ago. It ended badly, in a mess and a lot of anger.'

'It ended when you met my friend Caroline,' Belle said.

'I've been looking for you for months,' Donald went on, ignoring this, 'ever since I found out it was you who'd come asking for me, actually waited for me, and then, for a reason that escapes me, ran away. I want to talk, and I want to be allowed to meet Teddy. Will you come to lunch on Sunday, and bring him?'

'He's not your son, Donald.'

'I asked if you'd come to lunch. There'll be no embarrassment.

If you didn't know, Caroline's in Adelaide. She and the kids won't be back.'

'I'm sorry about your marriage, but you didn't seem to hear me. I said he's not your son.'

'Then there's no problem about us meeting.'

'There's an awfully big problem. I don't want to sit at your table or eat your food, let alone drink your wine. You kicked me out of your life long ago, and now you've paid someone to hound me. If Dan's a sleazy shit, you're the cunt who hired him.'

There was a pause while he stared at her, the smile vanishing. She was vaguely conscious of stagehands and dancers passing, intrigued by the signs of argument between them. A clenched-teeth squabble conducted in hushed voices, but the anger was unmistakeable. There'd be gossip at the matinee tomorrow, about her and the well-dressed gent – *and* their dispute. Bloody Eunice would interrogate her; even Teddy would be curious about it.

'Please come to lunch.' Donald's voice was deceptively quiet. 'If you don't, that will force me to the conclusion that you're afraid. Of what, I ask? I'll have to leave that to the court to decide.'

'What court? Don't try your snide lawyer's tricks on me.'

'I have some papers, Belle. Some documents. You and I need to discuss them rationally. If you refuse, I can ask a magistrate to open proceedings, and we'll both have to hire advocates and give evidence. I don't want to do that. I just want you to come to lunch and bring Teddy. Is that really so difficult? Sunday, shall we say twelve-thirty for one o'clock? You know the address.'

'You're not going,' Nuncie said. '*Surely* you're not going there. You'd be stark raving mad to go.'

352

'I'm not raving mad. I'm awfully scared. I need to know what the hell he's talking about. Documents, he said. What bloody documents?'

'It's a bluff, Belle. Legal crap.'

'Well, that's why I have to go. To find out. Because I can't sleep at night until I know.'

She expected the same surly housekeeper, but Donald himself met them when she rang the doorbell. Looking relaxed and casual in grey flannels and a plaid sports shirt, he greeted her with a welcoming smile, stooped to shake hands with Teddy and congratulated him on the great show, declaring it was the best vaudeville he'd ever seen.

The *only* one you've ever seen, Belle thought sourly as they were ushered into the living room. It appeared to her it had recently been redecorated, and much of the furniture seemed new. Donald opened a bottle of white wine being cooled in a silver bucket, and offered Teddy lemonade. A delicious aroma from the kitchen indicated roast lamb for lunch, and a new housekeeper – a distinct improvement, Belle thought – brought in appetisers. There were peanuts and crisps for Teddy, and olives and savouries for them; it was clear he had gone to a great deal of trouble, which really bothered her.

She had to contain her impatience while Donald had a running conversation with her son. He particularly wanted to know all about Sally, how and where they'd met. Teddy was happy to oblige. So for some time the two held an animated conversation that virtually excluded her; Teddy related the history of how the pair had made friends at Greta's dance classes, his regular walks home with Sally after school, how they'd lost touch after leaving the Cross, then the chance meeting again and their audition together. Donald appeared to listen with close attention.

'And the first show was a flop?'

'Terrific flop,' Teddy agreed readily. 'Hardly anybody came to see it, and sometimes there were only about ten in the audience.'

'That must've been awful.'

'Horrible. I had to go back to rotten school again, Mum went back to work at the hotel, and I didn't see Sally for weeks. It felt like we'd never meet again, but then Mum and Eunice met Mr Mendoza.'

'A lucky day, that one.'

'It certainly was.' Teddy grinned. 'A real beaut day.'

'But six nights and two matinees each week, that seems a lot. Don't you get awfully tired?' Donald asked.

'Not really. With packed houses, you never get tired.'

'Why is that, Teddy? What's the difference?'

'With a big full house, it's exciting. We got fed up doing the flop because nobody laughed or clapped. But when it's exciting, Sal and I don't get a bit tired then – we like it.'

'I suppose it's called adrenalin,' Donald said, and went on to explain this. He seemed engrossed, talking to Teddy – wanting to know every detail, which pleased Teddy but did not fool Belle. Donald Ferrier had never been engrossed in anything except his law books. But he was certainly giving a fine performance.

The roast lamb was delicious. There were crisp potatoes, peas, baked pumpkin, rich gravy and mint sauce. In over three years Belle had not lived in a place with a kitchen or a proper stove, so a meal like this had not been possible. Donald carved the meat, filling their plates, and Teddy had a second helping.

For dessert there was peach melba and ice-cream. He had a second helping of that as well, and pronounced the meal terrific, absolutely beaut. Belle could see he was being seduced; in all his life he had never known such close attentive interest from an adult, or the new luxury of having a housekeeper fuss over him and provide a meal like this.

Afterwards they had coffee on the side verandah, and Teddy wandered out to explore the garden. It was time to talk, but she waited for Donald to begin. All he wanted to do, it appeared, was enthuse about Teddy.

'He's a wonderful boy. Well-mannered. Talented. You should be proud.'

'I am.'

'He's a real credit to you.'

'Thank you, Donald.'

'I can't lay claim to his upbringing,' he said, then after a pause added, 'but I can prove he's my son.'

She put down her coffee cup with a clatter. Let the battle commence, she thought, and vehemently shook her head.

'I'm afraid not, Donald. Your child – son or daughter, whatever it was,' she said, 'was scraped out of my womb by that society doctor, that bloody butcher you sent me to. You insisted on an abortion, you gave me the money, and I had it done.'

'I can prove you didn't, Belle.'

'You can't prove any such thing,' she said heatedly. 'Look, I came to lunch as you insisted. It was a nice meal, and under other circumstances I might've enjoyed it. Now I'm leaving here, and you can go straight to hell with your bloody documents, whatever they are.' She started to rise, but his firm hand on her arm detained her.

'I'll tell you what they are. I obtained validated copies from the Registrar's office. A replica of a marriage certificate to George

Carson, June 1923, and the birth certificate of Teddy Carson, exactly five months and eighteen days later.'

Belle shrugged off his hand, but resumed her chair. She felt cold, knowing what was coming next. It was essential not to let herself be flustered. 'These things happen,' she told him. 'I met George on the rebound after we broke up. He was a randy bugger, all over me like a rash, and I needed that sort of consolation. He made me pregnant so I agreed to marry him.'

'Impossible. How do you have an abortion in May, and give birth to a new baby in November?'

'You're turning this charming house into a courtroom,' Belle said angrily. 'Trying to attack me like you harass hostile witnesses.'

'The dates, Belle. The dates prove you're a liar. We split up in March that year. In late April you told me you were pregnant – with our child. I went to the bank, drew the cash for the doctor. April the thirtieth.'

'I remember.'

'Do you remember a week later you wrote to say you'd had the abortion? That was the first lie. You didn't have it, Belle. You kept the child, kept the money, found a convenient husband, and you've been lying about it ever since.'

This, she thought, is where you turn to the judge and jury with a flourish and make your closing address. A decent father, able to handsomely provide for this child, tricked out of his paternal rights and here to make his claim. The vital thing was to remain unruffled; unlike in his courtroom the beleaguered witness here had the right of reply. But she must do it calmly, with composure.

'Proving I'm a liar, Donald, would be quite easy for you.'

'I'm glad you realise that.'

'I realise you've lost your wife and children. Now you've suddenly discovered that a foetus you wanted to get rid of is alive – a talented, well-mannered boy – and you want a share of him.'

'Cut it out,' he said, in reaction to the word foetus.

'Let's not pussyfoot around, that's what you want, isn't it?'

'No. I want a reasonable discussion. Some amicable arrangement.'

'But I don't want to be reasonable or amicable.' It was time, she thought, to reveal her sharp claws. 'And you don't realise how embarrassing this will be for you. Because I'm going to fight.'

'In court you won't have a hope.'

'Who said anything about a court? Gutter tactics, Donald. The tabloid press and even those gushing women's magazines will lap up a story like this.'

'You wouldn't dare.'

'Me? Think about it! "Eminent King's Counsel dumps pregnant chorus girl to marry her rich friend. Demands the chorus girl abort the child. But she can prove she didn't. She can also prove a butcher, a socially prominent surgeon, insisted she pay his fee just the same, which she did." And believe me I paid it, and went out of there intact. Can you even imagine what the newspapers will make of that?'

'For God's sake,' he said, shaken, 'all I'm asking for is a civilised arrangement —'

'Fuck being civilised. You weren't the least bit civilised when you married my friend Caroline and withdrew a previous offer to me, or when you told me to get rid of the baby.'

'I behaved like a shit, I admit it.'

'The readers will certainly come to that conclusion. And of course this'll get huge coverage, because it's Teddy Carson, and he's news. The sleazy papers will fight to get hold of it.'

'You'll ruin his life.'

'No, I'll ruin yours. Think of the almighty stink, the gossip and dirty jokes among your legal luminaries. The child star that Ferrier KC wanted aborted.'

'Christ almighty, Belle, you throw that kind of mud, it'll stick to all of us.'

'Not to Teddy. People might blame me; they'll definitely blame you. The mud will stick all right, Donald, it'll stick all over you like shit to a blanket if you don't back off. I brought him up, gave up a hell of a lot of things for him. Do you really think I'd let some bloody magistrate rearrange his life to suit you?'

She felt exhausted but triumphant. They walked home from Woollahra through the back streets to Glenmore Road. Donald had asked her to let him drive them, but Belle was adamant; she had no intention of allowing him to know where they lived. She made the excuse they had shopping to do and friends to visit. Teddy had shaken hands, asking if he could thank the housekeeper for the beaut meal. Belle had been proud of that, and had not missed seeing the blend of esteem and regret in his father's eyes.

They had finally come to an arrangement, dictated on her terms. He would make no public claim. And he must control his wayward friend Dan, making sure he didn't shoot off his mouth and create rumours. She made it clear George had been a fond and decent parent, and she did not want him to be humiliated. In return they would visit for an occasional Sunday lunch.

'Once a month,' Donald suggested.

'Not regimented visits like that, or it will become a chore to Teddy. I'll ring you from time to time to see if it's convenient.'

'It will be. What's he going to call me?'

'He can call you Donald. Seems logical – you're a friend of mine from the past. Now and then you ask us to lunch. Can we agree on that?'

'Don't have much choice, do I?' he replied after a long and reluctant pause.

He accompanied them to the gate, and stood there watching until they reached the corner. Teddy looked back and waved. Donald waved to him, torn between pride and a deep sense of loss.

Chapter twenty-seven

Dan Hardacre found it hard to conceal his scepticism. In fact, the more he thought about it, the less he believed it. Having spent Sunday with them, Donald now declared himself satisfied: young Ted wasn't his son after all.

'But you said you had proof,' Dan protested.

'I thought so,' Donald said, 'but wishful thinking is not legal proof. Still, you found them and we had a deal, so here's a cheque for five hundred pounds.'

'I was hoping it might be cash. I'm not very welcome at my own bank.'

Dan left after a brief drink, with a cash cheque in his pocket. Not quite the scenario he'd had in mind: he hoped to be greeted by good news, then seize the moment to point out he'd had far more expenses than anticipated, and request another two hundred quid. Or even test the water and see if he could get more.

But if Ferrier wasn't the dad, then who was? It wasn't George Carson. He could count, and he knew exactly when Belle had met George – at some local art show, of all places. And knowing his dates, he knew there wasn't time for them to make a kid; she was at least three months up the spout by the time George came along. It could only mean that Donald had to be lying. There was no one else in Belle's life at that time; he was the only possible candidate.

All of which would be of no public interest, he reflected as he drove back to Elizabeth Bay, except that young Ted was headed for stardom. He was no normal child any more, and people would be interested in this pedigree puzzle. He and little Sally were cute, and they were current favourites, especially since they'd sent up the so-called King Bobby, that jerk on the radio. Dan began to speculate on which newspaper to approach. *Truth*, the weekend rag that specialised in scandal, would be a likely prospect. It'd be worth finding out whether any journalist friends of his worked there.

Belle told Nuncie about the lunch. They sat in her office drinking tea while she gave a verbatim report. It was an implicit bond between them, one always there, but never mentioned since; Nuncie had vehemently opposed the abortion. It was her support and persuasion that had influenced Belle to keep the child. She could recall those awful weeks when she was so vulnerable after the abrupt rejection by Donald, with the added trauma of an unwanted pregnancy bringing her close to despair. Close to – although she always tried to erase this from her memory – a contemplation of suicide.

She would never forget the day of the appointment. They'd taken a taxi to the address in Rose Bay. Nuncie had insisted; they were not going to arrive like vagrants, she maintained. It was a secluded private hospital in a quiet street. The doctor was a lizard of a man, impeccable in a Savile Row suit, an old school tie and Italian shoes. He was not only notorious as an abortionist, but his hospital was a refuge for gunshot victims. Members of the feuding Tilly Devine and Kate Leigh gangs relied on Doctor Randolph-Smith and his clinic, where knife and bullet wounds could be treated safe from interference by the law.

When Belle told the doctor she'd changed her mind, he was not pleased. An appointment had been made, he declared, a surgical nurse was on stand-by; it would only take a half hour and it was too late for second thoughts. That was the moment when Nuncie reached out and gripped him by the rather flamboyant old-school tie. Before the doctor could protest she'd slipped the knot so it was tight around his neck, and while he went red in the face and ordered her to stop, she had examined it and pronounced it a fake.

'St Paul's College in London? I don't think so, Doctor,' she'd said. 'My brother went there and this tie is counterfeit. You can buy them in the markets, anywhere from Camden Town to Marrakech. You're a phoney, and so is your tie.'

'I'll call the police,' he'd threatened between clenched teeth.

'Good idea,' Nuncie agreed. 'Get the cops, and I'll call a reporter mate of mine. He'll bring a photographer, and we'll be a hot gossip item on the newsstands tomorrow.'

'A bluff,' he snapped, struggling free of her grasp, his hair – usually so sleek with brilliantine – becoming disarrayed.

'No bluff, sport. I could use the publicity for my new shop. Any exposure is good for business. How do you feel about a full facial all over page one, Doc?'

'Your friend has committed herself to the operation.'

'My friend, as a woman of good sense, has decided not to trust her body to you and your filthy curette,' Nuncie had bluntly informed him. 'She had the guts to come and tell you. Now she's leaving.'

'Not before payment, I assure you.' He'd been enraged, pressing an alarm button on his desk to summon his nurse and a muscular medical orderly.

Belle had taken an envelope from her handbag. It held seventy-five pounds given to her by Donald, more money than she'd seen in her lifetime. It was bulging, for the fee had been requested in single used notes.

'There's your payment.' She'd ripped the envelope and thrown the contents on the floor. 'It's worth every penny not to have a butcher like you touching me.'

Then she and Nuncie had walked out, while the nurse and the orderly scrabbled for the money.

They took a tram back towards the city. 'You are one crazy girl,' Nuncie said.

'It was Donald's lousy cash,' Belle replied, not caring if other passengers heard her. 'I'd rather the abortionist have it than send it back to him.'

Nuncie had laughed and thrown her hands in the air, declaring there was a third alternative she'd forgotten – they could've had a slap-up party for fifty of their closest friends at the Hotel Australia with that kind of money.

Belle remembered it with such clarity. And recalled Nuncie's deep emotion the day she'd brought Teddy here, the first time she'd ever seen him. Real friendship was about things like that – debts that need not be spoken of, but could never be repaid.

Belle and Eunice, unified by the success of their children, were being classed as friends. Each kept personal scrapbooks that soon became voluminous. No longer were Carson & Sharp an anonymous footnote in a critic's review. When they went into yet another show – another boxed credit on the bill in a bigger typeface, the size of their credit was increasing all the time – some of the newspaper notices were excellent, while others for the first time posed the question of whether it could last.

What would happen when Teddy Carson's voice broke?

What lay ahead when these talented children reached puberty?

Both mothers were indignant at the snide comments; they called it typical local sniping at success. Australians were good at building up and then undermining their favourites. 'Take absolutely no notice,' was Belle's advice, and Eunice was content to agree. Meanwhile there were new opportunities, and the future seemed more promising than ever. An advertising agency hired Teddy and Sally to promote its product, and Belle wrote one of her rare letters to George, telling him to borrow a radio set and be sure to listen on Sunday evening.

The broadcasting station was in the same building as the previous one they'd visited, above the Savoy Theatre. It had a larger studio, and Belle and Eunice sat in the viewing booth with the producer and an agency executive. Teddy and Sally stood either side of a microphone, with an announcer immaculate in his dinner suit at a lectern. All eyes were on the clock. From the control room the director signalled the announcer his cue.

'This is station 2UE. The time is six o'clock, and we present, live for your entertainment, fifteen minutes of songs with Carson & Sharp. But first, a word from our sponsor.'

On another cue Sally played an introductory few bars on the flute, then she and Teddy began to sing a jingle specially written for them:

> We clean our teeth twice each day,
> We clean them in the nicest way.

We always brush with you-know-what,
We clean our molars quite a lot.

They spoke the next lines.
'Your teeth are so white, Sal.'
'And you know why, Teddy.'
'*Pepsodrill*,' they chorused synchronously, then sang again:

You'll never have a dentist bill,
If you brush your teeth with – Pepsodrill!

It was fortunate their listening audience could not see the cherished pair, hands clamped to their mouths to prevent laughter, and only just able to compose themselves as music signalled the introduction for their first song.

Dear Belle, George wrote the following day:

It was most entertaining, all their songs and even the one about the toothpaste. I borrowed a set from work, and invited my good friends Jim and Betty Nelson, and of course Maureen in to listen. We weren't sure if we'd be able to hear it, but the wireless station in Canberra had what they called a relay, and apart from a bit of static we didn't miss anything. They sang really well together, and I'm not surprised the local paper here said they were popular. I'm glad you moved into a nicer place to live, and I hope with all this acting and singing, Teddy is still able to do his school work, as it would be a shame for him to lag behind again.

As I have mentioned Betty next door and of course Maureen in my past letters, I enclose a snap Jim took to show what they look like. I'm the strange bloke in the middle between the sisters, and Maureen is on my right.

Love to Teddy, and to you,
George

Belle studied the photo, and thought George appeared rather self-satisfied with his arms around both sisters. The one on his left looked . . . she searched for the words and in the end thought that plump and comfortable might fit. The younger one on the other side was clearly Maureen, who had a nice smile, and closer study made it apparent she was wedged much tighter against George than her sibling. In fact, Belle decided, she had a slightly proprietorial air – and he certainly looked more than a bit pleased with himself.

Fair enough, she thought, noting the wording 'and of course Maureen' used in the letter twice. It was a friendly letter, but she wished he hadn't made the predictable comment about school work. It was typical George, causing her to feel guilty that Teddy was missing quite so much. But with eight shows a week, some personal appearances that Ricky was insisting on, plus parts in radio serials now for the new George Edwards Company – how on earth did he have any time for school!

Belle began to sleep badly. She had stomach cramps occasionally, and was sick several days in a row, telling Nuncie it felt like morning sickness but since pregnancy was out of the question it was obviously indigestion. Nuncie said it was far more likely to be sheer exhaustion, sitting in the theatre each night, then taking the train every morning out to Homebush Studios because Teddy now had a regular part in a new family serial that was being broadcast live at breakfast time. Nuncie declared she was on a treadmill, and so was Teddy. It was about time to slow down, to stop overdoing things. For a start, she should organise to see a doctor.

Instead Belle consulted a herbalist recommended by Eunice, and was given a tonic to take three times daily. Nuncie, who was jealous of Eunice and thought her flighty and pretentious, angrily described this as the height of folly.

'The woman's a fool, and you're an idiot to listen to her.'

'She had symptoms just like this, and it cured her.'

'For Christ's sake, girl, see a *proper* doctor. Not some bloody quack who prescribes crushed elderberries and garlic.'

'Don't be ridiculous, it's full of aromatic and medicinal herbs.'

'It's full of bugger-all,' Nuncie said with a sigh. 'You're on such a daily grind you can't even take the time to look after yourself. I know success is a bloody nice change from poverty, but this is getting out of hand. You'll wear yourself out, not to mention exhausting Teddy.' She hesitated for a moment, then added, 'As a matter of fact, love, you won't like me saying this, but I think those two kids are being well and truly overworked.'

There was a letter for Belle at the stage door. Inside the envelope a message typed on Donald Ferrier's letterhead was succinct and alarming:

AS I DON'T KNOW YOUR ADDRESS THIS IS THE ONLY WAY
I CAN CONTACT YOU. MOST URGENT WE MEET TOMORROW.
DONALD.

His chambers were in an elite section of Phillip Street, convenient to the Supreme Court. His clerk met her at the lift, and conducted her to an austere room, much smaller than she'd imagined. The walls were lined with bookshelves containing bulky volumes of law reports. His wig and gown lay discarded on an armchair. The clerk collected these and left them alone. Donald abruptly handed her a cutting from a newspaper and she started to read it. She sat down in the chair, trying to control her shock.

'It was in last weekend's edition of *Truth*. I had no idea if you get the rag and had already seen it.'

'No, I don't get the wretched thing,' she said.

'Nor do I. I was warned it was in there. If you'd allowed me to know where you live I would've brought it around two days ago.'

'Who warned you?'

'Bloody Hardacre. Who else? The slimy bastard rang to say someone must've got hold of the story. He seemed to be amused.'

Of course, Belle thought. Dan had been paid his finder's fee and told to get lost. That wouldn't buy his loyalty. She read the cutting again. It was fortunately little more than an unpleasant and vicious paragraph at present, a single column on an inside page. But for her it was full of poisonous innuendo and foreboding.

PARENTAL PUZZLE

What mystery lies behind the family tree of a certain young stage star? Names at this stage must be withheld pending further investigation. A strange ambiguity conceals the truth. Is a certain well-known barrister the real parent of

this talented lad, or could he have been sired
by one who met his mother, married her, and
produced the child less than six months later?
Behind the footlights in theatreland gossip is
rife. It's a wise child who knows his own father,
according to the proverb, and *Truth* will assist in
this search for wisdom. Enquiries are proceeding,
and we will bring readers full details next Sunday.
Don't miss the revelation of *who's his father!*

'Next week! God almighty.' She felt sick with a helpless dismay.
'Can we stop this, Donald?'

'Not if they've got Hardacre feeding them details. I've got the name
of the journalist, but he's unavailable. Even if I could get to the editor
and appeal to his sense of fair play, I'd be laughed out of the office.'

'Then what's the answer?'

'I'm afraid we have to face facts, Belle. I doubt if we can prevent
the story. I can't take an injunction on the grounds it's untrue, can I?'
He looked carefully at her. 'That would be pretty stupid, wouldn't
it, us taking on a newspaper and having to lie under oath?'

'I expect so,' she replied unhappily. 'But on the other hand, I don't
suppose you really care if the whole thing does come out, do you?'

The moment the words were spoken she could see his face tighten
with anger. His hand slammed down on the desk and sent papers
scattering.

'That's bloody unfair, Belle, and untrue. It'll affect Teddy: they'll
be around him like a flock of vultures, so believe me, *I care*,' he
snapped furiously. 'Try thinking without extreme prejudice just for
once. Would I have asked you to be here if I wasn't concerned?'

'I'm sorry.' She flushed while apologising hastily. 'I really am. It's just such a shock. Dan Hardacre – he was once —' a lover, she almost said, 'once a friend. At least I thought so.'

'I've offered the bastard money to stop it. Two hundred. He didn't think he could do it for that. I made it four hundred, and he said he'd consider the matter.'

'So it's blackmail?'

'Of course. And blackmailers always return for more.'

'What'll you do?'

'Try to deal with him.'

'Is there any way I can help, Donald?'

'No,' he said firmly. 'Now that you're forewarned, just steer well clear of Hardacre. And the press.'

He pushed a buzzer on his desk and his clerk brought in coffee. While she drank it Belle looked at the newspaper cutting again.

'It's a wonder nobody's said anything to me, this is so obvious. Mind you, there've been a few odd looks, now I think of it. Most of the backstage crew seem to read *Truth*.'

'If anyone asks you, say it couldn't be Teddy,' he suggested. 'Just be mystified, and let's hope we can do something about it before Sunday's edition.'

'But how, if Dan's already fed them the whole story? We're far more likely to be bloody headlines.'

'Belle, stay calm, and for Christ's sake *don't you do anything*. I'll try my best, that's all I can tell you at this stage.'

In the next few days Belle began to be more aware of speculative glances. She even saw a copy of the paper in the corner of a dressing-room, left open at the page containing the story. The stage doorman had always been friendly; now his smile had a trace of something different, as though there was a question puzzling him, one he felt it best not to ask. Eunice, of course, was not so circumspect.

'Did you see that peculiar item in *Truth*?'

'Never read the nasty smutty publication.' Belle was brisk and casual. 'That rag is a terrible waste of good trees.'

'What have trees got to do with it?' Eunice looked bewildered.

'Paper is made from wood, Eunice. They cut down lovely old forests to provide newsprint.'

'Oh! Fancy that.' If Belle hoped to divert her, she failed. Eunice had a copy of the article in her handbag. 'You mean you didn't see this?'

'That silly story – a friend showed me. We spent ages trying to work out who it might be,' Belle said with a shrug that dismissed it as trivia.

'I thought it might be Teddy.'

'You can't mean it!' She laughed. 'His father back in Gundagai would have a fit,' she exclaimed and felt satisfied with her performance. 'He'd probably sue them.'

'Who else could it be?'

'That's what we're all trying to work out, Eunice dear.'

'Well, I expect we'll know on Sunday.'

'Perhaps. But don't forget, *Truth* is a paper that rarely lives up to its name.'

Although she managed to evade other confrontations, it was a long and stressful week. Early on Sunday morning Belle walked to the newsagent's at Rushcutters Bay, dreading the outcome. She bought a copy and sat on a seat at the tram stop, bracing herself for what she'd read. There was no report on the front page. That was some relief. She started going through pages until she reached the sports section, then in reverse systematically scrutinised every page again. She could hardly believe it.

There was no report anywhere in the paper. Not a mention.

Donald was in old clothes, washing his car in the driveway as she arrived. He watched her pay off a taxi and cross the street.

'It's not in there.'

'No, and it won't be. You didn't bring Teddy?'

'He's sleeping in. Then he has homework. How did you know it wouldn't be? What did you do?' she asked.

'Paid Hardacre his four hundred pounds. But first I told the police I was being blackmailed, and they marked the notes. When they arrested him his wallet was chock-full of evidence.'

'Will he go to jail?'

'I hope so. He's greedy and vindictive, which should hardly be a surprise to either of us.'

'But what about the story, and the journalist?'

'The journalist was fired for being so gullible, and his editor is grateful that I saved them from a defamation case. The story will go on a spike where all spurious stories go.'

'You're quite clever,' Belle said.

'Thank you.'

'And bloody ruthless,' she added.

'At times,' he said, 'if I have to be.'

Chapter twenty-eight

Teddy was thrilled. It felt wonderful to have a week's holiday between shows. Seven free days from the last night of the old revue until they started rehearsals for the new one. Ricky M complained it was too expensive to keep the theatre dark like this, but Belle insisted. She said the pair had worked hard without a break for far too long, they deserved a holiday; more than that, they needed one, however brief. Overcoming the inertia that had been troubling her, she arrived at his office like the Belle of former days, reminding Ricky they were still children, neither of them yet twelve years old, and refusing to leave until she received his grudging consent.

Although it was not entirely a holiday. Belle also tried to have Teddy written out of the morning radio serial for a spell, but Mr Edwards had a firm contract for his services and would not agree. 'Darby and Joan' was the most popular serial on the air. It ran at breakfast time and went out live, so none of the actors dared to make mistakes; if they did, they had to ad lib their way out of trouble. The producers and stars of the show, George Edwards and his wife Nell Stirling, were fond of Teddy, declaring everyone liked the cheeky character he played, and to lose him even for a time would cost them listeners. So every morning at six they had to catch a tram to Central, then the train to Homebush and a bus to the studio.

It was a rigorous schedule, and most days Belle found herself dozing on the return train journey. While she avoided admitting it, the herbalist's tonic had proved ineffective. In response to Nuncie's urging, she agreed to consult a doctor, but the pains eased. She was still easily tired, but she felt better and decided she had no need for quacks. To keep her friend from nagging she lied and said the doctor had diagnosed a minor tummy infection.

They were rarely home before ten each day, and even during his week off Teddy had to spend the remainder of the morning doing school work. When he protested, Belle said it was essential or the education inspector would be around making trouble, and the next thing he'd be back at Paddington Public, stuck behind a desk with the eight and nine-year-olds, doing the same lessons.

But the afternoons belonged to him. He and Sally went to the zoo. She lived only a few streets away from it, and to his surprise had never been there. Teddy appointed himself her guide; from his previous visit he knew the times when the animals were fed and the best places to view this. The trouble was, people recognised them and after that they spent the best part of their afternoon signing autographs. The queue seemed endless; when it shrank other people joined it. Teddy in particular disliked autographs because his handwriting was so cramped; he could see how they compared Sally's neat signature with his untidy scrawl as they walked away.

There were even more autographs to sign when they tried going down to Balmoral beach for a swim. One afternoon, to escape this routine, Teddy took her to meet Nuncie, and they had a hilarious time swapping jokes with Charles and Clarence, while Nuncie fed them chocolate biscuits and lemonade. But when he took her home and Sal enthused about Nuncie Billingsworth and her wonderful shop full of treasures, Eunice was furious.

She told Teddy he had no right, she disapproved of him taking her daughter to meet *that* woman; she was not fit company for children, altogether a curious creature, and it was *never* – did he understand that word? – *never* to happen again.

'But we had good fun there,' Sally protested, 'better than signing boring autographs all the time.'

'You heard me, Sally. She's abnormal and unsuitable.'

'I liked her, Mum. And besides, she's a friend of Belle's.'

'Belle's old enough to choose her own friends, but I have to say she has an odd taste in people. That particular person would never be a friend of mine.'

'She isn't abnormal or any of the things you said.' Teddy was upset at the derogation and tried to intervene. 'She's nice, and she makes jokes all the time. It's a joke when she says she's the only woman who has three balls.'

It was a mistake; he realised it instantly. Eunice stared at him, then demanded he go straight to the bathroom and wash out his mouth with soap. She had never heard such a disgusting remark. To think he'd taken her daughter to hear vulgarity like that! She made it apparent he would not be welcome at Mosman any more.

Belle consoled him, telling him not to let it spoil things. Eunice'd calm down in time. She liked to climb on her high horse, and was well known for getting her knickers in a twist – but she had a lovely daughter. For Sally's sake, they had to put up with her.

'We had a real great time at Nuncie's, Mum, and she ruined it.'

'She'd ruin a teddy bears' picnic, but don't tell her I said so. Let's take the ferry to Manly tomorrow, and I'll show you my old stamping ground.'

But even Manly was a disappointment. For a start, he missed Sally, and his mum seemed in an odd mood when they arrived there.

She liked the musicians on the ferry who played a song from *The Merry Widow* for her after she said she'd been in the original show, but when they walked through the town she made him stop while she gazed at a big weatherboard building that had a sign reading: PRIVATE HOTEL. ROOMS TO LET AT ALL HOURS. She looked at it for quite a long time, until Teddy tugged at her hand and asked why didn't they go to the beach, which was when he felt sure she was crying.

'Mum, what's the matter?' She swiftly brushed her eyes with the sleeve of her dress, and he knew for certain she was crying. 'What's wrong?'

'Nothing's wrong, darling. Just a silly old memory caught up with me for a moment. I used to know this place quite well.'

'Did you live here?'

'No, but I visited it now and then. It's a crummy old dump, but I was rather fond of it.' She smiled and took his hand as they turned in the direction of the Norfolk pine trees that fringed the ocean. 'Let's have a walk on the beach and an ice-cream.'

But going home on the ferry she seemed tired. She went to sleep against him, and didn't even hear the song from *The Merry Widow* when the musicians recognised her and played it for her again.

It was Nuncie's idea; a surprise treat for his birthday. She arrived in a car to collect them, a limousine with a uniformed chauffeur no less – an ordinary taxi cab was unsuitable for a special occasion like this, she told them. And for the occasion Nuncie had transformed herself into a different being, wearing a long evening gown with a fur stole, and a smart turban instead of her shabby beret.

'Golly,' Teddy said, 'you look real different, Nuncie.'

'I'll take that as a compliment, young master.'

'It is. You look beaut.'

'He means beautiful,' Belle said, joining them in the back of the hire car.

'I know what he means, dear. I expect the phrase we're looking for is done up like a . . .' – she was about to say a pox doctor's moll, but substituted – 'a bleedin' great Christmas tree.'

Belle had made a rare excursion to David Jones and bought a new dress and a chic hat. Nuncie's keen gaze tried to calculate whether she'd recovered from her troublesome ailment and she felt relief. Belle looked animated and quite gorgeous.

'Very stylish, Belle,' she approved, and was gratified by a dazzling smile.

'Where are we going?' Teddy wanted to know.

'You'll find out in good time, my duck,' he was told.

'Are we all set, Madam?' the uniformed chauffeur asked.

'All set, Box,' she said.

There was a barely muffled reaction from the front seat as he switched on the engine and drove down towards the stadium.

'His name is really Mr Tucker,' Nuncie confided to them in a stage whisper, 'but I decided to call him Box.'

Teddy smothered a giggle. Belle shook her head, trying not to laugh at this absurdity. The chauffeur, choosing to be unaware of it, kept his eyes firmly on the evening traffic. He turned at the intersection of Bayswater Road, and headed towards the city.

The Capitol Theatre on Campbell Street, in the heart of Chinatown, had once been a circus hippodrome, and after that became a flamboyant Picture Palace showing silent films. John Gilbert, Garbo,

Douglas Fairbanks and Clara Bow all charmed their audiences here. It was a huge, ornate building with marble walls and grandiose statuary, said to be the oldest theatre in the city now that so many others had been demolished. When the house lights dimmed on the packed audience the ceiling began to twinkle like a sky full of stars. Teddy gasped at the sight. From where he sat between Belle and Nuncie in the front row of the grand circle, they had the best seats with a perfect view of the stage and the magic firmament above.

A birthday surprise, Nuncie had promised him; it was a revelation to Teddy. He'd heard so much about the famous Capitol Theatre, and he and Belle had often walked past it on their way to see Florian, but he had never been inside it until now. Even better, the show was a special charity gala to raise money for an actors' home, and all his friends and favourites were taking part. Roy Rene, the famous 'Mo', and his wife Sadie Gale were on stage. He and Sal's first revue for Ricky M had been a brief spot in a show in which the couple had topped the bill. And there was George Wallace, big fat funny George. Teddy had played a runaway boy in one of his films, and at times could hardly act for laughing at George making faces at him from behind the camera. There were others he knew: Queenie Paul and Minnie Love, and the dancers from the new production of *White Horse Inn*.

Nuncie had been precise about her instructions. The show began at eight; she told the chauffeur they were to reach the theatre ten minutes before the curtain and stop at the main entrance, even if it meant queuing behind the other cars unloading their celebrities.

'You want to fetch up in front of all them photographers?' Mr Tucker (Box) had said, eyeing her in his rear-vision mirror, thinking he'd got a right peculiar bird on this job and no mistake.

'Exactly, Box old darling. No nearest corners or side alleys. I rely on you to deposit us on the red carpet, centre stage.'

'Depend on it, Madam.'

He was as good as his word. They arrived just as the governor, Sir Phillip Game, had been ushered inside, and when Belle got out with Teddy the cameras were not yet back in the photographers' cases.

'It's young Ted Carson,' one of them said, and becoming aware the elegant woman beside him was his mother, had asked her to join him for pictures. In a matter of moments the other photographers had set up their tripods again and popping flashlights were attracting spectators while Belle and Teddy posed for magazines and the morning papers. Some of the crowd stayed to witness this, and by the time they went into the foyer people were aware of them, waving and pointing Teddy out to their friends.

Belle was elated by their recognition, thoroughly enjoying this surprise night that Nuncie had arranged. It seemed a long time ago that they had celebrated his last birthday: eleven candles and singing their hearts out above the shop. But it was only a year, and so much had happened since. Extraordinary things. Dreams had come true. Could she have imagined back then there'd be a night like this?

Sitting in the dark, she was thankful she had made the effort to come. She'd almost asked to be excused from whatever Nuncie had planned. This morning there'd been real pain; she'd rested the whole afternoon, and it had done the trick. Now she laughed and applauded as if there was nothing at all wrong with her. And perhaps there wasn't; not if she could recover like this and feel so good. Even *look* good, the photographers had thought so. So had Nuncie!

She felt grateful to her friend. It was such a kind, thoughtful gesture: the whole thing so perfectly arranged, the best and most expensive seats in the house, even the arrival in time for photographs seemed a part of her design. An altogether lovely evening, she thought as the cast crowded on stage for the final curtain call, which was when Belle discovered the evening wasn't quite over yet.

Roy Rene waved his arms in the air to silence the audience, then in his familiar character Mo McCackie had them laughing as he shouted with his trademark splutter, 'Strike me lucky, where's that young friend?'

'Whose young friend?' George Wallace asked.

'*My* young friend.' Mo sent saliva in all directions, and the audience roared as Wallace ducked for cover.

'You haven't got a friend, Mo,' he bellowed.

'Fair suck of the sav,' Mo leered, 'I got friends by the thousands. Ain't I, Sadie?'

'No,' his wife answered, raising a laugh, while a single spotlight weaved around the crowd, making everyone wonder who it was seeking. It finally landed on Teddy.

'There he is, there's me young friend!' Mo bellowed.

'Don't give me the raw prawn,' Sadie Gale replied, 'it's Teddy Carson, and he's *my* friend.'

'And *mine*,' claimed George Wallace.

'And *ours*. Hello, darling!' Minnie Love and Queenie Paul waved at him.

'He's everyone's friend,' Mo agreed as the crowd started to applaud and Nuncie nudged Teddy into standing up. There were cries of recognition from all around the theatre as he did so.

'Twelve years old today!' Mo called. 'Good on yer, Ted, I'm saving up me pennies to buy you a razor.' He started to conduct as the cast sang 'Happy Birthday' and the audience joined in.

Teddy stood blinking into the spotlight as they sang. Beside him his mother and her best friend were awash with happy tears.

A month later when their new revue opened, it was clear to Teddy and Sally their mothers were no longer on good terms. Eunice had been tight-lipped about the charity gala; in her opinion it had been a typical sneaky trick of Belle's to organise his presence there, and she had clearly tipped off Roy Rene and the others to put on their little panto about his birthday.

Very manipulative, she said to Ricky on one of their torrid afternoon siestas together, pointing out the whole thing had been organised right down to the bloody photos that had been all over the morning newspapers. Lots of brownie points for twelve-year-old Teddy, and not a solitary mention of Sally.

'The Murrumbidgee Kid and his mum,' she said scornfully, aware how much Belle disliked the name. It was a label fast fading into oblivion, but with a little help she might be able to resurrect it.

Ricky M tried to relax her; he found the most effective way to do this was in bed, for he had no wish to see warfare break out among the mothers of his young luminaries now that they were earning him a small fortune. He stroked Eunice's shapely bottom, and whispered lewd Latino obscenities into her ear.

Despite his wishes, there was a growing rift. The Carsons did not pay visits to the Sharps in Mosman any more, where Eunice had moved house and rented a smart new apartment with views across the harbour. On the surface the two parents remained carefully neutral, but in private Belle admitted she could not stand the other woman's empty prattle, or the way she had begun to use Sally's earnings to pay for her lavish lifestyle.

Their own way of living remained unchanged; the room in Glenmore Road had been their home for nine months now, and Belle seem disinclined to move from there. It was convenient, she said: Teddy had freedom to ride his bike in the safe streets, and money was for saving in case hard times came again, not for wasting on high rents or for flaunting herself around town dressed like a tarty duchess. Everyone knew the acidic remark was aimed directly at Eunice, who had replenished her wardrobe with the latest fashions and, trying to get even, had been photographed at the opening night of the revue on the arm of Ricky Mendoza.

If Eunice's circle of friends and social connections were expanding, Belle's domain seemed to diminish. Nuncie remained a constant in their lives, but there were few others. Invitations to parties, once welcomed, were often rejected now. Teddy gradually became aware that apart from the hours in the theatre and at Homebush, he and Belle were spending a great deal of their time alone. Sunday, for instance – free from work – had always been the day for meeting friends, for cheerful gatherings and lunches; now they mostly stayed at home by themselves. He rode his bike in lonely contemplation, as he had once ridden it along the tracks by the Murrumbidgee; Belle stayed inside, reading or listening to the wireless they had bought or, more often than not, resting.

Something began to trouble Teddy: that same uneasy sense of impending change was threatening, although why it should be a threat he could not explain.

There was another problem. Ricky Mendoza had discovered that their personal appearances guaranteed an increase in audiences. An attendance at David Jones or the Grace Bros store on Broadway became a regular event. Posing in front of a photographic collage of their stage act, and signing photos for a queue of kids and their families was work Teddy and Sally both disliked intensely, but it augmented the box-office takings. Eunice was strongly in favour of it; Belle felt it was exploitation and made a token protest to Ricky M, but lacked the energy to argue when he read aloud to her a clause in the contract that stipulated an obligation 'At all times to assist in promulgating the show as required by the producer'.

'Don't forget, they're on a piece of the action, babe.'

It amused her the way he had apparently left his South American persona behind and become a New York Yankee, or a Hollywood huckster; it was also apparent but less amusing how she was being frequently overruled by Ricky with the help of Eunice. On the other hand, she told herself to stop complaining. Her son was a star. His name was up there outside the theatre, and on billboards. It was what she had been striving for, what had once seemed like a vain and hopeless dream; it had made her a joke in Brewinda Road, but they'd be singing a different tune there now, for it had all come miraculously true.

She tried not to remember what Nuncie had warned: that they were still just a couple of children, and overworking them was a serious mistake.

Donald said it was about time – far too long since their last visit – and he felt sure Teddy had grown. An inch, he thought when they arrived, and he said after lunch they'd measure him and keep a mark on the wall to record his progress. Teddy had been looking forward to the visit; he remembered Donald treating him like a grown-up, and he had fond memories of the roast. The housekeeper served another superb meal but Belle had no appetite. 'Indigestion,' she said, and she sat silent while father and son talked non-stop.

Donald had seen and enjoyed the new revue, particularly the sketch where Teddy appeared as Burlington Bertie and Sally was dressed up as a Salvation Army girl trying to cadge a penny from him.

'It was great fun. The audience laughed so much they nearly fell out of their seats. And they loved you and Sally as Snugglepot and Cuddlepie,' he enthused. This was surely a new Donald; Belle had never seen him so animated.

'You should've come backstage,' Teddy said, 'and met Sal.'

'I'd like to. Next time, if I can,' he promised, with a glance at Belle that seemed to ask permission.

After the meal Teddy played the piano and sang verses of 'The Road to Gundagai' for him, then told him about their early-morning train trips to Homebush, where he was a regular in the serial broadcast at breakfast time.

'You should listen to it, Donald. It's called "Darby and Joan". Mr Edwards is the producer and he plays four or five parts using different voices.'

'I've met George Edwards. Clever bloke. He put on a show called *Famous Trials*, and not only played the prosecutor, but the defence counsel, the judge and the prisoner as well. Imagine it – he could defend and prosecute himself, then cross-examine himself, and overrule himself as the judge.'

'Golly,' Teddy said, and they both laughed uproariously. The laughter was infectious, and Belle tried vainly to join in. She wished there was a spare bed where she could rest.

The housekeeper served them coffee on the side verandah.

'Donald, can I climb one of your trees?' Teddy asked.

'If your mum agrees. But pick a low one, we don't want you falling.'

'I'm used to climbing trees. I climbed some big ones back home.'

'I'm sure you did, Ted. You look like a tree climber. But you can't have any accidents, with you going on stage wearing a sling. Do you need a rope?'

'No,' Teddy laughed, 'these aren't big trees. They're easy peasy.' He ran to a thick camphor laurel, clambered up and waved as he perched on one of its branches. Belle waved back, then realised Donald was studying her.

'What's wrong, Belle?'

She turned to gaze at him carefully. 'Who said there's anything wrong?'

'It's obvious. You look exhausted.'

'Thanks for the compliment.'

'I'm worried. You barely touched your food. Hardly cracked a smile. Not at all like you.'

'I'm taking a tonic,' she said.

'Have you seen a doctor?'

'Now don't *you* start.'

'At least someone else is concerned about you.' Donald seemed gratified he had support. 'Your friend Mrs Sharp?'

'Eunice? She's too busy shagging Rick Mendoza.'

'Is that a fact?'

'Regularly. A matinee most afternoons.'

'Well, well!' He laughed at this. 'Then who's the one you meant?'

'Nuncie.'

'Oh, her.'

'Yes, her. I know you don't like her, but she's been my friend a long time. A better friend than most people could imagine. She wants me to see a quack.'

'Then she and I agree. Probably for the first and only time,' he said.

'I'll tell her. It'll give her a laugh.'

They watched Teddy scale another branch. He pretended to overbalance, and Donald jumped to his feet with genuine alarm. Belle shook her head. 'Take no notice of his antics.'

'Young monkey!'

'He likes you. He was pleased we were coming here today.'

'I wish you'd come before this.' He was happy at the rapport he'd established with Teddy, but still troubled about her. 'There's so much I don't understand, Belle. This stress – these late nights at the theatre, early train journeys to do radio serials . . . Do you have to set such a schedule – for yourself, or for him?'

'Wearing us both out, am I?' She gave a wry smile. 'You'd be surprised how exactly you mirror the thoughts of Nuncie Billingsworth – again.'

'But why? Tell me why it has to be such a rat race.'

Belle took her time in answering. She was not sure he would understand, but she had to try. 'Because he's talented,' she said. 'This is the hard part for an outsider to understand. In our business we know talent's important, but it's never enough. The world's full of talent. You need more: you need luck, a slice of fortune, being there, the right place, the right time. We had it when he was eight years old starring in that film. A moment of providence and we let it slip. People talk about seizing the day, but we wasted it. I'm trying not to let that happen again.'

'But it surely won't. Those two are virtual stars now.'

'*This* year. Memories are so short, Donald. I can name you stars of a few years ago who today are on the bones of their arse. Our best film director can't get work. He made some wonderful pictures, but everyone's forgotten them – and him.'

'Incredible.' He seemed to find it difficult to comprehend.

'Shocking, more like. It's a cruel business. So if George Edwards wants Teddy in his radio serials, it's another string to his bow and we accept – even if it is exhausting. And if a film comes along, we take that as well. It's what theatre people call the instant of serendipity, and this time we grab it and never let go.'

'Even if it is exhausting?' He gazed at her, repeating her own words. For the first time he noticed the dark circles below her eyes that the carefully applied make-up couldn't hide.

'A bit of rest will soon solve that,' Belle answered, leaving her chair and moving down the garden steps to put an end to the conversation.

'But this life you've just described won't allow that,' he said, following her. 'Do me one favour, Belle, please. Promise me you'll go and see a doctor.'

'I will.'

'Not like that. Promise.'

'Don't nag. I promise. Any other requests?'

'Yes. Don't leave it so long before the next visit.'

Later he asked if he could drive them home this time, and Belle agreed. They took the road that went past the locked and shuttered film studio, looking more derelict than ever despite rumours it would soon reopen under its new American management. Seeing it reminded her of Dan Hardacre. In the garden after lunch, Donald told her that he'd pleaded guilty in court and been given a two-year suspended sentence on condition no details of his blackmail attempt ever appeared in print.

Donald asked her permission to detour: he had something he wanted to show Teddy in Rushcutters Bay. They headed towards the yacht club, where he pointed to the row of masts lining the marina, and said one of the boats was his. Would Teddy like to go aboard for a look?

Teddy's eyes lit up with excitement. 'Can we go for a sail?'

'Next time we'll go sailing. But it's a bit late today, so we'll just explore and see the way things work. I'll show you the rigging. How's that?'

'Beaut,' Teddy said, jumping from the car and starting to run across the park towards the moorings. He passed a family packing up the remains of a picnic, parents and two young children, who seemed suddenly arrested in this task as they all gazed towards him.

'You want to come aboard, Belle?' Donald asked her.

'No, thanks. You two boys go and play at being sailors. But Donald – although it's been another nice day, don't take too much for granted.'

'I won't, believe me.'

Like hell you won't, she thought as he went down towards the marina to catch up with Teddy. The crafty bugger had sprung this surprise deliberately; now Teddy would be pestering her for another visit as soon as possible. She would have to be careful not to allow Donald too much latitude.

Yet it was strange; despite their turbulent history and the years she had detested him for his past treatment of her, she could no longer feel that same deep animosity towards him. A certain wariness, yes – it was natural she would be cautious – but she could understand his wish to be part of Teddy's life. She realised a great deal had happened since her shocked glimpse of him at the theatre that night with Dan.

As for seeing a doctor, she'd made a promise, and supposed she'd have to keep it. She should've found one and gone to him weeks ago, instead of fobbing off Nuncie with a lie. The trouble was, she could admit it to herself, she was bloody scared. It might mean an operation, weeks in hospital. If it was serious, it could decimate their savings . . .

The car was warm, the seats of the Daimler soft and comfortable. She was starting to doze off when she heard tapping on the glass beside her head. It was the woman from the picnic, wanting to talk. Belle wound down the window.

'We're right, aren't we? That boy . . . it is *him*?'

'Yes,' Belle said, pleased at the recognition.

'Teddy Carson?'

'That's right, I'm his mother.'

'Are you?' the woman said. 'Well, you should be ashamed of yourself.'

'What?'

'No wonder you're able to sit in your expensive car, exploiting him the way you do. We think it's absolutely disgusting.'

She turned and walked back to her family before Belle could reply.

The doctor was elderly, with white hair and kind eyes, which reassured her. He took her blood pressure, then asked her to remove her blouse and skirt, and to lie down while he examined her.

'I'm sure all I need is a proper rest and a tonic,' Belle asserted as she lay on the surgical table. 'I've been working quite hard and worrying a lot over the past few years, but my son's a success now and everything's fine and dandy —'

'A deep breath, Mrs Carson.'

'I can tell from your expression that my blood pressure's low. I'm sure I'm run down and anaemic, but I don't know why. After all, the hard slog is over. Those tough times are behind us.'

It was ridiculous; she could not stop talking. She paused only when he told her to breathe in or out, waiting for him to relax, to smile and tell her it was just a minor ailment or something easily cured. Talking non-stop seemed to be the only way to sustain her confidence.

'A tonic's always done the trick when I've been out of sorts. Cut down the grog, an afternoon rest and a vitamin tonic.'

'Perhaps you're right, Mrs Carson,' he nodded, 'but since I'm the doctor and I'm being paid for this, why not let me make the diagnosis?'

The stethoscope was cold on her skin. She wondered if she should tell him more about the pain that sometimes came in the middle of the night, keeping her awake so often, the pain that had been even more savage yesterday when that woman had berated her. She'd have told the bitch to piss off and mind her own business, but the sudden onset had been like a scalding knife in her guts; it had made her frightened, with sweat drenching her body and running down her face. The cold sweat had chilled her with fear and made her breathless. She had scarcely been able to speak by the time the two of them had returned from the yacht club, but did her best to show interest at Teddy's excited description of the boat, while all the time aware of Donald's probing gaze.

'Hot flushes,' she'd tried to tell him when they were alone for a moment. 'The change.'

'Have you even *got* a doctor?'

'Never needed one. Not a day's illness in my life.'

'Let's stop this, Belle. Cut the crap.' He'd frowned, impatient with her pretence. 'If I give you a name, will you promise to ring for an appointment?'

'If you insist.'

'Better still,' Donald resolved forcefully, 'I'll call him myself.'

'Are you sick, Mum?' Teddy had asked when he rejoined them.

'Of course not, darling. Fit as a fiddle.'

'Sometimes even fiddles need their strings adjusting,' Donald had said, and drove them home.

And now the doctor he'd insisted she consult was saying there'd have to be some tests, perhaps exploratory surgery, and he didn't want to unduly alarm her, but he thought she should be admitted to hospital.

No, not next week. Or even tomorrow. Immediately.

Chapter twenty-nine

There was still almost an hour before curtain-up, but the theatre was slowly filling. In their shared dressing-room Sally could hear the occasional clatter of seats and the murmur of voices through the tannoy speaker. People were coming in early to get out of the rain, at least that's what the stage manager had told her, and he hoped Teddy hadn't been caught in it. He was later than usual.

Sally made no comment. She knew he was late. He'd been progressively later each day for weeks now, and no wonder. The stage manager was a dill, she thought, with as much compassion as Ricky, or her own mother. Neither of them seemed to realise Belle's illness was serious. Everyone knew that after lots of tests and an operation, she had been sent home, then two weeks later had collapsed and been rushed back to hospital. She'd been there ever since.

No one seemed to know the exact details. Eunice had been typically vague about it – typically appalling, her daughter thought angrily – saying that she must find time to visit soon, but after all, she'd sent a get-well card to the hospital and had no reply. She felt sure it was nothing too alarming. Women had these problems at certain times, she announced, and perhaps Belle was having them early. It could hardly be that critical, or she'd have seen all these expensive doctors and specialists long before this. Her mother and

Ricky frequently speculated on what it must be costing, and who was paying the bill.

'What if Teddy isn't here for the show?' Sally asked when Eunice came to visit their dressing-room as she did every evening before curtain-up.

'Don't be silly, of course he will. He has to be.'

'But suppose he doesn't turn up? Last night he said she is really sick.'

'If that's true, it's up to the doctors. What on earth can Teddy do,' she said with a toss of her head and the acerbic note that so often of late accompanied any mention of Belle or Teddy, 'except get in their way? He most certainly *will* turn up, or there'll be one enormous row. Ricky doesn't tolerate that sort of nonsense from anyone, I can assure you.'

Eunice had left in a waft of expensive perfume, modish in a new silk dress. She was meeting a group of friends in the foyer, society people who'd come to see the show, she said, but would be back to check all was in order before they went onstage. She told Sally to get dressed and put on her make-up, then she might as well start catching up on her homework.

Sally did neither of these things. She found herself wondering if there was such a thing as a law permitting a girl to divorce her mother, in the same way that Eunice had divorced her dad. She rarely saw her father these days – there was never time for that or anything else: if they weren't performing in the actual show, they were rehearsing new routines for it or signing their names at the personal appearances that she and Teddy hated so much. After that came catching up on homework. School, where she once came top of the class when they went to Liverpool Street, was no longer enjoyable. Because there was a lack of time for regular attendance, she now went to Miss Fenwick's in Spofforth Street, Cremorne, which was truthfully not a school at all but a crammer for backward students. Miss Fenwick's also catered for the children of diplomats and overseas visitors, and was therefore not subject to the rules laid down by the Department of Education. Sally felt disadvantaged by it, and resented the way Eunice bragged to her friends as if it was an elite place of learning.

There were days – more and more of them lately – when she found herself wishing she and Teddy had never been at that audition together. Days when she regretted what had happened to them. For almost a year it had been fun, really *wonderful* fun, but too often now she felt engulfed by tedium and disillusion. Her mother and Ricky Mendoza seemed oblivious to her feelings, their only concerns the weekly house takings and their daily sexual romp that they called a love affair.

On the tannoy she heard the audience gradually settle into total quiet before the curtain rose, and then the fanfare for the opening dance routine. There was still thirty minutes before she and Teddy were to appear on stage for their first sketch, but where was he?

Now it really *was* becoming late.

She heard a tap on the door, and the assistant stage manager looked in, but before he could ask she jerked her thumb towards the corner screen where they changed costumes, and he smiled and went on his way. She heard him call out the other kid was in, thank Christ, and she tried to imagine what might happen if Teddy did not turn up.

It had been raining forever, it seemed to Belle. Leaden skies, the grumble of thunder and the swish of car tyres on the road outside.

A good day to be indoors, she thought, although not necessarily in here. But by evening the steady downpour had softened to a drizzle. From her bedside window she could see the raindrops glistening on trees lit by streetlights. People, small figures on the pavement below, were hurrying home wrapped up against the weather.

The nurse, the friendly one from Edinburgh who brought her extra morphine when the pain became too great, said the rain was more like Scotch mist now and it made her homesick. She'd also heard there was another tram strike, so she'd have to walk home after her shift, and that was a bit like Edinburgh too. Her name was Genevieve; she was a sturdy, cheerful girl in her twenties who had worked her way from Britain as a stewardess on a passenger liner and had later become a nurse, she told Belle, because it was less gruelling than her maritime adventures repelling drunken passengers and randy members of the crew. At St Vincent's she had graduated from washing floors and bedpans, and did everything possible to keep her patients happy. Belle thought the hospital would be sheer hell without her.

She looked at her watch; the curtain would be up by now, and she hoped Teddy had reached the theatre safely. The news of the tram strike was a concern. Taxis might be hard to find if the trams were off. She'd told him to take a cab to avoid getting soaked, because he was later than usual in leaving. Not only later, but seemingly reluctant to go. It was as if he'd begun to realise in the past few weeks that time might be precious, and their hours together should be cherished.

She fell asleep trying to think of all that must be done. George should be told. But writing to him or talking by phone was beyond her. Could she possibly ask Donald to do that? She was unsure; he'd done so much, insisting on paying for everything and arranging for her to be moved to a private room. She was deeply in his debt, and felt slightly uneasy and at a disadvantage because of it. Donald had wanted Teddy to move to his home, but she'd resisted that. He was staying at Neutral Bay with Nuncie, at least for now.

There were so many matters to resolve. Things to discuss with Nuncie, such a lot of things. Most important of all, she had to tell Teddy the truth, which was something she should've done years ago and which she dreaded.

Eunice was on Ricky Mendoza's divan with her pants off and her legs in the air as she felt herself coming and begged him to dig deep, to perform as he had never performed with his dick in her before, and Ricky, who liked dirty talk and loved to get Eunice inflamed because nothing was sexier than her kind of toffee-nosed sheila, went wild and did everything he was told until he felt sure the earth had moved for her. It had most certainly moved for him.

While they were still glued together and trying to regain their breath, he glanced at his watch and realised the curtain would be going up by now.

'You sure all's well backstage, doll?'

'I know all's well here, Ricky darl. That was a truly terrific performance.'

'We'll have an encore later.'

'You spoil me,' she murmured, knowing he would like this.

They had plans for the rest of the night, and well beyond it. The group of society friends were new investors, *her investors*, rich new friends from Mosman and Balmoral, and after the show she and Rick were giving them a party. Sally didn't know it yet, but she was being sent home in a taxi, while Eunice and Ricky would spend the night in a luxury suite at the Hotel Australia. It was a rehearsal for the future. Although both his wife and the Filipina mistress were still unaware of it, they were about to be given the heave, and Eunice was to become a partner in the business. She had nothing to contribute to it except a willing body and a total lack of business acumen. This suited Ricky M, who wanted incessant sex and a partner who could not read the balance sheet.

'Better get your arse in gear,' he said, stroking it as she squirmed with pleasure, 'and make sure the kids are set to go. We want to really impress those investors tonight.'

Teddy knew he was perilously late, but no taxis would stop for him. They went past filled with passengers because of the rain and the tram strike, and his only alternative was to run. By the time he reached the theatre in Pitt Street he was soaking wet and breathless, but had a rare stroke of luck as the stage doorman was not at his usual place in the cubicle, and nobody noticed his arrival.

The show was going well; he could tell this because the two comedians on stage rarely got more than a chuckle, but tonight the reception was full-bodied, their tag lines greeted by enormous belly laughs. He ghosted his way past the group of dancers and went down the stairs and into their dressing-room. Sally was alone in there, concentrating on her make-up. She hardly seemed to notice his arrival.

'Sal?'

'Hang on,' she said, and he had to wait for a moment until she turned and poked a face at him. She wore thick glasses, and a big moustache was fixed to her upper lip. She chewed on an improvised long cigar.

'So waddaya think, huh? You ever met my brother Harpo?'

Despite everything she made him laugh. She was amazingly, uncannily like Groucho Marx. 'Fantastic,' he said. 'You even sound like him.'

'I can walk like him, too.'

'I believe it, Sal.' He reached for a towel and tried to dry himself. 'But aren't we on in ten minutes?'

'Never mind that – what's the news? Is Belle any better?'

'I don't think so. She spent half the day asleep while I sat and held her hand. She can't eat anything and keeps saying she's fine, that she'll be better in a few days, but Nuncie cries most of the time when she's there, so it can't be good.'

'Won't the doctors tell you what's wrong?'

'They say she's as well as can be expected, but I don't believe it.' He took off his wet shirt and flung it in the corner, feeling angry and close to tears himself. 'Nobody will tell me the truth.' He took a deep breath. 'I'm puffed. I had to run all the way from St Vinnie's Hospital.'

'You better sit down,' Sally said. 'Sit on the chair and keep nice and still. I'll fix your make-up.'

Eunice was more than satisfied. So far it had been a gratifying and fulfilling night. And when the show was over it would be even better, for her investors would be writing their cheques at the party. By this time tomorrow she would have seen off Ricky's wife as well as the mistress, and Belle Carson would discover how much things had changed. She smiled at the prospect as she approached the dressing-room. Nobody knew the extent of the changes, least of all Belle and her son. Soon Sally would be heading the bill; she'd be the star –

doing her routines with Teddy, of course: Eunice had no intention of letting the kid go, she wasn't stupid, but it would gradually become apparent that he was now a supporting act. A long time had passed, but her memory was unforgiving. She had never forgotten Belle's goading that had led to their unseemly brawl that day in front of Hugh Bellamy.

She opened the door, and felt relieved at seeing Teddy's wet clothes on the floor. About to request he pick them up and try to dry them, she suddenly saw them both and screamed. Groucho Marx and a grotesque gargoyle were grinning at her, then giggling in delight, so obviously pleased with themselves that she utterly lost control.

'You stupid, wicked little bastards!' she shrieked at them. 'You wretched children, don't you realise that you're on stage in five minutes?'

The gargoyle laughed at her as if this was an irrelevance. She hit him across the face, shouting that he was a revolting little trouble-maker, she'd always known that, and this insanity was clearly all his mad idea. Sally tried to remonstrate and was roughly pushed aside. When Teddy attempted to protect her Eunice slapped him again, hard and viciously this time, the topaz ring on her finger cutting his face, which spurted blood.

Sally yelled at her to stop it, and her mother turned and began hitting her instead. They were both screaming as the assistant stage manager ran in, alerted by the turmoil. Not even the make-up on their faces could hide the flow of blood and the marks of her enraged blows. Eunice seemed uncontrolled, possessed by furies.

He had a disturbing image of both children, terrified and trying to back away from her as she flailed at them.

Chapter thirty

Ricky Mendoza spent a troubled night, trying to work out how to salvage a very awkward situation. Never before had he been forced to front an audience and apologise abjectly like that, informing them there had been a regrettable accident backstage, and the young stars Teddy Carson and Sally Sharp were unable to appear. He had tried to quell the outbreak of surprise and disappointment by offering a refund to anyone who did not wish to remain, announcing the show would continue after a short interval. To his dismay more than half the audience accepted the offer and left the theatre, including Eunice's new friends from Mosman, and presumably their promised investment with them. The rest of the show, decimated by this event, had limped towards a depressing final curtain to the accompaniment of more seats being noisily vacated.

He knew urgent decisions were imperative. The kids had been stupid and provocative, but Eunice's behaviour was the real problem. The silly bitch, why did she have to go berserk like that? If it happened to get into the newspapers – God forbid – the chances were that some government busybody would invoke the Child Welfare Act, and the department would flex their muscles and try to close the show. Even if that failed, as it doubtless would, the publicity would be destructive. The public's twelve-year-old darlings being beaten up backstage – by *his* paramour! The thought of it made him sweat with fear for what that could do to his image.

The theatre staff and the company must be sworn to silence. Meanwhile he kept coming back to the heart of the problem, the quandary of what to do about Eunice. He had no desire to give her up, and no intention of doing so, but for the moment he took the decision that she must be quarantined. He therefore moved her into a city hotel in case the press got a sniff and laid siege to her home. She was given strict orders to remain there and communicate with no one. When she pleaded to be allowed to see Sally, he said that was not an option at present. Not until he got this whole bloody mess untangled.

The first decision he made late that night was to close the show for at least forty-eight hours; it was pointless to think of raising the curtain until he could persuade the kids it would never happen again. Looking after them was his priority. Sally had point-blank refused to go home with her mother and wanted her father to collect her, but when he could not be located because he was a commercial traveller and away working on the south coast, the wardrobe mistress had offered her a bed for the night. Teddy had been taken by taxi to Neutral Bay, to the eccentric family friend who had looked after him for the past few weeks.

A meeting to restore peace was essential. He needed urgent help to broker this, so the second decision he took the next morning was to visit St Vincent's Hospital and call on Belle.

She was in a private room. Teddy was there with her, as well as the friend from Neutral Bay. Ricky thought Belle looked drained and quite haggard, but he kissed her and said it was such a relief to see her looking so well. He realised he had forgotten to bring flowers.

'I expect Teddy has told you about our little problem last night?'

'A little problem, was it?' Her voice was no more than a whisper, and he had to lean forward to hear. 'He said Eunice carried on like a pork chop at a Jewish barbecue, and he and Sal didn't go on.'

'Yes, that's about the truth, I'm afraid. A pork chop indeed,' he smiled at Teddy. The wound across his face had bled so copiously they had been concerned it would require stitches. It was now dry after treatment, but still vivid. 'What we need is a friendly chat to sort things out, Belle, and I'm hoping you can be there.'

'Of course she can't.' It was the large masculine lady who smoked cigars, and whose name he remembered now was Nuncie. An odd name for an odd body, he thought, but decided it was best to be affable.

'If the doctors prefer it, perhaps we could hold it here. But I think we all need Belle, one way or another, to bring a bit of commonsense to the situation. I'll do whatever you think is best.'

'How did he get the cut on his face?' Belle asked, trying not to flinch from a new shaft of pain that gripped her.

'Eunice did it.'

'Did she, indeed?' She looked at Teddy. 'You said you slipped and fell.'

'I expect he was trying not to upset you,' Ricky said hastily. His quick mind could see an opportunity here. It was clear Belle had not been told the full gory details, which meant Teddy did not want to press the matter. 'The fact is, she got agitated and started waving her arms around. And the next thing . . . well, she was wearing a ring that cut him. Unforgivable, the stupid woman.'

He saw Teddy's gaze on him, and held his breath. It was a shame about the wound. Eunice and her bloody topaz ring; he wondered if it might leave a scar.

'Was that what happened, darling?'

'That's pretty much it, Mum.'

'Then why not tell me?'

'It was a sort of accident. I didn't want to make a fuss.'

Ricky felt like smiling, but knew it might create the wrong impression. So he nodded, as if in serious confirmation of what Teddy had said. 'That describes it exactly. A stupid accident that contributed to a disastrous night. I know we can sort this out by talking to each other, Belle. But I need your input. These two have been such an outstanding success; we shouldn't let a silly misunderstanding like this spoil it.'

'When do you want to meet?'

'Is tomorrow possible?'

'Where?'

'Ideally, at my office. But here, if you wish.'

Belle hesitated, thinking about it. Another tremor made her want to call Genevieve for the blessed relief of morphine. Best not have them all here where she would be at a disadvantage, the patient in the bed, the object of their sympathy.

'Your office. Noon tomorrow.'

'You can't!' Nuncie objected vehemently. 'That's out of the bloody question.'

'I'll be there,' she said as firmly as she could, and asked Ricky to leave. She was tired and it might be best if Teddy went too. She wanted Nuncie to stay for a moment. She did not mind Nuncie knowing about her desperate need for morphine.

By the time they reached the hospital foyer Ricky had worked out what he wanted to say to the boy.

'I'm sorry we had to tell that small white lie in there, Ted old son, but it's for the best. You don't want to upset your mum, and nor do I.'

Teddy did not respond to his smile. 'If she wasn't sick I'd have told her the truth.' His eyes were on Ricky's face, and if looks could convey emotions he felt the little bugger hated him. 'I'd have let her know how Eunice kept hitting me across the face. And hitting Sally, too.'

'But Eunice is going to apologise. We'll sort it all out. Hey, there's a shop over there. How about letting me buy you an ice-cream?'

'No, thanks,' Teddy said, so promptly that it was a curt rebuff.

'At least let me give you a lift home in my car.'

'No need. I've got my tram fare to Neutral Bay.'

'See you tomorrow, then.' Ricky was equally curt in response to this further rejection.

'Expect so.' Teddy turned and walked away, receiving smiles of recognition from passing nurses.

Mendoza went out to his car, fuming. It was a Packard coupe, the latest model, and he was extremely proud of it. If Teddy Carson preferred to slum it on the tram, then let him. Cheeky little brat. But at least it was now certain their problem would be solved tomorrow. The show could reopen the following night.

A strange kid, he thought as he drove off, talented but strange. He'd never known anyone of that age refuse an ice-cream before.

Nuncie argued vehemently. It was ridiculous. Bugger Ricky M and the lot of them, it was an unreasonable ask. Belle was too weak. She needed morphine just to cope with the pain, let alone get out of bed. And besides, the hospital would never agree to her going walkabout like that. Her doctor would try to prevent her. And the matron would have a bloody fit.

Belle heard her out, while the pill Genevieve had given her brought a slow relief until she could speak. If her voice sounded exhausted, it was also edged with determination.

'If the matron won't agree then I'll discharge myself, and to hell with the consequences,' Belle said, 'but she knows, just as you and I know – as everyone in here knows – I'm not a long-term prospect. I'll be back here when it's over. Now I need to save my strength. And I need to talk to you about a lot of things. So for Christ's sake, Nuncie, be a dear love and please stop crying.'

Belle was at the meeting early. After a routine protest the night before the matron had grudgingly agreed she was within her rights. Insane, perhaps, but there was no law to prevent her attending a meeting, despite the calamitous consequences that would ensue. She was given a sleeping pill and she woke around ten, when she was helped to bathe and dress, and after close study in the mirror thought that, all things considered, she didn't look too bad. When Genevieve came to tell her the car was downstairs, the Scottish nurse's smile and her surprise confirmed this.

'Fantastic, Belle. If I didn't know better . . .'

Belle said it showed what careful make-up could do, and gratefully slipped the extra pills Genevieve gave her into her handbag.

She had a moment of concern when she reached the office building, for there were times the antique lift didn't work and she knew she could not manage the stairs. But the gilded cage descended, and Miss Cardew, Ricky's secretary of many years, was there to greet her. She took Belle upstairs to the conference room, sat her in the most comfortable chair, brought her a cup of tea and a plate of sweet biscuits – just to tempt her – although Belle said she couldn't eat a thing. Then Ricky entered, brisk and cheerful, followed by Sally and Teddy. Sally came and gently hugged her, then both children moved their chairs to sit close on either side of her. Their affectionate supportive gesture made her feel the effort to be there was more than worthwhile.

Eunice was the last to arrive. Belle thought she looked extremely glamorous – as if she had chosen to make an impact, she wore a knee-length dress that displayed her long legs, with sheer silk stockings and stiletto heels to accentuate them. Her hair was neatly coiffured, and French perfume enveloped Belle as they met.

'I was sorry to hear you were ill, Belle.' There was no warmth in the eyes that surveyed her.

'A little better now, thanks, Eunice.'

'That's good.'

'So we're all here, time to begin.' Ricky was clearly impatient to get the show on the road. 'We're grateful to Belle for coming from her sick bed. I think before we discuss anything else, Eunice has something she wishes to say.'

'I just want to apologise, to you both.' She smiled down at Teddy and Sally. 'I feel awful about what happened. I admit I got a shock, because it was almost stage time, and I lost my temper. I solemnly promise you it'll never happen again.'

'Good,' Ricky said, bouncing to his feet as if that was suitably disposed of, 'now what I suggest is this. Tonight the show will stay closed. Time for us all to have a little rest, to relax. Then tomorrow we arrange for Sal and Teddy to go on radio, to explain that all is well and we're reopening. We need to have an extra performance this week, for the people who cancelled . . . but for this I will pay you a special bonus . . .'

He smiled, an avuncular smile, waiting for their reaction. Eunice nodded her approval. The pair of them looked at the children on either side of Belle, who had so far not spoken a word. The children looked at each other. Everyone waited. The wait became extended and ultimately embarrassing.

'You agree?' Ricky asked them.

'No,' Sally said.

Belle was impassive; the others stared at Sally with disbelief.

'Why not?' Ricky was agitated, his arms wide and gesturing. 'You want other changes? Less autograph signings? I do my best to make you happy, I give anything you want within reason.'

'The answer's no,' Teddy replied.

'Don't be stupid!' Eunice began to shout, but Ricky quickly interrupted her, sensing the atmosphere, trying to be conciliatory.

'What do you mean "no"? No, you want more money? Or no, you want something else? Better conditions?'

'No, we don't want anything like that. We want to stop.'

'For a few days, you mean?' Ricky nodded as if this might be possible.

'No,' Sally said again.

'Will you stop saying *no?*' her mother shrieked.

'No I won't,' Sally replied. 'Tell them, Ted.'

'We've had enough,' Teddy told them.

'A gutful,' Sally added, supporting him.

'That's right, a gutful. We don't want to do it any more.'

'Did you hear him?' Sally asked. 'Do you get it now? We quit.'

'Belle, please. Talk to them.' Ricky seemed bewildered at the rejection.

All eyes turned to Belle. 'I already have talked to them. They came to see me last night in the hospital. We did rather a lot of talking.'

'Whose side are you on?' Eunice demanded, clenched hands betraying her fury.

'Their side, Eunice.'

'But you can't allow this to happen!'

'It's already happening.' Belle's voice was quiet, but as if she had saved it for this occasion they could all hear her firm enunciation.

'Just because I lost my block —'

'Long before that. You and your nasty, vicious behaviour the other night was just the finale. They've been tired of this for months, worn out and fed up with the routine, but none of us adults wanted to notice. It suited us not to see what was obvious – that they were sick to death of it.'

'But why? For God's sake, they're famous!' Eunice yelled.

'They're bored,' Belle replied. 'For a long time it was exciting, and it was fun . . . then it stopped being both.'

'Because of what I did the other night? Damn it, I have apologised for that.'

'And I told you that's not the main reason. Stop trying to put yourself in the spotlight, you silly egotistical bitch.' She saw Eunice's shocked face, and thought it was worth the pain. She skilfully palmed the last morphine tablet into her mouth. 'All you did was scare my son and make your daughter dislike you. She wants to go and live with her father – which could hardly surprise anyone who knows you.'

'Belle, please . . . Eunice, stop, enough . . .' Ricky Mendoza felt it was time to end the personal vilification and get back to the substance. 'We're all upset and tired. We shouldn't say things we'll regret.' He assumed his most engaging manner, aiming the charm at Sally in particular. 'You want a little holiday. Maybe we all need this. Perhaps we close the show this week, and all have a holiday, eh, *cara?*'

'No,' Sally repeated.

Ricky sighed. 'Belle, help me. Explain to them why they can't say no. I have an enforceable legal contract.'

'I think they have some ideas about that, Rick, if you decide on litigation.'

'If you do want to go to court,' Sally said, 'just remember that my mother signed my contract, so you'll have to sue her.'

Teddy laughed. Eunice looked at them both with what seemed like hatred. 'You're a nasty spoilt little girl,' she said to her daughter, 'trying to ruin everything.'

'Listen to who's talking,' Teddy told her.

'Well, that seems to take care of the meeting,' Belle said and she felt a great weariness. Today would take care of more than that. The old doctor had tried to be kind after the exploratory surgery six weeks ago, when it was apparent she had delayed too long, explaining that nothing could be done, which was why they'd sewn her up again without attempting to operate. He had predicted two or three months. She felt it might be sooner than that. Sooner would spare her pain, but it seemed unfair for it to end like this, with all her dreams in ruins.

Chapter
thirty-one

George Carson was ringing up the sale for a Silent Knight refrigerator when he saw Henry Gable beckoning imperiously from his office door. Excusing himself and handing over to an assistant, he hurried to the store owner.

'There's a phone call for you. I don't encourage it, as you know, but some person in Sydney insisted it's important.'

George apologised for the interruption to work, and picked up the receiver. A voice on the line said his name was Donald Ferrier, and he had some bad news.

Eunice came to the hospital the following night, bringing an enormous bunch of flowers. She was profuse with apologies for the way the meeting had ended in acrimony and stalemate, but with Belle's help they could still manage a miracle and save the show. Belle said she doubted it.

Eunice insisted it was possible. The temporary closure notices were up, but they could reopen in a week with not much harm done. A bit of publicity would fix it. Sally was the real problem; if Belle could manage to change Teddy's mind – and she and Ricky were both convinced he could be persuaded if Belle would only try – then Sal would eventually back down. If Teddy acquiesced, Sally would do likewise.

'I doubt it,' Belle said again. 'She has a mind of her own, and I don't think I can persuade him.'

'Please, at least try. You must. My daughter's gone crazy. She's locked herself in. Won't talk to me. Waiting for her father to collect her. She wants to live with him, then go back to school, full-time. It's sheer waste, a silly foolish waste. She can already read and write perfectly well. What else does she need from school? Does she want to end up some sort of underpaid teacher?'

Belle wished Eunice would either shut up or go away; wished she had the strength to shout at her. But her strength had been used up earlier in the day. There had been a brief visit from an anguished George, who had hurried to the city; poor George, trying to be encouraging and even cheerful, but failing dismally. She had never seen him weep, and his tears distressed her immeasurably. Then, after a rest and buoyed by painkillers, Nuncie had brought Teddy for what she knew would be his last visit.

She had thought she was prepared. So many times over the years she had rehearsed the way she would explain the details of his parentage. The simple facts, told quietly and rationally, she had always believed, would suffice. She had not taken into account the bewilderment that grew on the young freckled face, the confusion in his moist brown eyes that began to seem like an accusation, and his asking why she had misled him for so long. She tried to stumble on, but emotion had choked her, and Nuncie had sat him on her bulky lap and helped her finish. Nuncie explaining that it had all happened because of love – two people in love had created him, and another had offered him a loving home.

In the end he had hugged Belle, which felt like understanding and forgiveness, but it had left her drained. The last thing she needed was Eunice intruding like this. But Eunice was too insensitive to realise she was trampling on grief and cherished memories. She was still carping continuously.

'Why have they done this – after all we did for them? How can they just decide to stop? To walk away, give up a wonderful career and a fortune? Belle . . . are you even listening to me? For God's sake, don't you care?'

'Of course I care.' How could she not care? 'This small person whom you love,' Florian had said in a rare moment of sincerity, 'you're driven by a need to see him reach the top, to – well, what's wrong with a bit of dreaming? – to touch the stars.'

'Then *help* me,' Eunice pleaded, her face so close that Belle could feel her breath. 'Don't let these silly kids ruin it. You and I together, we'll *make* them go on. Teddy said we can't, but he's wrong. Of course we can make them go on.'

Belle felt corralled by a mouthful of capped teeth. She knew the only way she could get rid of this hateful woman was by telling her the truth.

'No, you can't. He's right,' she said. 'You can't make them go on. Nobody can.' Her remaining energy was ebbing. 'I'll never understand it . . . but I accept they've had enough; they don't like it any more. So you better accept it too, and stop talking a lot of silly shit, Eunice. If they choose not to get up on stage and perform, then not you, or me, or God – or even Ricky Mendoza – can make them do it. It's finished . . . it's over.'

'I can't believe this! I thought you'd fight! I was so sure you'd help me. What's happened to you?'

'I'm ill, Eunice. Or didn't you notice? My son's only twelve years old, and I've come to the conclusion I don't want him to spend his life doing something that makes him unhappy. And that's what matters in the end. Not *my* dreams for him, but his own dreams, whatever the future might be.'

'They're both far too young to decide what they want out of life.'

Oh, you silly fool of a woman, Belle thought, and found strength from somewhere to contest this. 'He's not too young,' she said hoarsely. 'Four years of earning a living in films, stage, radio – that's long enough to know his own mind. He's done more than I hoped for. Far, far more.' She paused for breath. It was becoming difficult to go on. 'He asked me if I was angry with him. How could I be angry? I told him I'm proud he did so well. But you don't understand that, do you?'

'How could I, when you're letting him throw away a good career?'

'That's *his* choice. I'm proud of him and I'll always be proud of him. Now please go. I'm very tired, and awfully sick of you and your bellyaching.'

She closed her eyes, hoping Eunice would leave. For a moment there was no movement. I can't give her a better cue than that, she thought, then heard a rustling sound, quick footsteps and the door closing. She opened her eyes.

To her relief Eunice had gone. So had the flowers.

At midnight when her shift finished, Genevieve stayed in the hospital to sit with Belle. She was weakening and had been heavily sedated. Genevieve knew how much pain the stress of the past few days had cost her patient. She was aware Belle had pleaded that her son be kept away from this last painful vigil; the lady with the beret and the barrister would be here in the morning, but that would be too late, she thought, and it was wrong that Belle should die alone.

For most of the night Genevieve sat feeling the life still in the frail hand, listening to murmurs and fragments of memory that meant nothing to her. Dancing in the street with Fred Astaire, borrowing money from Banker Burwood, queuing up to audition for silent films, chaps with wandering hands at the stage door when she was in the chorus. There was someone called Ross – it sounded as though she treasured the name – and another, Florian, who seemed to cause her pain even though she was full of morphine.

As the hours passed the voice became inaudible, the names and memories they conjured ceased. Genevieve watched her protracted breathing grow faint and falter until it stopped. She went to the window, opened it to let in fresh air and looked out. The rain had finally ceased, and a pale moon was now visible through the patchwork sky.

Sometimes, the nurse thought, there are people you come to meet too late. She wished she had known her patient better. She did realise, from her short acquaintance, that Belle's life had been like an exhilarating carousel, and that her death had left some awkward and unanswered problems.

Chapter thirty–two

The minister's voice was like the distant drone of something from the past. Teddy was trying to think what it might have been, then remembered the sound of Mr Miranda's lawnmower on Sunday mornings in Brewinda Road. It was a noise at odds with the cloudless blue skies and the ocean view below them, where fishing boats were drifting off the shore and a coastal steamer was far out at sea. But the boats were a part of the real world, he thought.

Not the strange cemetery world of headstones and burial chambers that were called crypts, with iron railings around them and even statues of angels with wings. Not the open grave and the wooden box with Belle supposed to be inside it. He felt none of it was real, and at any moment she might open the lid, step out and hug him, or else be furious with him as Eunice had been, and tell him she was angry because he didn't want to go on the stage any more.

Only she hadn't been angry. She'd told him she was proud, and thinking of it now he felt his eyes starting to water, because he had never loved his mother so much as that moment in the hospital. He tried to recall if there were times when he hadn't loved her, but couldn't think of any. Even the worst days, like the big row with the adjudicator at the talent quest, or when he'd had to fight kids at school who made jokes about her, or when her rotten friends

Sam and Mabel had run off and dumped him in that town. But that wasn't her fault, and he could still remember the wonderful feeling of relief when she'd come to rescue him from the police station. If he thought about his life, Belle was always there, such a special part of it. And now she wouldn't be, which was too difficult to imagine.

The minister was droning on. 'In my Father's house are many mansions . . .' Teddy tried to work out what that meant. Did the minister mean his own father, or was he talking about God? And if he was, why would God have a house with many mansions? Religion, he thought, was peculiar. Not that he knew much about it, because Belle used to say it was ritual bullshit, and he remembered Mrs Audrey Stevenson, the vicar's wife, asking her to kindly not speak like that, especially not in front of children. Clear as if it was yesterday, Belle apologising that Mrs Stevenson had overheard a private remark and taken offence, but she always spoke her mind to people, including her own son. Telling the minister's wife that language was a matter of communication, in this case between two people, and if a third happened to hear by accident or even by design, such as eavesdropping, that was her hard luck.

Just remembering it – how Mrs Stevenson had gone really red in the face and stomped off – made him partly realise why Belle had always had such trouble with people at home. It made her suddenly seem so real in his mind, as if she was not dead at all. He wondered what the others were thinking, the people who had come to say goodbye. He could see Nuncie standing opposite, with tears running down her cheeks. Charles was on one side of her, Clarence on the other, both looking different because they were in suits instead of their work overalls. Sally was there, but not Eunice; she'd asked her mum not to come because it would upset people – especially her and Teddy. So it was good she wasn't there. But a lot of others were, including friends like Greta Torrance, Ross Tanner, Helene LaRue and Chrissie, who smiled at him, and he remembered how they had sat together and watched movies at the Picture Palace.

One day at the Palace a film had been mistakenly run in reverse, going back to the beginning while the audience laughed and jeered. Thinking of it made him wish life could be like that. If time could go backwards they would still be living in Kellett Street and Belle would be alive. Ross would be there at nights arguing about art and politics with the circle while they drank four-penny dark, and he and Sal would still be walking home after school and wondering if Belle and Ross were lovers.

It was too painful; he tried to stop thinking about this before it made him cry. Instead he made himself wonder about the future. There was his dad, George, on one side, and his real dad, Donald, on the other, and while the minister kept on with his strange and boring speech about heaven and the afterlife and his Father's mansions, while they committed his mum to the earth, to dust and ashes, he tried to work out what was going to happen to him now that he had two dads.

Chapter
thirty-three

They met the day after the funeral in Donald Ferrier's chambers, which George knew at once was a mistake, for the territory was foreign to him, filled with law books all the way to the ceiling and a clerk who brought them coffee on a silver tray. It was Ferrier's turf, not his. The only other person present was Belle's friend Nuncie Billingsworth, who had sobbed her way through the funeral and most of the wake afterwards. She had been in a dress then, but now looked thoroughly out of place in baggy trousers and a man's shirt, having removed a beret when she arrived as well as stubbing out a cigar. He'd heard her name mentioned in the past, but never imagined she'd look like this. Still, Belle had always said she was a poppet – one of her words – with a heart as big as Sydney Harbour, and she had taken good care of Teddy, who liked her, and he supposed that was what counted.

It was strange meeting these people. Ferrier was in a smart suit, a fairly good-looking sort of bloke, being overly polite, asking them to sit down while he took on the job of pouring the coffee, making small talk about the countryside around Gundagai and asking if they'd had any rain. Over the years George had often speculated on who Teddy's real father might be, and felt almost certain it was Dan Hardacre, but now knew he couldn't have been further from the truth. A barrister, and a King's Counsel at that! Though he'd have been just a novice lawyer starting out when he knew Belle, and she must've been a young soubrette. He abruptly tried to drink his coffee, not wanting to dwell on the details of that episode in her life.

'I'll start by thanking you both for coming here,' Donald said, 'particularly in your case, Mr Carson. I expect it's a bit like a football team having to play what's called an away game.' He smiled as George looked surprised at his perception. 'But I think we should resolve this today, swiftly and amicably, for Teddy's sake.'

'I agree. But what do you mean by amicably, Mr Ferrier?'

'That we needn't have a legal stand-off, not on this matter. Miss Billingsworth is here because she can testify Belle acknowledged me as the father. She was present when Belle explained it to Teddy.'

'I'm aware of that.' George nearly added he had consoled the boy afterwards, but the other's interruption prevented him.

'There are other obvious ways to prove it if they're required.'

'You mean a blood test, things like that?' George was unsure what other tests there could be.

'If necessary.' Donald sipped his coffee. 'But any prolonged court battle would be terribly unfair on Teddy, and I think he's had enough grief for now.'

'That goes without saying.' George hated coffee, and wondered why he hadn't said so. Tea was his tipple, not this rather bitter muck. 'But why should we have a court battle?' he asked.

'We wouldn't – unless you dispute my claim.'

'I don't dispute it. I just won't recognise it, Mr Ferrier.'

'I'm not sure I understand. That seems like a contradiction to me – as if you're positioning yourself for a challenge.'

'That's legal talk. What I'm saying is, I hope to go back home tomorrow. And I reckon Teddy should come with me.'

'Just like that. Why?'

'Because I brought him up, me and Belle. I think it'd be a fair crack of the whip if I can go on doing that.'

'A fair crack of the whip? Is that really the basis on which you suggest we should resolve his whole future?'

Nuncie sat watching them start to argue, knowing who was going to win. The decent truculent bloke from beyond the black stump didn't have a bloody hope in hell against the silver-tongued favourite of the courts. He'd be going back home all right, to his job at Gable's and his friend Maureen from next door, but not with this kid. Not unless she intervened, and she wasn't sure if she should. It was an awesome responsibility Belle had dumped on her, deciding the course of a young life like this. Just because in her last few days she couldn't decide – didn't feel it fair to distinguish between the two, or perhaps wasn't strong enough to make such a choice – she had shoved the burden on Nuncie. Not only that; had pleaded with her to help break the news that Donald was his real father.

'I love you, girl,' Nuncie had grumbled, 'but you're giving me a right load of shit to shovel.'

But she'd been there, which was just as well. She'd done her best. And now she had one last job entrusted to her by Belle, she thought as she listened to them arguing.

'I really don't think whips should come into it, Mr Carson —'

'Forget bloody whips,' George said heatedly, a nervous movement as he pushed away the coffee cup, betraying his agitation. 'I meant it'd be justice – isn't that one of your favourite legal words? It'd be the right thing for me to have him.'

'Despite the fact that I can give him a far better life?'

'Maybe you can, Mr Ferrier. You can send him to a smart school, bring him up in a posh house, buy him things I'll never be able to afford. My house is a dump – at least that's what Belle always called it – but I'd gladly sell it to fight you in the court if I have to.'

'So much for peaceful resolve,' Donald said. 'The one thing you appear to completely forget is that he's my son. Ask Miss Billingsworth.'

'I don't need to ask. He's not your *real* son. He's never been it!'

'Now calm down, old boy. If Belle said that, then she lied to you.'

'Belle never lied,' George said, more quietly but with equal passion. 'She never told me who, but I've always known he wasn't mine. Not by blood, I mean. But I held him in my arms before he was an hour old. I've loved him, worried myself sick about him, seen him through all the childhood things – measles and colds, and wetting the bed. Taught him to walk, to ride a bike. Took him to school, tried to help him with homework, got upset and angry when he came home after a fight with a split lip. You were never his dad, not like that. Being his natural father was just something you did with Belle . . . a long time ago.' He hesitated a moment, as if unused to speaking at such length. 'Perhaps you were in love with her – I don't know that – but if you were it's strange you never even seemed to know she'd kept the baby. Or if you did know, you never bothered in all these years to see him.'

Donald had listened carefully, with a sort of courtesy, Nuncie thought. Like a polite counsel, nodding as if conceding that some of the points raised were valid before setting out to demolish them.

'Whatever I did wrong back then, Mr Carson, I want to make up for it now. I appreciate all you say, but in the end the law's quite clear. Teddy's mine, by every legal right.'

She could see failure on George Carson's face. Brave words and a bit of bluff could never beat the legal eagles, with their judicial precepts and precedents, and all the protective imperatives of the law. She sensed the man from beyond the black stump was about to admit defeat.

'How about a *moral* right?' Nuncie asked, and when they both turned to her, surprised by the intervention, she made them wait while she took a cigar and lit it. 'What happens, Donald, if this does go to court? I'm your star witness, right?'

'Nuncie, keep out of this. And do you have to smoke that filthy cheroot?'

She ignored him, blowing out a stream of smoke as he grimaced. 'What if your star witness decides George shouldn't have to sell his house?' Nuncie challenged him. 'Because her best friend, a girl she happened to love deeply, left her with a big problem. "If it ever comes to a fight over custody, I rely on you to tell the truth," she said.'

'What the hell are you talking about?'

'The foetus, Donald, the one you wanted to get rid of. *I* talked her out of it. *I* went with her to the abortionist – that horrible doctor – where she told him she'd changed her mind. And when he tried to heavy her, tried to pull rank and bully her, she chucked her money – *your* money, since you gave it to her – chucked it on the floor as we walked out. I don't think George should be allowed to risk everything he owns, just to be beaten by you in court. Which he undoubtedly would be.'

She had their complete attention now. Both of them speechless.

'I'm sorry to do this to you. It surprises me a bit, and probably surprises you, but I've grown to rather like you, whereas I hardly know George. But I think if Belle was in this room and heard what he said, I honestly believe she'd want him to look after her child, at least until Teddy is old enough to decide for himself. So consider me a hostile witness, Donald.'

The house looked just the same. Except that the neighbours in Brewinda Road were waiting in their front gardens, and waved to him. Teddy waved back with a sense of excitement, and just a trace of fear, because the gang and the kids from school must be hanging around somewhere, also waiting to see him.

But, to his surprise, his former best mate and old enemy, Herbie Bates, was standing there in the garden, alongside a friendly woman with a big smile on her face, who George told him was Maureen. He'd already said, in the train on their way home, that he and Maureen were real close, real good friends, and some day they might even make it official, if Teddy knew what he meant.

Teddy went and shook hands with Herbie, and then went to shake hands with Maureen. But she put her arms out, and it seemed natural to hug her, so he did. Later Herbie said to him that Ginger and the blokes wanted to meet up, and how about tomorrow?

Which was why he rode his bike down to the river, and felt a strange stir of memory: trying to swim across it, the first day he'd joined the gang, when George had saved him. This unchanged river that he'd known since his early childhood, the Murr-um-bid-gee; he remembered Larry the American director teaching him that. It looked just the same, the way he'd sometimes dreamt. The gang looked the same, too, a few years older and all of them bigger, waiting there, the whole mob. He remained poised on the bike, ready to pedal for his life in case of trouble, but they came close and stopped there.

'Came back, eh?' Ginger began, which was a pretty stupid thing to say, because there he was, but he decided to agree. No point in starting with a fight.

'Is she dead, your mum?'

'Yes.' He didn't want to talk about it, because it hurt and he was scared his eyes might start to water.

'I never seen a dead person,' one of the other kids said.

'I never saw her dead. Only in the . . . the box, you know . . . the coffin.'

'Shit,' Ginger said, 'did you cry?'

'Yeah.'

They all looked at him. He felt ready to start lashing out at them if they laughed, but no one did.

'S'pose I would too,' Ginger confessed. 'My mum said your mum was quite pretty. A bit peculiar . . . but pretty.'

Teddy nodded. It seemed friendly, but he was unsure.

'Our gang's still going. You interested?'

'Thought you didn't want me,' Teddy said.

'We changed our minds. Norm was crook on you, but he's moved away. So you can't be leader, 'cos I'm still leader. But everyone's voted, and they say you can be second in command. What do you think? If anything happens to me, you can take over.'

Teddy thought about it. In his mind he conjured a battlefield and the sound of gunfire. He wore an army captain's uniform. They were in a sandbagged dugout as stretcher-bearers carried in the bloodstained figure of Ginger.

'The major's bought it, sir,' Sergeant Herbie said. 'You're in charge now.'

'Thank you, Sergeant. Stand by to attack.'

It seemed so real. He realised they were all staring at him, waiting for a reply. Ginger was there with what seemed like an outstretched hand.

'Well, Ted . . . don't frig about. Are you in or not?'

'I'm in,' Teddy said, feeling a moment of great joy.

'Good on you, mate. Welcome home.'

They shook hands, and the others clustered around to be included in the greeting. Herbie said it was time for a swim, and they all ran down the bank, stripping off their clothes and diving in. Teddy looked up at the big river gum, and could see a familiar sight. He climbed up to where the rope was still suspended.

He stood balanced on the branch looking down at the river. *His river*, that he would show Sally when she came to visit, as her dad had promised she could. Tonight he was going to write her his first letter; he had so much to tell her. Just thinking about her made him feel exhilarated.

'Look out below!' he shouted, and they laughed and cheered as he swung on the end of the rope and bombed into the river with a joyous yell and a splash.

Acknowledgements

My research on film studios and theatres of Sydney in the 1930s was facilitated by two friends. Producer Anthony Buckley, with whom I've worked closely for many years, was a rich source of information on the film industry of the time. The late Alistair Duncan, author of *Actors Blood*, lent me books that provided an insight into the period's vaudeville theatres. I am grateful to them both, and if there are mistakes in any depiction of the era, the errors are mine.

I'm deeply indebted to Bryce Courtenay, who introduced me to Robert Sessions of the Penguin Group, and equally indebted to Robert himself and Ali Watts, who made the decision to publish this book. It has been a pleasure working with everyone at Penguin: Marina Messiha for the striking cover design; Associate Publisher Kirsten Abbott for her encouragement throughout; and my editor Saskia Adams, whose energy and expertise have been a driving force that was invaluable.

In conclusion, any similarity between the case of Karel Janacek on page 263 and the indictment of Egon Kisch in 1934, in which the notorious dictation test was applied and found to be illegal, is intended.

Brother Fish

BRYCE COURTENAY

Brother Fish is an Australian saga spanning eighty years and four continents. Inspired by real events, Bryce Courtenay's novel tells the story of three people from vastly differing backgrounds. All they have in common is a tough beginning in life.

Jack McKenzie is a harmonica player, soldier, dreamer and small-time professional fisherman from a tiny island in Bass Strait. Nicole Lenoir-Jourdan is a strong-willed woman hiding from an ambiguous past in Shanghai. Larger than life, Private Jimmy Oldcorn was once a street kid and leader of a New York gang. Together, they reap a vast and not always legitimate fortune from the sea.

Brother Fish *is an inspiring human drama of three lives brought together and changed forever by the extraordinary events of recent history. But most of all it is about the power of friendship and love.*

Jessica

BRYCE COURTENAY

Jessica is based on the inspiring true story of a young girl's fight for justice against tremendous odds. A tomboy, Jessica is the pride of her father, as they work together on the struggling family farm. One quiet day, the peace of the bush is devastated by a terrible murder. Only Jessica is able to save the killer from the lynch mob – but will justice prevail in the courts?

Nine months later, a baby is born . . . with Jessica determined to guard the secret of the father's identity. The rivalry of Jessica and her beautiful sister for the love of the same man will echo through-out their lives – until finally the truth must be told.

Set in the harsh Australian bush against the outbreak of World War I, this novel is heartbreaking in its innocence, and shattering in its brutality.

The Rose Notes

ANDREA MAYES

Charming, infuriating Dobie Kinnear, widower and manipulator extraordinaire, is battling to retain his wits, his authority, and his only daughter, Pearl.

Pearl, a hostage to her ageing father's needs, fiercely resents her role as Dobie's unofficial housekeeper. The years are passing on their southern Riverina farm, and still her life lacks meaning or purpose. She loves the farm with a passion but, tending her rose garden, she dreams of escape.

Then a stranger comes to Mamerbrook Farm bearing a secret from the past and a gift for the future. Along with an old scrapbook of roses, a hitchhiking angel, and an onion farmer with a knack for rescuing people, he will turn their world upside down . . . and change their lives forever.

House on the Hill

ESTELLE PINNEY

Belle Dalton has stardust in her eyes. It's the early 1920s in Far North Queensland, and the three Dalton sisters board with Mrs Sanders in the house on the Hill.

Lovely Belle, the youngest, a talented singer and dancer, tours with a vaudeville troupe as they follow the rodeos and shows of western Queensland. On the romance front, she's being pursued by handsome local Greek Nicos Alexandros, owner of the swankiest café in town. But will she choose marriage with Nicos or a life on the stage?

Molly reigns as head cook at King's Hotel, and can whip up any stylish gown down to the last bugle bead. However, happiness with her sweetheart Fred is threatened by a terrible twist of fate . . . Josie, the eldest, has bookish ambitions and a strong spirit, which will be tested to the full when her life takes an unexpected turn.

This heart-warming and colourful novel about the power of dreams brings to life Australia's exotic far north of days gone by, with its vibrant mix of cultures and personalities. *House on the Hill* follows three sisters' joys and heartbreaks – and the difficult choices they have to make that change their lives forever.

Jillaroo

RACHEL TREASURE

After a terrible argument with her father over their family property, 'Waters Meeting', Rebecca Saunders throws her swag in the ute and heads north with her three dogs. A job as a jillaroo takes her into the rowdy world of B&S balls, Bundy rum and boys. When she at last settles down to a bit of study at agricultural college, her life is turned upside down by the very handsome but very drunken party animal Charlie Lewis . . .

Will she choose a life of wheat farming on vast open plains with Charlie? Or will she return to the mountains, to fight for the land and the river that runs through her soul?

It's only when tragedy shatters her world that Rebecca finds a strength and courage she never knew she had, in this action-packed novel of adventure, dreams and determination.

The Stockmen

RACHEL TREASURE

Rosie Highgrove-Jones grows up hating her double-barrelled name. She dreams of riding out over the wide plains of the family property, working on the land. Instead she's stuck writing the social pages of the local paper.

Then a terrible tragedy sparks a series of shocking revelations for Rosie and her family. As she tries to put her life back together, Rosie throws herself into researching the haunting true story of a nineteenth-century Irish stockman who came to Australia and risked his all for a tiny pup and a wild dream. Is it just coincidence when Rosie meets a sexy Irish stockman of her own? And will Jim help her realise her deepest ambitions – or will he break her heart?

The Stockmen *moves effortlessly between the present and the past to reveal a simple yet hard-won truth – that both love and the land are timeless . . .*

The Call of the High Country

TONY PARSONS

In the heart of Australia's rugged high country, three generations of the MacLeod family battle to make a living on the land. As a young married couple, Andrew and Anne work together to make the very best of their property, High Peaks, but at what cost to their happiness?

In time the property will pass to their son, David. Handsome and hardworking, he is determined to become the best sheepdog handler in the land. Nothing is going to stand in his way – not even the beautiful Catriona Campbell, daughter of the wealthy graziers next door.

An inspiring and heart-warming saga of a family battling through hard times, of a love that defies all odds, and of dreams that won't be broken.

Return to the High Country

TONY PARSONS

In the beginning there had only been High Peaks, the MacLeod family property in the heart of Australia's rugged high country. Andrew and Anne MacLeod struggled on the land to give David, their only son and heir, a better life.

Wracked by grief following his father's death, David is determined to succeed. With the MacLeod love of the land running in his blood, and the beautiful Catriona at his side, he builds an impressive empire of grazing properties for the sons he hopes will follow him.

But grooming a suitable heir proves as challenging and heartbreaking as rural life itself. It is David's passion for his beloved high country, and the support of the women in his life, that keep his dream alive.

Here is a story that will transport you to the heartland of Australia's bush and keep you spellbound till the very last page.